Susan Meier is the author of over fifty books for Mills & Boon. *The Tycoon's Secret Daughter* was a Romance Writers of America RITA® Award finalist, and *Nanny for the Millionaire's Twins* won the Book Buyers' Best Award and was a finalist in the National Readers' Choice Awards. She is married and has three children. One of eleven children herself, she loves to write about the complexity of families and totally believes in the power of love.

Since 2002, *USA TODAY* bestselling author **Judy Duarte** has written over forty books for Mills & Boon, earned two RITA® Award nominations, won two Maggie Awards and received a National Readers' Choice Award. When she's not cooped up in her writing cave, she enjoys traveling with her husband and spending quality time with her grand-children. You can learn more about Judy and her books on her website, www.judyduarte.com, or at Facebook.com/judyduartenovelist.

D1550163

THE SPANISH MILLIONAIRE'S RUNAWAY BRIDE

SUSAN MEIER

NO ORDINARY FORTUNE

JUDY DUARTE

MILLS & BOON

First Published in Great Britain 2018
by Mills & Boon, an imprint of HarperCollinsPublishers,
1 London Bridge Street, London, SE1 9GF

The Spanish Millionaire's Runaway Bride © 2018 Susan Meier
No Ordinary Fortune © 2018 Harlequin Books S.A.

Special thanks and acknowledgement to Judy Duarte for her contribution to *The Fortunes of Texas: The Rulebreakers* continuity.

ISBN: 978-0-263-26468-5

38-0218

MIX
Paper from
responsible sources
FSC™ C007454

This book is produced from independently certified FSC™ paper to ensure responsible forest management.

For more information visit: www.harpercollins.co.uk/green

Printed and bound in Spain
by CPI, Barcelona

THE SPANISH MILLIONAIRE'S RUNAWAY BRIDE

SUSAN MEIER

To my mum, an avid reader,
who taught me to love every story.

CHAPTER ONE

RICCARDO OCHOA DROVE under the portico of the Midnight Sins Hotel on the Las Vegas strip. He got out of his rental—a black Mercedes convertible with white leather interior—and tossed the keys to the valet.

"Don't take it too far," he told the twentysomething kid dressed in neat-as-a-pin trousers and a white shirt. "I don't intend to be long."

He turned to enter the hotel and almost ran in to a gaggle of giggling women. "Good afternoon, ladies."

They stopped. Wide-eyed and no longer giggling, the women stared at him.

He hadn't been living in New York City for years without recognizing that his Spanish accent intrigued American women. As did his dark hair, dark eyes and the fact that he worked out five days a week. To them, he was exotic.

The woman wearing a strapless red velvet dress took a step closer. Her brown hair had been pulled into curls on top of her head. Her green eyes were sultry, seductive. "Are you going inside?"

He smiled at her. "As a matter of fact, I am."

"Maybe I should ditch my friends and join you?"

If he hadn't been there on business, he probably would have taken her up on her offer for a few hours of drinking and gambling. Just some fun. That might have morphed into a night of romance, but that was it. Not because he didn't believe in relationships. He'd seen them work. His cousins Mitch and Alonzo had married beautiful women and were as happy as two guys could be.

But some men weren't built for that kind of life. Riccardo had tried it and had had his heart ripped out of his chest and stomped on—publicly—when his fiancée left him two days before their wedding to reunite with her ex. Gowns had been bought. Tuxes had hung in closets. White-linen-covered tables had lined the rolling lawn of Northern Spain's Ochoa Vineyards, and she'd walked out without a backward glance.

Humiliation had caused him to swear off relationships, but over the next few years, he'd grown to appreciate the benefits of being single. Not to mention rich. When a man had money, the world was at his fingertips. Though it was his cousin Mitch who had started their company, Ochoa Online, Riccardo took the income Mitch's websites generated, invested it and made them millionaires, on the fast track to become billionaires. He more than earned his keep.

Which was why he was in Vegas. With the creative genius behind Ochoa Online away on an extended honeymoon, and one of Mitch's best customers having trouble with his daughter, Riccardo had to shift from moneyman to client problem solver.

"Sorry." He took the hand of the woman in red velvet and caught her gaze before kissing her knuckles. "I'm here on business."

She swallowed. "Maybe when your business is done?"

"I'm picking somebody up and driving us both back to the airport." Morgan Monroe, daughter of Colonel Monroe, owner of Monroe Wines, had run from her wedding. The Colonel wanted her home not just to explain, but for damage control. "I'll be here two hours, tops." He released her hand. "Maybe we'll be lucky enough to meet on my next trip."

"Maybe."

He nodded at her and her friends. "Goodbye, ladies."

The little group said, "Goodbye," and he walked toward the hotel door, which opened automatically. The sleek, modern lobby welcomed him.

He stopped at the concierge. "I'm looking for Morgan Monroe." Unlike his ex, Cicely, who'd at least given him two days' warning, Morgan Monroe had walked halfway down the aisle before she'd turned and run. Her dad had asked his staff to monitor her credit cards and the next day this hotel had popped up. "I'm told she's a guest here."

The fiftysomething gentleman didn't even glance at his computer. "I'm sorry, sir. We don't give away guest information."

"I'm only asking because her father, *Colonel Monroe*," Riccardo said, deliberately dropping the name of her famous father, "sent me."

The man's face whitened. "Her dad is Colonel Monroe?"

Riccardo unobtrusively slid his hand into his trouser pocket to get a one-hundred-dollar bill. "The same."

"I love his wine."

"Everybody loves his wine." He eased the bill across the polished counter. "He just wants me to make sure she's okay." And bring her home. But the concierge didn't need to know that.

The man casually took the bill off the counter and stuffed it into his pocket. "It's against policy to give you her room number, but friend to friend," he said, motioning for Riccardo to lean closer, "I can tell you I saw her going into the casino about an hour ago. I also happen to know she plays penny slots and loves margaritas. She's been in the same spot in the far right-hand corner every afternoon since she got here."

Though Riccardo groaned internally at the thought of getting a drunk woman into his car and onto a plane, he smiled appreciatively at the concierge. "Thank you."

He turned away from the serene lobby and faced the casino. Twenty steps took him down a ramp, out of the quiet and into a cacophony of noise. Bells and whistles from slots mixed with cheering at the gaming tables and blended with keno numbers. He inhaled deeply. He loved a good casino.

But he didn't even pause at the rows of slot machines or the game tables, where an elderly gentleman appeared to be hot at blackjack. He made his way through the jumble of people and paraphernalia to the penny slots in the far right-hand corner.

No one was there.

He looked to the left, then the right. He'd walked so far back the noise of the casino was only a dull hum behind him. The vacant slots around him were also silent.

Confusion rumbled through him. Though Monday afternoons typically weren't as busy as weekend afternoons, the entire corner was weirdly quiet.

"I'm telling you. When you have as little money as you guys have, you can't play the stock market."

Riccardo's head snapped up.

"But my cousin Arnie netted a bundle playing the market!"

"Because of a lucky guess." The woman talking sighed heavily. "Look, your primary goal should be to make money without losing any of your initial investment."

Curious, Riccardo followed the sounds of the conversation. He walked down the row and turned right, then stopped. Two cocktail waitresses, an old guy in shorts and a Hawaiian shirt, a young guy in a hoodie and two women leaned against the corner machine as a slim blonde in jeans and gray canvas tennis shoes counseled them.

"You can't guarantee you'll keep your initial investment buying individual stocks. Mutual funds mitigate the risk."

One of the waitresses saw Riccardo and nudged her head in his direction. The woman doling out investment advice turned, and Riccardo's mouth fell open.

He knew it was stupid to think Morgan Monroe would still be in the wedding gown she'd had on when she bolted from St. Genevieve church on Saturday, but he also hadn't expected to see Colonel Monroe's high-society daughter in blue jeans and canvas tennis shoes. Her long blond hair hung past her shoulders in tangled disarray. Her enormous blue eyes speared him from behind the lenses of oversize tortoiseshell glasses.

"Get lost, buddy."

He also hadn't expected her to snipe at him. Oh, he'd been sure there'd be a little resistance to his putting her on a plane and taking her back to Lake Justice, home of her father's enormous wine empire. But everything he'd read about Morgan portrayed her as a demure, sweet woman who loved charity work and took in stray cats.

Either the press had absolutely got her wrong, her dad had a really good PR machine, or Morgan Monroe had snapped.

Considering she'd gotten halfway down the aisle at her eight-hundred-person wedding and then turned and run, he was guessing she'd snapped.

He suddenly wondered if that's what had happened with Cicely. If she'd snapped when she'd called off their wedding—

His heart chugged to a stop. He hadn't thought about Cicely in years and today he couldn't stop thinking about her, comparing his situation to Morgan Monroe's. He didn't like remembering the humiliation any more than he liked being reminded that it was his own damn fault. Arrogance had made him believe he could make her love him, though she'd told him time and again that she had an ex she couldn't forget. And pride sure as hell went before his fall.

So, what was he doing getting involved with another runaway bride? Was he nuts?

No. He was helping a client. Plus, the situations were totally different. Cicely had been his fiancée. Morgan was the daughter of the owner of the biggest vineyard on Mitch's wine website. Riccardo did not intend to get *involved* with her beyond taking her home to her dad. This wasn't just a favor for their best client. It was the only way to keep the beloved, world-renowned Colonel from dumping them to start his own wine website and becoming their competition.

Morgan Monroe barely held back a sigh of annoyance with the guy staring at her. He was good-looking, obviously rich—if his tailored white shirt and Italian leather loafers were any indicator—and clearly confused, just standing there as if he had no idea what to do.

Guessing he had been startled to find someone doling out investment advice by the penny slots, she gave him the benefit of the doubt, and said, "There's a sea of machines behind you. You can play any one you want. And if you go at least a row away, you won't even hear us."

The surprise on his face was replaced by chagrin. "Holding a little stock seminar, are you?"

His voice wasn't exactly condescending. She really couldn't tell what it was. But if he thought she would let him insult these people who needed her help, he was mistaken.

"If I were, it would be none of your business."

The chagrin became a wince. "That's not true. I'm actually looking for you… Morgan."

Her chest squeezed. She'd expected her dad to come searching for her. But this guy didn't look like a private investigator. She glanced at the black trousers and fitted shirt again. Open at the throat, the white shirt revealed tan skin, as if he summered in the Mediterranean. With his accent, he probably did.

"*You're* a PI?"

"No. I'm a friend of your father."

That was infinitely worse. A PI she could handle. A friend of her dad's? That would take some finesse.

She turned to her group. "I'm sorry, guys. I'm going to need a few minutes. Just stay here. I'll be right back." She walked toward her dad's minion, pointing at the raised circular bar in the middle of the room. "There's a table open up there."

Heading for the bar, she assumed the guy would follow her. She used the two minutes of skirting people, slot machines and gaming tables to remind herself she was twenty-five, educated and in desperate need of some time alone. No matter how this guy approached this, she could say, "Tell my dad I love him and I'm sorry he spent a lot of money on the wedding…but I needed some air."

No. She couldn't tell a perfect stranger she needed some air. That was stupid. Her dad would roar with fury if she sent this admittedly handsome guy back to him without something concrete.

She reached to pull out her chair, but Handsome Spanish Guy beat her to it.

Giving her a polite smile, he said, "My nanna would shoot me if I let a woman get her own chair."

She sat. "Your nanna?"

"My grandmother." He sat across from her. "She lives

in Spain. Very much old-school. She likes men with manners."

So did Morgan. And, wow, she loved this guy's voice. Smooth and sexy with just enough accent to make him interesting.

But he was here because her dad had sent him. She shouldn't be noticing that he was attractive. Plus, she'd just walked out on her own wedding. After leaving one guy at the altar two days ago, she was not in the market for another. No matter how gorgeous.

She cleared her throat. "Okay. My dad sent you to find me—"

"I didn't have to find you. He knows where you are. He wants me to bring you home."

She gaped at him. "He knows where I am?"

"Did you think I just strolled into this hotel on a lucky guess?"

"No." As a former secretary of state and a current high-profile business owner, her dad had more money than God and resources to do things Morgan was only beginning to understand. She didn't need to know how her dad had found her. The point was, he had.

She pulled in a breath and released it slowly enough to get her thoughts together. "Okay, Marco Polo, here's the deal. The next two weeks had been blocked off for a honeymoon. My dad has an event in Stockholm two days after that, so I have to be home before he leaves. But that also means I don't have to be anywhere for another twelve days." She planted her backside a little more firmly on the chair. "I'm not going anywhere."

"Yes, you are. You left your dad with eight hundred confused guests filling the bed-and-breakfasts in town, waiting to see if you're okay, not to mention one very disoriented fiancé. You're not dodging the damage control."

She rose from her seat. "I didn't want the eight hundred

guests. Charles did. I didn't want the wedding reception at the vineyard. That was my dad's handiwork. I picked out the dress and my bouquet." Her eyes unexpectedly filled with tears and the emotions that had hit her as she walked down the aisle spiraled through her again. The betrayal. The sense of stupidity for trusting Charles. The sense of stupidity for being so trusting—period.

She very quickly said, "If you'll excuse me," turned and headed back to her cluster of new friends, not willing to let this stranger see her cry. Damn it. She'd thought she'd worked through all this in the plane.

She raised her chin. She *had* dealt with all this on the commuter flight to JFK, while shopping for clothes to change into in the big airport and on the flight to Vegas. That reaction to talking about her wedding was simply a release of stress. She was not unhappy that she'd left Charles. She seriously didn't care that her dad's life had been inconvenienced. She'd told them and told them and told them that she wanted a small wedding. No one listened, and eventually she'd let it drop. Because that's what she'd done since she was twelve, when her mom had died and she suddenly became lady of the house.

Not old enough to really know what to do, she'd taken her father's advice on everything. That had become such a habit she didn't even realize she'd let him pick the man she'd marry. For as much as her dad had nudged her in Charles's direction with frequent dinners at their home and trips to London, Ireland and Monaco that coincided with trips Charles was taking, her dad had also groomed Charles to be his son-in-law.

They'd seemed like the ultimate power couple until Charles's best man mentioned that fact at the rehearsal-dinner toast. Even he'd seen how Charles had been groomed and all Morgan had to do was wait until her fa-

ther's creation was finished to have the perfect man to add
to their two-person family.

The crowd had laughed, but her chest had pressed in-
ward, squeezing all the air from her lungs. His toast, no
matter how lighthearted, had a ring of truth to it. No.
More like a gong of truth. A whole Mormon Tabernacle
Choir of truth.

And Charles's response when she'd confronted him
after the dinner? He'd needed her dad's help. If marrying
her was the price, he'd pay it.

When she'd gasped, he'd said he didn't mean that the
way it sounded. He loved her. She was beautiful. Wonderful. A woman so perfect she was more like a reward,
not a price. He was sorry his explanation had come out
all wrong.

For the hours that had passed between the toast and her
trip down the aisle, she'd believed that.

But there was something about walking toward her des-
tiny, dressed in all white, looking sweet and innocent while
perpetuating something that felt very much like fraud,
that caused her feet to stop, her heart to break. Her dad
had controlled everything in her life, from where she'd
gone to school to how she dressed and who she'd invite
to their gatherings. The man she spent the rest of her life
with would be her choice.

"You okay?" Mary, the lead waitress for the afternoon
shift, studied her as she walked back to her little investment group beside the last row of slots.

She sucked in a breath and smiled. "I'm fine." She *was*
fine. Though Charles was history, she wasn't writing off
her dad completely. This was a hiccup in their relationship.
A time for her to take a breath, sort out what she wanted,
maybe come up with some new rules for how she and her

dad would relate. Then she would go back to Lake Justice. Then they would talk.

And no gorgeous Spaniard with a sexy voice was taking her back before she was ready.

CHAPTER TWO

RICCARDO STAYED AT the two-person table in the bar. From the raised vantage point, he could see Morgan as she counseled her little band of friends. She was a lot stronger than he'd imagined. He didn't want to admire her for it. It was his job to bring her home. But he had to admit to a twinge of respect that she could hold her own. Which was good. He didn't want to feel like he was riding roughshod over her by forcing her onto the plane. He wanted her to see the error of her ways and go home voluntarily to do her duty to her ex. That was more than Cicely had done for him.

He winced. Seriously. He had to stop comparing the two. At least Cicely had talked to him two days before their wedding and been honest. Morgan had just run. She'd embarrassed her groom. Embarrassed her dad. Shocked her guests. And now she wanted to give stock seminars?

Okay. That did speak to her state of mind. Ignoring something wasn't always a sign of indifference. Maybe she wasn't ready to handle it yet.

Who was he? Doctor Phil? It was not his job to fix her, just to get her home.

Of course, it wouldn't hurt to keep her mental state in mind as he guided her to see the error of her ways and agree to come back home with him.

That's what Mitch would do. And Mitch was their people person.

When the small group broke up, Riccardo glanced at his watch. Twenty minutes had gone by. Their flight left in an hour and a half. But it was a short ride to the airport. Of course, he should probably add packing time in there. He might not have luggage, but she did.

Or maybe not.

She'd run from the ceremony, jumped into her car and had gotten to Lake Justice's small municipal airport in a matter of minutes. She'd caught the commuter flight that just happened to be leaving for JFK International, and that's why they'd lost her. The plane had taken off as her dad's people were pulling in to the small airport parking lot.

He could imagine her arriving at Kennedy in her gown, stopping at the first shop she saw and buying some jeans, T-shirts and those superspiffy canvas tennis shoes.

He laughed into his beer before he finished it in one long swallow. He seriously doubted she would want to take home any of the clothes she'd bought if they were anything like what she was wearing now. But he would be more sensitive, more Mitch-like, when he approached her this time.

Except she'd better not call him Marco Polo again. Marco Polo wasn't even Spanish.

The group dispersed. Morgan took a seat at the last slot machine. She pulled her comp card out of her jeans pocket, inserted it into the poker machine and started playing.

Riccardo rose, tossed a few bills on the bar table and ambled over to her. He sat on the seat of the empty machine beside hers. "So… Our flight leaves in an hour and a half. I know it's a short ride to the airport, but we do have to go through security."

"*Your* flight leaves in an hour and a half."

"*Our* flight. You're coming with me. You're too nice of a woman to leave your groom upset and wondering what the hell happened."

"I seriously doubt Charles is upset. We'd had a disagreement the night before. He thought he'd talked me out of being angry. But I'd never been angry. I was hurt. Which means, once again, he didn't hear what I was saying. Only what he wanted to hear. When I get home, he'll have a ten-point plan for how we can fix things. And he doesn't even really know what's wrong. I have twelve days until I have to be back and I'm taking them."

He wanted to argue, but saw her point. Something had caused her to run from her own wedding. But it sounded like Charles didn't care to talk it through. All he wanted was to fix things. That wasn't very romantic. Or sensitive. Or even nice.

He hated having to drag her back to that, but all he had was her version of things. He knew what it was like to be the brokenhearted groom, totally confused—

And, once again, he was thinking about his own situation, which was entirely different and completely irrelevant. If he was going to take Morgan Monroe home, perhaps he would have to get her to talk about whatever it was that had hurt *her* and caused *her* to bolt, and stop thinking about Cicely. Then Morgan would feel better about returning to Lake Justice, and Mitch wouldn't come home from his honeymoon to find his biggest client gone—and becoming their competition.

He leaned his elbow on the poker machine and studied her. When he'd first seen her, she'd seemed out of place. But really, in her jeans and T-shirt, with her long hair casual, she looked like the average slot player on a Monday afternoon.

He nodded at her machine. "You like poker?"

She peeked over at him, her blue eyes a pretty contrast

to the tortoiseshell glasses. "To be honest, I'm just learning to play."

"That would explain why you threw away the chance for a straight flush."

"Odds are I'm not going to get it."

He bobbed his head in a sort of agreement. "Yeah, but when the machine gives you four cards in a row in the same suit and you have two open ends, your odds go up."

"Odds are odds."

"What are you? An accountant?"

She glanced over at him. "Yes."

He remembered the little stock seminar and felt like an idiot for not realizing that. He knew she was educated but he'd never thought a society girl would pick such a practical major. Her dad only talked about her charities. He'd made her sound like a sort of helpless Southern belle though they lived in upstate New York.

"You're like a CPA?"

"I *am* a CPA."

Her machine gurgled the music of a lost game and she hit a few buttons to make her bets and start the next game. Cards appeared on the screen. She threw away two twos.

His eyes narrowed. "What are you doing?"

"Two twos don't pay out."

"No. But three of a kind does. So does two pair. Starting off with two twos you have a good chance of getting another two or another pair and both of those hands pay."

"Chump change."

He laughed. "What?"

"I want to win. I don't just want to keep playing."

That was a weird strategy if ever he'd heard one. And he'd certainly heard his share in Monaco. "Who taught you that?"

"The guy who was sitting beside me on Sunday night."

"He was a professional gambler?"

"No. He manages a couple fast-food restaurants."

"And you thought this made him a genius poker player?"

She tossed her hands in the air. "Hell if I know."

He scooted over to get closer to her. He'd take this opportunity to become her friend and eventually she'd spill the story. He could sympathize and in a few minutes they'd be in his rental, heading for the airport.

"Okay, look." He pointed at the ranking of hands. "See this list here? This is what pays out and how many points."

"I know that."

"If you have a pattern that you use all the time, the machine will become accustomed to it and use that against you."

Her pale blue eyes narrowed.

"If you only go for what seems like a sure thing, it will set you up so that you keep getting those opportunities, then never give you the cards you need to make the hands, so that you lose all your money."

"Oh." She thought about that a second. "I should shake it up? Not play the same way all the time."

"Exactly. But on another trip." Now that they were friends, or at least friendly, they could talk about her wedding in the car. "Right now, we need to get you home."

She looked over at him. "We have to leave this very second? What's a few more hands going to hurt? I just want to try out what you told me."

He'd expected a bit of a protest. Maybe an argument. But getting her to think about her fiancé must have caused it to sink in that she had to take responsibility for what she'd done. She hadn't even blinked when he mentioned leaving.

He caught her gaze and saw a muddle of emotions in her blue eyes. Sincerity? Regret? Or maybe fear? She wasn't exactly returning to a celebration.

A twinge of guilt rippled through him for pushing her. The least he could do was teach her some strategies.

"Okay. A few hands."

"And you'll show me what to do?"

"Sure."

He didn't know how it happened, but a couple of hands turned into forty minutes of playing, which put them behind the eight ball. Though she'd seemed to have had a good time and was definitely a quick study, the fun had to end now.

"Okay. That's it now. Time to go."

She hit the button to cash out and got the little slip that told her she had thirty-eight dollars coming.

"Huh."

"What?"

"Thirty-eight dollars." She caught his gaze. "Hardly seems worth it."

"Most people who gamble enjoy the game."

"Really? Because I've seen video poker games that are handheld. Our cook, Martha, has a ton of them. It's how she fritters away time waiting for doctor appointments or bread to rise."

He shrugged. "People enjoy the game."

"Yes, but she doesn't spend money playing. She owns her handheld machines and can *enjoy* anytime she wants."

He sighed.

"If it's all about playing a game, enjoying a game, why not just buy the game? Why involve betting?"

"Are you trying to ruin Vegas for me?"

She laughed. "No. I mean, come on. If playing the game is the attraction and not gambling, why not just use a hand-held poker game?"

This time his sigh was eloquent. "Do *not* ruin Vegas for me."

"I'm not ruining it. I'm just pointing out that your argument doesn't hold water."

"You're a stickler for logic." And obviously so was her fiancé. Anybody who'd have a ten-point plan to fix their canceled wedding had to be logical. Was that how they'd ended up together? Two people who were so much the same it seemed inevitable that they get married?

"I *am* a stickler for logic. So sway me. Why do you really come to casinos?"

He looked into her eyes again and saw the quiet remnants of pain, even though she was very good at pretending she was fine. If talking about himself made her comfortable, calm enough that she'd be compliant through their trip, then so be it.

He shrugged. "I come to Vegas for the people, the crowds, the noise, the excitement." He couldn't stop a smile. "You never know who you're going to meet here. You can sit beside a sheikh at a blackjack table and end up a guest at a palace. Or meet the daughter of a rock star and end up backstage at a concert."

"Interesting."

She glanced around. The way her eyes shifted, he could tell she was seeing the place from a new perspective. If only for a few seconds, her sadness lifted.

"It's about people for you."

"Yes." It was one thing to help her get comfortable, quite another to let this conversation derail his plans. He'd be happy to discuss anything she wanted, just not now. He pointed to the exit. "But we'll talk about it on the way to the airport or on the plane."

She slid off her chair. "I have to pack."

"You have five minutes! I'm serious. *Five.* I'll get the car."

She nodded.

He started walking away but turned back. "And, honestly, I have no idea why you'd want these clothes. If I were you, I'd leave them."

She laughed.

A strange sensation invaded his chest. Even in those big glasses, she was incredibly beautiful. Add adorably logical and laughing—

He yanked himself back from the feeling that almost clicked into place. Attraction. He wasn't worried that he'd fall for her. His heart had been sufficiently hardened by Cicely. So the pullback was quick, easy, painless. Especially given that Morgan had also publicly dumped some poor guy.

He headed out to the valet. When the kid returned with his rental car, he gave him a good tip for being speedy. He slid behind the steering wheel and locked his gaze on the door. The first five minutes had already passed, so when a second five minutes ticked off the clock he got nervous. The third five minutes had him slapping the steering wheel. She'd ditched him.

He shoved open his door, apologized to the valet for needing a few more minutes and raced into the lobby, hoping to see her checking out at the registration desk. But the place was quiet.

The concierge slipped away from his station and ambled up to him. "Your friend left."

He spun to face the short, bald man. "What?"

"She checked out, rolled her suitcase through the casino—not the front door—and slipped out of one of the back exits." He cleared his throat. "I probably shouldn't have watched her, but it's kind of hard not to see a beautiful woman rolling an ugly black suitcase through the casino."

Riccardo pressed his fingertips into his forehead. He'd been duped. And in the most obvious, simple way. She'd used up all their time, gotten him to trust her and just walked away.

He was an idiot.

No. He had trusted her.

Hadn't he told himself he should never again trust a pretty girl?

Morgan entered her new room at the hotel right beside Midnight Sins. She felt just a teeny bit bad for deceiving the handsome Spanish guy. Not just because her dad had made him a pawn in a game that didn't have to be a game—she only wanted her twelve days to think about what to say, and how to handle him when she went home—but also because he was interesting. And fun. In a weird way, it was nice having someone so curious about her, even if it he was only asking her questions to figure out how to get her on the plane with him.

She took a shower, fixed her hair and slid into a slinky black dress she'd bought at one of the many shops in Midnight Sins. She wasn't here to have fun, but she didn't intend to sit in her room and mope, either. She'd spent her entire life semisheltered. She'd had a path at university. She'd had a path with Charles. And her dad had had too big of a hand in creating those paths. For the next twelve days, she did not want a path. She just wanted to live. Breathe. And eventually figure out an explanation for running that would appease the man who'd spent his life first fighting in wars and then preventing them.

Right now, living meant getting a salad, maybe having a gin and tonic and going to a show.

She grabbed her small beaded evening bag and left her room. Though she'd never been to Vegas before, she'd happily discovered that once she checked in to a hotel, she didn't need to leave for anything. She could sleep there, gamble there, eat there, buy a bathing suit in a shop and sunbathe at the hotel pool. She would be right under Handsome Spanish Guy's nose and he would never find her because he'd have to check hundreds of hotels. And then he'd have to find someone willing to tell him she was a guest.

The odds were absolutely in her favor.

Happy, she took the regular elevator to the first floor then a designated elevator to the rooftop restaurant, where she had a reservation.

The maître d' greeted her effusively and led her to the private table in the corner. With its walls of windows, the restaurant provided a view of Las Vegas that astounded her. She sat, smiled at the maître d' and took her menu. A minute later she gave her drink order to a friendly waiter and he left her alone to decide what she wanted to eat. She should have at least glanced at her food choices, but the view from forty stories up was too captivating. Lights and color twinkled silently below. Beyond the city, the desert was so dark she swore the world ended at the city limits.

The blackness in the window was interrupted by a strip of white. Something shiny winked. She saw the reflection of a hand.

She spun around and there was Handsome Spanish Guy. The man who wanted to take her home.

"Who are you anyway?"

"Riccardo Ochoa." He pointed at the seat across from her. "May I join you?"

She tossed her hands in despair. "No! What part of 'I'm trying to get some peace and quiet' do you not understand?"

"Well, most of it—since *I* come to Vegas to meet people and have fun."

"I came here to rest my brain. I know I have to go home and face all of this but I just want a breather."

He sighed, pulled out the chair opposite her and sat. "You are not going to make this easy for me, are you?"

"Why do you care?" She sighed. "Look. Whatever my dad is paying you, I'll double it."

"He's not paying me. He's a client of my cousin's firm."
He made a quick signal to summon the waiter and ordered
a Scotch.

When the waiter left, she said, "And my dad threatened
to walk if you didn't bring me home."

"Something like that."

"Well, I hate to disappoint you but if you're counting
on taking me home to keep him as a client you're going
to lose him."

"Well, I hate to disappoint *you*, but I've never failed on
a mission. Never. When I promised to return you to Lake
Justice, you were as good as home."

She shook her head. "So arrogant."

He laughed but the humor didn't reach his eyes. "Sweet-
heart, I'm Spanish. We invented arrogant."

"It must have really hurt your pride that I lost you." She
frowned. "How did you find me so quickly?"

His Scotch came with the drink she had ordered. He
took a long swallow. "Your credit card."

"*My* credit card?"

"Your dad got you that card when you were at university, right?"

"Yes, but I took it over. I pay the bill."

"He still has the number and his name is on the account.
Yesterday, he realized he could log in online. Now, every
time you use it, he sees where you are."

She slapped her evening bag on the white linen table-
cloth. "Damn it." She'd been so stressed out, she'd completely forgotten that.

"You're not getting away from me." He smiled. "Unless you have another card."

"I don't." She sighed. "Well, I do, but my dad's staff
got me that one, too." She drank her gin and tonic in one
long gulp, thinking through her options, which, right at
this moment, stunk.

"Sort of a little too attached to Daddy, maybe?"

She rose. "That's actually the point."

No matter what hotel she checked in to, her dad would know her location from the charge record. No matter where she flew, same deal. She could rent a car, but that would be on a card, too, and even if she drove a hundred miles away, every time she stopped for gas her dad would know where she was.

She started toward the restaurant door.

Riccardo jumped up. "Really? We're going to play this game?"

He pulled a few bills from his pocket and tossed them on the table. When he caught up to her at the elevator, he said, "There's nowhere for you to go. You're trapped."

Oh, she knew that better than anybody else.

She cast him a sideways glance. As long as her dad knew where she was, there would be someone coming after her. If this guy failed, her father would just send somebody else.

She'd already fooled Riccardo Ochoa once. She liked her odds with fooling him again. And she had a plan. She and her mom had spent many a week in Chicago shopping. She could think things through there just as well as in Vegas. She'd never get Riccardo to fly her to Chicago. But after a bit of time together, she might be able to convince him to drive her there. And she had just the way to do it.

"Do you have a rental?"

"Yes. But I'll be getting rid of it at the airport."

She turned, facing him. His gaze rippled from her bare shoulders, past the shimmery sequins of the bodice of her dress to the hem where her skirt stopped midthigh.

The quick look was as intimate as a caress. A light flickered in his dark eyes. She would bet if this guy was interested in her romantically, there wouldn't be a dull moment. Their summer vacation wouldn't be a trip to

Europe to meet with clients. He'd take her somewhere hot and steamy—

She stepped back, away from him. The last thing she wanted was a man attracted to her when she hadn't properly dealt with Charles. But she also needed this guy. She had to keep their relationship platonic.

"I don't want to fly. I don't want to be in Lake Justice any sooner than I have to be. Drive me—" She felt a prick of conscience, but desperation overwhelmed it. She was twenty-five. *Twenty-five.* And her dad was theoretically kidnapping her. This was her only move. "Instead of forcing me to fly, and I'll have a few days to think things through, while my dad calms down." She caught the gaze of his very suspicious black eyes and smiled prettily, innocently. "I just want a couple of days of peace and quiet. A car ride will give me that as well as give you something to tell my dad about why it's taking you so long to get me back."

Those dark eyes studied her. "You won't run?"

"No."

"You won't sneak out of a hotel room in the middle of the night?"

"You'll have the only keys to the car."

He still deliberated.

She stood quietly, but confidently. She didn't intend to sneak out, steal the car, or ditch him. True, she wanted him to take her to Chicago to extend their trip for an additional few days, but she'd cross that bridge when they came to it.

"Okay."

"Good. Just let me get my bags."

He laughed heartily. "Right. This time I'm coming with you."

CHAPTER THREE

THEY STEPPED OVER the threshold of her hotel room and Morgan immediately ducked into the bathroom. Riccardo ambled into the small room, but not far. He wasn't letting her get much more than an arm's distance away from him until they were at her daddy's vineyard.

His conscience grumbled a protest. When he'd accepted this assignment, he'd done it out of desperation, to protect everything he and Mitch had built. He hadn't thought much about the situation beyond the fact that Morgan had dumped her fiancé and she needed to come home and explain herself. Then she'd told him a bit about her fiancé and he'd felt sorry for her.

Then she'd duped him and now he was super suspicious of her.

But he couldn't stop thinking about her ex's ten-point plan and the sadness he'd heard in her voice. If he were to guess, he'd say she genuinely believed her fiancé hadn't loved her.

She stepped out of the bathroom wearing jeans, a tank top and the gray canvas tennis shoes. The curls had been combed out of her long blond hair and she'd pulled it into a ponytail. Her glasses were gone and he suspected she'd put in contacts. She looked innocently beautiful. So beautiful that he could probably disabuse her of the notion that her fiancé hadn't loved her. There wasn't a man on the planet who wouldn't fall for that face.

"You may not like my clothing choices but they are going to come in handy driving across the country."

He couldn't argue that. Or the fact that she was beginning to look really cute in jeans. Not quite hot. More like sweet and cuddly.

Thank goodness. Sweet he could resist. Hot? The way she'd looked in that form-fitting black dress? That was his wheelhouse. Instinct had almost taken over and he'd wanted to touch her, to smooth his hands along the lovely curve of her waist. But he hadn't because he was smart. And now she was dressed like a good girl, not the kind of woman a man played with. She was perfectly safe.

So was he.

In the hall outside her room, he took the handle of the cheap black suitcase that she'd probably bought at the worst shop she could find in the airport on her way here.

"I'll get this."

She smiled sweetly. "Thanks."

He wanted to trust that she really was this compliant, that the promise of several days on the road to calm her nerves had satisfied her. But his pride still stung from the way she'd ditched him at Midnight Sins.

They rode down the elevator and she used her credit card to check out. Then she motioned for him to follow her to an ATM. She withdrew cash three times, getting as much money as she could before the bank shut her off.

"Planning your escape?"

"No. Paying for my own food and hotel."

"You could use the credit card for that. Your dad's going to know where you are. Might as well just roll with it."

She said nothing, simply walked out the front door, her head high, as if it took great effort to preserve her pride, and his damn conscience nudged him again.

He scrambled after her. "It's not like I'm kidnapping you."

"If you were, I could at least call the police. As it is, with my dad behind your taking me away, you're more like a jailer."

"I'm not a jailer."

"Sure you are. You're keeping me from going where I want to go."

They strode the short distance back to Midnight Sins and he tossed his car keys to the valet, who rolled his eyes as he raced away to get Riccardo's rental.

"I don't know what he has to complain about. He gets a tip every time he takes or brings back my car."

She laughed.

His spirits rose a little. If she could laugh, then he shouldn't feel too bad. Because she was right. With the way all this was going down, he *was* her jailer. Or her guard. Which meant she probably felt like a prisoner.

The valet returned and handed the keys to Riccardo, who gave him a tip way beyond what he deserved.

He stowed Morgan's suitcase in the trunk before getting behind the wheel. "I just realized that I don't have anything to wear for five days on the road," he said. "I'd planned on flying to Vegas and back to Lake Justice in the same day."

"I'm sure we'll pass a discount store along the way."

"Discount store?" He glanced over at her as he started the car. He didn't like being judgmental, but he was just about positive she'd never seen the inside of a big-box store.

But, of course, *she* wasn't going to shop there, she was sending him there.

Because she had a low opinion of him?

Probably.

He shouldn't care. No matter what she thought, she

wasn't a prisoner. And he was more like the accountability police than a jailer. He was taking her back to deal with the fallout from her canceled wedding so that cleaning up the mess didn't default to her dad or her undoubtedly shell-shocked fiancé. He was doing a good thing, and on some level, she had to agree or she wouldn't be on the seat beside his.

He pulled the gearshift into Drive and eased off the hotel property into the traffic of the Vegas strip. In the time that had passed since his arrival, they'd transitioned from afternoon to evening. Hotel fountains now spewed water through glorious colored lights. Neon signs began to glow.

Realizing he had no clue where he was going, he took his phone out of his pocket, set it on the dashboard and said, "Directions to Lake Justice, New York."

After a few seconds, his GPS told him to turn around. He glanced at the green road sign up ahead and sighed. "We're going the wrong way."

Morgan didn't reply.

The GPS took him to the first street where he could make a right. He turned around and headed out to the strip again, except in the opposite direction.

"Okay. Now, we're on our way."

She said nothing.

Fine. They could spend the next four or five days in total silence and he'd be happy. She'd probably be happy, too. She'd said she wanted time to think things through. Well, he would give it to her. Jailers or guards or even accountability police didn't try to make friends with prisoners. They just got them to their destinations.

He refused to feel guilty.

Refused.

Except she'd said her fiancé didn't listen to her. The

idiot had thought she was angry, when she was hurt. Hurt enough to run out on a wedding with eight hundred guests.

Curiosity begged him to ask her about it. Especially since this was nothing like his own past. His fiancée had gone back to the love of her life. Morgan had run to nothing. No one.

The fact that she was quiet made him feel like scum. Even more than when she called him her jailer.

It didn't take long until they were on the highway, headed northeast to pick up the roads that would take them east. When they left the lights of Las Vegas, the world became eerily dark. Time passed. Riccardo wasn't sure how much because he'd been so concerned with getting Morgan into the car that he hadn't checked his watch to see when they'd started out.

He shifted on his seat, uncomfortably aware that he'd awoken at six o'clock that morning in the eastern time zone. And it was now after ten at night, mountain time. Midnight in New York. No wonder his eyelids were scratchy. And he couldn't even remember the last time he'd eaten.

"Want to stop to find someplace to stay for the night and get dinner?"

"Sure."

Her reply wasn't exactly perky or happy, but she didn't sound sad anymore, either. Ten minutes later, the road signs for a town began to appear, including one that named the available hotels and restaurants. He took the exit and drove to the first hotel.

With Morgan standing beside him, he booked a room for each of them using his own credit card. When he handed her key to her, she gave him the cash to cover her room. Then she took the handle of her suitcase and headed for the elevator.

"Don't you want dinner?"

She stopped and faced him. "I'll eat breakfast."

She turned toward the elevator again, got in and disappeared behind the closing door.

He almost cursed. But not quite. She might not be angry with *him* but upset with the situation. And the situation was her doing, her problem. Not his. It was not his fault she had no support system. He'd rescued one damsel in distress—Cicely, who had been heartbroken over losing the love of her life—and that had ended in *him* being humiliated. He had learned this lesson and refused to fall into the same trap. He was a driver—he'd settled on that instead of jailer—not a knight in shining armor.

Besides, he needed something to eat. He didn't even have a suitcase to drop off in his room. He could go now.

He walked to the sliding glass door of the popular chain hotel. It opened automatically and he turned to the right. A twenty-four-hour, diner-type restaurant was within walking distance. He strolled over, found a booth and ordered a burger and fries.

When his food arrived, his stomach danced. But when he picked up the hamburger and opened his mouth to take the first delicious bite, he remembered that Morgan had been in a restaurant, menu in front of her, when he'd barged in on her and reminded her that he'd always be able to find her because of her credit card. She'd been in that restaurant because she was hungry. No matter what she'd just said.

He sighed, put the burger back on his plate and hailed the waitress again.

"Is something wrong?"

He smiled. "Actually, it looks and smells delicious but I left my friend back at the hotel. Could I get a burger and fries to go for her?" The waitress nodded but before she turned away, he lifted his plate. "And could you put this in a to-go container, too?"

She took his plate. "I'll be glad to."

Twenty minutes later, he arrived back at the hotel with a bag containing two orders of fries and two burgers. Remembering her room number, he pushed the elevator button for her floor and inhaled deeply as the little car climbed. When the bell chimed, he stepped out and walked down the hall.

He hesitated at her door but only for a second. His nanna would shoot him for letting anyone go hungry, especially a woman in his custody.

He knocked twice and waited. After a few seconds, her door opened as far as the chain lock would allow.

"Checking up on me, Mr. Jailer?"

"No." He displayed the bag of food. "I bought you a hamburger."

"Leave it outside my door. I'll get it."

"Come on. Let me in. I'm sorry for my part in this but I made a promise and I keep my promises. If you're angry, it's because you don't like the idea of going back and facing the music."

She closed the door, undid the chain lock and opened it again. "No. I'm angry because I honest-to-God thought I'd get almost two weeks to think all this through before I had to go home and settle things with my dad and Charles." She motioned him over to the small table at the back of the room. "I should have laughed at the best man's dumb wedding toast, but what he'd said was true. My dad *had* groomed Charles to be his son-in-law and I'd fallen in line like a fluffy sheep. I would like a few days to consider all sides of the argument I'm about to have, so I'll know what to say and I can win."

His curiosity about how she hadn't seen what was going on and had been a sheep almost overwhelmed him. But if he asked for specifics he'd become involved and he didn't want to be involved. Rescuing Cicely had been enough.

He pulled the containers out of the bag and set them on the table. "You can think the entire drive." She didn't reply, but he noticed she also didn't say no to the food. "The orders are the same. Bacon burgers and fries."

She smiled stupidly. "I haven't had a burger in years." She peeked over at him. "Not since college."

"Really?"

"There's a lot of fat in beef."

"I know. I love it."

She shook her head then sat on one of the two chairs at the table. "At least I don't have to worry about fitting into a gown."

Taking his cue from her, he sat on the chair across from her. "There is that."

She bit into the hamburger and groaned in ecstasy. "That's so freaking good."

He laughed.

She tried a fry and her eyes closed as she savored it. "I can't eat like this the whole trip. We have to have a salad now and again."

"Noted." He also noted she hadn't called him a jailer again and she was making small talk. He bit into his burger and his stomach sighed with relief. He ate three bites and four fries before he realized she'd gone silent again.

She did have things to work out before she talked to her dad. But his curiosity rose again. Plus, he didn't want her to be sad for five long days. Surely, he could hear the story without wanting to jump in and fix things for her.

"What did your fiancé's best man say in the toast that made you feel like a sheep?"

She shrugged. "That my dad had groomed Charles to be his *son-in-law.* Not even my husband. *His* son-in-law." She shook her head as if she could shake away the anger. "But it wasn't all about the toast. The toast merely confirmed odd, disjointed thoughts I'd been having for a few months before the wedding. My first doubts appeared while we were planning. I realized that Charles insisted on his own way a lot."

"Were you one of those brides who'd planned her wedding when she was six and got mad when he asked for a few changes?"

"No. It was more that he had this grand, elegant event planned, and since I was sort of clueless about what I wanted, I went along."

"Makes sense."

For the first time in hours she held his gaze. The sadness was gone from her pretty blue eyes, but not the confusion.

"Yes. At the time, it did."

"But eventually it didn't?"

"No, eventually I saw that he got his own way a lot. That he always told me what we'd be doing. Everything from vacations to whose Christmas parties we'd attend."

"Ah."

"Then I noticed that if I tried to get something my way, he'd bulldoze me." She suddenly closed the lid on her container of food, which was still half-uneaten, and bounced out of her seat. "You know what? That's enough about me and my almost wedding to Charles." She tossed her container in a wastebasket under the small, wooden desk and turned to him with a smile. "I'm tired and I'm talking about things I haven't even worked through."

He understood why her realizations infuriated her enough that she was done talking. Cicely had been all about getting her own way about their wedding, too, and he'd wanted so much to make her happy that he always fell in line.

"I knew somebody like that. We were engaged."

"What happened?"

"She called off the wedding."

She grimaced. "Like me?"

"No. She called it off a few days before so we had a chance to cancel things like flowers and the caterer."

"I'm sorry."

"Hey, I didn't tell you that to make you feel worse. I wanted you to understand that I've dealt with someone who was selfish, too. Cicely didn't let me have a say in our wedding and though she didn't exactly bulldoze, she did have a knack for always getting her own way."

Morgan laughed.

He smiled. "I'm glad you're feeling better."

Her head tilted and her eyes met his. "I don't feel better. I may never feel better. I was suffocating in that dress, walking down the aisle. Turning and running was like saving myself...like a survival instinct." She drew in a breath and huffed it out again. "But I upset people. And I'm not used to that. I'm not used to putting myself first at the expense of others. When I turned and ran, I lost the girl who would never in a million years hurt another person. So, no. I don't feel better. I may never feel better again."

The next morning, he brought breakfast sandwiches to her room. Morgan suspected that was to keep her moving, but he need not have worried. She didn't intend to slow him down. She wanted him to trust her again. When they reached the point in the highway when one simple turn would take them to Chicago, she wanted him to be willing to take it.

"Can I help with your suitcase?"

A week ago, she wouldn't have minded a man being deferential to her. Now? She just wanted to do things herself. To *be* herself. But she wouldn't argue something so stupid and risk alienating him. She let him wheel her bag out to the parking lot.

When they had settled in the car, she pointed up the

road. "I see a few stores along there. Do you want to drive over and get a pair of jeans? Maybe a clean shirt or two?"

He laughed. "Do I smell bad? Or are you prolonging the trip?"

"Neither." She pulled in a breath. There was no time like the present to start the campaign to get him on her side. "As I told you last night, I'm normally a very considerate person. Now that the shock is wearing off, part of the real me must be coming back."

He glanced over. "I get that."

"Do you?"

"Yeah, I thought about what you'd said about how you felt when you bolted, and I realized there probably isn't a person in the world who doesn't understand the feeling of suffocating when you're with someone who always has to have their own way."

Though he didn't know that her dad was really the one suffocating her, she smiled. "Thank you."

The conversation died as he drove them to one of the big-box stores. As they got out of the convertible and headed for the door, she realized she was okay in her jeans and canvas tennis shoes, but in his expensive white shirt and black trousers he looked like he'd just stepped off the Las Vegas strip—at one of the better hotels. People were going to stare.

The automatic doors opened as they approached. When they walked inside, he got a cart.

She frowned at him. "What are you doing?"

"I need clothes for three or four days." He nodded at his shiny handmade Italian loafers. "I'm not wearing these anymore. I want tennis shoes. Even with two of us to carry things, there'll be too much for us to tote around."

"I'm not talking about the clothes. What are you doing being so familiar with a shopping cart at a retail store?"

He laughed. "I came to this country a few years ago.

And I've been exploring ever since. I don't shop at stores like this often but I've investigated them."

It was a real struggle not to laugh, then she wondered why. If she moved to Spain, she'd probably investigate things, too. At least she hoped she would. Lately, she was beginning to realize she didn't know herself at all. Oh, she knew she was kind, a decent human being. But she'd taken a job at her dad's vineyard that wasn't even remotely challenging. She'd let it blow by her that her dad had thrown her and Charles together. And she'd been complacent with Charles. Where was the little girl who'd wanted her life to be an adventure?

She didn't even have to wait for the answer to pop into her head. That little girl had grown up and realized she had only one parent and if she displeased him she'd be all alone.

That was really the bottom line to her battle. Her dad was her only family. She loved him and didn't want to fight or argue. But she was an adult now, not a little girl, and she couldn't let him go on telling her what to do and how to do it. She had to take her life back.

Still, her dad was a brilliant, powerful man, accustomed to getting his own way. Could she make him see he was suffocating her? And if she did, would he stop? *Could* he stop?

Or was the real solution to her problem to leave? Permanently. Pack her bags. Get an apartment. And never see him again.

The thought shot pain through her.

That's why she needed the few days. To adjust to the fact that the conversation she needed to have with her dad just might be their last.

Riccardo recognized that his familiarity with the store totally puzzled Morgan, but within minutes he was preoccupied with getting himself enough clothes for what would probably be another four days on the road.

They returned to the rental car, drove back to the highway and were on the road for six hours before they stopped to get a late lunch. They drove and drove and drove until afternoon became evening and evening became night and—honestly—his backside hurt.

"I think we should stop for the night."

She shrugged. "Okay."

"I thought I'd shower and put on clean clothes, then we could get something to eat."

"Sure."

Her one-word answer didn't annoy him. It simply made him feel funny. After almost two days together, hearing bits and pieces of some of the most emotional, wrenching parts of her life, it seemed weird that she was back to behaving as if they were strangers. It was good that she was no longer calling him her jailer, but he knew there was something she wasn't telling him. He'd thought through her scenario—her dad grooming her fiancé and her fiancé being clueless—and nothing about that screamed running away and needing almost two weeks to get your head straight before you could go home.

Something bigger troubled her.

Except for the times they'd found radio stations, the inside of the car had been silent. She'd had plenty of time to confide in him. But she hadn't.

When they reached another hotel chain at a stop just off the highway, they got out of the car, registered and went to their rooms.

Showering, he told himself that it was stupid, maybe foolish, to want to hear her full story. Once he dropped her off at her father's vineyard, he'd probably never see her again. At the same time, he thought it was cruel to put her in a car and drive her home, and then not say anything to her beyond "where do you want to eat?" If they'd flown, they could have stayed silent for the hours it would have taken to get to Monroe Vineyards. But driving was a whole different story. The long days of nothing but static-laced music or the whine of tires should be making her crazy enough to talk if only to fill the void, but she kept silent.

He stepped out of the bathroom and put on a pair of his new jeans, a big T-shirt and tennis shoes. They had dinner at the diner beside the hotel, where she focused on eating her salad, not talking, then he went back to his room and fell into a deep, wonderful sleep. He woke refreshed, took another shower, put on clean clothes again and firmly decided Morgan's life was her life. Her decisions were hers to make. He wasn't going to ask her about either.

Just as he was about to pick up his wallet and the rental car keys, his phone rang.

He looked at the caller ID and saw it was Colonel Monroe.

He clicked to answer. "Good morning, Colonel."

"I'd expected to hear from you yesterday."

"Things weren't exactly cut-and-dried with your daughter."

The Colonel sighed heavily. "What did she do?"

Not about to admit how easily she'd duped him, Riccardo turned the conversation in a different direction. "You know she bolted from her wedding for a reason."

"What reason? Seriously? What could be important enough that she'd humiliate herself that way?"

He'd never thought of the fact that a runaway bride humiliated herself. Especially not with Cicely. He'd only seen his side of the story—that two days before his wedding the woman who was supposed to love him told the world she didn't by calling off the wedding. It had been humbling, but worse than that, it had hurt. Hurt to the very core of his being. He'd seen himself as her knight in shining armor. The real prince she was supposed to marry. The guy who would make her life wonderful. And in the end, she'd thrown it all back in his face and left with the man who had crushed her. She'd proved that good guys don't win. Bad guys do.

"You think she humiliated herself?"

"Sure, Charles and I might be left holding the bag, but we're also the ones talking to confused guests. What we're hearing is that everybody thinks she's a little crazy or selfish...or both."

He pictured the small town of Lake Justice, filled with concerned friends and neighbors, all expressing sympathy to Charles and questioning Morgan's sanity. But he knew Charles had hurt *her*. Now the idiot was sucking up sympathy, at the expense of Morgan's reputation.

"She's got a lot of explaining to do, and I sure as hell hope she's got a reason that doesn't make things worse. She already looks like a fool. Has she said anything?"

Riccardo winced. If she looked like a fool it was because Charles and her dad had made her into one. At least Riccardo wouldn't betray her trust.

"No. She hasn't really said anything."

"This is so not like her. None of it is. She was always so quiet and so quick to do what needed to be done."

Another picture began to fall into place in Riccardo's head. A picture of Morgan taking orders from her famous, powerful dad. Never arguing. Never complaining. Just falling in line.

The sheep metaphor became clearer.

"Maybe it's difficult being given orders by the man who was once secretary of state."

The Colonel laughed. "I know. I do have a tendency to be bossy."

"I wouldn't say that you're bossy. More accustomed to being in command."

"Of the foreign policy for an entire country," he said wistfully. "One word from me could have started World War Three. But it never happened because a good soldier is a diplomat first." He sighed. "And I guess that takes us back to my daughter."

"She wants a little time to think."

"She doesn't have time. We need to issue a statement."

Riccardo's brow furrowed. "Issue a statement?"

"I have business contacts who couldn't stay and wait for her to return and explain herself. So does Charles. The sooner we get something out, the better."

"I'm not sure anybody really cares—"

"*You're* not sure? I didn't send you to be sure. I sent you to bring Morgan home. I need to deal with this, and the best way is to get her out into the charity-ball circuit with Charles so that people stop talking about her."

Totally confused, he said, "You'd send her out with Charles? As if nothing happened? Don't you think that would only start people talking again?"

He laughed. "Well, look at you, giving me advice. How many wars have you averted, son?"

Riccardo grimaced.

"How many kids did you raise?" Without giving Riccardo a chance to answer, he said, "Bring her home." Then he hung up.

Riccardo shoved his phone into his jeans pocket, picked up his wallet and car keys and walked to the hotel-room door, righteous indignation making his blood boil. He thought of Morgan again, living with the Colonel, always coming under his command, and sympathy for her exploded. Worse, her dad wasn't just demanding she return home. He would stick her back with the jackass who had hurt her.

His protective instincts kicked into high gear but he instantly stopped them. He'd already made up his mind

that this was Morgan's problem, not his. He couldn't interfere. If that wasn't enough to pull him back, the interests
of Ochoa Online were. Mitch had a lot on the line. The
Colonel had warned Riccardo about his plan to build his
own wine website to compete with OchoaWines.com the
night *before* the wedding. Morgan running had actually
been good for Mitch and Riccardo because it forced the
former secretary of state to offer the one thing, the *only*
thing, that would give Riccardo a reason to go after his
daughter: an end to his plans. If Riccardo would just go
to Vegas and bring Morgan home, the Colonel wouldn't
build his competing site.

He had to take her home. No more hemming and haw-
ing around. No more being kind to a woman he really
didn't know. He had to fulfill his promise.

He found Morgan in the lobby and they decided to have
breakfast at the little diner where they'd eaten the night
before. After ordering, he glanced at her angelic face. Serious blue eyes. Pert nose. Full lips. He had to take her
home, but he couldn't let her walk totally clueless into the
mess she'd find. He had to at least lead her in a direction
that would alert her that she needed to be prepared for the
worst when she returned to Like Justice.

"I talked to your dad this morning."

She winced. "He's still angry."

"Yes. But he also gave me the idea that some of your
guests haven't left yet."

She sighed. "A lot of people decided to use traveling
to the wedding as an opportunity to take an early fall vacation, tour the local wineries, that sort of thing." She
caught his gaze. "But what you're really telling me is that
I'm not going to go home to a private resolution. I'll have
an audience."

"You might actually arrive to find a bunch of people
waiting with popcorn and soda, hoping to see a show."

She sighed, combed her fingers through her hair and shook her head. "Here I was wondering if I could get ten minutes to talk to Charles without my dad. Now I have to wonder if I'll get any privacy at all."

"You don't think your dad will let you talk to Charles alone?"

"No. That's part of the reason figuring out what to say is so difficult. If I knew I would talk to them separately, I'd say one set of things to Charles and one set to my dad."

"Makes sense."

"But figuring out what to say to them together, or even how to convince my dad to leave the room so I can talk to Charles first…it's almost impossible."

"All the more reason to be prepared with good answers when you get home."

She gaped at him. "Haven't I been telling you that all along!"

Her feistiness made him laugh. "Well, look at you getting all sassy with me. Like you were in Vegas." He pointed at her. "You need to remember this. How you feel. So that when you get home, you can make demands."

"Make demands? To my father?"

"Okay. Maybe not make demands. But tell him what you need."

She laughed. "That sounds good in theory but I doubt it will work. If I can't make him leave the room so I can have a private conversation with the man I thought I was going to marry, I don't see how I can make him realize he's suffocating me. The way I see this playing out, I either have to go back to the way things were, or I have to go out on my own. Which will make him so angry, I'll probably never see him again."

Saddened, Riccardo studied her, finally understanding that was the real reason she was delaying going home.

She truly believed she'd either have to go back to being a sheep, or she'd be nothing at all.

"Surely, there are other choices."

"I couldn't even get my way about my own wedding. My dad still sees me as the twelve-year-old I was when my mom died. He always believes he's doing the right thing for me. There's no malice intended. So, of course, he doesn't understand if I disagree. Which is why I rarely disagreed. Until now. Until something inside me froze and just wouldn't let me walk down that aisle."

The waitress arrived with their food and Riccardo thanked her. He waited until she'd completely walked away before he leaned across the table. He might have decided not to interfere, but it wouldn't hurt to give her a little guidance so she'd find the answers herself.

"Maybe walking down the aisle, your subconscious was telling you it was time to grow a pair."

Her mouth fell open. "Is that what you want me to go home and tell my dad? Oh, hi, Dad. I left my wedding because my subconscious was telling me to grow a pair?"

"What's he going to do? Arrest you?"

"Disown me." She picked up a square of toast to butter it, but put it down again. "Look, all this must seem very funny to you. But it's oddly life-and-death to me. I don't want to lose my dad. I lost my mom. And I don't have aunts or uncles, siblings or cousins. I have no one. I don't want to lose the only other family I have. So, while I appreciate your sentiments, you don't understand. I can't just go home a totally different person. I have to figure out how to behave so that things change but he still accepts me."

"You can't just be yourself?"

She tossed her hands. "I don't even know who *myself* is."

"I think—"

"Don't think. From here on out, just drive. Let me think."

Riccardo said, "Fine," and dug in to his eggs and home fries as if his life depended on it. He'd been working to stay out of her drama, but when he couldn't help giving her advice, his thanks was to be scolded. So, fine. He was out.

CHAPTER FOUR

MORGAN'S CHEST TIGHTENED. She hadn't meant to insult Riccardo. Especially since she wasn't angry with him for making suggestions. She was angry with herself because she honestly could not figure out what to say to her dad or how to say it. In her head, she'd rehearsed something snappy and snarky—not quite as crude as Riccardo's suggestion—but a potent little "Dad, it's my life, and I'm going to live it the way I want."

And she'd pictured her dad frowning. He wouldn't yell. Even if she yelled, he wouldn't. No, no. He'd frown in disappointment. Then tell her something like, "You're choosing to toss away the benefit of all my years of experience."

She'd determined there were six comebacks to that. But her dad would have even better comebacks to all six of those.

Because that's what he'd done for a living for twelve years: outtalk world leaders, some of the smartest people on the planet.

How was she going to best that?

They finished eating, got into the car and stayed silent for two hours. Morgan used the time to have unsuccessful conversations with her dad in her head until the car made a noise that sounded like a bump.

Riccardo immediately slowed the car.

Bump.

Bump.

Bump.

"Damn."

She gripped the dashboard as Riccardo eased the car off the highway. "What is it?"

"A flat tire."

She glanced at him incredulously. "This is what a flat tire feels like?"

"Yes. We probably ran over something sharp and it took this long for the air to seep out."

"You think we ran over something?"

He peered across the seat at her. "Unless somebody punched it with something sharp on purpose."

She shook her head. "I didn't do that, Mr. Jailer."

"I know." He chuckled. "I haven't let you out of my sight long enough for you to find something sharp and jam it sufficiently into the tread that a tire would go flat. If you'd done it while I was sleeping, the tire would have been flat in the morning."

He turned off the engine, pushed open the door and got out.

He'd actually thought that through? Wondered if she'd be idiot enough to ruin a tire?

She shoved open her car door and scrambled after him. "You still don't trust me!"

He sighed as he pushed the key fob to open the trunk. "It's not my job to trust you. It's my job to get you home. No talking, no thinking, just driving. Remember?"

She combed her fingers through her hair. She'd hated making him angry at breakfast. She wasn't the kind of person who lashed out at anyone. Plus, he'd been good to her. He didn't deserve her anger. "Sorry about that."

He said nothing.

"Really. I don't generally act like this, and I feel bad about insulting you."

He pulled in a breath and studied her for a second. "Okay. Apology accepted. But only because the quiet car this morning about drove me nuts."

"You were bored?"

"Weren't you? We've done nothing but drive and eat for days. It's getting old."

She had a little too much on her mind to be bored, but maybe that was the problem. Maybe if she'd stop thinking, an answer would come.

"I wasn't bored. I was trying to come up with something to say to my dad. But apparently thinking isn't helping, so maybe it's time to talk. Except not about my dad. Surely, there are a million other things we could discuss."

Standing in front of the trunk, he considered that. "You're right. The only time we fight is when we talk about you going home. Better to stay away from that. Agreed?"

"Agreed."

He smiled his acknowledgment and her heart kicked against her ribs. Good grief, he was gorgeous. A Nebraska breeze blew his dark hair across his forehead and above brown eyes that were sharp and curious. Warmth flooded her. She dropped her gaze, but it landed on a full mouth that had her wondering what kissing him would be like.

"Let's see if this thing has a spare." He turned his attention to the car again.

She blew out a quiet sigh of relief that he hadn't seemed to notice the way she was looking at him, before she peeked into the trunk and watched him lift the carpeting to reveal a spare tire and some tools. He dropped the tools and tire on the ground then crouched beside the flat. Using the long shiny thing, he eased off the hubcap.

His broad back stretched his knit shirt to capacity then

tapered into a trim waist. His blue jeans encased an absolutely perfect butt.

He peered over his shoulder at her. "Taking notes?"

Her face heated. She hoped he was talking about the tire change and hadn't seen the way she was studying him. "No. But maybe I should. If my dad kicks me out, I might need to be able to do things like this."

She regretted the words the minute they were out of her mouth. Talking about her dad was supposed to be off the table.

He rose, took the second tool and put it under the car's bumper to raise the tire off the road. Cars drove by but the silence from Riccardo was deafening.

Finally, he said, "No trust fund?"

Glad he'd found a way to redeem the conversation, she admitted something she rarely told anyone. "A healthy one, actually."

"So, you'll probably never have to change your own tire."

He might have great eyes, a mouth she wanted to kiss and a nice butt, but the man was back to insulting her. "Look at the pot calling the kettle black. What do you do for a living that lets you drop work at a moment's notice and traipse around the country ruining other people's privacy?"

"You mean what do I do for Ochoa Online?"

"If that's where you work."

He turned and picked up the third tool, crouched beside the car and began unscrewing the bolts that held the tire in place. "Yes. That's where I work."

She slid her gaze from his broad back to his bottom, along muscular thighs currently holding him balanced in front of the tire he disconnected. He had to be strong not to grunt or groan or even sway.

The cool September air suddenly grew warm again.

She forced herself back into the conversation. "So you own a company?"

"Technically, my cousin Mitch owns Ochoa Online." His attention taken by the tire and the conversation, he didn't even glance at her. She took advantage and ran her gaze along the muscles of his arms as they flexed with every twist of the big wrench.

"I'm the money guy. I create and watch our budgets and five-year plans. I monitor sales. And the minute more than thirty dollars in profit comes in, I invest it."

Her brow furrowed. "Thirty dollars?"

"I was teasing."

Annoyed with herself for being so distracted by the flexing of his muscles that she'd made a dumb mistake, she didn't reply.

After thirty seconds of nothing but the sound of interstate traffic whizzing by, he said, "Probably not a lot of teasing goes on at your dad's dinner parties."

"More than you'd expect." Curious about him, and his connection to her father, Morgan brought back the subject of his job. "So, my dad pays to be on your wine site?"

He rose, reached for the spare and carried it to the car. "No. We list his wine and get a commission on everything he sells through our site."

Wow. No wonder taking her home was so important to him. "You make a lot of money because of him, don't you?"

"People like brands. Status. Especially when it comes to wine. Your dad himself is a brand, the epitome of status."

A breeze ruffled his dark hair again but this time it brought the scent of his aftershave to her. She'd smelled it in the car for days, but right now with him making changing a tire look sexy, as he talked about things that made her realize he was pretty damn smart, she began to wonder about him. Who he was. How loyal he had to be to his cousin to take on the task of bringing home a runaway bride. And good grief, why was such a great-smelling, smart, sexy guy still single?

Flustered by her thoughts while he was blissfully unaware that she was practically lusting after him, she said, "Are you telling me my dad's wines only sell because of his name?"

"Your dad's wines are excellent. Name or no name, he wouldn't get on OchoaWines.com if Mitch didn't like the flavor and quality."

She laughed. "Really? You'd have turned down Colonel Monroe?"

"Not me. Mitch." He twisted the wrench, fastening the bolts for the new tire, causing the muscles of his back to ripple. "He has standards for the products he sells. A reputation for offering only the best. People shop at his sites because they know they don't have to look anywhere else. He has the best. So, he'd turn down Queen Elizabeth if her products didn't meet his standards."

"That would be interesting to see."

"No one's ever turned down your dad?"

She thought for a second. "No. Even when things start going wrong, my dad has the ability to guide any conversation in the direction he wants it to go."

"Which is why you're worried about talking to him."

Because they'd agreed not to discuss this, she simply said, "Yes."

He rose, dusted his hands on his thighs and caught her gaze. "You really think he'd kick you out of his life?"

Part of her wanted to remind him they said they weren't going to talk about her situation. The other part wanted another person to understand so she wouldn't think she was just this side of crazy for not being able to live that way anymore.

The other part won. "Not in the way you're assuming.

He wouldn't say, 'That's it, Morgan. You're out of here.' He'd tell me he was disappointed in me and treat me differently, coolly, until I fell in line again."

"That's a hell of a way to live."

"Actually, it was a very easy way to live in some respects. I knew exactly what he wanted from me. A respectful daughter who helped him in his business. In fact, I think the blame for Charles rests as much on me as it does on him. I dated Charles because I knew it was what my dad wanted. He wanted me with Charles. So, I was with Charles."

Riccardo stared at her, a confused expression on his handsome face. "That's just sad."

The wind raised her hair and she tucked it behind her ear. "No. It was life with my father. Walking down the aisle, I realized I wanted more."

"More?"

She almost blurted out that she wanted somebody like him. Someone strong and interesting. Someone who listened to her opinions. Gave her choices. But after running away from her wedding, another man was the last thing on her mind. As it was, if her dad shut her out, she'd have to create an entire new life, without family, and probably with only a handful of friends who'd be okay with going against her dad. She didn't need the added complication of this handsome Spanish guy.

But, oh, he was tempting.

"I don't know how to describe *more* except to say I realized I'd never had the chance to see who I am. What I'd do if I didn't have one of the smartest men on the planet making my decisions for me before I even knew there were decisions to be made."

"I think I get it. Your dad looked down the board, knew he'd want grandkids, found a suitable guy and introduced him into your world."

"That's it exactly!"

He picked up the old tire.

Happy he understood, she bent over to gather the tools. "It's like you were in our living room."

He tossed the tire into the trunk and took the tools from her. "I know a bit about bossy patriarchs. Mitch and I are modern thinkers, but our dads aren't. Our granddad was worse." He looked up at her. "It's why Nanna's so strong. Not opinionated, but strong."

"Your grandmother, right?"

"Yes. She was married to a guy two generations above me. My father and Uncle Santiago are strong, but apparently their father was like a stubborn bull."

"My dad's not a bull, but he's stubborn. But not like you'd think. He doesn't dig in his heels and fight. He has this look."

She tried to imitate her father's expression when he was unhappy with something she said.

Riccardo shook his head. "Sorry. That wouldn't get me to change my mind."

"How about this one?" She raised one eyebrow as she squinted.

"I'd probably offer him a laxative."

"Stop!" A laugh escaped her. "I don't want to make fun of my dad. I just want to show you that he can be intimidating."

"I already know that."

She nodded. "That's right. He got you to come after me by threatening to pull out of your company."

"Among other things."

"He knows how to find a weakness and exploit it."

"So, you have to figure out how to be strong. Sometimes it isn't what you say but how you say it." He closed the trunk and said, "'Dad, thank you very much for the benefit of your experience but I've decided to go in another direction.'"

She sighed. "He'd pour a brandy, offer me a seat on a Queen Anne chair by the fireplace in the den and ask me to explain the direction."

"And you'd say, 'I'm not ready to reveal particulars yet.'"

She deepened her voice, imitating her dad. "'It sounds to me that you haven't thought it through.'"

He raised his voice an octave to sound like a woman. "'Nope. I'm good. Say, did you see the Patriots won another game?'"

She laughed. Really laughed. "He'd know I was deflecting and just bring the conversation back."

"And you deflect again. Until he can't remember what you were talking about."

She gazed up at him. "I wish it was that simple."

"I'm not saying that you'd get it right the first time. You'd need to practice."

"Like in a mirror?"

"You could do that. But the best practice would be engaging in conversations with him. See what works. Toss what doesn't."

"I can't do that. I have to set things straight as soon as I get home." She swiped her windblown hair across her face and behind her ear again. "I don't want to give him the impression that things can go back to the way they were. I want to have the conversation the minute I see him. But that just confuses things because I also need to talk to Charles. I have this horrible feeling that I'll be in on this dual discussion, talking to Charles about breaking up and my dad about our future. And nobody will hear me. It'll be a mess."

"I thought you said your dad was leaving for Stockholm?"

"He is. Two days after my honeymoon was supposed to be over."

"So, go home after he's gone. Talk to Charles first, then talk to him."

She stared at him. "That's brilliant." The wind blew her hair across her face and she whisked it away again.

"You got some dust on your face."

He brushed his finger along her cheek and Morgan's heart stuttered. The whole world seemed to stop. The touch had been as gentle as the breeze, but it had the power to steal her breath. Add that to him standing so close, smelling fantastic, looking even better and actually listening to her, and her brain almost couldn't process it.

With their gazes locked and the sound of the interstate a dull hum behind them, her heart beat so hard she swore she could feel it. She'd give every cent in her considerable trust fund to be able to kiss him.

"There's another reason to delay going home. If you go back now, he's going to have you go out into the charity-ball circuit with Charles."

All thought of kissing him fled. "What?"

"He thinks that's damage control."

Fury roared through her. "That's insanity!"

"He's saying it's a way to stave off gossip."

"It's a way to get me back with Charles!" She tossed her hands and stomped away, yelling, "Damn! Damn! Damn!"

A car suddenly pulled up behind them. The driver rolled down his window and called, "Everything okay here?"

"Yes! We're fine," Riccardo answered. "Flat tire. We fixed it."

The older man nodded toward her. "Everything okay with your friend?"

Riccardo laughed. "Yes. She just got bad news."

"Okay." The man pulled his gearshift out of Park. "You

should stop at the next town to make sure there's enough air in the spare."

"Will do!"

The man drove off and Morgan just stared at calm, casual Riccardo. Had she been with her dad, she would have been embarrassed that a car had stopped because she was having a fit. With Riccardo she didn't even feel a blip of discomfort. And neither did he. It didn't bother him that she yelled, tossed her hands, even stomped a little. He hadn't called her unladylike. Hadn't reminded her people could see.

The strangest sense filled her. For as sexy and smart and fascinating as he was, he was also very calm and collected. She didn't have to be on guard or on her best behavior around him. She was with, arguably, the best-looking, sexiest man she'd ever met, and she was comfortable.

That thought brought her up short.

Comfortable? The man had virtually kidnapped her. And the way he looked at her had made her want to kiss him.

Kiss him.

She didn't know what she was feeling around him, but it sure as hell wasn't comfortable.

They did stop at the next town. Riccardo checked them into a hotel so she could take a break while he had the tire inspected at a garage. She showered, put on a clean outfit and watched mindless TV as she waited for his call. When her room phone finally rang, they decided to get dinner after he showered.

She combed her hair and primped a bit, making herself look the best she could in cheap jeans, telling herself she was not trying to be attractive for him. She just wanted to look her best.

Eventually, he called again and he instructed her to

meet him in the lobby so they could walk to the restaurant beside the hotel.

When she got to the reservation desk, he already stood there, handsome in his new jeans and plain blue shirt and smelling like someone sent straight from heaven.

As they walked to the nearby restaurant, she reminded herself that she still had a fiancé. Reminded herself that this guy making her feel things she never felt before was also carting her home to her dad. She couldn't be comfortable or happy around him. She had to stay focused.

Riccardo's steak sizzled as the waitress set it in front of him.

Morgan glanced at it longingly. "That sounds delicious."

"I know it will be." He peered at her salad. "You really should eat more red meat."

She poked at a piece of bacon. "This is kind of red."

He chuckled. "You have an interesting sense of humor."

She wished she could just say thanks. But the truth was she wasn't anything like the person she'd been with him for the past few days.

"No, I don't. With you I just sort of say what jumps into my head. That's why you laugh. But most of it is meaningless."

"Everything in life doesn't have to have meaning. Otherwise, we'd all be extremely serious and extremely tired."

"I had been!" She hadn't meant to say that. Once again, it had just popped out and she said it because she was comfortable with him, when she shouldn't be.

She squeezed her eyes shut. "See what I mean?"

"You were being honest. Isn't that what you're trying to do? Find the real you? The honest one?"

"I didn't realize I'd have to be a bumbling idiot to find her."

"You're not a bumbling idiot. You're normal. Normal

conversation ebbs and flows. Sometimes people say things that sound funnier when they come out than the person had intended. Sometimes people blurt things out by instinct." He reached across the table and took her hand. "But that's how the person you're talking to actually gets to know you."

She pulled her lower lip between her teeth. He probably thought she was thinking that through. The truth was, the feeling of his big hand wrapped around hers sent warmth cascading through her. He was gorgeous. Sexy. Honest. Real. And so easy to talk to. She longed to open up completely, tell him every darned thing in her life, then kiss him senseless.

Which was insane. Ridiculous. Riccardo Ochoa wasn't merely taking her back to her dad, she also had Charles at home. Somebody she'd thought she'd loved, but she didn't. She shouldn't even *want* to get involved with another man.

She *didn't* want to get involved with another man.

She was simply really, really attracted to Riccardo. *Physically.*

It had to be nothing more than a physical attraction. She didn't know him well enough for what she felt to be deeper. And he most certainly didn't have the kindness and compassion she kept attributing to him. Otherwise, he wouldn't be taking her back to her father.

For once, she was glad he'd stuck to his guns taking her home. It proved he wasn't the nice guy she believed. He was a man with a mission. She was just a means to an end for him.

As long as she remembered that, the physical attraction she felt for him would fade.

Riccardo saw the battle in her eyes and immediately changed the subject. How she handled her life wasn't his concern, but she was so lost it was hard not to offer her counsel. Still, it was wrong. Especially when the things he'd just told her only seemed to confuse her more.

They finished dinner making polite conversation about Mitch, his websites, Mitch's new wife, Lila, and Lila's mom, Francine. At age ten, Lila had told a social worker about her mom's alcohol abuse and she'd been shuffled into foster care and gotten lost in the system. She and her mom hadn't seen each other in fifteen years and Mitch had been instrumental in bringing them together.

Riccardo had told the story to have something to talk about that could take him and Morgan through dinner and the walk back to the hotel, but watching her face in the elevator back to their side-by-side rooms, he knew the story had affected her.

"I lost my mom at twelve and she lost her mom at ten?"

"Yes." He wouldn't have told her Lila's story if he'd remembered how old Morgan had been when her mom died. But maybe it was good that he hadn't. It was the first normal curiosity he'd seen in her eyes since this trip began. Though her story and Lila's were different, they'd both lost their moms.

"So how did Lila end up?"

"Happy. She works for us. Her mom, too. They had some open, honest conversations, but the bottom line was they had missed each other." He paused. "No, I think they longed for each other. That's why they didn't quit when the discussions got difficult. I was proud of them both."

The elevator doors opened but she didn't get out. Instead, her head tilted and she studied him. "Are you really this emotional?"

"Excuse me?"

"You really seem to get emotional about other people's problems."

He directed her out of the elevator. "First off, Spaniards call it passionate. Second, look who you're comparing me to. A dad who constantly manipulated you to get his own way, and a guy who had to have an older friend fix him up with his daughter. Of course you see me as being emotional. You've lived in a world with two duds for a decade."

Morgan laughed then squeezed her eyes shut as if she hated admitting it, but she said, "True."

"And Charles didn't stop there," Riccardo said, enjoying her laughter. When she laughed, her tension left. The confusion in her eyes dimmed. And he didn't have to regret his part in taking her home. "Oh, no. He went all the way and let his older friend groom him."

"Um, take a look in front of you." She laughed again. "I can't even figure out how to explain running from my wedding. It's not as if I was such a great prize myself."

"You are a great prize." The words came out soft and filled with regret that her dad had skewed the way she saw herself.

She stopped at her door, but she didn't use her key card to open it. She glanced at Riccardo, her pale pink face illuminated by the light beside her door. "I'm a twenty-five-year-old woman who doesn't know who she is."

"You have to know you're beautiful."

She caught his gaze. Her long black lashes blinked over sad blue eyes. "Physical things fade."

"You're pretty in here," he countered, touching her chest just above the soft swell of her breasts. "When you're sixty, eighty, a hundred, you'll still be compassionate."

She shook her head. "You don't know that. We just met. Aside from the fact that I ran from my wedding and my dad's a bit of a control freak, you don't know much of anything about me."

"I know that you connected with Lila's story and felt bad for both Lila and her mom."

"Because I understood."

"Other people dismiss Francine as being selfish, weak. Most are sad for Lila. You felt sorry for both."

"There are two sides to every story."

"And maybe that's what you need to tell your dad."

As she thought that through, the air around them stilled. She swung her long blond hair over her shoulder. Her head tilted and she smiled. "You know what? Maybe it is."

Silence hung between them as they stared into each other's eyes. The warmth in her big blue orbs touched his heart, but the lift of her lips sparked a small fire in his belly. Everything male inside him awoke. The urge to kiss her tumbled through him.

Fighting it, he forced himself to return her smile, though he had to clear his throat before he could speak. "Good. Think it through on the drive tomorrow, while I'm listening to country music, counting the bugs that die on the windshield."

She laughed.

He should have turned, walked the few steps to his own room and gone inside. Gotten away from her. Instead, he stayed right where he was.

"I wish I had time to meet Lila before I had to talk to my dad. If nothing else she might be able to give me a nice ice-breaker line."

He wished he could comb his fingers through her long yellow hair. "You have the oddest sense of humor."

"And in a way, it's interesting to experiment with it." She caught his gaze. "Particularly since it seems like you don't judge."

"I don't."

"How do you do that?" Her eyes told him that this was important to her. Probably because she'd grown up in a house with nothing but judgment.

He shrugged. "I let you be you. It's been sort of fun watching you root around, trying to find yourself." Because the more layers she peeled back, the more he liked her. Really liked her. Not just in a sexual way, but as a person.

The urge to kiss her set his instincts in motion. His upper body leaned forward. His head began to descend—

He jerked himself to a stop.

What the hell was he doing?

Angry with himself, he pulled back and rubbed his hand along his nape, avoiding her eyes. All this time he'd been feeling an attraction, but he'd been confident that he'd never follow through because she was sweet. And he liked sexy. Yet, somehow, she'd managed to merge the two.

Because he'd been helping her. Talking to her. Growing to like her.

Just as he'd done with Cicely.

He took another step back. "I'll see you in the morning."

She smiled that smile again. The one that had shifted his definition of sexy to include everything that she was. "Okay."

He said a quiet "Okay," and walked to the room beside hers as she used her key card to open her door and disappear behind it.

Memories of falling in love with Cicely crept into his brain. This time, he didn't try to stop them. Not because he wanted to remember the humiliation, but because he needed to remember that sometimes his urge to be a knight in shining armor blinded him to the truth.

And the truth was Morgan didn't want to go home. Yes, she said it was because she wasn't ready to face her father. But that only made her desire to escape stronger. She might not bolt in God-knew-where Nebraska, but once they got closer to Chicago she'd have plenty of chances to run. Especially if his guard was down because he was beginning to like her.

He tossed his key card on the dresser, thankful they

only had another few days of driving. The closer they got to Chicago, the more he would watch her.

Just as he convinced himself he could keep it all under control, his phone rang. Glancing at the caller ID, he groaned. He squeezed his eyes shut for five seconds before he popped them open and answered.

"Good evening, Colonel."

"I expected my daughter to be home by now."

"I told you we were driving—"

"And I told you I wanted her home! *Driving* wasn't the order I gave you! I want her on a plane *now.*"

That's when it all came together in Riccardo's head. *This* was the guy Morgan knew she'd be talking to when she returned to Lake Justice. No matter how many times she called her dad a diplomat, the Colonel that Riccardo kept encountering was a hothead. Her confidence would shatter when confronted by this angry, manipulative man, the man she didn't want to lose from her life because she'd already lost her mom. He was her family. She wanted to keep him. Yet, the Colonel knew how to push her buttons and Riccardo was certain he'd use every weapon at his disposal to get her to fall in line.

He paced to the bathroom as two options hung before him. Save himself and tell the Colonel she'd be on a plane tomorrow. Or save her. Which meant she could try to escape when they got close to Chicago. It also meant more time together. More time for her to tempt him.

Except now that he had his bearings, she wouldn't tempt him anymore. He could be as stubborn as her father. He did not have to worry.

"Did you hear me, son? I want her home tomorrow!"

Riccardo's last remaining piece of knight in shining armor rose in him. It was small, but it was powerful. He could not send Morgan home until she was ready. And he wasn't an idiot. He would not make the mistake he'd made with Cicely twice.

"Respectfully, Colonel, Morgan will be home when she gets home."

Then *he* hung up the phone.

He perched on the lip of the bathtub and ran his hands down his face. He might have saved Morgan, but he'd also taken the first step that assured the Colonel would dump OchoaWines.com, create his own wine site and sweet-talk their clients away from them.

He worked out the numbers in his head. An undertaking like creating a monster website and stealing a hundred clients wouldn't happen over a weekend or even a week. Also, Mitch didn't get back to New York for another week. So Riccardo had a little time to play with.

And he *would* eventually take Morgan home. She just needed a few more days to bolster her confidence.

But not in the car. Not getting close to Chicago, where she could potentially ditch him—

An idea leaped into his brain and his head snapped up. She needed someone to talk to? Nanna was smart and strong. Strong was her middle name. And then there was his mom. Also a smart woman. Those were the people she should be talking with. Not a jaded playboy, who found her so attractive he was having trouble keeping his hands off her, but two women who knew how to deal with demanding men.

CHAPTER FIVE

MORGAN SHOWERED THEN put on a T-shirt and slid into bed. She tried to sleep, but she couldn't stop thinking about Riccardo.

He'd almost kissed her. He might think she hadn't noticed, but she had, because the same feelings were running through her. And this time it wasn't just physical. Riccardo Ochoa was a wonderful person. She'd been seeing it all along. But tonight, his goodness had somehow connected with her attraction and the way she'd felt had been gloriously scary.

Remembering those thirty seconds as his head was descending toward hers made her breath shimmy. Every cell in her body had been ready for the touch of his lips on hers. But he hadn't taken that last step, hadn't kissed her, because it was wrong.

He might be unlike anybody she knew—unafraid to talk, wise about family and relationships and amazingly good-looking—but she still had a fiancé at home. Until she dealt with Charles, she shouldn't be attracted to anybody, let alone kissing somebody.

Her room phone rang and she almost jumped out of her skin. Thinking it might be Riccardo, she grabbed for the receiver, but just as quickly yanked back her hand.

She should not be excited to talk to him.

The phone rang again.

But she was.

She squeezed her eyes shut. This was a mess.

The phone rang a third time and she reminded herself that if Riccardo was calling it was probably for something about their trip. She very cautiously answered it. "Hello."

"Good evening, Ms. Monroe. This is the front desk. Mr. Ochoa left a wake-up call for you for tomorrow morning at seven. You need to approve it."

Relief flooded her. "Yes. Yes. It's fine. Thank you."

"Thank you and have a good evening."

She hung up the phone a bit confused about why Riccardo hadn't called her himself, but glad he hadn't. His not wanting direct communication said he didn't have feelings for her—

Or he could have just called the front desk and given the wake-up call order for both of them because it was convenient, and the hotel had a policy that said the clerk taking the call had to follow up.

His feelings for her weren't neutral. The man had almost kissed her. And her feelings for him weren't neutral, either. She'd wanted him to kiss her.

She turned off the bedside lamp and settled under the covers, forcing her mind off Riccardo, and it jumped to Charles.

Here she was attracted to a man—no matter how foolishly—and she hadn't even really broken up with Charles.

Guilt consumed her. Though she was fairly certain he would realize her running from the church meant they were through, the need to make it official pounded through her.

She sat up and clicked on the lamp again. Lifting her cell phone from the bedside table, she didn't let herself think about the time difference, didn't consider that

Charles might be with her dad. She simply dialed his cell number and waited until he answered.

"Hello." A quick pause. "Who is this?"

His voice was thick and groggy. She did the calculations in her head and realized it was after midnight in Lake Justice, and he was in bed. But in a way, that was good. It meant he was nowhere near her father.

"I'm sorry, Charles. It's me. Morgan."

"Morgan." His voice was instantly stronger, as if he'd come to attention. "Where are you?"

"That's not important." She didn't want to have a long, drawn-out conversation. She just wanted to apologize and make sure he understood she wasn't coming back to him—wasn't going out on the charity-ball circuit to smooth things over. She couldn't be attracted to Riccardo then go home and pretend nothing had happened. Lots had happened. Too much for her to tell Charles, and maybe too much for it to be his concern anyway.

She knew they'd have to talk again, more seriously—especially about selling the condo they'd bought and returning gifts—but they could have that discussion when she got home. For now, she simply needed to end it.

"Look, I'm really sorry for everything. Running. Leaving you to deal with the mess. But I know you probably realized that my running from our wedding meant there was a problem."

She expected him to say something like, "Nothing we can't fix." Instead, he softly said, "Yes. It's kind of hard to ignore a woman who'd rather go on the lam than marry you."

"I'm so sorry. Everything just closed in on me."

"And we did have the fight the day before."

Relief filled her lungs with air again. He sounded like he more than understood. He sounded like someone who'd adjusted. "Yes. We did."

"It took me 'til yesterday for it to sink in, but I got it. The toast from my best man didn't bother you because it made you think I didn't love you, but because it prompted you to realize you didn't love me."

Her breath caught. His level of understanding amazed her. Surprised her a bit, too, since it had taken her two days in Vegas and a few on the road to come to that conclusion.

"Our dating and engagement all fell together so easily, so pat, that I don't think I ever really took the time to figure out what I felt."

He sighed. "I get it. And I'm okay. Your dad's another story, though."

"I know."

"You're going to have your hands full when you get home."

She winced. She might be settling some things with Charles, but her biggest problem still remained. "I know that, too."

The conversation died. Twenty seconds ticked off the clock. He drew a breath. "So, this is it?"

"Yeah." Her heart drooped a little bit. "I hope we can still be friends."

He laughed. "Women always say that."

"That's because we have to like someone as a friend to even consider marrying him."

"Yeah. Right." He took another quick breath. "Look, I have to go. Can I tell your dad you're fine?"

He might have adjusted, but he was still her dad's errand boy.

But it wouldn't hurt for him to tell her dad she was okay. "Yes. Sure. Tell him I'm fine."

Another silence, then Charles softly said, "Goodbye, Morgan."

"Goodbye, Charles."

She hung up the phone, a sense of relief filling her.

Charles might not have been the man of her dreams, but he was a good person. And she'd done the right thing by calling him.

She turned off the lamp and settled on her pillow again, but the strangest feeling suddenly hit her. She was free.

Free.

No longer engaged. Not under her dad's thumb. Her own person for the first time since she was twelve.

And traveling with a man who tempted her.

The next morning, Riccardo waited for Morgan at the registration desk of the hotel. When she arrived, she barely looked at him. And who could blame her? He'd almost kissed her the night before. She'd have to be a total idiot not to have seen it.

She wasn't in the state of mind to have a fling. And he was about to defy her father—to take her to Spain rather than take her home. He didn't want to have another Cicely on his hands. But he wasn't going to let Morgan go back to Lake Justice until she was ready. So, he had to be smart. *He was being smart.* Taking her to his nanna to get the help she really needed.

They checked out, and as they walked to the lobby door, he said, "Give me your phone."

She glanced up at him. "Why?"

"Do you know phones can be used to track people?"

"Yes."

"Well, last night I told your dad we'd be home when we got home. I don't think he took it too well."

She shot him a curious look.

"He was angry enough that he might send someone after us. We have to get rid of anything he can use to find us."

He dropped their phones into a trash can just outside

the hotel door. They walked up to the Mercedes and he patted the hood. "Including this."

She peered across the black car hood at him. "We're going to stop driving?"

"Yes."

Her eyes widened. "We're gonna walk?"

He laughed. "No. We're just going somewhere we can stay for a few days."

She peeked at him. "I've always loved Chicago."

"I was thinking more about Spain."

Her confused expression became downright pained. "Spain?"

"My family's vineyard. You can meet my mom and nanna, watch how our families interact. Watch how I relate to my dad. Or better, watch how my cousin Alonzo's wife, Julia, relates to her dad. He owns a vineyard, too."

She gaped. "Really? You think I'm so bad I need examples of normal behavior?"

"No, but I think a couple of days around a real family—a big family, counting Nanna as the matriarch and my dad and his brother and their families—would give you some perspective. You say you want to think things through? Vineyards are beautiful in Spain. And quiet. That's where you need to be."

Morgan gaped at him.

The man had almost kissed her the night before. *Almost kissed her.*

And now he was taking her to Spain to meet his family?

The obvious jumped into her head. That he liked her enough to want her to meet his family, but she quickly crossed that off with a big red marker. They'd known each other for a few days. And he *hadn't* kissed her. He'd pulled back. If he was taking her across an ocean, it wasn't for romance, but to make sure her dad didn't find her before he left for Stockholm.

That was a good thing. If she could wait until after he left for Stockholm before she went home, she could talk to Charles first and have another few days to get her bearings before she had to explain to her dad that their relationship had to change.

Hiding out in Spain was not such a bad idea.

She sucked in a breath. "Okay, Marco. Let's go."

He glared at her across the car hood. "Marco Polo was not Spanish."

She laughed. "Right."

"I'm mean it. No more calling me that."

She studied his big dark eyes. "You take your heritage very seriously."

He directed her into the Mercedes. "If you think I'm bad, wait 'til you meet the family."

He got behind the steering wheel as she slid into the passenger seat. Calm as always, sexy as hell, he started the car and she couldn't help wondering what it would be like to be meeting his family for real, as his girlfriend.

The returning thought shocked her so much that it jarred her demanding father out of her head and started a whole new chain of thoughts. She was a runaway bride. His family was old-school, steeped in tradition. They would probably think her absolutely crass.

But she didn't really have anywhere else to go. She had three hundred dollars. Without her credit cards, she was sunk. And going to Spain was the perfect plan. She sincerely doubted her dad would find her there.

As they returned the Mercedes to a rental-car agency and Riccardo called a friend and arranged to use his jet, her thoughts went around and around. By the time the plane was ready for them, she was still nervous. But she didn't want to talk about this with Riccardo. She'd already behaved like a crazy woman with him. It was time to start keeping some of her thoughts to herself.

Luckily, the stress and constant travel of the past few days caught up with her, and five minutes after the jet was in the air, she fell asleep and didn't wake up until the pilot's announcement that they should fasten their seat belts for the landing.

Noting the warm cover tucked around her, she felt incredibly guilty. "Sorry."

Riccardo shook his head. "Don't be sorry. I slept most of the flight myself. Besides, you'll be glad you slept. When we land it will be a little past eight in the morning."

"I slept sixteen hours!"

"No. There's a time difference between the US and Spain. Besides, you clearly needed the sleep. Nothing to worry about."

She pulled her bottom lip under her teeth. There was a lot to worry about. A thoughtful guy like this had to come from a nice family. Two weeks ago, she would have charmed their socks off. Now, she'd left a groom at the altar and was hiding out from her dad.

"Your family's going to think I'm crazy."

The jet began its descent. "Not hardly."

"Seriously?"

He shrugged. "Have you ever heard the story of why Mitch started his company in the US rather than Spain?"

"No."

"Mitch's brother, Alonzo, stole his girlfriend."

Her eyebrows rose. "Oh."

"Mitch had been angling to start Ochoa Online for years, but his father, Santiago, would never give the go-ahead. Then all hell broke loose when Mitch found Alonzo and Julia in his bedroom."

Morgan about swallowed her tongue. That made running from her wedding look like small potatoes. "That's awful!"

"It was." He leaned across his seat a bit, getting closer, as if telling her a secret. "They swore nothing had happened. That Mitch had actually walked in on their first kiss, but Santiago was so afraid the scandal would split the family apart that he decided Mitch needed to go away and he offered the start-up capital for the business."

Morgan pressed her lips together to keep from laughing. "Oh...that's—"

"Scandalous. I know."

She laughed and lightly slapped his forearm. "Stop acting like this upsets you. You're loving telling this story."

His eyes sparkled. "I am."

Morgan swallowed. She could drown in the humor in his dark, dark eyes. And maybe that was the real reason for the anxiety tripping through her. She shouldn't be going anywhere with this man who tempted her, let alone across an ocean. But here she was, on a jet, landing in Spain.

She took a breath to clear those thoughts, because it was too late to do anything about it now. "Then what happened?"

"Mitch told his dad he would only leave if the money Santiago provided for OchoaWines.com would be a loan, not an investment."

"That doesn't sound so bad."

"Santiago might not be Colonel Monroe, but he's a family patriarch. He wanted Mitch's business to be part of the family's enterprises."

"And your cousin didn't?"

"He saw an opportunity. In his mind, he was giving up everything. The price was autonomy. And he paid all the money back. With interest. So the family lost nothing."

"Clever."

His smile warmed. "So, Mitch goes to America and creates Ochoa Online and does what no one guessed he would do. He adds other wines to the site. Santiago flipped. Mitch reminded him it was his company, not the family's, and *that* argument got so big everybody forgot that Alonzo stole Julia from him."

After half her childhood of being raised with only a father, and no other family, the magnitude of what that fight must have been like nearly overwhelmed her. "I'm not quite sure I'm ready for your family."

"The trouble is long past. Mitch gives Ochoa Vineyards the prime spot on his website and doesn't take a commission from their sales. He makes a ton of money for the family. Plus, he got married a few weeks ago."

She nodded. "To Lila."

"Yes."

"The woman who spent her childhood in foster care because she got lost in the system."

"Yes."

"Wow, you people are like a soap opera."

"Not really. We're just family. I told you all that so you would see my family will barely bat an eyelid when they meet you. We have our own skeletons."

The plane landed. They waited quietly for the pilot and copilot to come out of the cockpit and open the door.

Though she felt a little cheap and tawdry after hearing that story, Morgan's interest in meeting Riccardo's family had about quadrupled.

The copilot walked out, opened the door that lowered the stairs and wished them a good day in Spanish. Fluent in that language—and three others—Morgan thanked him, then walked out of the jet and stepped into a world of green covered by the most amazing blue sky.

A limo awaited them beside the hangar of the private airstrip. As she and Riccardo walked toward it, the driver opened the back door and Morgan saw an older woman sitting on one of the two bench seats that faced each other.

Riccardo said, "That's Nanna."

Small, classically beautiful with black hair with ribbons of gray streaking through and bright dark eyes, Riccardo's nanna didn't look anything like any grandmother Morgan knew.

After they got settled on the seat across from her, his nanna handed Riccardo a glass of red. "I miss you like the sun in winter."

And she didn't talk like anyone Morgan knew, either. She was sultry. Intriguing.

"Very funny, Nanna." Riccardo laughed. "You miss Mitch more."

Nanna sighed eloquently. "You boys. Always a competition." She faced Morgan with a smile. "And this must be Morgan Monroe."

"She's the daughter of—"

"Colonel Monroe." Nanna sized her up in one quick glance. "You ran from your wedding."

Morgan said, "Yes, ma'am," as Riccardo said, "Nanna!"

Nanna looked totally unrepentant. "What? You already told me all that. Besides, I'm an old woman. I might not live long enough to rehash the basics and Miss Monroe looks like someone who appreciates candor."

Considering his family had bigger, better secrets, Morgan didn't mind talking about her own indiscretion. "I also don't want to tiptoe around the subject. So, here's the story. I got halfway down the aisle, realized I was making a mistake and got myself on the commuter to JFK before anyone could stop me."

Nanna laughed. "I'd have paid to see that. I bet your dad is angry."

Riccardo mumbled, "He is." Then he looked out the window.

Morgan's heart gave a funny catch. He was pulling himself out of the conversation, more or less handing her over to his grandmother—

She suddenly realized the real reason he'd brought her to Spain. He was on the hook with her dad. Responsible for her. Yet they'd gotten so close in just a few days that he'd almost kissed her. Getting involved with her would be like professional suicide. He'd brought her to Spain so she'd have his family to entertain her, and he wouldn't have to worry about what was growing between them.

Disappointment began to rise but she stopped it. She didn't want to get involved with him, either. She was only a few days out of the most serious relationship of her life. She did not want to be falling for another man.

Putting distance between them was the right thing to do.

So, she let him stare out the window on his side, and she turned to look out the window on hers. The morning sun glistened off the dewy grass beside the road that threaded through the valley.

Nanna pointed at the rows and rows of green leaves that Morgan knew sheltered their grapes. "We started off as one vineyard and got lucky enough to buy the neighbor's." She poured Morgan a glass of wine. "We combined them and now we have an empire almost as big as your dad's." She smiled. "Bigger if you count what Mitch and Riccardo have done with their online presence."

Taking the wine, Morgan laughed. "*You're* the one who's competitive."

Nanna smiled. "I prefer to be called feisty." She turned to Riccardo. "So, you came home to help with the grapes?"

That brought his gaze back from the window. "The grapes?"

"It's about to be harvest time." She laughed. "Surely

you haven't been away so long you've forgotten. I expect Alonzo to announce it's time to pick any day now."

Morgan glanced at the seemingly endless fields of grapes. It would take hundreds of people to get all this harvested on time. "You pick by hand?"

Riccardo glanced at her. "Yes."

She held her breath, caught in the gaze of his captivating brown eyes. Of all the things Morgan had thought might happen in her life, falling for a stranger was not one of them. Sexy or not. Handsome or not.

These feelings she had were so far out of her comfort zone that she worried running from her wedding had changed her too much. Morgan Monroe, the real Morgan Monroe, did not fall for strangers.

She faced Nanna again. "Up until a few years ago, my dad had our grapes picked by hand, too. I've helped."

Nanna clapped her hands. "Excellent! We get lots of laborers from town." She leaned close to Morgan. "Even some tourists volunteer. But everyone in the family also picks." She flicked a glance at Riccardo.

Riccardo said, "It'll be fun," though he sounded less than enthusiastic.

Nanna didn't seem to care. "Yes, it will be." She smiled at Morgan. "Have you brought a gown?"

The quick change of topic made Morgan blink. "A gown?"

"There'll be a ball when Mitch and Lila return."

"I barely brought any clothes. I'm not even sure I have enough underwear."

Nanna's musical laugh echoed through the limo. "No problem. I love to shop. Let's get you settled in then you and I will head into town." She frowned. "You do have a credit card, right?"

She winced. "I tossed them in Vegas when I realized my dad could find me by watching my purchases."

Riccardo pulled his wallet from his pants pocket. "Here. Company card. Spend as much as you like. We can expense it."

Nanna clapped with glee. "We are going to have such fun."

Riccardo held back a grimace. He was happy Nanna liked Morgan, but his afternoon would not be fun. He might not have kissed the runaway bride in his custody, but he almost had. If he had, his explanation to Mitch for why he'd refused to take her home would have been infinitesimally worse. Especially since he wasn't 100 percent sure he wasn't doing what he'd done with Cicely—falling for a woman who might not have feelings for him, as much as she needed him.

He thanked God he'd stepped back from that kiss, and determined with every fiber of his being to get this situation back on track. First, get Morgan settled with his nanna. Second, come up with an explanation for Mitch about why she was in Spain instead of Lake Justice. Third, let Nanna guide her on what to say to her father to get her life back.

He turned to Nanna. "When is Mitch expected?"

"He didn't pin down a time. But the ball is Friday next week. They promised to be here a few days before that."

That gave Morgan time to get her bearings. She could even meet Lila and go to the ball. And after that, her dad would leave for Stockholm and she could go home.

The driver pulled the limo onto the lane for Ochoa Vineyards, toward the original stone mansion. Built centuries ago, it was a great two-story house, beautiful even. But if the transfixed expression on Morgan's face was anything to go by, she saw far more.

"It's gorgeous. Like time stood still."

"Not on the inside," Nanna commented casually. "The

first floor has been renovated to be the business offices for the vineyard, along with a lovely gift shop." She leaned in close to Morgan. "There's a huge ballroom in the back with its own entrance. The basement is our restaurant. We only serve dinner. And the second floor has two apartments. One for me. One for Marguerite and Santiago, Mitch's parents."

"Wow."

Nanna took Morgan's hand and led her out of the limo. "I'll bet the home of your vineyard is every bit as lovely."

"It's nice," Morgan agreed, as Riccardo climbed out behind her. "But there's not a lot of charm. It's stuffy." She glanced at the big house. "Look at the lines in the stone. This house seems like it's been here forever, lovingly guarding its occupants."

Nanna slipped her arm across Morgan's shoulders and gave her a quick hug. "That's exactly how I see it."

The driver opened the trunk to get their baggage, such as it was. When Nanna saw Riccardo's duffel and Morgan's small black suitcase, she clicked her tongue. "Seriously, you and I are going shopping as soon as we get you settled."

She hooked Morgan's arm with her own and guided her down the cobblestone sidewalk that led first to a duplex and then to Ochoa Vineyard's newly constructed condos.

Riccardo said, "I see the building is done."

"Yes. Lucky for you," Nanna said over her shoulder. "Alonzo and Julia are in the one side of the duplex and Mitch and Lila will be taking up the other. Poor Francine has been staying with Santiago and Marguerite."

It was why the family had decided to build eight condos. With Mitch getting married and Lila's mom being folded into the clan, their group was growing. Add other guests and businessmen and women who came and went, and they needed more space.

Following Nanna and Morgan, Riccardo said, "We'll be the first to stay in the new condos?"

"Yes. Francine will be returning to New York with Lila and Mitch. It seemed foolish to move her over for only a few days." Nanna tossed him a puzzled frown. "I thought you'd go to your parents' house?"

His parents' home at the second vineyard was only two miles down the road, but as sympathetic as he'd become to Morgan's problems, he hadn't forgotten how easily she'd duped him in Vegas. His plan might have been to bring her to Spain so he could get some distance from her, but he didn't think it was a good idea to be two miles away. Just in case she got it in her head that she could trick him again.

"I'd be happy in a condo."

"Very well."

Nanna directed them to the yellow stucco building and into an elevator in a quietly elegant lobby with a marble floor and a modern crystal chandelier. "Not letting us stay on the first floor?" he asked.

As Nanna pressed the button that started the car moving, she gave him a curious look. "You can stay on the first floor." The elevator stopped and the doors opened onto a wide hall showcasing doors to four separate condos. "But I'm giving our guest a room with a view." She turned to Morgan. "It's a peaceful, panoramic view of the vineyard."

Morgan said, "Thank you."

But Riccardo got a funny feeling in his stomach. He shouldn't feel odd that his nanna wasn't putting them on the same floor. They'd had separate rooms while driving across the US. They weren't romantically involved. They weren't even friends. In Nanna's mind, there was no reason to keep them together. Especially given that his grandmother didn't know Morgan had tried to lose him in Vegas. All she was doing was giving their "guest" the room with the best view.

But he got a weird, itching sensation along his skin, thinking of her on one floor and him on another.

Nanna punched in a code and opened the door to the first condo. Like a proud owner, she offered Morgan entry. "Everything's compact. Two bedrooms, two baths." She pointed to the right. "Sitting room." And to the left. "Kitchen."

Morgan glanced around appreciatively. "It's lovely."

Riccardo agreed. The place was exceptional. The duplex had been built in a rush and had simple, plain architecture. The condos had been lovingly designed with arches, rich hardwoods, Carrera marble and wrought-iron accents.

The driver arrived with their bags. Morgan took hers with a smile. "It's kind of light. I can carry it to the bedroom myself."

Nanna nodded her approval. "Come on, Riccardo. Let's get you to your room." She addressed the driver. "His bag is going to the first floor."

"Actually, I'd like to stay up here. On the second floor."

The driver stopped. Nanna frowned. "Here?"

"Well, there's no need to have people on two floors." Riccardo suddenly felt young and clumsy. He couldn't tell his grandmother Morgan had already tried to escape once. At least not in front of Morgan. "It's a safety thing."

Nanna laughed. "We're in the middle of Northern Spain's beautiful rolling hills. We don't even have a neighbor for miles."

"What if there's a fire?"

"Alarms will go off." Nanna sighed. "But there's no reason why you can't stay on the second floor. So, fine. I'll put you in the suite next door." She consulted a small blue book she pulled from her skirt pocket. "I have the codes for all the suites. Let's go."

Morgan stopped them. "Give me twenty minutes to

shower and put on clean clothes, and I'll be ready to go shopping."

"Great. Meet me downstairs. I'll have the limo wait while I freshen up, too."

"Sounds good."

Nanna directed Riccardo out of Morgan's condo. "I think your dad and Santiago want to talk to you."

About Colonel Monroe, no doubt. Though Ochoa Online wasn't part of their business, they were protective of it, and they'd want to know what was going on. But that might be good. It wouldn't hurt to try different explanations on them so that when Mitch arrived Riccardo would know which one worked. Particularly since Morgan would be spending the rest of the day occupied—and sort of guarded—by his grandmother.

In the hall, Nanna gave him the code for the lock to his suite. He took his bag from the driver, using the same explanation Morgan had—it was light enough he could handle it. The driver left, but before Nanna could follow him, he caught her arm.

"Don't forget that Ms. Monroe is a runaway."

"Runaway *bride*."

"No, just plain runaway. She gave me the slip once in Vegas. Her dad is leaving for Stockholm next week, and she says she's going home then, but until she's safely on a plane back to the States, she's my responsibility. I brought her here to see how a family works. But also, so that you can talk to her. Help her sort out her feelings, figure out how to deal with her demanding dad."

"It would be my honor."

"Great." He loved his nanna's enthusiasm, but he also wanted to be clear about Morgan. "But I don't want her running again. Don't let her out of your sight today."

Nanna pointed a finger at him. "Shame on you for thinking she'd run."

"I don't know her well enough to *think* anything. I do *know* that she fooled me once. I'm not getting so comfortable with her that she does it again."

"Fine."

"Thank you."

Inside his condo, he showered and put on a clean pair of jeans and clean T-shirt. He tagged his dirty clothes for laundry, glad he had a tux and a few suits at his parents' house.

Clean and refreshed, he left his condo at the same time Morgan did. As she closed her door, she said, "Hey! Are you coming shopping with your nanna and me?"

His gaze cruised from her sandals to the top of her head. She wore shorts and a tank top, appropriate for the still-warm September weather, and though she'd clearly combed her thick yellow hair, it fell about her in wild waves.

He sucked in a breath, reminding himself she was the daughter of a client and a woman in emotional trouble, but he still wanted to tease and flirt with her, and that was worse for his sanity than the threat that she might bolt.

"Uncle Santiago wants to see me. My dad will be there, too."

"That's right. I remember your nanna saying that." She winced. "Sorry they're going to grill you about me."

"I'm not sure they are." He directed her to walk to the elevator. "But even if they do, I can handle it." He pressed the down button. "Besides, they might want to talk about their investments. They aren't part of Ochoa Online, but I handle most of the family's money."

"That's right. You're the moneyman." She smiled. "Probably the most important person in any business."

The elevator arrived. He shook his head as he motioned for her to enter. "My ego isn't delicate. You don't have to coddle me—" *or try to compliment me into trusting you* "—because I don't own Ochoa Online."

"I'm not coddling you. I'm an accountant, remember? I know how important your job is."

He said, "I remember," but confusion rolled through him. He'd been so suspicious of her, then attracted to her, then suspicious again, that he'd barely thought of her as a worker in her dad's company, a certified public accountant. But just then, when she'd reminded him she was an accountant, he saw a glimpse of the woman he'd found happily giving the stock seminar beside the slot machines. The supersmart CPA in glasses and gray canvas tennis shoes. Not the confused runaway bride. It was weird—

No. It was Morgan. The real Morgan. Honest. Honorable. With a warm smile and a big heart. And *that's* why he'd wanted to kiss her. In the few days they'd had in the car, she'd gone from being confused to being herself.

And he liked her. Who wouldn't? She was a likeable person.

The elevator door opened. She exited first and he followed her out, his gaze unwittingly sliding from her shoulders to her butt. Her perfect butt. She was warm, funny, intelligent and sexy—

What the hell was wrong with him?

She was as forbidden to him as a person could be. Not only the daughter of a client, but also a woman who needed him. The absolute wrong kind of person for him to be interested in. Yet, he couldn't seem to stop himself from noticing everything about her.

They reached the door and he opened it for her. "Enjoy shopping with Nanna."

She smiled at him. "I will."

She all but raced up the cobblestone walkway to the limo, where his Nanna awaited her. "I hope I look okay."

Nanna kissed her cheek. "We'll get you an outfit at the

first store. Maybe a cute dress with a big sun hat. Something chic and European," she said, holding the limo door open. "Then we'll have lunch. After that we can purchase the rest of what you need."

What Morgan said was lost as she entered the limo, but only an idiot would have missed the happiness in her voice. And *that* was what he wanted. Morgan to see real life with his happy, always fun grandmother, so she'd know what she was missing and be able to explain the future she wanted to her dad.

Once she got a dose of Nanna, she wouldn't want to run. She'd want to learn as much as she could. If there was one thing he'd realized about Morgan, it was that she was curious about what she'd missed. As long as Nanna was helping her figure things out, she'd happily stay with her. There was no reason to worry that she'd try to escape. Just as he'd planned, he could keep his distance from her.

He crossed the driveway between the cobblestone path and the huge Ochoa Vineyards mansion and shook his head, wondering why that realization hadn't gotten rid of the odd feeling in his stomach.

Morgan was a good person, trying to figure out her life before she had to talk to her domineering dad. She wasn't going to betray him. He shouldn't have this emptiness in his gut as if…

He turned the feeling around in his head, trying to figure it out. When the answer came, he squeezed his eyes shut.

As if…he missed her.

Damn it! That's what the weird, itchy feeling was about. He didn't mistrust Morgan. He felt odd about being away from her because he didn't want to be away from her. They'd spent almost every minute of the last few days together and he had grown to like her. That's why it felt so odd that his grandmother was separating them. Why watching her drive off had seemed wrong.

He missed her.

Damn it!

If he didn't watch out, she'd be his second Cicely.

He absolutely had to stay away from her.

He entered the first floor of the mansion, walking past the gift shop and down the long hall that led to his Uncle Santiago's office. With every step he took, his trepidation grew. He had done the right thing for Morgan, but his uncle and his dad would be more concerned with the Ochoa family than Morgan's situation with her dad.

He took a long breath, reminding himself that that was why he was going to Uncle Santiago's office. To convince his uncle and father that bringing Morgan to Ochoa Vineyards was the right thing to do, and that he could handle Colonel Monroe.

If he couldn't convince them, he'd never convince Mitch.

He opened the door and Santiago rose from behind the big mahogany desk. A tall, trim man with black hair and serious dark eyes, the CEO of Ochoa Vineyards could be intimidating.

"Uncle Santiago."

"Riccardo. Good to see you."

Seated on a chair in front of the desk, Riccardo's dad—Carlos, a younger version of Santiago—also rose.

"Riccardo!" He hugged his son. "Welcome home!"

Motioning for Riccardo to sit, his Uncle Santiago cut right to the chase. "We heard you brought a guest."

Riccardo sat on the chair beside his dad's. "Yes. Morgan Monroe. I think she could benefit from some time with Nanna."

Santiago frowned. "With Nanna?"

"Morgan ran from her wedding. It's a long, complicated story, but when she really opened up about her dad, I knew I was in over my head. I figured Nanna could help sort this out."

Riccardo's dad said, "Ah."

Santiago sat back in his chair. "Nanna's good with people."

"Exactly."

The room got weirdly quiet. The conversation wasn't over by a long shot, but nobody said anything.

Finally, Santiago drew a slow breath. "You know that we're on the cusp of harvest?"

"Yes, and I'm glad to be here. Happy to help."

Carlos glanced at Santiago, then at his son. "We understand what happened with Morgan. She's got a powerful father. And we all know how difficult powerful men can be to live with."

Because his father was one of those men, Riccardo had to hold back a smile. "But?"

"We're at the most critical time of our year. This is Alonzo's first year of being in charge of the harvest. He'll choose the time we pick the grapes."

"And I think he's earned the right," Riccardo said.

"We do, too, or we wouldn't have given him such an important responsibility." Santiago sat back in his chair. "Our problem is that your guest comes with trouble at a time when we don't need trouble."

"She's fine."

"When her dad figures out where she is, he will most likely send someone after her."

"He already sent somebody after her. Me."

His father held his gaze. "And you failed him. Now he will send somebody else."

He looked from his dad to Santiago. "Are you saying that you want us to leave?"

"No. We want you to watch her. Every second of every day."

Riccardo's dad agreed. "Nanna is a wonderful person for her to talk to, but she's nobody's bodyguard."

Riccardo looked from his dad to his uncle. "First, I don't think Morgan's dad is going to figure out where we are. We ditched our phones. Got rid of the rental car in an obscure city. Flew here on a private plane."

Santiago frowned. "You don't think he'll figure out that you'd bring her to your family for protection?"

"He might. But this is a guy who worries what people think. He doesn't want any more bad publicity. The canceled wedding was disaster enough. Sending a contingent to Spain or even flying here himself would cause a stir. He's not going to give the press a chance at another story. He'll keep a lid on this. Which works in Morgan's favor. He won't do anything to make any waves. And that gives her the time she needs to decide what to say when she does go home."

Santiago rose, dismissing him. "Okay. We'll trust you on this. If it's peace and quiet she wants, we have it in abundance. If it's something fun and interesting to do, she can help harvest grapes. But I warn you. If she's using us to insult a former diplomat or make some sort of public spectacle, we will not be pleased."

He rose. "Morgan's not like that." He'd been with her in a silent car for days, listening to her story in bits and pieces the few times she'd talked. At no point had she ever behaved like someone who wanted to hurt her dad—

But what if all that good behavior had been a ploy?

No. He didn't for one second believe it. She would not hurt her dad. She loved him.

"I saw genuine emotion in her eyes when she spoke of her dad cutting her out of his life. She does not want to lose him. She *does* want to be in the right frame of mind when she talks to him so that she can effectively argue her case."

That he'd seen in her eyes every time he looked at her. He'd heard it in her voice every time he'd talked to her.

His father sighed. "Yes, Riccardo, but if you're wrong, you won't be the only one to suffer. The family could be drawn into something that could end up an international scandal."

He hadn't thought of that. Or the impact on his family. He'd only seen his attraction, his fear of getting involved and Morgan's need for somewhere to stay until her dad left for Stockholm.

"I'll handle it."

"When she's not with Nanna, you must be with her."

"If that's what you want, that's what I'll do."

He walked out of the office. When the door closed behind him, he blew his breath out on a long sigh. For as much as he didn't want to tempt fate, he was going to have to stick to his runaway bride like glue.

CHAPTER SIX

DINNER WAS AT seven with cocktails at six thirty. Riccardo stopped at Morgan's condo at twenty past six. He knocked twice and she opened the door.

"Ready?" His gaze involuntarily rippled from her blond hair, which she'd pulled into a curly ponytail with a sunny yellow flower, to her blue strapless sundress, down her bare legs to white sandals. "Wow. You look amazing."

She fastened a slim bracelet on her wrist, calling attention to the porcelain skin of her bare arms, but also reminding him of how beautiful she was. She'd been cute, sweet, pretty, in blue jeans and T-shirts. But dressed up? With makeup? And all that gorgeous hair? She was a knockout.

"Once Nanna filled me in on how many family dinners we'd be having, my shopping list doubled."

He laughed, but the collar of his white shirt suddenly felt tight. The air-conditioned condo heated. He was back to being an up-close-and-personal bodyguard, and back to being face-to-face with his attraction.

"I couldn't very well wear that shiny black minidress to any of your nanna's dinners."

The heat in the room intensified. That little black dress had molded to her curves like a second skin—

He sucked in a breath and told himself to remember the

conversation with his dad and Santiago. Morgan Monroe was potential trouble to his family. But more than that, she was vulnerable, like Cicely. Any feelings Morgan got for him could be nothing more than appreciation. He'd never again get involved with a woman who needed him. That was part of how he stayed happily single. No entanglements. No messes.

"And by the way, I intend to pay you back for every cent I charged to your card."

"That won't be necessary. I told you. We can expense it."

She caught his gaze. Her eyes held a tinge of something he couldn't quite interpret. "I want to pay you back."

That was so unexpected that for a second he almost lost himself in her beautiful blue eyes. But he caught himself. *No entanglements. No messes.* That was how a smart man stayed out of trouble.

She led him to her condo door and headed to the elevator as if she'd been in this building a million times. It wasn't until they were outside, on the cobblestone walkway, that he realized the last thing either one of them had said was about her insistence on paying him back.

He might not be allowed to be attracted to her, but he also wouldn't be rude. He forced himself to think of something neutral to say. "So, you're comfortable?"

"Yes. You have a beautiful estate."

"Technically, all this property belongs to the main house. My home, the house I grew up in—" he turned and pointed behind them "—is back there."

"I know." She smiled, her blue eyes lighting up when she caught his gaze, and everything inside him shimmied. When she was happy, there was no one prettier. "On the way back from shopping, Nanna had the limo stop so I could see the second vineyard. I met your mom. We had tea in the lovely backyard that fronts all those rows of grapes."

His spine stiffened. "You met my mother?"

"It would have been impolite to take the tour of the second vineyard and not go to the house to say hello."

Yes. It would have. The insulted feeling rumbling through him was ridiculous. Why should he care that Morgan had met his mother, that he didn't get to introduce them? It had been kind of Nanna to show her around, have her meet some of the people she'd be dining with tonight.

Everything was fine.

They walked up to the front entry of the mansion, then through the echoing foyer, past the gift shop and corridor that led to the vineyard offices and up the wide, circular stairway.

"This house is fabulous. It's hard to believe it's centuries old."

"Good maintenance."

"To be able to keep it this nice, I'm guessing your family never went through hard times."

At the top of the stairs, he motioned for her to walk down the hall. "Every family goes through hard times. Every business goes through hard times."

She stopped walking. "You just separated family and business."

"So? Though Ochoa Vineyards is the main client of Ochoa Online, they are two different companies. And I work for Ochoa Online. Not the vineyard. I'm more involved with my family than their vineyard."

"That's not how Nanna sees it. Everything's one big tangled vine to her. She never separates family and business."

He thought about that for a second, about why it would be significant to Morgan. "Your father doesn't separate family and business, does he?"

"No." She smiled at him. "And that's why I think Nanna

was the perfect person for me to talk to. Our situations are the same. Technically, we both live at our jobs. She gave me a wonderful new perspective and a few inventive ways to approach my dad. Especially now that I have a plan for how to talk to him and Charles separately."

Relief rippled through him. His nanna had done exactly what he wanted. Morgan looked and spoke stronger than ever.

The sense that this was the real Morgan struck him again. She'd grown up a bit after running from her wedding. She'd also faced her demons—or at least had a plan to face them. She'd definitely changed some, but she was balancing out now, and this was her new normal. Stronger than she had been. Wiser than she had been. But her real self.

He looked over at her.

She smiled.

And the oddest sensation fluttered through him. He almost wasn't sure how to relate to the real her.

Calling himself all kinds of crazy, he pushed the buzzer that announced them and opened the door before he led Morgan through a small foyer and into the sitting room. Everyone in his family except Mitch and Lila sat on one of the tufted chairs or milled near the bar.

Spotting Morgan, Nanna broke away from a conversation with Santiago and his wife, Marguerite.

She caught Morgan's hands. "Darling. Thank you for the lovely day." She kissed both her cheeks. "And if you don't take that sun hat with you when you leave Spain, it's mine."

"It's yours. There aren't many functions where I'd wear it," Morgan said with a sigh. Then she laughed. "Unless I go to the Kentucky Derby in the spring."

Nanna slid her hand beneath Morgan's arm and directed her away. "Have you ever been?"

"No. My father's not a horseman. I think he's crazy, though. We have acres and acres of land that aren't planted. We could easily put in a stable."

"So, you ride?"

"I love to ride!"

Her voice drifted off and Riccardo realized he was standing in the doorway like an idiot, watching her as if transfixed. He'd think it crazy, except she did look really pretty and it was fun to see that the confused woman he'd found in Vegas wasn't so confused anymore.

He walked to the bar.

Mixing drinks behind the polished wood, Alonzo said, "What can I get you?"

"A beer."

"Coming right up." Riccardo's tall, dark-haired cousin pulled a bottle from a small refrigerator, opened the lid and handed it to him with a glass.

Alonzo's wife, Julia, sauntered over. Looking stunning in a pink dress, with her yellow hair pinned above her ears, Julia was the picture of a wealthy man's wife.

She caught Riccardo by the shoulders, stood on tiptoes and kissed his cheek. "I feel like I just saw you."

He laughed. "Mitch's wedding was only a few weeks ago."

"It's nice to have you around for more than holidays."

He said, "It's nice to be here." But Morgan's laugh floated to him. He automatically glanced around until he saw her, sitting on a sofa, Nanna on one side, laughing. Lila's mom, Francine, on the other.

He angled his thumb toward them. "I should go over."

Julia frowned. "Why? Nanna's entertaining her. Besides Francine seems happy to have another American around. We should let them chat."

Not wanting to make a scene, he smiled graciously. "Of course."

"Plus, you haven't said hello to your mother yet." Julia took his arm and turned him in the direction of his parents. "Go."

He walked to the corner where his parents and Mitch's parents chatted. His mother caught him in a huge hug. "Riccardo!"

"I heard you met Morgan today."

His mother's dark eyes lit up. Like Marguerite, she had a pinch of gray in her black hair, but only enough to add interest. Her simple dress was the color of a summer sky.

"Such a lovely girl. And such an odd story about her wedding. Her dad sounds like a tyrant." Then she frowned. "Why did you agree to help him?"

"I thought I was doing a good deed. Plus, he's a client."

His mother sighed. "Always a client."

His dad chuckled. "The boys are making an honest living, Paloma. Never discourage a child who knows how to make his own money."

Even though his dad's words were positive, when he caught his gaze Riccardo saw the warning in his father's eyes. Neither his dad nor Santiago would say anything to embarrass Morgan, but they didn't want any problems. It was his job to make sure there were none.

He said, "Right," as his gaze involuntarily drifted to the woman in his charge. Helping Morgan could ruin a big chunk of Ochoa Online or bring trouble to Ochoa Vineyards in the middle of harvest. But it wasn't because of Morgan. It was because of her dad. She was innocently beautiful, laughing with his grandmother. Her dad was the tyrant.

By the time he glanced back, his parents' conversation had changed from Riccardo to a possible trip to Greece in the winter. His mom was a yes. She loved Greece. Marguerite was intrigued. His dad wanted to see China and

Santiago thought it was time they went to America. Miami Beach or maybe Vegas.

Alonzo took his arm and pulled him aside. "Come over here," he said. "Talk to the people who aren't semiretired and always planning their next trip."

Riccardo laughed, but Francine's louder laugh burst through the room, along with Nanna's and Morgan's. Whatever they were talking about, Morgan was having fun.

He'd loved the times she'd laughed with him. Loved the sound. Loved the way her eyes lit up. If she were anybody else, he would be wooing her with flowers and wine, late dinners, long nights in bed—

He cleared his throat to bring himself back to the present. Not only were thoughts like that wrong—he'd vowed he wouldn't romance another woman on the rebound—but they would also drive him crazy.

Alonzo began a discussion of this year's grape crop and Riccardo was grateful for the easy topic. Soon the staff announced dinner and they all walked to the dining room, where Nanna sat at the head of her table. His parents sat to Nanna's left and Mitch's parents sat to the right. Francine sat next to Mitch's parents, with Alonzo and Julia filling in beside them. Riccardo pulled out the chair beside his mother for Morgan and sat beside her.

As salads were served, Nanna directed the conversation to Alonzo and the new responsibilities he'd been assigned this year. Proud, he began sharing his plans, including the desire to buy the neighboring vineyard.

Everyone expressed approval.

Riccardo glanced at Morgan, who was staring at the dish in front of her.

"I see you finally got a proper salad."

She turned to him with a smile, her eyes bright and filled with laughter. "Yes. Thank goodness. It's lucky I tossed my wedding gown in the trash can of an airport bathroom. That turkey will never fit again."

He loved her American way of looking at things. Loved that she'd called her gown a big bird. Loved that she hadn't lost the odd sense of humor that had developed when she realized she'd never again fully be the old Morgan Monroe.

But telling her that would be too intimate, so he said, "American women want to be too thin."

She laughed. "Do you think you'd like a chubby version of me?"

He didn't think she was flirting, fishing for a compliment. She only said what was on her mind. He wanted to tell her he would probably like her no matter what size she was, but though he might have said that in the car, trying to help her get her thoughts straight, he couldn't have that kind of conversation with her now. Their discussions for the next few days would have to be surface, superficial.

Disappointment filled him, but he quickly shook his head to clear it. What was wrong with him? He should be glad his one-on-one time with Morgan was done. He'd already had to berate himself for missing her when she went shopping with Nanna. He could not let them get close again.

Before he got the chance to say anything, Nanna directed the conversation to Morgan. She didn't mind talking about her famous dad, making Riccardo's family laugh with her misadventures as his hostess, or her years at boarding school in New England. Julia interjected a few stories about her boarding-school experience and Alonzo joined in.

When they retired in the sitting room for after-dinner drinks, Morgan huddled in with Julia, talking about friends and silly things they'd done as kids. Though Morgan had been told the story of Julia stealing Alonzo from Mitch, she never gave any indication that she knew. Riccardo's dad continued the discussion of the neighboring vineyard that might come up for sale and suddenly it was almost midnight.

Morgan yawned. "Oh, my goodness. I didn't realize how late it was getting." She rose. "I think I'd best get myself to bed."

Riccardo set down his drink. "I'll walk you over."

"There's no need," Morgan said with a smile. "I'll use the time to unwind. It's a beautiful night."

"I insist."

Nanna frowned at him, but he got an obvious nod of approval from his father and Santiago.

When they were outside, under the star-filled sky, she said, "It was nice of your uncle and dad to want to make sure I got back to the condo safely."

Because she wasn't looking at him, he rolled his eyes. The old coots were afraid she'd run and bring the wrath of her father down on them at harvest time. But she didn't need to know that.

"They want all guests on the estate to be treated well."

"In spite of your scandals, your family is very nice."

"We're just normal people." He knew he wasn't supposed to get into any deep, thoughtful conversations with her, but this was something she needed to hear. "Every family has things happen. The trick is to forgive and move on."

"Yeah, well, it remains to be seen if my dad agrees."

He winced and said, "He will," but he let the conversation die. He already loved her laugh, missed talking to her and was seeing the real her, but he couldn't—wouldn't— get involved with another woman who needed him.

They reached the building, walked beneath the crystal chandelier in the lobby and into the elevator. The ride was short. In less than a minute, they were stepping into the corridor facing the doors to their condos. She walked to hers. He walked to his.

As she punched her security code into the keypad, she said, "I'm so confused about the time zones that I'm not even sure how long I've been up."

She pressed the final button and opened the door, but before she could go into her room, he said, "Technically, the nap we took on the plane counts as last night's sleep."

"Yes. I wouldn't have been able to keep up with Nanna if we hadn't slept. And I'd have lost out on a great chance to see the light."

"The light?"

She shrugged. "You know…the way. The path."

He laughed. "What *did* you talk about with Nanna today?"

"My wedding. She asked about it. So, I told her."

"You told her everything?"

"Yes. Riccardo—" Her voice softened and her eyes became liquid pools of blue. "After talking to your grandmother, I understand why you brought me here and I really, really appreciate it."

He might not get involved with women on the rebound, but there was no denying that he liked Morgan. Especially her honesty. He didn't get a lot of that in the superficial dating life he'd created for himself, and for the first time he realized how much he missed true intimacy.

When he didn't say anything, she caught his gaze. "Maybe we're both tired?"

He had to be. Otherwise, he wouldn't be standing by yet another door with Morgan, wishing he could kiss her. Wishing he could comb his fingers through the thick strands of her hair. Wishing he didn't have to walk away.

But he did. She might be the most honest woman he'd ever met, but she was about a week out of a serious relationship. Plus, he was still her keeper, still responsible

for her to her father. If the Colonel didn't like the idea of
Riccardo not bringing her home, he'd probably explode
if he thought the man he'd chosen to protect her wanted
to seduce her.

He took another step back. "Good night."

She smiled. "Good night."

Everything inside him responded to that smile. The
urge to kiss her rose, swift and urgent, a blinding need as
sweet as it was desperate.

He forced himself to turn, to walk across the corridor
and into his own condo.

CHAPTER SEVEN

A KNOCK AWAKENED Morgan the next morning. She grabbed her new pink satin robe and ran into the main living area of her condo. "I'm coming!"

Though it was foolish, she wished it was Riccardo. From the second he'd turned from his door and sauntered over to her the night before, her stomach had been in knots. Her chest had tightened. Her breaths felt shivery. He hadn't seemed to be able to pull himself away from her, and she was absolutely positive he was going to kiss her.

Just the thought had been delicious. Scary, yet wanted. Her throat got so tight, she'd have paid every cent in her trust fund to swallow—

But for the second time, he hadn't kissed her. He'd gone into his condo, leaving her with no choice but to enter hers, and the disappointment had been like an ache in her chest.

She'd tried to prevent her mind from jumping to the logical conclusion, but that was like telling her brain not to think of the color blue. The realization popped into her head like a neon light.

She liked him.

Not the way she'd liked Charles, the convenient, easy man who was always around. She liked Riccardo the way a woman was attracted to a man. A man who made her pulse skip and her insides quiver.

And he liked her, too. Enough to almost kiss her twice.

But when she answered the door, Nanna stood in front of a smiling man who pushed a cart with a tray of buttery croissants, a large bowl of fruit and a pot of coffee.

"I normally drink tea," Nanna said, motioning for the tall man to bring in the cart. "But for you and Lila, I'm more than happy to join you with coffee."

"That's very sweet," Morgan said, tightening the sash on her robe, fighting misery that made no sense. Even though it had been hard for Riccardo to walk away the night before, he *had* walked away. Maybe because he didn't want to get involved with the daughter of one of his biggest clients? Maybe because he still saw himself as being responsible for her?

And that seemed wrong. Now that she had her bearings, she could as easily spend the time before her dad's trip to Stockholm in Paris, and Riccardo would be off the hook. He did not need to be her keeper anymore. She was fine. She could leave.

Of course, if she left, she probably wouldn't see Riccardo again. If something didn't happen here in Spain, whatever was going on between them would be nothing but a few thoughts, a few almost kisses, a few nice conversations, easily forgotten when he got back to his real life in New York City.

"Are you okay, dear?"

Morgan's head snapped up. "Yes. Yes. I'm fine. I was just thinking about when I go home."

"Oh, honey. Of course you are."

The gentleman with Nanna slid the cart beside the table that sat between the kitchen and the arrangement of the sofa and club chairs that formed the sitting area. Nanna thanked him in Spanish and he left.

Morgan's training immediately kicked in and she said, "Please. Have a seat."

Nanna sat at the far end of the table. "Thank you." She frowned. "Are you thinking about going home because you're still afraid of talking to your dad?"

"No. Thanks to you, I have that all sorted out now," Morgan said, as Nanna took a croissant and offered the plate to her.

The knife Nanna had picked up to butter her croissant stopped. "Then what?"

She didn't think it appropriate to tell Nanna that just thinking about kissing her grandson made her shiver. So she said the first thing that popped into her mind.

"If I leave too soon I won't get to meet Lila and I'd love to talk to her."

"Why is that?"

"She grew up without her mom. Not the same way I did, but she still had to fend for herself, learn everything on her own. In all the thinking I've been doing since I ran from my wedding, I'm starting to wonder if I might have missed some things growing up without a woman to guide me."

"What do you think you've missed?"

"Well…" She thought about the crazy, wonderful feeling in her stomach the night before when she and Riccardo stood looking at each other, not speaking about much of anything, but not able to walk away. If she'd had normal teenage years, a mother to ask questions and dates with men her father hadn't chosen for her, she might have grabbed Riccardo's shirt collar, pulled him down to her level and kissed him.

But she couldn't tell his grandmother that.

Still, there were plenty of other things she'd missed out on. "Do you know I've never cooked beyond breakfast."

Nanna's face fell. "Seriously?"

"My last two years at university I had an apartment, but I really didn't prepare meals except eggs and toast, pancakes, French toast. My dad had made breakfasts for us when the cook had days off. I'd learned the basics watching him."

"And that's it? That's what you think you've missed?"

Embarrassed, she fumbled with her silverware. "That and a few other things that aren't easily explained. After hearing about Lila, it just seems talking to her would help me get a bunch of things straight in my own brain."

"She'll be home in a few days."

Morgan wasn't sure she had a few days. Her head said the smart thing to do would be to leave, get Riccardo off the hook and hope they met again. The crazy feeling in her stomach told her to stay. Spend enough time with Riccardo that he might call her when they returned to the States.

"In the meantime, I could give you a cooking lesson or two."

Morgan snapped back to reality. "I'm sorry. What?"

Nanna shot her a curious look. "I said I could give you a cooking lesson or two."

If Morgan's dad kicked her out and she ended up on her own, trust fund or not, she'd need to be able to cook more than eggs, but that hardly seemed like a reason to prolong her stay.

"Thanks, but…"

"I made these croissants."

Morgan looked at the flakey croissants that had melted in her mouth. Even if she decided to leave, she still had a day or two of planning to get herself off the estate. She could probably request the use of a limo and go to an airport without having booked a flight—she still had Riccardo's credit card to pay for a ticket—but that could mean hours waiting at the airport for the next flight to Paris.

And she couldn't get help from Riccardo or anyone in his family. If her dad found out they'd known where she was going, he'd blame Riccardo. So she had to leave on her own. To do that she had to get access to a computer.

"I'll show you my favorite websites to find recipes."

Her brain perked up. "Websites?"

"I do everything on the computer these days." She paused. "Actually, my tablet is much easier to keep on the counter while I'm cooking."

"You work from a tablet?"

Nanny smiled. "Yes. I might be old but I'm not crazy. Computers are better."

Maybe this was her answer to whether she should stay or go? If life was so easily going to give her access to the internet, maybe she was being nudged to leave.

"What time should I come to your residence?"

"First, we need to take a trip into town for your gown fitting. Then we can come back here and make our own lunch."

"Here? In *this* condo? Not your kitchen?"

Nanna laughed. "The tablet's portable."

The relief of having access to the internet was briefly overshadowed by her hatred of deceiving Nanna, a smart woman who wouldn't be easily fooled for long. But she didn't want to give away her plan and risk making her dad angry with Nanna if he discovered she'd helped her. She had to act as if everything was fine.

"Sounds great."

They finished their breakfast and Nanna left to get ready for the trip to the seamstress. A household employee arrived a minute later to get the breakfast cart. Glad her father had insisted she learn four languages, she smiled at the middle-aged man.

"With whom do I speak about arranging for a car to take me somewhere?"

Stacking the dishes to make pushing the cart easier, he said, "Dial three-four-seven on the phone and you will be connected to household services."

That would get her off the vineyard to an airport. Now, all she had to do was get a ticket.

After the butler left, she showered and slid into a pretty blue dress and white sandals.

Happy, she picked up the big sun hat and sunglasses and walked out of her condo to meet Nanna for the dress fitting. As she pressed the elevator button, Riccardo's door opened.

She turned with a smile, but when she saw he wore only a white bath towel knotted around his waist, her mouth dropped open.

"Where are you going?"

He was male perfection. Broad shoulders, muscular legs, strong thighs and a flat stomach. Her heart thumped in her chest.

This was why she couldn't figure out what to do. She was absolutely getting feelings for Riccardo, and she believed he was getting feelings for her. Why else would he jump out of the shower to see her? But every time they got close, he pulled back. If she left now, he'd never contact her when they returned to the States.

Something had to happen between them. Something strong. Something important. So that he'd call her when they returned home—or she'd feel comfortable enough that she could call him.

"You're not going off the estate, are you?" He tightened his hold on the towel at his waist, taking her eyes to his flat stomach.

She had to clear her throat before she could answer. "I'm having my gown for the ball fitted this morning. Nanna's taking me."

"Oh, okay. Good."

Water drops clung to his wet hair and shoulders. He'd obviously raced out of the shower to catch her to find out where she was going…

She sighed. He still thought of himself as her keeper, thought of her as his responsibility.

The disappointment she'd been fighting all morning settled on her shoulders like a snow-covered coat. The silence in the little hall became deafening. He wasn't getting feelings for her the way she was for him. She was just another task on his to-do list.

She turned away and punched the elevator button again. The damn thing was taking forever.

"You look pretty in blue."

She closed her eyes and savored the compliment before she faced him again. "Thanks." She kept her voice light, friendly, though everything inside her wanted to walk over, place her hands on his gorgeous chest and kiss him. "You look very nice in your towel."

He laughed. "There's that sense of humor I've been missing."

She longed to bridge the space between them, to be close enough to touch him, close enough that she could flirt, but she stayed rooted to the spot. She had no idea what he felt for her. One minute he was silent, a man only interested in her because he was her keeper; the next he was telling her she was pretty. And she'd just officially broken off an engagement. It didn't seem right to be this attracted to another man so soon.

She was a mess.

Her whole life was a mess.

"You call it a sense of humor. I call it saying stupid things."

"To-may-to, to-maw-to." He smiled. That's when she noticed the morning stubble on his chin and cheeks. The sheen of desire in his dark, dark eyes.

Her heart felt like it did a cartwheel.

There was no point in trying to talk herself out of this attraction. It was alive and well and scaring her silly.

"I'll see you later." Riccardo's eyes took another stroll down her blue dress and her bones felt like they melted.

"See you later." She turned and quickly got herself into the elevator, away from him. When the door closed, she pressed her hand to her chest. Freedom had multiplied the sensations running through her when he looked at her. Her pulse had scrambled. Her breath stalled. And all the while he'd smiled at her as if to say if she wanted him, really wanted him, she could have him, but she'd have to be the one to make the first move.

Where another woman might have reveled in the power of it, Morgan froze. He was sexy and strong, and she was just finding her feet. It would take years for her to catch up to him in confidence. Forget about ever having his swagger.

Plus, she was leaving. If not now, in a little over a week, when her dad went to Stockholm.

She closed her eyes, but she could still feel the warmth of his gaze on her. Curiosity about kissing him rose in her like a tsunami. The thought of leaving seemed so, so wrong.

Downstairs, she stepped outside, grateful the air was cool. Nanna stood by the limo, cell phone to her ear. When she saw Morgan, she waved as she said, "Yes, darling. I hear you loud and clear. Never out of my sight. Not for one second." She clicked off the call and smiled at Morgan. "We are ready?"

No. She wasn't ready at all. Freedom was airy and light and wonderful, but scary. Risky. At the same time, she didn't want to leave.

Still, was it fair to stay and keep Riccardo on the hook for her just because she was curious? She knew he'd been the person talking to Nanna. Making sure his grandmother watched her. He had to be tired of it.

The dress fitting took only an hour. Because Nanna

had promised to teach her to cook, they returned to the vineyard to make lunch. Nanna went to her apartment to change clothes and Morgan slipped on a pair of her jeans and a big T-shirt.

Thirty minutes later, Nanna arrived with her tablet. "First we're going to make a dessert my friends call the better-than-sex dessert."

Morgan laughed. "Better than sex?"

Nanna tossed her a look. "Just trust me." She walked to the island counter. "It needs to be refrigerated before we can eat it, but that gives us time to make the paella."

Nanna pulled the dessert recipe up on her tablet, then placed a call to the kitchen to have everything they needed for the paella and the dessert delivered to Morgan's condo. When the ingredients arrived, they began cooking.

And it was easy. The condo was stocked with pots and pans, bowls and utensils, dishes and silverware. Everything required was at their fingertips or a phone call away to the staff, and following recipes was just like following instructions for chemistry experiments.

They ate the paella and dessert for lunch, and Morgan groaned with ecstasy. "That dessert is fabulous."

Nanna laughed. "I told you." She rose from the table. "Now it's time for my nap." She headed for the refrigerator. "But I'm taking the leftover dessert with me."

Dessert in hand, Nanna walked to the door. Morgan opened it for her. "I'll see you at supper."

Nanna stopped. "Oh, no, dear. I'm sorry. There is no family dinner tonight. It's Saturday night. Everyone has plans."

"Plans?"

"Marguerite and Santiago are going out with friends. Riccardo's parents are having a private dinner at home. Alonzo and Julia are also staying in." She paused, caught

Morgan's gaze. "I just assumed you would be doing something with Riccardo."

She almost told Nanna that Riccardo had said nothing to her, but stopped herself. Anybody who jumped out of the shower to ask where she was going wouldn't let her have supper alone.

She smiled at Nanna. "I'm sure we will."

Nanna kissed her cheek. "I'll see you tomorrow."

She closed the door and leaned against it, excitement bubbling through her. Tonight would be their first private dinner since they were on the road, when she'd looked like a street urchin. Tonight, she would dazzle him.

She spent an hour doing her toenails and fingernails, soaked in a bubble bath for another hour and then washed her hair. Dressed in pink silk pajamas, she was about to do her makeup when she had a flash of inspiration. She called the kitchen and had them bring up four different kinds of wine, and she slid them into the kitchen's wine cooler. She had no idea what Riccardo had planned, but no matter where they went for supper, even if it was only the family's restaurant, she could invite him into her condo for a glass of wine afterward.

She might be inexperienced but she wasn't dumb.

Eight o'clock that night, alone in her condo, wearing a sundress she hoped didn't scream "I've been waiting for you," with her hair fixed in a fancy style and her lips a striking shade of red, she was bored and miserable.

She paced the sitting room feeling like an idiot. She couldn't be angry with Riccardo for not showing up. He hadn't invited her to dinner. He hadn't even mentioned dinner. And she was an adult. He probably figured she could find her own food. On an estate with a restaurant, she should certainly be able to get something to eat.

She sucked in a breath. She wasn't hungry for food, but she did feel the need for comfort. A little sugar could go a long way right now. Especially if it came in the form of a better-than-sex dessert.

She was just about to call the kitchen to see if they had the recipe when she noticed Nanna hadn't taken her tablet. She hit a few keys and saw it hadn't been password-protected. She easily got in and opened the app that got her on the internet.

Her hand paused above the screen. Riccardo wasn't interested in her and she was about to make a fool of herself because she kept making ridiculous assumptions. Maybe it really was time to go.

Without further thought, she typed in the name of a popular airline and almost made reservations on the earliest flight to Paris—two days from now, but her fingers stopped again. It seemed dishonest to take off without telling Riccardo. Even with him ignoring her, she couldn't seem to deceive him.

She cleared the screen without making the reservation and looked up the recipe for the dessert. With her life back to being a confused mess, she wanted her pudding.

Though it was now long past eight, she called the kitchen. Speaking Spanish, she asked for the ingredients she needed to make the dessert. While she waited for them, she ducked into her bedroom, yanked off the dress, combed out her hair, wiped off the red lipstick, took out her contacts and threw on old jeans and a T-shirt.

She returned to the sitting room, sliding her big glasses on her nose just as there was a knock on her door. She opened it to find someone from the kitchen staff and the ingredients she'd asked for.

She refused to think about Riccardo as she pulled a glass baking pan and two big bowls out of the cupboards and went to work. The crust was first since it had to be cool before she could put the cream cheese filling on top. She mixed the butter, nuts and flour together, spread it out on the bottom of the baking dish and put it in the pre-heated oven.

Fifteen minutes later, the timer rang. Pot holder in hand, she pulled out the finished crust and beamed. Perfect. It was all so easy, she felt like a dolt for not cooking her entire life. And for caring what Riccardo thought. She would go home to a whole new life. A life where she wasn't just an equal with her dad, but she could cook. Take care of herself.

As the crust cooled, she gathered the cream cheese, whipped topping and vanilla extract and blended them using a hand mixer Nanna had shown her was in the cupboard. Relaxation filled her. She'd been told her mother had been an excellent cook and now she understood why she'd taken the time to prepare meals though they had a staff. Preparing food came with a wonderful sense of accomplishment.

With the wet ingredients blended, she opened the confectioner's sugar and measured a cup and a half, dumping it on top of the cream-cheese filling. She turned on the mixer and dipped the beaters into the powdered sugar and—*poof!*—she was covered in white dust.

It surprised her so much she screamed.

CHAPTER EIGHT

RICCARDO WAS JUST about to punch in his key code, when he heard Morgan scream. He raced to her door, damning his family for insisting on locks and steel doors he couldn't break down. He banged on the door, calling, "Morgan!" as he tried the knob. It gave—because she hadn't locked it—and he shoved open the door and raced inside, only to find Morgan standing by the counter covered in white powder.

He laughed.

She gave him an evil look. "What exactly do you think is so funny?"

"Oh, my gosh. You…" Another laugh escaped. Even the lenses of her big glasses were covered in white. "What were you doing?"

She took off her glasses, whipped a paper towel off the roll and cleaned the lenses. "I was cooking."

He sniffed the air. "Smells good."

"That's the crust of the dessert your grandmother taught me to make this afternoon."

"And you decided to make it again because you were bored?"

Her chin lifted. "No. I got hungry for it."

He pointed at the powder-covered countertop. "You should have gotten hungry for a sandwich."

Her chin rose a little higher, clueing him in that she was

truly angry. And he supposed she had a right to be. The entire family had other plans that night. He'd expected to be out of his meeting with Alonzo in time to take her somewhere. But Alonzo kept talking about wanting the third vineyard, needing the house for himself and Julia, in spite of the fact that the seller had finally provided the purchase price and it was way over what the vineyard could afford to pay.

Meaning Riccardo had totally abandoned Morgan.

"I wanted dessert."

Not sure how to make amends, he took a paper towel and brushed off her shoulders. "Your back is comically clean."

"Ha. Ha."

"Oh, come on. Don't pout. It's very funny to see somebody covered head to toe in white stuff in the front but perfectly clean in the back."

"Yeah. It's hysterical. I'm going to change."

"It might be a better idea to finish making your dessert first." Avoiding a glare, he glanced around. "How much more do you have to do?"

She sighed and walked back to the mixer. "I just have to beat this powdery stuff in, then make instant pudding."

"I could help."

She hesitated. He almost wished she'd tell him to go back to his room. It was too late for dinner. And damn if she wasn't adorable trying to be domestic.

"Maybe a little supervision isn't a bad idea." She eyed him skeptically. "Do you cook a lot?"

"Enough to know that you don't put mixer beaters into dry powder sugar and expect to stay clean."

He walked over to the counter and pulled a large spoon from a side drawer. He folded the white powder into the cream-cheese filling a few times, then said, "Okay, try it now."

She lowered the beaters and in under a minute it was blended. "I suppose I should thank you."

He leaned against the counter. "That would be nice."

She peeked over at him. "Thank you."

He looked into her pretty blue eyes and saw a combination of chagrin and desperation that made him long to hug her. But he remembered he didn't get emotionally involved with needy women or even nice women. He didn't do relationships. He had simple, uncomplicated flings. That was why his life was easy.

"You take all this too seriously, you know."

She picked up the bowl and began layering the cream-cheese filling onto the cooled crust. "All what?"

"Normal stuff. Things you think the rest of us know but you don't. Lots of it is common sense. And for the rest there's YouTube."

She looked over at him, studied him for a few seconds, then laughed. "YouTube?"

He shrugged. "Sure. Take that box of pudding mix. I'll bet if you Googled it, you could find a YouTube video on how to make it."

She presented the box to him. "Directions are right here."

"Sure. You had the directions for the white stuff, too, but you ended up covered in powder."

"Very funny."

"At least now you know you won't do that again."

She peered over at him. "No. I won't. I'm not that stupid."

"Actually, you're not stupid at all." He spotted the wine in the cooler and strode over to grab a bottle. He hadn't meant to leave her unattended through dinner. He owed her some company for a little while.

While she made the pudding, he found two glasses and

poured rich red wine into them. "This is last year's. My dad thinks it's too sweet. I think it's perfect."

She took the glass, sampled the wine and smiled. "I like it."

She poured the pudding onto the layer of cream cheese then slid the pan into the refrigerator. "I'm guessing you're hanging around because you want some of that dessert."

He laughed. "Yes and no." Knowing it was time for the apology he should have made right away, he said, "I'm sorry I left you alone this evening."

She didn't accept his apology, but looked away. She might have thought that made it appear like she didn't care but it actually told him just how much she had cared.

"It takes an hour to be firm enough that we can cut it."

He lifted the bottle of wine. "We can kill time with this."

She shrugged. "Okay. Sure."

He headed for the French doors. "Have you used the deck yet?"

"Your nanna has kept me kind of busy."

"Then you're in luck. There's a full moon. You can see for miles."

Nerves rattled through Morgan. It wasn't the perfect evening she'd seen in her head, but he was here and he was staying for a while. Plus, hadn't she thought that morning that she could have him but that she'd have to make the first move? This might be the night she got the chance.

The air was warm and the sky was clear. A huge golden moon watched over the silent vineyards. A woman who'd just walked away from a wedding, broken up with a fiancé and learned to cook was alone on a deck with the first man who'd ever really attracted her.

Yeah. This was going to work.

She sat on one of two chaise lounges on the well-appointed deck. There was a round glass table in the corner that would be perfect for morning coffee and a small square table sat between the two chaises. Riccardo set the wine bottle there, as he lowered himself to one of the chaises.

"So Nanna tells me you know what you're going to say to your dad."

Tonight she didn't exactly want to talk about her dad, but the conversation had to start somewhere. This was as good of a place as any.

"I have a general idea, but it's not like I made a PowerPoint presentation with slides." She shook her head with a laugh. "Your grandmother thinks that I should go home, tell him I'm not happy with our relationship and then leave."

Riccardo peered over. "Leave?"

She ignored the feeling that zinged through her when she looked into his eyes. Especially since the expression in them seemed so neutral.

"She thinks that if I try to argue he'll best me. But if I take a stand and leave, but tell him where I'm going—the address to my new apartment—ultimately he'll come to me willing to talk…or maybe listen."

He took a long breath, as if thinking through what she'd said. "That idea has some merit."

"But?"

"He's a busy guy." He glanced at her. "Men do things differently than women."

"No kidding." She was on pins and needles, thinking this might be her chance to make a move, and he was talking about her dad. Men certainly did do things differently than women.

"I'm serious. The man runs a huge business and he's still an advisor to more people than you and I even know. Heads of state come to him for advice all the time. What if you leave, one of his friends has a crisis and asks for help and he's tied up for weeks?"

The nervous torment of wondering how to make the first move disappeared. She silently held his gaze, not quite sure what he was telling her.

"You could be sitting in an apartment in New York City, waiting for a call that he's not even thinking about making because he's handling a crisis."

"You're saying I'm not that important to him?"

"No, I'm saying that people are creatures of habit. He's accustomed to solving problems. Accustomed to being called upon. To dropping everything to fix the world. And while he's doing that, you'd be sitting alone, thinking he doesn't care about you when really he's just busy."

She let all that slide around in her brain. It was the reality of their relationship. Not that her dad believed everything in the world was more important than she was. It was more that he was a statesman, a diplomat. It was his calling. If someone needed him, he went.

And she would be waiting for a phone call that wouldn't come.

She shook her head, jarring the picture of her sitting by a silent phone out of her brain because it was wrong. She was an adult. If she spent her time waiting by the phone for her dad to call? That was on her. Not him. She should be out having a life. *Her life.* Not being part of her dad's.

"Oh, my gosh."

"What?"

"You're right. Though Nanna got me thinking in the right direction, you just filled in the blanks. I need to move out of my dad's house. But not because I don't want him to find me. Because I need my own life. I also need to get a job somewhere other than the vineyard." She finished the wine she'd been sipping in a quick swallow and refilled her glass.

"That's not what I said."

"It didn't need to be what you said. That's the conclusion I came to after thinking through what you said." She tapped his arm. "Come on, Riccardo. I'm twenty-five and I still live with my dad. I can't complain about him running my life when I'm not doing anything to run it myself."

Riccardo just stared at her. Had she just taken the advice he'd given her and twisted it to make his problem worse? If she told the Colonel he'd helped her decide to move out, the old man would forget everything he knew about diplomacy and shoot Riccardo first and ask questions later.

"You're getting ahead of yourself."

"I don't think so." She took a sip of wine, then rose from her chaise with a laugh. "Your nanna thought leaving was a way to make him realize that I was serious. But the truth is, the best way to make him realize that the way he sees me needs to change is for *me* to change."

She walked over to the railing. Moonlight spilled over her hair and gave her face a radiant glow. "I wasn't a spoiled child. From the time I was twelve, I was my dad's hostess and that wasn't easy. I never saw myself as dependent upon my dad. I saw us as a team. But I never realized that team was holding me back from becoming me." She took another sip of her wine. "I'm a CPA, for heaven's sake. I could change the world."

He took a long gulp of his wine, almost afraid to talk for fear of making things worse. In the end, he could only argue the obvious. "CPAs don't change the world."

"Oh, yeah?" She turned from the railing, her face radiant, her smile so bright it competed with the moonlight. "How do you know?"

"Because I'm a CPA and I haven't changed the world."

"Really? Look around you. You could have stayed in

your parents' home, working a low-level job for this vine-yard, cashing in on your family name. Instead, you left."

"Because there was nothing for me here."

She opened her arms, waving her wineglass out over the railing. "You just made my point. There is nothing for me at my dad's vineyard, except to be his employee and hostess. As both of those, I'm under his command. Out here in the world, I can be anything."

"You're a CPA."

"Exactly!"

Riccardo's head spun. He set his glass on the small table, rose from the chaise and walked over to her. "I meant, you can't be *anything*. You have to work within the parameters of your degree."

"I know that. I'm just thinking out loud. And we've al-ready decided I'm not stupid."

He'd never thought she was. From the second he'd seen her giving the stock seminar behind the slot machines, he'd realized she was more than the woman portrayed in the press. More than a woman in trouble. He'd just never realized how perfect she was. How wonderful.

Her smile grew. She glanced out over the rows of har-vested grapes. "Maybe I'll get a job here."

"What?" Wonderful or not, she couldn't stay here. If the Colonel thought he or Mitch helped her escape, he'd bring the full force of his power down on them.

"I know Ochoa Vineyards is fully staffed. I was talking about Spain. I'm fluent in Spanish, French and Italian and Mandarin. I love Europe." She began to pace. "I need to put together a résumé. Start looking at companies, seeing if there's anywhere I want to work. Any company looking for someone with my skills."

"Once again, I think you're getting ahead of yourself."

"I don't!" She set her glass on the round glass table, walked over to him. "I'm behind where I'm supposed to be. True, I got some experience working for my dad's companies, but my work was pretty much low-level stuff."

"Everybody starts at the bottom."

She considered that. "Okay. Good. Since I've already started at the bottom, what you're saying is that I need to find a next-level job."

Riccardo groaned. "I'm not saying anything. I'm not giving advice. I'm not making recommendations."

"I know. I don't need your advice. I've got this."

She stood on her tiptoes and pressed a quick kiss to his lips.

As if realizing what she'd done, she froze in place.

Their gazes caught.

Temptation roared through him. So swift and so strong, he didn't have time to combat it. She was sweet. She was funny. And she drew him in a way no woman ever had before.

His hands went to her shoulders, his head descended and his lips pressed to hers with the determination of a man taking what he'd wanted for what seemed like forever.

His lips slid across hers, tasting a hint of the sugar that had covered her face when he'd arrived, sending a bubble of laughter through him, causing him to take the kiss deeper, to open his mouth and encourage her to open hers. When she did, he plundered. She was like a rare treat, water to a thirsty man.

She rose to her tiptoes and gave as good as she got. As desperate as he was, she nestled against him and that's when warning bells began to chime.

Not because she was a woman who had just gotten out of a relationship, but because of who he was. Right now, he could take anything he wanted from her and she'd let him.

And then he'd know real regret. Because he wasn't a man who settled down, not anymore. He was a man who had flings. If they did what he wanted to do right now, he'd walk away tomorrow morning without looking back, and he'd hurt her.

He broke the kiss and stepped back quickly. "Okay. That's the last time we're going to do that."

She blinked. Her big blue eyes seemed bigger, shinier. "Why?"

He walked over to the small table between the chaises, picked up his wine and downed it. "You may not understand this now, but you're not in any kind of condition to make the decisions you think you want to make."

"*I* think *I* want to make? There were two of us in that kiss."

"Okay, let's look at this purely from my vantage point. I got involved with a woman who was fresh off a relationship. We were together two years and when her old boyfriend came back, she dropped me. Even after all the time we dated, after accepting an engagement ring, planning our wedding, she'd never gotten over her ex."

She fell to the chaise beside him. "Wow."

"No matter how angry I wanted to be with her, I had to recognize that I was as much to blame as she was. She was emotionally vulnerable. I didn't think I'd taken advantage of that. But I sure as hell didn't give her time to heal." He shook his head. "No. I thought I could help her heal. But the real bottom line was she wasn't ready. And here you are a week after running from your wedding. You haven't even officially talked to Charles yet."

Her head came up. "Yes. I did. I called him."

His heart stumbled. "You did?"

She nodded. "I couldn't very well be looking at you in nothing but a towel when I hadn't settled things back home."

He laughed.

"You think that's funny? You think I want the feelings I have for you? I've fought them at every turn."

"Well, keep fighting them because this—" he motioned from him to her and back to himself again "—is wrong."

"I don't think so. I fought it and fought it and fought it and what I feel keeps getting more and more real."

"Okay, then how about this. Getting dumped in such a public way, losing a woman I adored, changed *me*." He caught her gaze. "I decided relationships weren't for me and I learned how to have fun without getting involved. I could easily take what you're offering and walk away." He shook his head. "This time I wouldn't get the broken heart. You would."

He turned then, not giving her a chance to reply. He walked through her condo, to his own, where he closed the door, trying to make himself feel safe. Not from her. From himself. He'd never been so tempted by a woman before.

Then he realized his lips still tingled. He pressed two fingers to his mouth. *She'd kissed him.*

And he'd liked it. Really, really liked it. And not just sexually. Morgan was sweet and funny and smart. *Everything about her* called to him.

He pushed those thoughts out of his brain. She might find him attractive, she might be ready to move out of her dad's house, get another job, start another life, but only a week ago she'd been ready to marry another man.

What if she went home, and in the familiar surroundings of her life realized she'd made a mistake?

What if she went home, saw Charles and changed her mind?

The risk was too great.

With this being his second time of making the same mistake, the potential humiliation was off the charts.

He should stay away from her. But he couldn't. He had a father and uncle who wanted to make sure she wouldn't bring trouble to Ochoa Vineyards. Little did they know, she already had.

CHAPTER NINE

MORGAN WAS EATING a croissant from a basket sent over by Nanna the next morning when there was a knock at her door. Done with hoping it was Riccardo—because she'd made an idiot of herself the night before and she didn't want it to be him, she was surprised when she answered and found him on the threshold.

Wearing chinos and a white shirt, he looked like a businessman on casual Friday. Which, unfortunately, appealed to the CPA in her. Her heart tumbled. Memories of their kiss sent warmth through her. But she could not fall in love with him. As he'd said the night before, she wasn't emotionally ready. It shamed her that he'd had to spell it out for her. To remind her that she'd need time to heal from one relationship before she could start another. But she wouldn't let him see that. She'd embarrassed herself enough in front of him.

Glad she'd dressed in jeans and a T-shirt before coming out of her bedroom that morning, she smiled innocently, as if their conversation the night before hadn't happened. "What's up?"

"Today's an off day." He shrugged. "I thought I'd take you to town, buy you lunch."

"You're not in charge of my happiness." It made her feel weird to say it, but it was true. That was another lesson she'd learned after spending the entire day primping, fancying herself up, to see him—only to have him not show up when she thought he should. From here on out, she would stand on her own two feet. Think for herself. Protect herself. Entertain herself.

"I'm fine. I'll find something to do." She pointed to the kitchen island, where Nanna's tablet still sat. "Maybe I'll cook something."

He laughed. "No. I don't want you to be bored and I don't want you to leave Spain with negative feelings after our conversation last night. Let me show you around."

Because he asked, didn't order, she softened a little. He was right. She didn't want to go home with weird feelings about him. He'd given her the chance to think through her life when her dad wanted him to take her home. And they had gotten along well until she'd kissed him. It only seemed fair that she capitulate, go with him and give them both back the good feelings they'd had toward each other.

"Okay, give me ten minutes to dress."

His eyebrows rose. "Ten minutes?"

"Seriously. I'll just change into a sundress and slip into sandals."

"No makeup?"

"Are we meeting royalty?"

He laughed. "No."

She headed for her bedroom. "Then I'm fine."

"It's very warm. You should also bring that sun hat you bought with Nanna."

She stopped. It struck her as odd that he remembered an offhand conversation from dinner the first night she got there. Charles sometimes couldn't remember important things she told him. Riccardo even remembered insignificant details. It filled her heart with something indescribable, then she pushed that thought out of her head.

He wanted nothing to do with her.

And who could blame him? The woman who'd canceled *his* wedding had just left a relationship when she'd met him. It was either a terrible coincidence or a cosmic joke that they'd met right after her breaking up, but she understood.

Anything between them would be foolish.

She slipped into a pink sundress, found her sunglasses and snagged the big sun hat Nanna liked.

When she returned to the sitting room, he was staring out at the deck—where she'd kissed him the night before, then he'd kissed her.

Really kissed her.

Her breath wanted to stutter. She stopped it, suddenly realizing that it might be her own fault she was getting feelings for him. Every time something happened between them, she infused it with meaning. Maybe if she'd let herself see the real Riccardo, and stop making a big deal out of everything, these feelings would disappear?

He turned from the window. "You look great."

There. See? Here was her first realization. He was a man who complimented her. Because she wasn't accustomed to being complimented, she lapped up his praise as if it had more meaning than it did.

He was right. They needed an outing together. But not so they could remain friends, but so she'd see how badly she continually misinterpreted him.

"And I'm all ready to go."

They walked outside to a red Porsche that sat in front of the condo building. He opened the door for her—like a gentleman, nothing romantic about that at all—and she slid inside.

As he drove them into the small town where she'd shopped and lunched with Nanna, he pointed out various vineyards, and places he and Mitch had played as kids. In town, they walked along cobblestone streets fronting small businesses in buildings that looked a lot like gingerbread houses from fairy tales. He told her stories about the baker, the hardware store owner and the tavern owner, who was a friend of his, making her laugh enough to remind her that he was a nice guy. A friendly guy. And though that was good, it wasn't a reason to fall in love. He treated everybody well.

With the warm sun beating down on them, and the soothing tone of his voice washing over her, she began to feel normal again, except smarter. The sheep in her had died the day she ran away from her wedding. Her thoughts really had cleared in Spain and she had a plan for her life. True, Riccardo had helped her, but maybe it was best not to think about that. It brought all kinds of appreciation to the surface and made her like him again.

And she didn't want to like him. It was too soon. Her emotions were scrambled. The cautious part of old Morgan Monroe resurfaced and she let it. Casual Morgan did nothing but get her into trouble.

They decided on the bistro across from the park for lunch, sitting at a wrought-iron table with matching chairs. The town wasn't crowded, but tourists strolled the streets. As they finished eating, a mime took up residence at the edge of the park.

She pointed across the street. "Look at that."

"He's a regular."

"He's very good."

"Eh…he's so-so."

She gaped at him. "Really? So-so? Can you juggle three oranges?"

"Anyone can juggle three oranges."

Morgan held back a laugh. Finally, a flaw. The arrogance she'd seen in Vegas was back. And she couldn't resist teasing him.

"Do you want to go over and try?"

He gave her a funny look. "You don't believe me?"

Suddenly feeling a little crazy for pushing him, she batted her hand. "Never mind."

He shoved his chair back. "You don't believe me."

"It doesn't matter if I believe you or not."

He took her hand and forced her to stand. "Come on. No one calls Riccardo Ochoa a liar."

She couldn't help laughing as he all but dragged her across the quiet street.

When they reached the mime, he said, "Can I see those?"

The mime tilted his head in question as his face twisted in confusion, clearly getting his point across without saying a word.

Morgan pressed her hands to her chest to keep from hugging him. "You're so good!"

The mime bowed.

Riccardo sighed.

The mime bowed to him and handed over the three oranges. Riccardo took them and juggled them like an expert, even throwing one behind his back without missing a beat. The small crowd that had gathered applauded.

Done, he handed the oranges back to the mime then took her hand. "There. See. I can juggle."

She laughed and pointed behind him as the mime picked up a forth orange and began to juggle more oranges than Riccardo had. "I think you've just been bested."

He faced the mime. "Are you challenging me?"

The mime shrugged.

Laughing, Riccardo took the four oranges from his hands and juggled them with ease. But when he stopped, he didn't lay down the four oranges, he picked up a fifth.

Like a pro, he juggled the five oranges. The growing crowd cheered.

The mime took the five oranges from Riccardo and

juggled them but not with the ease Riccardo had. When he stopped, he picked up a sixth orange. He barely managed to juggle all six, but he did it.

The crowd clapped.

Grinning, the mime handed the six oranges to Riccardo.

But Riccardo shook his head, then he bowed. With a laugh, he said, "You are the better juggler."

The mime strutted in a small circle. Riccardo applauded him, then dropped some money into the hat the mime had sitting on the ground for donations.

Walking back to the Porsche, Morgan said, "What did you just do?" She glanced back at the mime, then at Riccardo again. "You'd juggled the five oranges much better than the mime had. You'd have easily done six. Why'd you give up?"

He said nothing.

"Oh, my gosh! You lost on purpose!" The craziness of it caused her to stop walking.

He opened the car door for her.

She stared at him as she rolled the whole thing around in her brain. "You didn't want to embarrass him."

He pointed at the door and she scrambled over and got inside. He closed the door and rounded the car, getting in behind the steering wheel.

"Admit it." She almost added, *You lost on purpose because you saw how he bobbled the five oranges and didn't want to embarrass him.*

But when the truth of it sunk in, she closed her mouth. He wouldn't want credit for that. She glanced at the mime, who was happily juggling his oranges, bowing when someone tossed money in his hat, and her heart swelled. She wasn't falling in love with Riccardo Ochoa because she was needy…or because she was on the rebound. He was a great guy. Unlike anybody she'd ever met. And very much like somebody she'd want in her life forever.

* * *

Riccardo walked her to her door, annoyed with himself for challenging the mime. It had been easy enough to get out of the contest when he saw the man wasn't as skilled as he was. But Morgan had seen right through it.

Because she was smart. And he *loved* that she was smart. The combination of beauty and brains just about had him mesmerized. But that was the problem. They weren't right for each other. She was a woman who'd just got out of a serious relationship, and he was a guy who had built protective walls because he'd been hurt by someone who'd just got out of a serious relationship.

He could not like her. He would hurt her. Or she would hurt him.

But even that line was blurring now, which meant he liked her a lot more than was advisable.

They stopped at her condo door. She punched in the key code. "Why don't you come in. It's four hours 'til dinner. There's plenty of time for us to have a glass of wine on the balcony."

He glanced outside at the place where they'd had wine the night before, where he'd helped her come to another conclusion and where she'd kissed him.

The power of that simple kiss snapped through him and he wanted nothing more than to kiss her again. To drink wine and laugh. Except that would only make him like her more. As it was, he was dangerously close to letting go, letting himself enjoy her company. Then, when she left, when she got home and realized how much she'd missed her life, he'd barely be a passing thought. And if he as much as moped one day over her, his family would think he was an idiot.

It was one thing to fall for one woman who'd been on the rebound. Falling for a second would make him the world's biggest fool.

Which was why he said, "No. Thanks. I'm going to look at some accounts before dinner."

She smiled. "Why don't we have the glass of wine, then I could come over to your condo and help you do whatever it is you have to do."

He laughed. "Right. I'm going to audit accounts after a couple of glasses of wine?"

"I said one glass."

"I saw how you are with wine. I saw you refill your glass twice last night without even hesitating."

"Because it was good."

The simplicity of her answer soothed his agitated soul. But that was what being with her did to him. Made him happy. Calmed him down. Made him feel like he'd found his place. Like he wasn't the one helping her. She was the one helping him. And in a way she was. He hadn't realized how empty his life had been without intimacy until he'd met her.

"Thanks." He longed to run his fingers through her hair, to be allowed to touch her. Just to have contact. But none of this was real for her. Oh, she might think it was, but being away from her dad, Charles, the gossip about her running from her wedding, had put her in something of a protective bubble. She'd be strong about some things when she returned home, but she would realize she missed others.

Maybe even Charles.

"How about if I help before the wine?"

He stepped back. "No. I'm good. We'll both have enough wine with dinner at Nanna's tonight."

She nodded, opened her condo door and walked inside.

He shoved his hands in his trouser pockets as his heart drooped. It was cruel of fate to find him a woman to bring him back to life after Cicely, to remind him of all the things he'd wanted, to long for things he'd thought were beyond his reach. Because Morgan wasn't any more able to give them to him than Cicely had been.

He turned and headed for his condo. He was thankful she only had a few more days before she could go home, but when he walked inside his quarters that odd feeling struck him again. The one he'd had the day they'd arrived in Spain…

That he missed her.

That his life just wasn't complete without her in it.

He knew what was happening. Despite his best efforts and all his good arguments, it would hurt when she left.

Morgan dressed in a peach floral sheath dress for dinner that evening. Nerves pricked at her stomach but she ignored them. She'd stood by her door after she'd gone inside that afternoon, waiting to hear Riccardo leave but he didn't. For a good five minutes, he stayed in the hallway, in front of her door.

She'd thought he would change his mind about the wine, thought he might actually be changing his mind about everything. God knew she was. Every time she tried to tell herself she wasn't in the right frame of mind to be making emotional decisions, he did something wonderful and she would know she wasn't falling for him because she was vulnerable. She was falling for him because he was a man worth loving.

She couldn't even think about him without losing her breath.

In the end, he'd walked away and gone to his condo to look at his accounts, but they were having dinner that night with the family. They would have five minutes alone walking over and five minutes walking home—then there would be time at her door. He might kiss her again. Or maybe she would kiss him…

Twenty minutes went by with her pacing in front of

the sofa, waiting for him to knock on her door. When she recognized they'd be late if they didn't leave now, she wondered if he'd decided not to walk her over. He'd never actually said he'd get her for dinner, but it was common sense to go to family meals together. They were on the same floor of the same building. He couldn't, wouldn't, "ditch" her.

When another five minutes went by, she knew she either left now or she'd be late. Rationalizing that he could be on the phone with someone or napping, she realized that if she waited for him she'd look like an idiot who couldn't even walk herself next door.

She stepped into the hall and stood staring at Riccardo's door.

She could knock. If he answered, she could say something light and fun, like, "Hey, we're going to be late if you don't get a move on."

But knocking on his door seemed hopelessly desperate. She refused to be desperate. She might want to kiss him. She might even be falling in love. But Morgan Monroe was not desperate.

She raced along the cobblestone path and up the stairs to Nanna's. She did as Riccardo always did, pressed the doorbell, but walked inside without waiting for someone to answer.

She entered the sitting room with a smile. "Good evening, everyone."

A general greeting came from his family, as Nanna walked over and escorted her to the sofa. "Get her some wine, Alonzo."

Alonzo complied and brought her a nice glass of red. Taking a sip, she glanced around surreptitiously and didn't see Riccardo.

She wanted to ask. But what was the point? If he was on

the phone with someone, no one at Nanna's would know. If he was napping, same deal.

Still, no one seemed concerned that he was late, and when dinner was served and he still wasn't there, no one mentioned it. No one mentioned him all night.

At the end of the evening, Julia rose from the sofa and said, "Time to get moving." She caught Alonzo's hand and pulled him from his seat before she turned to Morgan. "Riccardo asked us if we'd walk you home."

Her breath froze at the mention of his name until she realized what Julia had said. "He asked you to walk me home?"

"Yes," Alonzo said. "He had a long day, and said he was too tired to join us for dinner, but didn't want you walking home alone. Especially since our town house is on the way."

He wasn't at dinner because he'd had a long day?

She'd been with him most of the day and she wasn't tired—

Unless he just plain didn't want to see her?

He hadn't wanted to come to her balcony for wine, didn't want to have dinner with her and now didn't want her walking home alone?

The insult of it built like storm clouds on the horizon.

The *nerve* of that man. He looked at her like she was his favorite jelly on a croissant, then avoided her?

Julia hooked her arm through Morgan's. "Let's go."

As they started for the door, a new sense of insult rose in her. Not only did he not want to see her, but he also had somebody walk her home as if he was afraid she'd escape. He couldn't seem to let go of his commitment to her dad to watch her.

Okay. In fairness, she had almost bought a ticket to leave. But to *protect* him. Not to get away from him.

Alonzo and Julia deposited her at the door to the condo

building and she rode up in the elevator in silence. She didn't even look at Riccardo's door, just powered through the hallway and into her own quarters.

Fuming, she fell into a fitful sleep but her phone rang what felt like only minutes later. She groggily said, "Hello?"

"It's time!" Julia's excited voice burst into Morgan's ear.

They'd talked about needing to pick the grapes very, very soon. "Probably tonight," Alonzo had said at dinner, and having lived on a vineyard most of her life, Morgan understood.

She whipped off the covers. "I'll be ready in five minutes."

"Someone will drive you back by ATV. Wear jeans."

Not taking even two seconds to think, Morgan jumped into jeans and a long-sleeve shirt. The heat of the day gave way to cooler nights and she wasn't taking any chances. In less than five minutes, she was in the hall, pressing the button for the elevator. Grapes had to be picked when they were at the perfect stage of ripeness. Once they hit the peak, a vintner had very little time to get them harvested. With a vineyard as large as the Ochoa family's that was a monumental task, especially harvesting by hand.

Waiting for the elevator, she didn't think about Riccardo, didn't glance at his door. He could sit and spin for all she cared.

The elevator finally came. She jumped in, rode to the first floor and raced out to the grounds of the main house. Nanna waved her over.

Walking to Riccardo's grandmother, she said, "*You're* picking grapes?"

"I haven't missed a year since I married Santiago and Carlos's father. I'm not stopping now."

Three ATVs pulled up to the cobblestone walk. Alonzo

drove one. Julia drove the second. Riccardo drove the third.

Nanna gave her a quick shove. "Go on. I'll ride with Alonzo."

Annoyed that Riccardo had avoided her, she walked toward Julia's ATV.

But Riccardo caught her arm. "You come with me."

Before she could argue, someone else jumped on Julia's ATV.

She raised her chin and slid on behind Riccardo. "I'm surprised you're willing to take me."

He shoved the vehicle into gear. "Are you kidding? Let you alone among hundreds of people with access to the road?"

She couldn't believe he was still guarding her, couldn't believe he didn't understand that letting her run away would end his responsibility.

"You do realize that if I left you'd be off the hook?"

He turned around to gape at her. "Off the hook? Your father would shoot me."

"I am a twenty-five-year-old woman. All you have to do is tell him I wanted to leave and you didn't want to go to jail for holding me against my will."

For some reason she couldn't fathom, that made him laugh. He turned around and hit the gas, and the ATV roared to life.

Out of stubbornness, she'd avoided sliding her arms around him. But as the thing bumped and jerked along the rough path, she had no choice. Forced, she slid her arms around his middle.

She closed her eyes, trying to dispel the tingles that whispered through her. In her mind's eye, she saw the abs her hands currently rested on. Wet from his shower the morning she'd seen him in only a towel.

She popped her eyes open to stop the vision, and saw

they'd made it to the vineyard's staging area. Huge construction lights lit the rows of grapes, mimicking daylight. A cart held food and coffee. People stood in a huddle getting instructions from Santiago or lessons with the small shears required to cut the grape stems from Carlos. Trucks arrived with more pickers. Laughing townspeople and tourists piled out and headed to Alonzo for gloves, baskets and shears.

Riccardo got off the ATV and offered his hand to help Morgan off. She all but batted it away.

"I can get myself off an ATV."

"Fine. Let's go to my dad for instructions."

"On how to pick grapes?"

He sighed. "Yes."

"I grew up in a vineyard. I've picked grapes."

"Great. Then we'll go to Santiago for our assignment and Alonzo for our shears and baskets."

"Fine." Her head high, she marched to Santiago. He started giving her an assignment, but Riccardo took the sheet from his hands. "She's with me."

Santiago smiled and Morgan cursed old-world cultures that still thought women were helpless. Out of respect, she said nothing to Santiago, but when she and Riccardo were alone, heading back to his ATV after getting gloves and baskets from Alonzo, she snatched the paper from his hands.

"I can find my way alone."

"Or you could just get on the ATV and ride out with me."

Morgan stopped by the little red all-terrain vehicle. "Great. Nothing like feeling you're in prison."

Riccardo got on the ATV. "You're not in prison. You're free to do anything you want."

She slid on the ATV. "Really? I can leave tomorrow?"

"Absolutely. I'll come with you."

"The point is to get away from you."

"With the three hundred bucks you have left?"

Assuming she'd have his blessing, she'd intended to use his credit card, but she supposed that was off the table now.

She made a sound of exasperation as the ATV took off toward their assigned rows. He'd chase her down in Paris but wouldn't have dinner with her that night. Sure. That made sense.

When the vehicle stopped, she jumped off, grabbed her basket and shears and stormed to find her place.

But in the vines, her anger suddenly disappeared. The night was cool, not cold, and the air so refreshing she took a long breath to enjoy it. With her gloves on, she angled her shears on the stem of her first cluster of grapes and snipped. They fell into her hand and she set them in her basket, the way her mom had taught her when she was six.

"I see you do know how to do this."

"Did you think I was lying?" She wouldn't look at him. She knew he had some sort of conciliatory expression on his face and she'd add that to his good looks and instantly forgive him for refusing to be around her, for sticking her with Julia and Alonzo and for basically telling her he'd follow her if she left. She didn't want to forgive him. She wanted him to like her.

There. She'd admitted it. She felt like a silly teenager with a crush on an older boy, but it was what it was. If she could figure out a way to get to Paris without him monitoring his own credit card, it wouldn't matter.

"I just thought that since it had been a while, you might have forgotten."

A new pain hit her. She remembered the night her mom had taught her where and how to cut the grape stem, her mom's laugh as it echoed through the vineyard and the many nights after that they'd picked together.

"You never forget the last thing you did with your mom."

* * *

Riccardo's heart stumbled to a stop. She'd tried to keep the sadness out of her voice, but he'd heard it. In all the time they'd spent together, she'd barely mentioned her mom.

"Why don't you tell me about her?"

She did the thing where her chin lifted and it almost made him laugh. She was like an adorable kitten trying to pretend she was a lion. His growing feelings for her spun through him again, but he easily stopped them. He'd spent most of the night reminding himself of the humiliation and embarrassment after Cicely canceled their wedding. Falling in the same trap twice would be infinitely worse. Able to keep himself in line now, he could spend time with her, even have fun with her.

"No, thank you."

"It's going to be a long night if we don't talk."

When she didn't reply, he said, "In all our conversations, you've never even told me her name."

"Montgomery."

"No. What was her first name?"

"Montgomery was her first name. It was her great-great-grandfather's last name. They gave her the name to honor him."

He chuckled. "And to make her life miserable in kindergarten."

Morgan shrugged. "She never mentioned that. She always talked about how she loved it. How it made her feel connected to her roots."

"I understand that." He felt the same way about his family. "Santiago and my father might be old-school sometimes, but my family is bound by tradition. Honor. A reason to make good grades at university. A reason to make my family proud."

She softened a bit. "Yes. That's obvious."

The noise of harvesters arriving to take their rows

ebbed and flowed around them. Riccardo was sure that would cause Morgan to clam up. To his surprise, she kept talking.

"My mom was busy. A lawyer with some impressive clients. But she always made time for me. Every couple of months, we'd go shopping in Chicago."

He remembered her guessing they were going to Chicago when he'd told her they were going to Spain, and felt like a heel for not realizing there might have been a reason. He'd spent so much of their time together working not to fall for her that he'd missed some pretty important things.

They snipped more grapes, carefully laid them in their baskets.

"She taught me how to know what looked good on me and what didn't."

Eager to keep the conversation going, he said, "Which is why you have a great fashion sense."

She shook her head. "I seem to remember you making fun of the clothes I bought at the airport and in the casino shops."

"I'm sure there wasn't much to choose from."

"You are such a charmer."

"Yet, you're mad at me."

"Because you don't trust me."

"The price of not going back to Lake Justice is being under my supervision. And it's not like I'm a hard taskmaster. You have your own rooms. You come and go with Nanna. If you want freedom, I'll arrange for the family jet to take you home."

Snipping a stem, Morgan considered taking him up on that. She was infinitely stronger than she had been the day she'd run from her wedding. She'd already talked to Charles. If her dad insisted on being in on the first conversation when she got home, it wouldn't make any difference. She could leave Riccardo Ochoa to the rest of his Vegas-going, probably womanizing life.

A little boy of about three came racing up to Riccardo. He tugged on his pant leg, talking in rushed Spanish that blew right by Morgan.

Riccardo reached down and swooped him up, into his arms. Speaking clear, slow Spanish that Morgan easily understood, he said, "And how are you, Jesse?"

The little boy gave him an earnest look. "Do you have candy?"

Riccardo laughed and reached into his pocket, pulling out some individually wrapped treats. "Did you think I would forget?"

A woman wearing jeans and a T-shirt, with her dark hair caught up in a bandana, ran up to them. "I'm so sorry!" She took the little boy from Riccardo's arms. "Jesse! I told you to stay with me!"

"He's fine."

The woman's face softened. "Yes. Thank you." She lightly pinched her little boy's cheek. "Tell Riccardo thank you for the candy."

The little boy grinned shamelessly. "Thank you."

Morgan watched the exchange over the grape stems she snipped. He looked really good with a child. Very natural. He didn't have any nieces or nephews so she wondered how he'd gotten that way.

"You've very good with kids."

Watching the woman leave with her little boy, Riccardo said, "Yes. I like them."

The question that had burned inside her since watching him change a tire tumbled out. "How come you're not married?"

"I told you. I nearly was married. When it didn't work out, I changed my life." He shrugged. "It's kind of nice being rich and single. I can go where I want. Do what I want. I like being alone. Being my own person."

Her head tilted as she studied him. "Don't you feel you should be carrying on the family name?"

"My cousins are doing that."

"Don't your parents nag you about grandkids?"

He laughed. "Once in a while I get a sigh from my mother."

That made her laugh, too. "I'll bet."

"But I like being single. My life was complicated when I was engaged. Now it's easy. I don't want to go back."

Though their situations were totally different, she understood what he was saying. She didn't want to go back to her old life, either. No matter how firm she was with her father, he was still Colonel Monroe, former secretary of state with high-powered friends and unfettered ambition. Like it or not, some of that would always spill over into her life.

If Riccardo didn't like complications, he didn't want her.

She wished that knowledge didn't sting so much, but it did. For the first time in her life she felt she was genuinely falling in love with somebody, and even if he had feelings for her, he didn't want them.

They said nothing for a few minutes as they snipped stems and filled baskets. Alonzo drove up in an ATV pulling a cart. He took their filled baskets and left empties. The conversations of the other pickers floated around them as a dull hum. Not clear enough to hear, but ever-present.

"You offered me your family jet a few minutes ago?"

He snipped a grape stem. "Yes?"

She took in a long breath, blew it out slowly. "I may want to take you up on it. I'm ready to talk to my dad, but I wouldn't mind a few days in Paris. That way, by the time I get home, he'll have left for his summit and I can meet with Charles privately." She shrugged. "You know. Give back the ring. That sort of thing."

He frowned. "I never saw you wearing a ring."

"I'd left it in my bedroom for the ceremony so we could get the wedding ring on without fumbling." She took another quick breath. "Anyway, when my dad gets home, everything will be settled with Charles and my discussions with my dad won't have to be about the wedding, but can be about our future as father and daughter."

"That makes sense."

"It really does."

"What are you going to say?"

"What we talked about on the highway, while you were fixing the tire. I'm going to say, 'Dad, I love you but we need some boundaries.'"

He laughed. "I didn't say that."

"I took your original idea and enhanced it."

"Do you know how you'll stand your ground?"

She stopped her scissors and looked across the grapes at him. "I'm moving out, remember?" She'd kissed him to thank him for helping her think it through, then he'd kissed her. Deeply, passionately, as if she was the second half of his soul.

He caught her gaze with dark eyes filled with longing. "Yes, I remember."

Her heart wanted to leap out of her chest, but no matter how much yearning she saw in his eyes, he wouldn't take the steps to fall in love with her.

She looked at her grapes again. "Yeah, well, that's why my first order of business will be to polish my résumé. I used Nanna's tablet that night to write it quickly. But it still needs some finessing."

"Do you have any idea where you want to work?"

"I think I've decided on New York City."

A few seconds passed with her heart beating heavily in

her tight chest, as a new thought struck her. If she moved to New York City, they could find each other. It would be their chance to date, to have a normal opportunity to get to know each other. More time for him to realize he could have all those things he'd always wanted, to trust that she wouldn't leave him. That he could give her his heart.

All it would take would be one word of agreement from him now, one hint that he would see her when she was in New York City.

He said nothing.

Disappointment began to rise in her, but she quashed it. He could be too busy with the grapes to notice she was waiting for his reply.

She tried again. "Maybe you could help me find a job?"

"Maybe."

All her patience with him evaporated like night mist in the sun. "Maybe? Seriously! You drag me across an ocean to protect me from my dad but won't help me find a new job?"

He sighed. "Okay. Yes. Mitch and I know a lot of people. We could probably help you find a job."

"Sheesh. If it's that much trouble, don't bother!"

"Don't be mad."

"I'm not mad. I just thought we'd become friends."

They *had* become friends. And if he thought they could stay friends while he helped her find a job, helped her find a place to live, helped her adjust to city life, he would be all over it.

But what he saw in his head when he envisioned her being in his life in the city wasn't two friends. He saw himself stealing kisses, laughing at private jokes as they walked through condos with a real-estate agent, finding her in the tangles of his sheets and covers when they woke up the next morning. And one day she'd realize she'd gotten involved with a man before she was ready and she'd dump him. He'd been with Cicely for two long years, but even that hadn't been enough. There was no point in finding each other when she moved to the city. She needed years to heal and, like an idiot, Riccardo was falling in love now.

Though she was clearly exasperated with him, they finished their picking time talking about the nonthreatening topic of the places she'd like to work. It didn't surprise him that the United Nations appealed to her and he knew with her dad's background she could get a job without him. He expected to be relieved. Instead, it gave him an itchy feeling to realize just how little this woman needed him. His job, his money, meant nothing to her. She could have it all, get it all, without him. If she liked him, it was for himself. Not for anything he could give her. He guessed that was why he found her so appealing, and that made him doubly sorry that he had to let her go.

When their work was done, they returned to the condo building. Getting out the elevator, they stepped into the hall where he'd almost kissed her, where she'd seen him in nothing but a towel, where he'd seen the interest in her eyes turn to awareness.

Ignoring the feelings that washed through him, he began punching in his key code. "Let me know when you want the plane."

"You really are going to let me go."

He shrugged, pretending he didn't understand what she was saying. "Now that I know your plan, I trust you. Just let me know when you want to go and I'll arrange it."

He peeked over and saw the sadness in her pretty blue eyes. Though it crushed him, he pushed open his door and walked away from her.

CHAPTER TEN

THE ALARM ON the old-fashioned clock woke Morgan a little after one on Monday afternoon. Before she'd fallen into bed, she'd taken a shower and slipped into a T-shirt and panties. After adding a pair of jeans, she ambled into the condo's main room and found a cart with coffee and some croissants and a note from Nanna telling her Lila and Mitch had arrived that morning and the women had congregated in Nanna's living room to talk.

She buttered a croissant and ate it as she found sandals, put them on and raced into the hall for the elevator. There was no sign of Riccardo as she waited for the little car, or on the first floor of the condo building or even the cobblestone walkway to the mansion. But it didn't matter. His mind was made up. He didn't even want to see her in New York City. He'd said he'd changed after being hurt and liked his life. He didn't want the complications of a relationship. It hurt, but she accepted it.

Done with her croissant, she ran up the big half-circle stairway and down the hall to Nanna's apartment.

She rang the bell, but didn't wait for anyone to answer. She walked inside and found her way to the sitting room where Nanna, Marguerite, Paloma, Julia and Lila's mom, Francine, sat with a small brunette with laughing eyes, who had to be Lila.

Nanna rose, kissed both her cheeks and turned her to face the new addition to their group. "This is Lila."

Lila stood up and gave her a hug. "You do realize there was a picture of you racing away from your wedding in all the London papers."

Morgan winced. "I'm sure the furor will die down soon."

Lila sat on the big ottoman between the sofa and a club chair and patted a spot beside her. "Sit."

She sat with Lila as Marguerite got her a cup of coffee. "Thanks."

"You're welcome. And thank you for helping with the harvest last night."

Lila looked from one woman to the next. "Oh, my gosh! You guys harvested last night?"

Paloma said, "Yes."

Morgan winced. "Am I the only one who took a nap?"

Marguerite laughed. "Probably."

Lila stood up. "Go, you guys! Seriously. We've been talking since I got here! You must be exhausted."

Nanna staunchly said, "We're fine."

"No, you're not," Lila insisted. "Go and get some sleep. You know I'm okay on my own."

"Actually," Morgan said, "I had a wonderful sleep."

Lila turned to her. "Great. We'll entertain each other while my husband talks business with his father and uncle."

Morgan said, "Sounds good."

After a round of hugs from everyone for Lila, the room cleared. Lila faced Morgan. "We should go to the pool."

Glad Nanna had insisted she buy a swimsuit, Morgan said, "I'd love that."

They left Nanna's residence and walked down the stairs and to the building with the two town houses. Lila pointed at it. "This is my stop. How about if we meet in ten minutes?"

"Okay."

Morgan raced back to her condo, put on her new one-piece swimsuit, sunglasses and the big sun hat and met Lila on the cobblestone path.

As they wandered to the huge blue pool surrounded by a sleek blue walkway and chaise lounges with aqua- and sand-colored pillows, Lila said, "I've never met a runaway bride before." She laughed. "Let alone one so famous."

"I'm not famous. My dad is."

"Well, you may not be famous in the way you think you are, but you're sort of the talk of the vineyard."

She winced. "Sorry. I don't mean to be trouble."

Lila took off her cover-up and sat on a chaise. "You're not trouble. Riccardo's mother and Marguerite are just sort of awestruck." She laughed. "No one's seen Riccardo spend this much time with one woman since Cicely."

Lila had the kind of earnest expression that inspired confidences and for two seconds Morgan was tempted to tell her she'd fallen head over heels for Riccardo. Instead, she stuck with the truth. "He thinks of me as a responsibility."

"I know! That's what makes it so funny. Paloma said apparently the only way to get Riccardo to stick with one woman is to put him in charge of her."

Glad she hadn't spilled her guts, Morgan said, "Is he really that bad?"

"He doesn't flaunt his affairs, if that's what you mean. He's discreet and happy."

"So he says."

"It's a shame, though, because before Cicely, he wanted the whole deal. Wife, kids, a summer house at the beach." She thought for a second. "In a way, it's like he's half the person he used to be."

She remembered him with the little boy in the vineyard. "He told me that before Cicely he wanted to be married."

"He did." Lila leaned closer. "In fact, I think that was why he took up with her. He was more in love with the idea of starting his family than with her."

"Was she pretty?"

Lila's face softened. "Only someone interested in Riccardo would ask that question."

"It doesn't matter. He told me he wouldn't get involved with a woman on the rebound—and since I just broke up with my fiancé, I guess I am. But, worse, he's also said he likes his life just as it is. When I mentioned moving to New York City for a fresh start, he didn't even want to help me find a job."

Lila's mouth opened in disbelief. "He likes you."

"As a friend."

Lila shook her head. "No. For him to be so cautious, he must really be getting feelings for you."

"Yeah, well, it soon won't matter. He's offered me the family jet to go home."

Lila caught her hand. "You can't! Riccardo is such a wonderful guy and it's broken my heart to watch him go through everything that happened with Cicely. But the real tragedy is that he intends to live his entire life without what he really wants. If he likes you, he could be getting back to normal."

"No. This is fate, Lila. We met at the absolute wrong time. I have trouble with my dad to straighten out. I just broke an engagement. I'm everything he hates."

Lila laughed. "I doubt that."

"Yeah, well, if he should decide to change his mind, he can find me in New York."

Lila shook her head sharply. "That's where he hides. He'll drown himself in work until he feels okay again, then pick up his old life where he left off. You have to do something now."

Morgan said, "I can't." Because it was true. She might be falling in love with Riccardo, but she wouldn't force him into anything, lead him into anything. That's what her father and Charles had done with her. She refused to lure him into a relationship. He had to come to her of his own volition.

Dinner that night was at Santiago and Marguerite's. Riccardo had worked late so he wasn't surprised there was no answer when he knocked on Morgan's door. She'd probably gone to the main house herself. He walked over to the mansion, his hands in his trouser pockets, the moon a sliver of light in the sky.

When he pressed the buzzer announcing his arrival, a butler opened the door for him. Mitch's parents were old-school and still made good use of the household staff, which added to the formal atmosphere when Riccardo entered their sitting room.

His eyes unerringly found Morgan. He told himself he only looked for her because it was part of his job. But his breath stumbled when he saw her. Her pale green dress somehow made her big blue eyes more dramatic and accented her long yellow hair. She sat on the ottoman with Lila, with Mitch on the sofa behind them. From the easy camaraderie between Morgan and Lila it was clear they'd been introduced and had begun getting to know each other.

He had the sudden, unexpected sense that his duty to her was over. In the same way that her calling Charles had made her feel free, having Mitch home freed him from being solely in charge of their best customer's daughter.

"Good evening, everyone." He took a seat on a club chair across from a long sofa where Nanna, his parents and Marguerite sat. Santiago relaxed on the second club chair. Francine sat on the third.

"You're late," Nanna scolded.

"I was working."

Mitch said, "On what?"

"I've gone through all our customer accounts so you have real numbers on which wines are selling the best. Just in case you have to make some phone calls."

Marguerite groaned. "No work at dinner!"

Riccardo's mom seconded that. "Family time is family time!"

That was when it hit him that his entire family was in the room. With the addition of Julia, then Lila and her mom, the group had swelled in what seemed like the blink of an eye.

Something soft and warm rippled through him. The family that had almost been blown apart when Alonzo stole Julia from Mitch had healed itself in the most magnificent way.

The butler announced dinner and they filed into the dining room. Everyone took seats, leaving him and Morgan beside each other again.

Calmer and more comfortable than he'd been in a long time, he pulled out Morgan's chair for her. He'd ended any possibility of a romance between them and he'd cemented that by being neutral with her while they harvested grapes. He might be pining for what they could have had, but she looked adapted. As if what he'd been saying to her had finally sunk in.

She sat, giving him a smile over her shoulder. "Thank you."

He took the chair beside her. "You're welcome."

With so much family, one big conversation wasn't convenient. The discussion split in half. Nanna, Mitch's parents and Riccardo's parents talked about past harvests.

Alonzo, Julia, Mitch and Lila talked about Greece, one of the places Mitch and Lila had visited on their honeymoon. Morgan easily slid into that discussion and Riccardo soon followed suit.

After dinner was eaten, Alonzo rose and tapped his spoon against his wineglass. "Everyone," he said, calling everyone's attention to him. "I…" He glanced at Julia. "*We* have an announcement."

Julia's face reddened sweetly, endearingly, and Riccardo knew what was coming.

"I'm pregnant!"

Marguerite put her hand on her chest. "I'm going to be a grandmother?"

Santiago pulled in a sharp breath. "Our next generation begins," he said reverently, then he rose, picking up his wineglass for a toast. *"Salude!"*

Riccardo glanced at Morgan. Tears filled her eyes, but they were happy tears. He suddenly, unexpectedly pictured her with her own kids and his breath caught.

He could see her with a little blonde girl and a dark-haired boy.

He shook his head to clear it. He didn't want to think about her that way.

Because it would mean she was happy with another man.

He might be able to let her go, but he wasn't a saint. He did not want to see her future.

CHAPTER ELEVEN

FROM THAT POINT on Riccardo kept himself away from her as much as possible. Imagining her with children was too painful to contemplate. He couldn't handle any more goodbyes at doors, or conversations that only reminded him how perfect she was. Nothing could change the fact that she wasn't even two weeks out of a relationship, that she would go home to a new life, with a new attitude, and want her freedom to enjoy it all.

The night of the ball, he walked out of his condo, dressed in his tux. No one had told him to escort Morgan, but it was simply common sense that he should.

Preparing himself to see her looking wonderful in her gown, he knocked on her door and waited. When there was no answer, he knocked again and waited again. It was too late for her to be in the shower, too late for the noise of a hair dryer to be drowning him out.

She had to have already left for the ball.

Misery invaded his chest. He tried to deny it but he'd been looking forward to escorting her tonight. She'd be leaving the next day. He'd probably never see her again, and he'd missed the chance to walk her over.

After a short ride in the elevator, he stepped out into the warm evening. He looked up the cobblestone path thinking she might only be a little ahead of him.

And she was…on the arm of his cousin Lorenzo.

Fury shuddered through him before he could stop it. He couldn't believe his mother had called her sister to get an escort for Morgan. The insult of it rattled along his bones, ignited his blood.

Entering the mansion through the front door, so he could go through the receiving line, he first greeted Mitch's parents, then Mitch and Lila.

After hugging Mitch and kissing Lila's cheek, he said, "You look radiant."

Always the kidder, Mitch said, "Thank you."

"Even on your best day, you're not radiant," Riccardo said, then he turned to Lila. "This is when we officially say welcome to the family."

"Thanks," Lila said through the soft laugh she'd only found once she and Mitch had become serious. Her face glowed with happiness. So did Mitch's, if Riccardo allowed himself to be honest.

Longing rippled through him. Not for marriage or kids, but for that connection. Since Cicely he'd believed it trite, or maybe something for other men, but getting to know Morgan had awakened all those yearnings again.

He turned to leave the receiving line and saw Morgan laughing with Lorenzo. Stealing his night. But he knew the anger that shuffled through him was wrong.

He walked directly to the bar. "Whiskey."

He named a brand that cost enough to make most people's heads spin. But he didn't care. He'd helped Morgan get through her problems, brought her to Spain, and he wouldn't even get twenty minutes with her tonight before she boarded a plane tomorrow.

"She's over there."

The sound of his grandmother's voice almost made him drop his drink. When he realized Nanna was talking about Morgan, he wanted to pour his very expensive whiskey over her head.

"Why would you be pointing out Morgan to me when the family invited someone else to be her escort?"

Nanna looked confused. "You were just mumbling about someone getting on a plane tomorrow, I assumed you were talking about Morgan."

Damn it! Now his craziness was spilling over into reality.

"She looks pretty in that dress, doesn't she?"

He glanced over and saw the front view of gorgeous Morgan Monroe in a tight yellow gown. Though he'd followed her up the cobblestone walk to the ballroom, he'd only seen the full train in the back. He hadn't realized the dress beneath was formfitting.

"Yellow's her color."

"I like her in blue." He mumbled that, so his grandmother wouldn't hear it. Louder, he said, "I should go say hello to Lorenzo."

Nanna grabbed his arm before he could move. "No. We're getting ready to eat. And you're at the main family table, so you can escort me over."

He said, "Okay," then wondered where Morgan would be sitting. But even as the question popped into his head, he realized that's why his mother had called Lorenzo. Morgan wasn't family—or even extended family, as Lila's mom was—so she wouldn't be sitting at the family table.

Lorenzo had been called upon to entertain her.

The relief that poured through him made him laugh. No one was keeping them apart. No one had seen him falling for Morgan. His thoughts had been nothing but his own imaginings. He'd been foolish to get so worked up.

The dinner sped by amid toasts to Lila and Mitch. When the dancing started, he had every intention of asking Morgan to dance, just to show himself he was fine—making mountains out of molehills because of stupid feelings he shouldn't have. He also wanted a minute to talk to her about her arrangements for the next day, when she went home.

But when he finally found a chance to slide in and ask her, she looked at him with her earnest blue eyes and his heart stumbled in his chest.

No matter how much he told himself he didn't want the feelings he had for her, he had them. He wouldn't do anything about them. She was only two weeks out of a bad relationship. And he didn't want to end up with a broken heart.

Still…

Was it wrong to want to have a few hours with her? Was it wrong to want another kiss? Just one more kiss? He'd paid the price of rescuing her from her dad, flying her to Spain, connecting her to women who could help her move on…

Didn't he deserve this night?

One measly kiss?

He swore to himself that he wouldn't hurt her or let himself get hurt. He wouldn't touch her beyond a kiss, but they deserved a night—one night, one kiss—before she left.

An ache built inside him, not just to touch her, but also for the innocence Cicely had stolen from him. What he wouldn't give to see only Morgan's goodness, the fun they could have together, the life they could create, and not the myriad consequences that could rain down on him when the whole damn thing imploded.

Because it would. She couldn't have real feelings for him. She would go home and soon forget everything that happened between them.

But he wouldn't. He'd remember her forever.

* * *

Morgan had spent the entire night watching Riccardo over Lorenzo's shoulder. She didn't know why he seemed to be spending the majority of his time at the bar, but her heart skipped a beat when she saw him walking toward her and Lorenzo. And suddenly he was there.

He nodded to her. "Morgan."

She said, "Good evening," but told her heart to settle down. If there was one thing she'd learned about the Ochoa family, it was that they were steeped in tradition, polite to a fault. Coming over to say hello, Riccardo was only being courteous. He'd made his feelings about her very clear. And stayed away from her for days to prove he meant it. She would not make a fool of herself.

He shook Lorenzo's hand. "And it's good to see you, too, cousin."

Lorenzo smiled. "My pleasure."

"I wonder if you would mind if I had a few dances with your date."

Her heart did the funny, shivery thing again. She told it to stop. This was nothing but a duty to Riccardo.

Lorenzo all but bowed. "Of course."

"Actually, because we're in side-by-side condos, it makes sense for me to walk her home, too."

Lorenzo said, "That's not necessary."

"No, but it's my pleasure." Riccardo laughed. "I'm releasing you of your duty. Go," he said, motioning around the room at the elegant crowd, which included eligible women. "Enjoy yourself."

Though he didn't look pleased, Lorenzo walked away. Riccardo faced her. "I'd love a dance."

She'd love an explanation. But she wasn't about to ask him for one and embarrass herself. If he wanted to dance with her and walk her home, it wasn't to enjoy her company. It was only out of respect for his family's sense of honor.

She curtsied, the way she'd been taught by her mother when she was very, very young, and the gesture was mannerly. "The pleasure is mine."

The band began playing a waltz and she smiled politely as he took her into his arms. As the smooth material of his tux slid across her hands, her breath stuttered in and fluttered out. Every man in attendance wore a tuxedo, yet not one of them looked as casually elegant, as sex-on-a-spoon gorgeous as Riccardo.

"Are you enjoying the evening?" Damn! She sounded like a hostess at one of her dad's stuffy parties.

His head tilted. "I think the better question is are you enjoying it?"

"Yes." Her voice came out as a nervous squeak and she had to fight not to squeeze her eyes shut in misery. In that second, part of her was glad her dad had sheltered her from this. The other part was still miffed. If she'd had the normal teenage girl experiences with boys, she wouldn't be making a fool of herself right now. "You're an excellent dancer."

"Part of my training."

She smiled. "Mine, too."

As he expertly swirled her around the room, her nervousness seemed to float away.

Just when she thought she would be okay, he caught her gaze. "You look amazing tonight. Do you know you're probably the most beautiful woman I've ever met?"

That made her laugh. "Really? You're going to use lines on me?" But part of her wanted to believe it. He was the most handsome man she'd ever met. He'd totally redefined sexy for her. No, actually, what he'd done was introduce her to sexy. In a world where everybody wore Oxford cloth shirts and chinos he was silk and swagger.

He swung her around. "I would never use a line on you."

"Oh, now, I think you're just lying."

"Okay, say I didn't mind falling back on a line or two every once in a while. In this instance, it's not a line. You are the most beautiful woman I've ever met."

The song ended and they stopped dancing, but their gazes clung. The whole world shifted. Just as he had introduced her to sexy, he was changing something else in her world. Not the way she saw herself, but how she saw relationships. What it was supposed to be like between a man and a woman.

There was a closeness, almost an arc of electricity connecting them. Capturing them. Making her feel linked to him, open to anything he wanted, as the world—a world she never knew existed—came to quivering life.

The music began again. This time it was a slow song. He pulled her close, nestled her against him and her eyes drifted shut as the sensation of being held to him trembled through her.

They danced the rest of the set knitted together or an arm's distance apart. Their arc in place. Their connection never broken.

Too soon, the guests of honor left, along with their parents, then Nanna and Riccardo's parents.

Alonzo gave a good-night toast, then took Julia's hand and escorted her from the ballroom, ending the party.

The crowd dispersed, everyone heading out the front entry to gather wraps or hats. Riccardo faced her. "We can leave through the private entry."

"Yes. Thank you. That would be great."

She stumbled over the words because she had no idea what would happen next. Their doors were side by side, bedrooms a whisper away. It seemed totally wrong to end a night of being held any other way than making love.

So nervous she thought she'd die from it, Morgan held out her arm. "I'm ready."

He gave her a long look. Everything inside her shivered, as she realized the double meaning she might have given him. Still, it was what she wanted.

After a beat, he took her arm and led her to the doors in the back.

But he said nothing.

She sucked in a breath to still her nerves and hopefully strengthen her voice. "I'm guessing this is a shortcut."

"Yes. To the back entrance."

"Okay."

They reached the discreet double doors and he opened them. They walked to the condos under the dark sky. Clouds hid the stars, promising rain in a few hours. He released her arm and opened the condo building door, granting her entry first.

She smiled. "Thank you."

At the elevator, he pressed the button, and the doors opened automatically. She stepped inside. So did he.

They rode in silence and goose bumps appeared on her arms. For as sure as she was that the evening should end in lovemaking, nerves changed her mind. They'd only known each other two weeks. They'd kissed once. She was crazy to think he wanted to sleep with her.

She was never so grateful as when the elevator stopped on the second floor and she could race out. When she reached her door, she turned to say a polite goodbye, but he was right behind her and she almost bumped in to him.

His eyes were as black and intense as the sky had been. "You're running away?"

Her chest tightened.

He took a step closer. "Why?"

The reasoning in her head in the elevator had sounded so good. But here? At her door? Caught in the gaze of his dark, brooding eyes...she couldn't remember a word of it. "I'm not sure."

"I think you're avoiding my question."

"No. It just was a long night and I think I'm confused."

"About?"

She sucked in a breath. "You want me to say it? To admit that I think there's only one way this night should end?"

"No. I want you to tell me that you're attracted to me." His voice cascaded over her like warm honey. He took the final step that separated them. "I want you to tell me that you want me to kiss you."

She did. Oh, good God, she did. But he didn't move. Didn't say anything else. And she realized he really was waiting for her.

"I do."

He leaned closer. "You do what?"

"I want you to kiss me."

CHAPTER TWELVE

THE KISS BYPASSED being warm and sweet and went directly to hot and steamy. Morgan didn't care. Every cell in her body tingled to life as if awakening from a long, unnecessary sleep, and she wanted more. She rolled to her tiptoes, put her hands on each side of his face and indulged.

Their tongues twined. Stuttering breaths mingled. His hands slid down her bare back, hesitating at the bustle-topped train of her gown as if frustrated, then slowly cruising up her naked skin again, raising goose bumps. When he reached the slim straps at the edges of her shoulders, his fingers skimmed beneath the satiny material but stopped. The kiss slowed. The heated encounter reduced to soft brushes. Harsh breaths leveled. Their lips pulled apart as he raised his head.

Morgan opened her eyes to find his squeezed shut. He popped them open with a muttered curse.

"This is wrong."

"Really?" Her slight whisper filled the small lobby, as frustration filled her. All she could think about was touching him. Kissing him. Belonging to him. She couldn't believe he thought this was wrong.

"I shouldn't be forcing you in to this."

Confused, she just looked at him. "Forcing me?"

"Tempting you?" He smiled ruefully. "Right now, when

you're scared and confused I seem like the answer to all your problems. But as soon as you get home, move to New York City, get a new job, you'll put all this behind you."

She listened to every word he said, twisted them around, searching for meaning, and eventually said, "You don't think there's something between us?"

He shrugged. "I know there's something between us, but I also know you're going home tomorrow and we're probably never going to see each other again. It would be so easy to fall into bed together, but then you'd regret it."

"Regret it?" Her heart kicked against her ribs. "I waited my whole life to feel what I felt with you tonight."

He shook his head. "You're going to feel a hundred different things when you get home. And one of them is going to be happiness that you didn't do anything to mess up your life."

"My life already was messed up."

"No, I mean that you didn't make any commitments, any promises." He caught her gaze. "You really will be able to start over when you get home."

She turned that over in her head until she remembered that the real bottom line was that he might have feelings for her but he didn't want them.

Hadn't he said it a million times?

And he was strong enough to fight them.

Because he liked his life simple. No complications.

She stared at him, feeling like an idiot as her heart splintered into a million pieces. Not only had she found her first love; she was getting her first heartbreak.

She stepped back. "You know what? You're right." She smiled at him as her pride swelled, refusing to let her try to convince him he was wrong for fear that she'd beg. Love was new for her. The all-encompassing sensations told her she was in over her head, not experienced enough to handle it and certainly not experienced enough to walk into a situation with someone who didn't feel the same as she did.

The pain of just the thought almost paralyzed her.

She pulled in a breath. "Thank you for a lovely evening."

She heard Riccardo say, "You're welcome," as she turned and walked into her apartment. Her gown shivered and swished as she went directly to the phone. She dialed the number for the household staff and not only ordered a limo, but she also asked if the family jet had been reserved for her. A manager came to the phone and assured her that it was blocked off for her use and if her plans had changed it could be available to her in two hours, the time it would take to get a pilot.

She thanked him and hung up the phone.

Then she let herself cry. For being naive. For being so lonely she'd fallen for the first man who was kind to her. And for being back to being lonely again.

When her tears slowed, she almost began packing. Then she realized she wanted nothing that would remind her of this time. She might have fallen in love but it had been a foolish thing to do, the silly, heartbreaking meanderings of someone who had imploded her life and then set about to pick up the pieces and restore some semblance of normality.

But in her naiveté, she'd fallen for the man who had helped her, and he'd had to tell her what a fool she was.

Riccardo woke the next morning a little after ten, ran his hands down his face and dressed for breakfast with the family. Everyone had been out late the night before so the meal would be more of a brunch. They'd laugh and talk about the ball, mostly gossip, but good-natured gossip. His nanna loved to talk about a party as much as she loved to attend one. Everyone would be there, including Morgan.

He paused at her door before shaking his head and walking to the elevator. She wouldn't want to see him. And he shouldn't want to see her. He couldn't believe he'd been so desperate as to want one real night with her. But he had. And then it had taken the willpower of a saint to pull away from her.

And that kiss?

Walking to the main house, he reminded himself he couldn't think about that kiss. This morning, he had to appear unaffected. Nonchalant. He'd just barely gotten them out of a potentially sticky situation at her door the night before. He didn't want to hurt her now.

But the kiss had been everything. He'd probably remember those few hours at the ball for the rest of his life. He'd probably always wonder what it would have been like if he could have taken the next step.

Sadly, though, he knew there was only one answer to that. She'd realize two or three months—or maybe two years, as Cicely had—into their future that she'd fallen for him out of need, necessity, when she was vulnerable, and she'd break it off.

It was better to part now.

He trudged up the stairway and down the hall, upset with himself, but ready to be cool and distant. He rang the bell and let himself in. Everyone was already in the dining room. He took his seat at the end of the table, and realized that for the first time since he'd brought Morgan to the Ochoa home, he didn't have someone to sit beside.

Mitch was the first to notice him. "Well, look who the cat dragged in."

"Cats didn't have to drag me anywhere," he replied with a laugh. "I danced off my whiskey." He almost added, *Where's Morgan?* His tongue itched to say the words, but his brain reminded him that he wasn't supposed to care. To his family, he was nothing more than her caretaker.

Julia sighed. "Everybody stop talking about drinking. I had to pass up France's best champagne last night."

"Poor baby," Mitch teased.

But Alonzo took her hand and kissed the knuckles. "It will be worth it."

Julia's entire demeanor changed as she gazed into his eyes. "It will."

Riccardo had never seen Mitch look at Julia the way Alonzo did. But more important, he'd never seen Julia look at Mitch the way she looked at Alonzo.

He shook his head to clear it of the thought that had seemed to come out of nowhere, and when he did, his gaze collided with the empty chair beside his.

He couldn't believe she was missing her last meal with the family. He wondered if Morgan was sick—then he remembered she'd turned away rather quickly the night before. Maybe the break he'd thought so simple hadn't been? Maybe she was so upset she didn't want to eat breakfast with his family?

An odd sense tumbled through him, regret so intense he could barely breathe. He never, ever, ever wanted to hurt her.

"So, Riccardo, I'm surprised you're here," Nanna said, then sipped her tea. "The limo's scheduled to take Morgan to the airport in ten minutes. I thought you'd accompany her."

That news cut through him like a knife. She wasn't supposed to leave until two. He'd hoped to catch a glimpse of her. To say goodbye.

Julia teared up. "I am so sorry to see her go."

Lila said, "Me, too. Did she invite you to the girls' weekend in Paris?"

Paloma said, "I think she invited all of us. Mani-pedis and margaritas."

The women laughed.

His father said, "I'll miss her."

Santiago said, "Me, too. I don't think anybody's ever hugged me goodbye quite that hard."

Marguerite said, "Best guest we've ever had."

Everybody laughed, but Riccardo's blood stopped pumping through his veins. Though he kept himself from embarrassing himself, he couldn't stop his brain from jumping to the obvious conclusion.

She left without saying goodbye to him.

She'd said goodbye to everybody but him.

He'd brought her here, talked her through everything in her life, wanted to kiss her so many times he'd ached from it...then she left without saying goodbye?

It hurt. Oddly. Passionately. So deeply his muscles trembled. But he forced himself not to care. He couldn't care. What they had was some sort of temporary thing a woman got for a man who helped her. She did not love him. She had needed him.

Twenty minutes later, he, Mitch, Alonzo and their fathers walked out of Nanna's home, down the circular stairway and toward the conference room.

Riccardo said nothing as his cousins and uncle talked about the third vineyard. Mostly how they would pay for it since Alonzo and Julia would need a house, a big house for the children they planned to have. He wasn't brooding over Morgan not saying goodbye. Technically, they'd said their goodbyes the night before—

But he felt empty. At a loss. He'd guarded her, protected her from her dad, brought her to his family. Enjoyed her company. Shared kisses that had touched his soul—

Didn't he deserve a goodbye?

The answer crept into his conscious. He would have deserved a goodbye if he hadn't hurt her the night before. He hadn't seen it at the time, because he was so grateful he had the strength to pull himself away from her. But looking back, remembering how she'd walked into her condo, he saw it. The droop of her shoulders. The sadness in her eyes.

They reached the conference room door but before his father could open it, the sound of his grandmother calling his name echoed down the corridor.

"Riccardo! Riccardo!"

All five men stopped. When she reached them, she said, "I'd like a moment with Riccardo."

Santiago said, "Of course."

Puzzled, Riccardo stepped out of the way to let his father, uncle and cousins pass. His dad closed the door behind them.

Nanna said, "Go after her."

"What?"

"Go after Morgan. She's only got a short head start. They have to load her bags, run preflight checks. If you take one of Mitch's motorcycles, you can catch her before the plane takes off."

"No. I don't want to catch her." He did. He desperately did. He wanted to tell her he was sorry for hurting her. He wanted to kiss her senseless. Beg her to stay. "I don't know what you think you saw happening between us, but I kept her from being another Cicely. I rescued Morgan and she was grateful. But neither of us did anything we'd regret. And when she gets home and is settled in New York City, she'll thank me. She'll realize what she thought was happening between us was only appreciation."

Nanna's brow winkled. "Is that what you think?"

"It's what I know. I went through this with Cicely, remember?"

"I remember Cicely, but I also remember that she loved her ex. Always loved her ex."

Riccardo just looked at her.

"Morgan didn't love Charles. At best, she thought of

him as a friend. Are you saying you're letting her go because of Charles?"

"No. I'm letting her go because she's only two weeks out of her relationship."

"No, she's two weeks out of a prison her dad created for her."

He ran his hand across the back of his neck, remembering that she'd barely spoken about Charles. That her concern had always been for her dad. Not losing her dad. She might have wanted to see Charles, but it had been to give back the ring. To set things straight.

Still…

"It doesn't matter. An engagement is an engagement and she just ended hers."

His grandmother heaved a long-suffering sigh. "So you're willing to let her go back to her fiancé?"

"She's not going back to her fiancé."

"You think not?" Nanna's eyes narrowed. "You hurt her. Only a complete moron would have missed it when we said goodbye this morning. She talked about seeing Charles, about how nice it would be to talk to him." Nanna shook her finger at him. "You thought you were a rebound for her? Charles is going to be the real rebound man. She'll go home to Charles, who will comfort her, and that will be how they will get back together."

He thought about everything she'd gone through. How her freedom had been so hard-won. "She wouldn't— I mean she might revert to some of her old behaviors with her dad. But she's a new person. She wouldn't want her old fiancé back."

"Maybe."

There were too many options in that one little word. The possibilities spun through his brain.

"Think it through. The fiancé she left will be the one

to help her pick up the pieces from the broken heart *you* gave her."

Riccardo shook his head. "That's all wrong. Backward. She needed help getting away from him. I gave it to her. I can't be the reason she ends up with him."

"Then go after her."

"I can't!"

"Oh, Riccardo." Nanna's eyes softened. "If you don't, you will not get another chance. You will lose another love."

When he said nothing, not wanting anyone to realize how quickly he'd fallen for her, she caught his forearm. "I saw how you looked at her."

He thought of Alonzo and Julia and wondered if that's how he'd looked at Morgan. With his heart in his eyes.

"I saw how she looked at you. Like a woman who's found the one man she wants to spend the rest of her life with."

Just the thought that she might really love him opened his heart. Air began filling his lungs again.

"If you've never trusted me about anything else. Trust me on this, *Nene*."

"I do trust you."

He finally saw what she saw. They might not have known each other long, but she'd been a blank slate when he met her. Not a woman pining for a man who had left her, but a woman who had no idea what love was.

He'd realized he was falling for her the night before he shuffled her off to Spain. If this empty ache in his chest was any indication, the falling was over and he was in love.

And he'd let her go.

Morgan's car sat in the lot of the municipal airport right where she'd left it. She jumped in and began the short drive to her father's vineyard.

She was strong now. Wise and strong. There was no point in going to Paris, waiting the two days before her dad's trip to Stockholm. Her dad would be at the house when she got there.

She didn't care. She was in the throes of her first heartbreak. She'd stupidly fallen in love in two weeks. With a man who didn't want to be in love. Another woman would turn to her father for comfort. She girded herself to prepare for his wrath.

Though part of her thought her dad was the one who might need to prepare himself for her. She wasn't the sheep who'd run from her wedding. She would speak her mind.

She pulled the car in front of the house, got out and headed for the main door. She stopped and took a breath. Then she twisted the knob, gave a push and called, "I'm home."

Her father started down the quietly elegant wooden stairway, Charles behind him. "We know. We saw someone open the gate and alerted security. You're lucky you weren't arrested."

He reached the bottom of the stairs. She longed to throw herself into his arms, to tell him her heart had been broken, to get the comfort only a father could give.

She straightened her shoulders. "It's nice to see you, too, Dad."

"You're not getting snippy with me, are you?"

"No, but I'm also not going to play sheep anymore."

His face contorted in confusion. "Sheep?"

"You and I will talk in a minute." She looked past him, smiled warmly. "Charles."

He reached out and hugged her, a soft, sweet hug that spoke of their friendship. She almost broke down. But they had things to talk about. She called upon the well of reserves she had way deep down inside her to keep her composure.

"Let's go into the den."

Charles said, "Sure."

They headed to her dad's den and the Colonel exploded. "What is going on here!"

"I'm going to talk to Charles, to apologize in person. Then I'm going to talk to you."

"No! No! No!" her dad sputtered. "I've spent two weeks apologizing for you! I'll have my time now!"

"I never asked you to apologize for me. But more than that, even you should respect Charles's right to get a better explanation than the brief apology I gave him over the phone."

She turned and walked with Charles into the den.

Riccardo counted the minutes it took to get from the small Lake Justice municipal airport to Monroe Vineyards. He'd gotten to his family's private airstrip a few minutes too late and cursed Morgan's ability to get away. He'd made a few calls and finally got a jet from a family friend and told the pilot to punch it, yet he'd still arrived in the United States an hour after Morgan.

When he got to the gate for Monroe Vineyards, he scanned his brain for the code to get inside, hoping they hadn't changed it since the night after Morgan's wedding, when he'd met with the Colonel to talk about him going after her. He punched in two sets of numbers before he got it right and suspected the wrong attempts had probably set off an alarm, but he didn't care. He raced to the house, jumped out of his rental vehicle and ran to the front door.

When he stepped into the quiet, formal foyer, he met Colonel Monroe. "You're the second person today to get inside my compound without my authorization."

"You should change more than one number when you reset your gate lock."

"There are twenty-four digits in that code. How did you know that I only changed one number? Better yet, how did you know what number changed?"

He hadn't. He'd guessed. Still, he pointed at his temple. "Mind like a steel trap." He looked around frantically. "Where's Morgan?"

"Talking to Charles in the den. Seriously, they've been in there an hour. I tried to get in twice—she threatened to disown me. What the hell did you do to her, son?"

"They've been in there an hour?"

"Yes! I think—"

"Don't think!" he said, suddenly understanding Morgan's frustration that day she'd told him not to think. "Which way is the den?"

"Down that hall and to the right, but—"

Riccardo didn't hear the rest of what the Colonel said. He ran down the hall and whipped open the door. "Don't get back together with him! You belong to me!"

It took a second for his surroundings to sink in, to see the brown leather sofa, huge mahogany desk, cold fireplace and two shell-shocked people.

"Riccardo?"

The man Riccardo assumed was Charles turned to Morgan. "This is Riccardo?"

"Yes."

He shook his head with a laugh as he rose. He leaned down and kissed Morgan's cheek. "We'll talk again."

Riccardo's blood all but boiled. "No. You won't."

Charles laughed and left the room.

Morgan rose from the brown leather chair. "I belong to no one." She said the words quietly, succinctly, but inside her heart thundered. She didn't consider belonging to him as being a possession, but more of a commitment. But he'd hurt her, confused her so many times, he had some explaining to do.

He caught her hands, brought them to his cheeks. "I'm sorry."

"Sorry?" Fear raced through her. That didn't sound like the declaration of a man who wanted her to belong to him.

He let go of her hands and ran his fingers through his hair. "I'm saying this all wrong." He squeezed his eyes shut. "When you were gone this morning, I wouldn't admit it, even to myself, but I hit rock-bottom. Worse than when Cicely left me. I loved you in a way I'd never loved anyone. We had little more than a handful of days, and half of them I tried to stay away from you, yet I loved you."

Her heart pounded in her chest. Her throat closed. The urge to tell him she loved him, too, bubbled up then bubbled over, but she fought to keep her mouth closed. She might be new at running her own life, but she knew what she wanted. Truth. Honesty. Reality. She wouldn't misinterpret him again.

"What happened to the worry that our relationship was just some sort of rebound thing?"

"My nanna reminded me of a few things. Mostly that you hadn't loved Charles. You'd left a trap not a relationship. Your feelings and Cicely's would have been totally different."

"Thanks… I think."

He shook his head. "Don't you get it? What happened between us was real."

Tears of happiness filled her eyes. "It certainly feels that way to me."

"When Julia said she was pregnant I could see you with a child, *our* child." He took a step closer. "That's why I was so afraid to be around you."

She smiled. "That's very romantic."

"Then there were the times I almost kissed you."

Her smile grew. "Those were nice." She raised her eyes to meet his. "But the actual kissing was better."

He laughed. "Infinitely better."

It was all so terrifyingly wonderful that Morgan needed the words. The real words. Spoken clearly. On their own. Not as part of an explanation.

"And you love me?"

"Yes. I love you."

A laugh spilled out. Relief and joy collided and danced. "I love you, too."

"And you're sure?"

She laid her hands on his chest, reveling in the fact that all this was real. He was hers. They were going to start a new life. A rich, wonderful life of family and honesty. There would be no more pretending to be somebody she wasn't.

"Riccardo, I've had twenty-five years of being who everybody else thought I should be. You're the first person who was worth fighting to be myself for."

He laughed, then put both hands on her cheeks and kissed her, his mouth both clever and desperate. As it sunk in for both of them that this was real, the kiss slowed. Desperation became tenderness.

When they finally broke apart, he said, "I think we should get married."

"I think we should date. I don't mistrust what I feel, but I'd actually like to have the experience of dating."

He thought about that. "You are moving to New York City?"

"Yes. But I'm thinking of getting my own apartment."

He caught her around the waist and tugged her to him. "Not a chance."

Then he kissed her again until her blood warmed and any worry she had about him disappeared. And she knew they were going to have a wonderful life, just as surely as she knew her dad would have one of his fits when he heard the news.

But they could handle him.

They could handle anything.

EPILOGUE

RICCARDO AND MORGAN married almost exactly a year later. The day of her wedding, she didn't have a mom to help her dress, but she had a nanna, three moms—Paloma, Marguerite and Francine—and Lila and Julia.

"I wanted her hair up." Julia pouted as she hoisted her three-month-old son on her hip.

"You hush," Paloma said. "Riccardo likes her hair down."

Julia gasped, horrified. "Morgan, please tell me you are not going to be one of those wives who does everything her husband says."

Morgan laughed. "Riccardo should be so lucky."

She turned from the mirror. She'd chosen a simple formfitting satin gown to let her lace veil be the showstopper. Flowing from the tiara at the top of her head to ten feet behind her and accented with pearls and sequins, the veil was the epitome of elegance.

Lila clapped. "You look perfect."

Francine walked over and hugged her. "So beautiful."

Paloma, Marguerite and Nanna wiped tears from their eyes. "Such a special day."

The knock at the door had the women scrambling for tissues. "Just a minute."

When Paloma gave the all-clear, Nanna opened the door.

The Colonel began to enter, but seeing his daughter, he stopped. "Oh, my goodness."

Morgan saw the tears in his eyes and she walked over and hugged him. "It's okay."

"No. It's not." He choked back tears. "You look so much like your mother."

She gave Julia a nod and the new mom quietly hustled everyone out of the room.

"You don't often talk about mom."

He pressed his lips together before he drew a long breath. "It's very difficult to lose the love of your life."

"I know. I'd only lost Riccardo for a couple of hours and I thought my life was over. I can't imagine how you felt."

He walked toward a window that looked out over the garden, where the wedding would be held. "This entire past year, I've been wanting to tell you how proud I am of you."

She laughed. "Really? I thought I'd made the past year difficult."

He pivoted from the window. "No." He winced. "Well, at first, but as everything began to sink in, I realized I hadn't been a very good mom."

Morgan walked over and took his hand. "You've always done the best you could with what you had."

He conceded that with a nod. "I've tried." He caught her gaze. "My mistakes, though, could have really hurt you."

"Nah," she said, batting away his concern. "I think Mom was always looking down on us, making sure you didn't go too far."

He laughed through his tears, then pulled a hanky from the pocket of his perfect black tux.

After wiping his eyes, he took her arm and tucked it in his. "Ready to go marry that Spaniard of yours?"

"Yes." The word came out with glee. She was so full

of awe that everything had worked out the way it had that her chest hurt.

He patted her hand. "And you know, of course, I'm expecting grandchildren." He laughed. "Not that I'm telling you what to do."

"Oh, you'll get your grandkids," she assured him. "The Ochoas are all about family."

* * * * *

NO ORDINARY
FORTUNE

JUDY DUARTE

To my personal hero, who always has my back, even when I'm spinning around like an ice-skater going for the gold. Sal, I love and appreciate you more than you will ever know.

Chapter One

Schuyler Fortunado had always been a family rebel, and she felt more like one today, as she drove her sporty red BMW down the highway, the back seat loaded down as if she planned to live out of her car for the next several weeks.

Granted, she hadn't actually packed the dry cleaning that hung from the rear passenger window or the bag of groceries she'd left on the back seat. She'd planned to drop them off at her condo back in Houston before starting out on her latest adventure earlier today. But she'd been so intent upon solving a family mystery that she'd hit the freeway and hadn't looked back until she'd stopped in the Texas community of Columbus for gas. The clothing would stay in the back seat, but she'd tossed out the almond milk and smoked Gouda that would go bad without refrigeration. Then, armed with a Venti coffee, she'd taken off again.

She glanced at the clock on the dash. It was late afternoon, and the traffic had slowed to an annoying rate. When her cell phone rang, she again looked at the dash, where her father's name was displayed on the screen. Kenneth Fortunado didn't take time out of his busy day for small talk, so she assumed he'd gotten wind of her latest escapade and wanted to voice his disapproval.

She was tempted to turn up the volume on the radio and let the call roll over to voice mail, but she answered instead. "Hey, Dad. What's up?"

"I didn't call to chat, Schuyler. What in the hell are you up to this time?"

"Not much. Just taking a little road trip and listening to some oldies."

He paused for several beats, no doubt reminded that she favored the same music her grandmother used to listen to, along with everything else they'd had in common.

"Where *are* you?" he asked, and not very nicely.

"I'm on a Fortune hunt."

"Oh, for Pete's sake. I told you to let that go."

"Yes, I know. But I can't ignore the fact that our family is related to the Fortunes."

"That's not a *fact*, Schuyler. You have no idea who my biological father was, and quite frankly, I could not care less."

He'd already made that clear, but Schuyler was determined to uncover the truth. And, contrary to what her father might think, she was nearly 99 percent certain that his mother's married lover had been Julius Fortune. It had been an easy conclusion to reach. The dear, eccentric woman Schuyler had called Glammy, thanks to a childhood speech impediment, had all but spelled it out during the many chats they'd had before her death.

"Daddy," Schuyler said, "I can't believe you're not the least bit interested in meeting your birth father. Or at least getting to know some of your biological relatives."

"Forget killing the damned cat, your curiosity is going to be the death of *me*—and before I get a chance to retire and enjoy life. Can't you focus on something else? Like going back to that art school or taking another acting class? You could even write that style and fashion blog you told me about."

"It's a vlog, Daddy. Besides, I can hardly concentrate on any of that when I'm so close to solving the family mystery once and for all. And don't blame this on mere curiosity. This isn't a personal quest. I'm doing it as a tribute to Glammy."

He blew out a ragged sigh that mimicked a grumble. "I suppose it shouldn't be surprising that one of my six children would turn out to be so much like my mother."

He said that as if it was a bad thing, although Schuyler wouldn't take offense. Glammy had been a little too flamboyant and over the top for the successful, straitlaced real estate mogul, but Kenneth had loved his mom. "I'll take that as a compliment, Daddy."

Out came yet another sigh over the line, this one softer and more controlled than the last. "I didn't mean that badly, Schuyler. It's just that I'm not a free spirit like my mother was. Or like you are. So I can't relate."

Both Glammy and Schuyler had embarrassed the poor man on several occasions, although never intentionally. But life wasn't meant to be boring. Nor were people supposed to be left in the dark about their past. "I'd think you'd be interested in meeting your blood kin."

"Even if your assumptions are correct, and I'm not saying they are, you do realize there was a confidentiality agreement in effect."

"I didn't sign anything."

"Dammit, Schuyler. Your grandmother did, and that's good enough for me. You need to let sleeping dogs lie—or you just might end up getting bit in the butt when you least expect it."

"Aha," she said triumphantly. "Sounds like an admission to me."

"I'm not going to admit or confirm squat."

"Maybe not, but I'd bet my trust fund that your father was Julius Fortune."

"Speaking of that trust fund, you're welcome to get a real job and join us at Fortunado Real Estate."

Schuyler could almost see him wince while making that offer, although she knew it was sincere and that he'd do whatever it took to make room for her in the family business. But they both knew that she'd never be a good fit, so she would make it easy on him, as well as herself. "I'm really not into office or corporate jobs, so that would never work."

Her father didn't immediately respond, which was just as well. They'd gone round and round on just what it was that Schuyler might actually be "into." As a result, he'd created a healthy trust account for her, just as he'd done for Glammy. He'd also threatened to cut Schuyler off on occasion, like the time she'd told him she wanted to move to Italy. He'd assumed she'd wanted to find herself, but it was more than that. She'd gravitated toward her college roommate's parents, who'd owned a villa there.

There was good reason for that. Calista's family not only welcomed her as a guest in their home, they accepted her and appreciated her uniqueness.

Schuyler wished she could say the same for her own parents. It grated on her to be the only Fortunado who was never taken seriously—and just because she danced to the beat of a different satellite radio network.

She might pretend as if it didn't bother her, but at times, disappointment rose up and smacked her in the face, taunting her with the fact that she wasn't like the others in her family. Yet how could she even try to compete with any of them? One of her brothers was a doctor, for goodness' sake. And her older sister was so determined to move up the company ladder that she'd become a workaholic.

None of that mattered, though. Schuyler wanted more out of life than that. Only trouble was, she wasn't quite sure just what "more" was. But she'd figure it out one of these days. It was just a matter of time.

A heavy silence strained the line. Finally, Daddy said, "Please don't embarrass me or the family."

Schuyler rolled her eyes. It seemed that her family shouldn't be so quick to be embarrassed. "Believe it or not, I've never set out to do that on purpose. And I'll be extra careful this time."

"I know, Schuyler. But…"

Again with the silence. Then his intercom beeped in the background.

"Listen, honey. I've been waiting for this call, so I have to go." As usual, Schuyler was saved by the corporate world in which her brilliant, business-minded father had made millions, all without the help of the Fortune family coffers he might have tapped into— had he been born on the right side of the blanket. "Just remember what I said."

"Got it, Dad. Don't embarrass myself or the family."

The call ended without a goodbye.

Schuyler turned up the volume on the radio dial, just in time to catch the beginning of the Beatles song "Can't Buy Me Love." She belted out the lyrics she knew by heart and continued her drive, wishing there was some way she could convince her well-meaning father that he didn't need to use money to keep her in step—or to buy her affection. He already had it free and clear.

She didn't particularly like being so different from everyone else in the family. Deep inside she feared that she'd never live up to their expectations, so as a teenager, she learned to embrace her inner maverick.

And that's what she was doing now. As she peered out the bug-splattered windshield, she hoped she didn't hit any more traffic in Austin. If she continued at this pace, she'd reach the Mendoza Winery offices before they closed.

If truth be told, she was nearly as eager to meet the

Mendozas as she was the Fortunes. There'd been quite a few marriages between the two clans. And from what she'd learned, Alejandro Mendoza, the owner of the winery, had a lot of handsome, single cousins. If Schuyler played her cards right, she'd be able to charm one of them into providing her with the info and the intros she needed.

Besides, it wasn't a total fact-finding mission. She'd heard their business was expanding, and she'd like to get a closer look at the inner workings of their company. At least, that's the excuse she'd give them for showing up today.

That wasn't too big of a stretch. If what she'd heard was true, their stock was going to soar in value. So she might be interested in making a personal investment.

The Houston society papers had pegged her as a ditzy trust fund baby, no matter how many charities she spearheaded. But they were wrong. And she had an impressive financial portfolio to prove it.

Either way, she hadn't set herself up for a difficult role. She was a people person, and she'd also taken several improv classes at the local junior college. So how hard could it be to win over the Mendozas and then move on to the Fortunes?

Despite the cool afternoon breeze, Carlo Mendoza had worked up a pretty good sweat as he unloaded the company truck and lugged cases of wine into the family's distribution center at Austin Commons.

Six months ago, his cousin Alejandro had asked him if he'd be willing to relocate to Austin, become the Mendoza Winery vice president and take charge of refurbishing the small, on-site restaurant.

Most of Carlo's friends had expected him to decline the offer and stay put. At thirty-five, he'd made a name for himself in Miami, working in the food-and-beverage industry. He'd managed several floundering restaurants and, in a short period, had turned them all around. He'd done the same thing with a run-down nightclub, which was now one of the most popular beachfront nightspots in Florida. But he'd jumped at the chance to become a part of the growing family organization in Texas.

Within hours of entering city limits, he'd gone right to work, planning the expansion and remodel of the eatery, overseeing the demolition and reconstruction, creating the perfect ambience and then hiring a talented chef who came up with an impressive menu.

Carlo usually preferred to stick close to the winery, as well as La Viña, the name they'd chosen for the new restaurant. But Alejandro was in the process of expanding the family business by opening a retail shop in Austin Commons. Plans were also under way for a new wine bar and a nightclub, both of which would be located on a popular downtown street. So that meant they all had to pull together.

Carlo had no more than stacked another case of wine on the cart he would wheel inside when Esteban, his father, stepped out of the distribution center. "Is that the last of it?"

"Not quite. I still need to unload the chardonnay."

After that, he would head for The Gardens at the nearby Monarch Hotel, where he'd scheduled an important tasting this evening for a group of chefs and restaurant owners attending a big culinary conference. This was the Mendoza Winery's chance to get its best vintages in the right hands, and Carlo had gone all out when setting it up. There'd be tiny white lights adorning the trees, exotic flowers on linen-draped tables and an impressive variety of gourmet cheese, crackers and hors d'oeuvres.

When Carlo had first come up with the idea of hosting carefully planned tastings, his cousin had given his hearty approval and said, "That's your baby. Run with it."

So Carlo had done just that. And up until an hour ago, things had gone exceptionally well. Then the model they'd hired to pour wine for the tasting called and said she was sick. As soon as the line disconnected, he'd immediately contacted the agency and asked them to send over a replacement. There was a lot riding on tonight's event. If things went as planned, it would launch the winery into the big leagues.

Carlo could, of course, serve the wine himself, but he'd rather be free to schmooze with attendees and lock down the sales he expected.

He glanced at his wristwatch, a TAG Heuer Carrera he'd purchased last summer, and swore under his breath. It was getting late, and the agency had yet to call back or to send another hostess. They'd told him they'd try their best to find someone. Hopefully, they wouldn't let him down.

When a car engine sounded, he glanced over his shoulder to see a red late-model BMW approaching. After parking in front of the office, next to the truck Carlo was unloading, the driver, a petite blonde, climbed out, shut the door and locked the car. When she spotted him watching her, she flashed a pretty smile.

The sight of her face alone was enough to set a bachelor's blood on fire. Add that to a pair of black skinny jeans that hugged her feminine curves and a colorful, gypsy-style top that suggested she had a playful side, and it took all Carlo's restraint not to let out a tacky wolf whistle.

She gave a little wave, as if they'd met before, then closed the distance between them with the grace and assurance of a woman who knew she had the power to knock a man off his feet. She also bore a remarkable resemblance to singer Carrie Underwood, which was merely an observation on Carlo's part. He didn't give a damn if she could carry a tune in a bucket. As long as she could pour wine, she'd work out just fine.

He'd run in the upper circles of Miami society long enough to recognize the black Chanel purse and the snazzy red Beamer, both of which announced that she lived the good life. Or that she hoped to one of these days and was trying her best to fake it until she did. He supposed that also meant she wouldn't come cheap, but at this point, he didn't care. He was desperate.

"Thank God you're here," he said. "I'm Carlo Mendoza, the one who placed the call to the temp agency. You're just in time. Let me show you what we need you to do."

She pulled up short, her expression sobered and her brow creased ever so slightly. Then her pretty smile returned and she reached out to shake his hand. "Schuyler Fortunado, at your service."

Not much took Schuyler by surprise, but when the handsome Latin hottie set aside the box he'd been carrying and swept toward her, she didn't much care what project he had in mind for her to do. She was up to the task, especially since he bore the correct last name—*Mendoza*.

He also had the perfect looks. He was tall, with dark hair that curled at the collar and expressive brown eyes. A killer smile revealed white teeth against a tanned complexion. He was definitely what she'd call eye candy. If she were a casting director, she'd sign him in a New York minute to star as the romantic lead in a major production.

She had only one question. How did he fit into the family hierarchy?

Black slacks and a white button-down shirt—crisply pressed, rolled up at the sleeves and open at the collar—announced that he was in upper management. Yet a light sheen of sweat from his labor suggested he wasn't afraid of hard work.

He reached out to shake her hand. The moment his fingers touched hers, an electrical current shimmied up her arm, giving her heart a jolt that made her pulse go wacky. She wasn't sure if he'd felt it, but she was having one heck of a time keeping her mind on the reason she was here and on the cover story she'd concocted.

"I'm glad the temp agency was able to get ahold of

you," he said. "And that you were available to help out this evening. You're a lifesaver."

Okay, so he clearly thought she was someone else. Did she dare correct him? Or should she let the mix-up play out?

"Have you ever poured wine at a tasting before?" he asked.

"No, I haven't." How hard could it be? "But don't worry about my lack of experience. I'm a fast learner."

"Consider this more of a cocktail party, only the drink options are various vintages from the Mendoza Winery. We have a lot of important and influential people attending, and your job will be to make our wines look good."

Schuyler was no stranger to parties or the nightlife. Why not play along and assume the temporary gig? It would be a fun way to get her foot in the door with the Mendozas.

"This particular tasting will be held at the Monarch Hotel," Carlo added. "It rained for the last several days, but the weather is on our side today, so we're going to have it outdoors in the garden."

"Sounds like a perfect venue." Schuyler wasn't the least bit familiar with Austin, so she didn't have a clue where that might be or what to expect from the outdoor setting, but she pasted on a big no-worries, I've-got-this smile.

He scanned the length of her from the top of her head to her strappy black heels and back again. "You look great, but I'll have to get you something else to wear."

"What'd you have in mind?" She slapped her hands

on her hips, shifted slightly to the right and taunted him with a playful grin. "A French maid's costume?"

His brow furrowed, which only lent a serious but more gorgeous air about him. "No, I meant something classy. There's a women's clothing shop just down the street. I'm sure they're still open, so we can stop there."

A smile tugged at her lips. Who would have guessed that it might come in handy to have those clothes from the dry cleaners still hanging in the back seat of her car?

"Actually," she said, "you're in luck. I happen to have an outfit with me. That is, if a black cocktail dress will work."

"That's great. Now just one last question. Do you have any experience with wine?"

"Other than drinking my share of it?" She laughed.

When he frowned, clearly not finding any humor in her response, she added, "I'm no connoisseur, but I'm not a novice, either. I know the difference between a cabernet sauvignon and a merlot. And while I don't have a wine cellar, I do keep several nice bottles at home. Also, my old college roommate's family owns an Italian villa that's surrounded by vineyards, and I spent a couple of summers there."

Finally, his expression softened, and he smiled. "You're going to work out perfectly."

Schuyler thought so, too. That is, as long as the temp agency didn't get in the way by sending someone else and blowing her chance to prove herself as the lifesaver he'd claimed she was.

Feeling a bit heroic, she strode to her BMW with a spring in her step. After unlocking the passenger door, she reached for the cocktail dress protected in plastic and hanging from the hook above the rear passenger window. She'd no more than clicked the lock button on the remote when she heard someone clear his throat.

She turned to see who it was, only to spot a silver fox and four dark-haired men, all handsome as heck and standing in an office doorway. She assumed they were related to Carlo, since they all clearly bore a family resemblance.

The older man standing front and center grinned and asked, "Aren't you going to introduce us to the lady, *mijo*?"

"Sorry," Carlo said. "Dad, this is Schuyler Fortunado, the model the temp agency sent as a replacement. She's going to be our hostess this evening."

The dashing older man offered a flirtatious grin. "I'm Esteban Mendoza, Ms. Fortunado, the father of this tribe." Then he introduced the younger men as Mark, Rodrigo, Chaz and Stefan.

Each of the Mendoza brothers was attractive in his own right. That is, if you liked the tall, dark and handsome type. Even Esteban had a debonair, heart-strumming appeal.

The DNA gods had been good to this family, and Schuyler was in her glory. Just look at the collection of hunks she'd stumbled upon. If she had to choose, she'd say that Carlo was the pick of the bunch. Either way, she'd never met a male—young or old—she couldn't charm. She was definitely going to enjoy her investigative work.

"Now that you've met my family," Carlo said, "let's

check out the setting for tonight's event. It's a short walk to the Monarch Hotel, where we've set up the tasting. Come with me."

That wasn't going to be a problem. Schuyler would gladly follow the Latin hottie anywhere.

Chapter Two

Just twenty minutes ago, the sun had disappeared into a kaleidoscope of color on the western horizon. All the while, Carlo stood next to a magnolia tree adorned with white lights and watched this evening's tasting unfold the way he'd planned it.

Several waiters, supplied by the hotel, carried trays of appetizers and moved about the garden, offering the smiling chefs and restaurant owners a variety of crackers, gourmet cheeses and hors d'oeuvres specially prepared to enhance the taste of the vintages being served. But it was the lovely blonde hostess pouring wine and entertaining the culinary experts with both her charm and wit who'd captured Carlo's full attention.

He must have caught hers, too, because every now and again, Schuyler looked across the garden, her blue eyes sparkling, and offered him a confident smile. Then she returned to her work.

She was a born hostess, it seemed, and he thanked his lucky stars the other woman had had to cancel tonight.

Just look at her. She rocked that curve-hugging dress she'd had hanging in her car. It was sexy, but not overly revealing. Classy, but still within the right man's reach.

But it was more than her outfit and pretty face that he found appealing. She had a natural effervescence, a confident demeanor, as well as an uptown style. And as a result, she'd done a good job of convincing the attendees that they should stock up on the best wines they'd ever tasted.

Schuyler flashed the label of a bottle of Mendoza zinfandel at the people gathered at her table, then poured them each a generous taste. Soft jazz played in the background, but it didn't drown out the sound of approaching footsteps.

Carlo glanced over his shoulder and spotted his father moving toward him.

"Looks like another successful tasting," the older man said.

"You're right. We've had several significant orders already. And once this group goes back to their fine-dining establishments, word about our wines will spread."

"And what about Schuyler? How's our temporary hostess working out?"

"A lot better than the last woman the temp agency sent us." She was prettier, too, which was why Carlo had been studying her with more than just business on his mind. He liked a woman with a playful side, especially since that usually meant she wouldn't expect a long-term commitment.

Carlo had already experienced a failed marriage and wasn't about to make that mistake again. He was too much like his father, he supposed.

"I'm proud of you, *mijo*. You put a lot of work into this evening, and it shows."

"Thanks." Carlo had never lacked confidence, at least not in the business world. Still, his father's praise meant a lot. "I've always gone above and beyond to pull off a successful event, but it's even sweeter when that success benefits the family."

"Sounds like you're settling in here."

Carlo stole a quick glance at his father, but he didn't see a need to respond.

"Are you happy you came to Austin?" Esteban asked.

"So far, so good. Why?"

"Don't get me wrong, *mijo*. But you have to admit, in the past, you sometimes got bored with a job after a while and moved on to what you'd called bigger and better things."

Carlo would like to object, to tell his father that he'd always had good reason to make a job change from one restaurant or nightclub to another, but some of what he said was true. Sometimes boredom had played a role. "Don't worry, Dad. That's not going to happen this time."

"I'm glad to hear that."

The two men continued to watch the tasting, as well as the pretty blonde hostess.

"You had a lot of friends in Miami," his father said. "And a busy social life. I worried that you'd miss all of that."

"Not really, although I'll admit it's been a bit of an adjustment." It had been six months since Carlo had turned over the keys to his ocean-view apartment and drove to Austin. Yet his enthusiasm for both La Viña and Mendoza Winery was stronger than ever. "I'm still in contact with some of my friends and making new ones. Besides, this position is a good fit, especially since I'm working with family."

"It's been a good change for me, too. So was reuniting with my brother. That took a huge weight from my heart."

"I know." Carlo, as well as his brothers, had noticed the positive changes in their father ever since he and Orlando had buried the hatchet. After a decades-old riff, everyone had been shocked to learn that Esteban had actually fathered Orlando's son, Joaquin Mendoza. The man Carlo thought was his cousin was actually his half brother. Recently, Orlando and Esteban had forgiven one another for the past, and Esteban was now getting to know Joaquin as his son.

"You're watching Schuyler with a keen eye," his father said. "Are you waiting to see if our temporary hostess makes a mistake? Or are you planning to follow up this tasting with a romantic evening?"

"She's not going to screw up. Look at her. She's in her element."

Esteban chuckled and slapped a hand on Carlo's shoulder. "Apparently, she's caught your eye, *mijo*. And something tells me you don't plan to thank her for a job well done and then send her on her way."

"Let's see how the rest of the night unfolds." Carlo glanced at his watch. Things would be winding down soon. The chefs and restaurant owners would be heading to dinner, and that left him and Schuyler to debrief following the tasting.

He knew better than to mention that plan. Of all Esteban's sons, Carlo was the most like their father, a dynamic, charismatic guy who had an eye for pretty women—and a bit of trouble with commitment. Yet none of that seemed to matter. Neither of them had ever had a shortage of dates.

"Schuyler keeps glancing this way," his father said. "So I'd venture to say that she's got her eye on you, too."

It seemed that way. And she wasn't looking at him like an insecure employee hoping to get her boss's reassurance. No, Carlo could spot sexual interest in her eyes.

In a few minutes, he'd ask her to celebrate the successful tasting by joining him at dinner. And something about that playful gleam in her pretty blue eyes told him she wouldn't turn him down.

Schuyler was having the time of her life. The garden setting was perfect, the evening festive. She'd never sold wine before, but she knew how to talk to people. And she'd soon found those in attendance, all men and women in the culinary industry, to be worldly and interesting. By the end of the tasting, she'd snagged several large-scale orders for the winery, and she'd had a fabulous time in the process.

As the chefs and restaurant owners filed out of the garden and the hotel cleanup crew moved in, Carlo made his way to the linen-draped table where she'd been stationed for the past hour or so.

"You were amazing," he said. "I couldn't have asked for a better hostess."

"Thanks for the vote of confidence. I never realized that work could be as fun as a cocktail party."

"I suspect you've attended your share of those."

She answered with a flirtatious grin, which he lobbed right back at her. From what she'd seen so far, all of the Mendoza brothers were gorgeous, but she had to admit that Carlo was by far the most attractive—and appealing. She couldn't pinpoint one single reason for making that conclusion. Actually, there were several—his drop-dead good looks, the playful intensity in his gaze, his confident air. On top of that, she also respected the way he'd orchestrated tonight's event then stood back and watched it all unfold the way he'd planned.

There was clearly more to him than met the eye. There was something under the surface that also sparked her interest, a sexy yet teasing style that gave her reason to believe he might be as interested in having fun as she was.

Some people shouldn't expect a romance to last forever, Glammy had said, *and I'm one of them. Why compromise my dreams and values just to be accepted? Doing that will only lead to failure, disappointment or heartbreak.*

Schuyler had to agree with her grandmother's philosophy. As the middle Fortunado daughter, she was used to coming up short in her parents' eyes more often than not.

Admittedly, she wished her father would be proud of her—just the way she was. Not that she'd suffered any lack of confidence because of his disappointment over the years. After all, she'd honed an innate ability to change direction whenever she needed to, something she considered a valuable asset, especially when there were a lot of miserable people in this world who'd do better if they followed their hearts.

"I can't begin to thank you for stepping up at a moment's notice," Carlo said. "You really knocked it out of the park tonight. Would you be interested in pouring wine at our future tastings?"

"Sure. Why not?" Talk about getting her foot in the door with the Mendoza family. Now she wouldn't have to mention anything about a possible investment, although the idea intrigued her.

Carlo tossed her a heart-strumming smile. "That's great. Let's celebrate a job well done."

"Good idea." Schuyler didn't always experience the joy of accomplishment, but she did tonight. Was this how her sister Maddie felt whenever she closed a big deal? She shook off the thought and asked, "Would it be okay if I tried some of the Red River merlot? I told everyone it was my favorite Mendoza wine, even though I'd never had your label. I wouldn't want my nose to grow and sprout leaves."

"Like Pinocchio, huh?" Carlo chuckled as he reached for two clean glasses and set them on the table.

"Exactly. I loved that story, especially the cartoon.

Besides, I have a thing about being honest." While that was basically true, a niggle of guilt rose up inside, reminding her that she'd neglected to admit that she wasn't the woman he thought she was.

Had he been impressed enough with the job she'd done that she could tell him about the mix-up? Would he get angry? Or would he laugh and let her hang around him and his family for a while?

She'd called Nathan Fortune yesterday as a follow-up to a letter she'd sent him last week. But before making a five-hour drive to visit him in person, she wanted to get a better feel for the renowned Fortune family. Who knew what the Mendozas might reveal or what questions she might have after talking to them.

Carlo pulled the loosened cork from one of the half-full bottles and made a generous pour. Then he handed a glass to Schuyler.

She thanked him and took a sip, savoring the hint of black cherry. No wonder some of the chefs had raved about it. "This is very good."

"I'm glad you like it." He held up his glass to the outdoor light overhead, flicked his wrist ever so slightly and watched the wine swirl. Then he returned his attention to her. "So how'd you like working this event tonight?"

"I had more fun than any of the attendees." And standing outside under a canopy of twinkly lights adorning tree branches with a handsome Latino made it all the better.

It was, however, getting a little chilly. She took another sip of merlot, hoping it would warm her from the inside out. Yet she still gave a little shiver.

"You're cold," he said.

"Just a little. It's not bad enough to run back to my car for a sweater."

"I'm not sure if I told you that's a pretty dress. It was perfect for the tasting tonight."

"I have plenty more like this one at home."

"I'd be disappointed to learn that you didn't. I assume that means you like to go out on the town."

"Every chance I get." She offered him another spunky grin, noting his playful expression. Apparently, he was enjoying her company as much as she enjoyed his.

"You've got to be hungry," he said. "I certainly am. Why don't you join me for dinner?"

"I'd like that. Just give me a chance to freshen up. I'll use the hotel restroom."

Ten minutes later, after running a brush through her hair and reapplying her lipstick, Schuyler stopped by the registration desk in the front lobby. She needed a place to stay while she was in Austin, and the Monarch was certainly convenient.

After checking in for the night and getting a key, she returned to the garden, which was now empty—thanks to the efficiency of the hotel cleanup crew.

"Ready to go?" Carlo asked.

"Yes. Are we walking or driving?"

"If you're okay with Italian food, we can walk. There's a great little restaurant a few blocks from here."

"I love all things Italian." And Latin, it seemed.

"Then let's go. It's close to the office, so you can get a sweater or jacket from your car, if you want to. Either way, it's a short walk."

When he offered her his arm, she took it, hoping to absorb some of his body heat. "Lead the way."

Carlo blessed her with a dazzling grin that could turn a girl's knees to mush. Then he guided her along the sidewalk to the street.

Her heels and the soles of his loafers tapped a steady beat, and while she should probably remove her hand from his forearm, she enjoyed his warmth, as well as the taunting scent of a masculine soap that complemented his sea-breezy cologne.

"How long have you worked for the temp agency?" he asked.

Uh-oh. She hadn't minded playing along with the identity mix-up at first, but she wasn't ready to reveal her hand quite yet. What if he had some kind of commitment with the agency that he thought had sent Schuyler as a substitute hostess this evening? What if he reneged on the job offer to hostess future tastings?

She'd have to face that possibility, but maybe it would be best to tell him over dinner—or even dessert.

"Would you believe this was my first time on the job?" she asked.

Okay, while that wasn't an out-and-out lie, it wasn't completely honest. But still, it was somewhat truthful. She'd never been a hostess for a wine tasting before.

"Well, you'd never know it from my vantage point. You were a champ."

Moments later, they approached Rossi's, a small

brick building with a black wrought iron railing that provided an enclosure for curbside dining. Several portable heaters supplied warmth for a few couples who'd taken a seat outdoors.

"Inside or out?" Carlo asked.

"It doesn't really matter to me."

"Then let's take the first available table." He opened the green door for her, just like a gallant Latin lover, and she entered the small restaurant that boasted white plastered walls and dark wood beams.

The place had an old-world charm, right down to a colorful mural on the east wall and a rustic fountain in the back. And if the aroma of tomatoes, basil and garlic was any clue, the food had to be good.

"Two for dinner," Carlo told the hostess.

"This way." The hostess reached for two leather-bound menus, then led them to a linen-draped table, which was adorned with a red rose in a budvase and several flickering votives.

Carlo pulled out Schuyler's chair, and she took a seat. Then he sat across from her.

The hostess handed them the menus. "Your waiter is Alfonso. He'll be with you in a moment."

Moments later, a short balding gentleman in his fifties stopped by their table, introduced himself and took their drink order.

"We'll have a bottle of Mendoza merlot," Carlo told Alfonso.

"Nice choice, sir."

Schuyler couldn't help but smile. "Did you choose

this place because of the food they serve—or because of their wine selection?"

He leaned forward and said, "The food is excellent. And for that reason, we offered a tasting here a couple weeks ago. The customer reaction was so positive that the owner placed an order. So I'd also like to be supportive."

Schuyler set her menu aside. "So tell me. What's it like working for a family business?"

"It's pretty cool. We all get along—and we have a common goal. We want to see the winery be the best it can be."

"That's nice." Schuyler supposed Maddie felt the same way about Fortunado Real Estate.

Carlo studied her for a moment, and a slow smile stretched across his gorgeous face. "You've got pretty eyes."

"So do you," she said. "Some women would trade just about anything for long, thick lashes like yours. I hadn't noticed until I saw them from this angle—and in the candlelight."

"Thank you. As a kid, my brothers used to tease me about them."

Siblings could sometimes be cruel without meaning to. "I'll bet that made you feel bad."

"No, it made me double up my fists and let them have it."

She laughed. "I'll bet it did. So did you guys fight a lot growing up? I'd imagine, with all that testosterone flowing, there'd be some pretty big power struggles."

"Sometimes, but it was usually just in fun."

When Alfonso returned with their wine, they grew silent, waiting for him to uncork the bottle and pour them each a glass. Then, after telling them he'd be back with water and to take their order, he left them alone.

They'd hardly taken two sips when Carlo's phone rang. He glanced at the display, then said, "I don't normally take calls at the dinner table, but this one might be for you."

Schuyler arched a brow. What made him say that? Who knew she was here—other than his father and brothers?

"Yes," Carlo said. "Speaking."

His brow furrowed as he pressed the phone closer to his ear. "Oh, yeah? No, that's not a problem. At least, not yet. Can we talk about this tomorrow?" After a moment, he nodded. "Thanks."

Schuyler leaned forward, wondering if he'd tell her who'd called—and why he thought they'd want to speak to her. She'd never been especially patient.

"That was the temp agency we've been working with," he said. "They were apologizing because they couldn't find a fill-in for the hostess who canceled out on us."

Uh-oh. Schuyler bit down on her bottom lip. Too bad she hadn't been up-front with him when she'd first arrived. Or given him her cover story about wanting to make an investment. He probably would have accepted her help anyway. And she would have saved herself from an awkward moment.

His eyes narrowed as he speared her with an assessing look. "So who are you?"

* * *

Schuyler's eyes widened, and her lips parted. Apparently, Carlo wasn't the only one who'd been thrown off stride by that phone call from the temp agency.

He leaned forward, his arms braced on the table, and waited for her answer, which she seemed to be pondering. That wasn't a good sign.

Several beats later, she brightened. "You know..." She lifted her index finger and gave it a little twirl in the air between them. "It's funny you should ask."

"I don't find it funny. Why did you lie to me?"

"Whoa, now just wait one minute. The only thing that was the least bit dishonest was the fact that I never set you straight when you assumed I was the woman sent by the agency. But other than that, I was up-front with you. My name is Schuyler Fortunado, I know a little about wine and I spent two summers at a friend's Italian villa."

At this point, he questioned everything about her.

"All right," he said. "Then assuming that's true, why'd you let me believe the temp agency had sent you?"

"I can be a little impulsive at times, and I like to have a good time. Serving wine at a classy event sounded like fun. Besides, it was pretty obvious that you needed my help."

He didn't doubt any of that, especially the part about his needing her help. And while he was still suspicious, he had to admit that she fascinated him. Why not enjoy his time with her this evening, even if only to discredit her?

"Okay, I can buy the fact that you had fun tonight. You're also a natural at serving wine and schmoozing. What kind of work do you do?" Modeling immediately came to his mind. Acting, too. And if that were the case, she had to be pretty successful at it. That car she drove and the purse she carried weren't cheap.

"Actually, I'm currently unemployed."

He wondered why. She'd admitted to being impulsive. Had she walked off her last job? Had she been fired? Temporarily laid off? And what position had she held up until that time?

Rather than pepper her with those questions, he asked, "How do you pay the bills?"

At that, her smile faded. "You're about to learn that I'm honest, even if it's not something I care to admit."

Oh, wow. Was she a high-end call girl? If so, he hadn't seen that coming.

"My father set up a trust fund for me," she said, "so I really don't have to work. But that doesn't mean I'm not looking for the right job."

A trust fund baby, huh? Daddy's little girl, too.

"Are you an only child?" he asked.

She laughed. "Sometimes I wish that I were, even though we're all fairly close. I have three brothers and two sisters."

"And they're all supported by trust funds?"

"No, just me."

Carlo lifted his glass and took a slow, steady sip. The woman was as interesting as she was gorgeous. He was usually pretty good at pegging people, but he wasn't having much luck with her tonight.

"My brother Everett is a doctor," she added, "and my sister Maddie works for my father's real estate company. But I'm more of a free spirit who dabbles in the arts, so my dad feels compelled to take care of me, like he did my grandmother."

Carlo wasn't used to women being that open and up-front—assuming that Schuyler was being forthright now.

She fingered the stem of her wineglass, then looked up and caught his eyes. Her beauty alone was staggering, but the sincerity in her gaze nearly stole his breath away. "Just so you know, I'm not always going to be on the family dole. I've gone to college and traveled abroad. I just haven't quite figured out what I want to do with my life, and at twenty-five, I don't think that's too unusual."

"No, I don't suppose it is. I went through a time in my life when I was unsure about what I wanted to do." At twenty-five, after his divorce, he'd been forced to reevaluate his future, and that had left him a little out of step for a while.

"Apparently," she said, her blue eyes glimmering, "you've got your life all sorted out now."

"In time, it all came together." He studied her in the candlelight, the lush blond locks, the heart-shaped face. Some men could lose their heads over a woman like her. That is, if they didn't drown in those sparkling blue eyes first.

But Carlo wasn't about to let his hormones run away with him. "I'm glad you came along when you did, but that doesn't explain why you happened to be at the distribution center in the first place."

She lifted her wineglass and took a sip. "I'd heard some interesting things about the winery and wanted to check it out for myself. I might even want to purchase some stock."

He supposed that was possible, and while he wanted to believe her, he was still a bit skeptical.

"So tell me," Schuyler said, "have you lived in Austin all your life?"

"No, I'm originally from Miami. I moved here six months ago."

"And you're working for your cousin now." It wasn't a question. The lady must have done her homework. But he supposed that wasn't so hard to figure out.

"Your family must be pretty close," she added.

They hadn't always been, but things were looking up between his brothers and his cousins. "I guess you could say that."

"Is your side of the family as close to the Fortunes as some of the other Mendozas are?"

Now there was a question that didn't sit right. Something about it was...off.

"Okay," he said. "What are you really up to?"

"Nothing," she said.

Yeah, right. "You can't play a player, Schuyler. Whatever scheme you're cooking up, I've probably already attempted it myself."

She blinked, and her lips parted. For a moment, he found himself softening. But he didn't dare let down his guard. "Listen, I can't be bought, sold or conned.

But there's one thing that might persuade me to open up and answer your questions."

"What's that?" she asked as if she seriously wanted to know what might tempt him.

"The truth."

Chapter Three

Schuyler hadn't meant to be deceitful. Nor had she tried to "con a con man." So it really ought to bother her to have Carlo assume that she was playing him. But in reality, she was a bit turned on by the fact that he wasn't like other men—and that she couldn't charm him into submission, like she was often able to do.

As Carlo continued to stare at her as if reading her innermost thoughts, as if he understood her better than anyone else in the world, she realized, for some inexplicable reason, that she actually wanted him to.

"Who *are* you?" he asked again, his demeanor cool and unaffected.

Admiration and attraction went up another notch. "I told you before. My name is Schuyler Fortunado, but you can also call me Schuyler Fortune."

He furrowed his brow, clearly confused—and unconvinced.

She'd better explain. "Gerald Robinson's father is my grandfather—which makes Gerald my uncle. But my father was illegitimate and kept secret from the family."

"But why'd you show up here, at the Mendoza Distribution Center?"

"Because I want to get to know the Fortunes. Rather than pop in on them unannounced, I decided it would be best to take a slow-and-easy approach in meeting them. And since the Mendozas have strong family ties with them, I thought I'd start with you."

"I'm not going to be very helpful."

"Maybe. Maybe not. Either way, you have to admit that today turned out to be a win-win for both of us. You needed my help. And I needed to meet someone who knows the Fortunes, even if it's by six degrees of separation."

"You also need a job." Carlo sat back in his seat, no doubt stretching out his legs under the table. "Money, too, I suspect."

So he didn't believe what she'd told him about the trust fund and thought she was in it for a payday. That's where he was wrong.

Schuyler lifted her wineglass and took another sip. "Contrary to what you might think, the Fortunes' wealth has nothing to do with this. You see, just like my uncle, Jerome Fortune, aka Gerald Robinson, my father is a self-made man."

"So you say." The intensity of his gaze nearly bored into the very heart of her, but he was way off.

"Why are you so skeptical of me?" she asked.

"Shouldn't I be?"

"I suppose it's only natural." She blew a little sigh out the side of her mouth. He wasn't going to be an easy man to win over. And oddly enough, that made him all the more appealing.

"Just to be clear," he said, "the Fortunes are experts at recognizing impostors and gold diggers."

"No doubt they are, but I can assure you, some people don't need a famous name to be successful. If you're smart and the cards are in your favor, you can make it to the top. And my father is as smart as they come. He's lucky, too. A real King Midas. He parlayed a winning lottery ticket into real estate, and his investments paid off. He now lives in the most exclusive area of Houston and owns an agency in a downtown high-rise, with branches in Austin and San Antonio."

"Fortunado Real Estate?"

"That's us. So, you see, we don't need the Fortunes' money."

Before Carlo could answer, Alfonso stopped by the table with a basket of bread, olive oil and balsamic. Then he took their orders.

When they were alone again, Carlo picked up the conversation where they'd left off. "If your family has plenty of money, why the interest in the Fortunes?"

"Actually, my father and most of my siblings aren't interested in forging a connection. At least, that's what they told me." She reached into the basket, removed a warm slice of bread and tore off one side of the crust.

"I suspect they're curious, but they're not sure about making any changes to our family dynamics."

"And you're not concerned about that?"

Schuyler wouldn't mind seeing a slight shift in the Fortunado family dynamics. For one thing, she'd like to see artistic expression valued as much as an advanced degree or a head for business.

"I'm more open-minded than the other Fortunados," she said. "So I decided to check out the Fortunes for myself."

Carlo studied her once again, as if he still couldn't buy her story. She lifted her wineglass and took a drink. Dang, it was good. No wonder those chefs had been impressed.

"Believe it or not," Schuyler said, "I'm as honest as the day is long."

"Except when you hold back information."

"Well, that's true." She popped the crust into her mouth. Mmm. Homemade and fresh from the oven.

"It seems to me," Carlo said, "that you'd be better off talking to Ariana Lamonte, who wrote those articles and blogs for *Weird Life* magazine about the Fortunes."

"I already did." Apparently, he didn't realize she'd done her homework. "Her articles actually convinced me that my suspicion was right and triggered my quest. And by the way, in case you didn't know, her last name is Fortune now. She married Jayden Fortune from Paseo, Texas."

"So your visit to the Mendoza Winery Distribution Center was plan B?"

"I hope that doesn't hurt your feelings."

At that, he laughed. "I'm just on the periphery of the Fortune family, but I can get you an introduction if you'd like one."

"That's great. And I promise that I'll watch from the outside. I don't mean them any harm. Think of me as an investigative reporter."

"And a damn pretty one at that."

Now, that was an interesting way to toss out a compliment. But then again, with the way he looked and his sexy style, it was easy to see Carlo had plenty of practice—no doubt from a string of sexual conquests over the years.

"Ariana can probably provide you with a better introduction to the Fortune family than I can," Carlo said.

"You're right. And once she and her hubby get back home in a few weeks, I plan to talk to her about doing that."

He scrunched his brow, creating a crease in his forehead, but it didn't mar his gorgeous face in the least. "Where are they?"

"They're out of town while she researches a new book about people who embody the Texas spirit."

Before Carlo could respond, his cell phone rang again. He glanced at the screen. "Believe it or not, I'm not usually a rude dinner companion, but I need to take this call. If you'll excuse me, I'll step outside and answer it. But I'll make it quick."

She nodded. Like Daddy had taught her since she was old enough to join the family at the dining room table, business always came first.

Once, when Schuyler was in high school, a friend

called her while they were having dinner. Her father threatened to take away her cell phone if she answered. Yet two minutes later, he got a call and took it. When he finished talking, she pointed out the inconsistency, which made him angry. He lifted his finger and shook it at her. *Here's the rule in this family, Schuyler. When a phone call earns money, you answer it.*

Moments later, Carlo returned to the table. He'd no more than taken a seat when he leaned forward and zeroed in on her like a con man who'd found his mark. "I have a proposition for you. I need your help again, and I'll do whatever you want if you agree."

Schuyler raised her eyebrows. "Whatever I want? Just what would this job entail?"

"Now who's being skeptical?" Carlo laughed. "There isn't anything unsavory about it. I need someone to represent the Mendoza brand at another special tasting. You just have to do the same thing you did this evening. Pour wine and get people to drink it—and hopefully buy it. I'll pay you well for your time."

"I told you before. This isn't about the money. I don't have to work a day in my life unless I want to."

And if truth be told, she wanted to hostess again for Carlo.

"So what do you say?" he asked.

She was always up for an adventure. So she reached across the table to shake his hand and seal the deal. "It'll be a pleasure doing business with you."

In spite of his better judgment, Carlo had been listening to Schuyler half in amusement, half in curiosity.

But things got serious the moment he took her hand and felt the unexpected strength of her small grip, the softness of her skin and the heat of her touch. Desire slammed into him, nearly taking him out at the knees.

He tried to play it cool, to hide his sexual attraction, but he'd never met a woman like her before. And he probably never would again.

Granted, he'd been skeptical of her the moment he'd learned the temp agency hadn't sent her and she'd let him believe that they had. In some ways, he supposed he was still a bit leery, but she seemed sincere.

She was also gorgeous and as intriguing as hell. Besides, she was the best hostess they'd had yet. And she was damn good for business. Bottom line? He was going to take a gamble and believe her story.

"The next tasting is on Thursday evening," he said. "Are you available to work that night?"

"Three days from now?" She tucked a strand of hair behind her ear, revealing a good-size diamond stud. "Sure. I'll be in town for a while."

She didn't say how long she intended to stay, and even though he was growing more and more curious about her plans, he didn't ask. "Thanks for being flexible," he said.

"Hey. That's practically my middle name." She flashed him a dazzling smile, then leaned forward. "So tell me about this 'special' tasting."

"There's going to be another convention in town. This one is for a group of software execs. So I called the people in charge and set up a special preconference event. We negotiated a discounted price, and they liked the idea."

"Is it going to be in the Monarch Hotel gardens?"

"No, this one will be held at the winery. We're sending a bus to provide them with transportation to and from the hotel. Then, after they have a tasting of our best vintages, we'll serve them dinner."

"Sounds like an exciting evening for a group I'd expect to be a little dull and boring in real life."

Carlo laughed. "Leave it to a party girl to make that assumption."

She gave a little shrug, followed by a playful wink.

"Actually," he said, "a lot of thought goes behind my invitation for a special tasting. Those executives all live in various parts of the country, so I figure they'll order several cases each and share it with their friends when they get home. It's a good way to get the wine into the hands of consumers outside Texas."

"I like the way you think."

"Hey, when you have a good product or business, the best promotion is word of mouth."

"Looks like you've thought of everything."

"I try to." He leaned back in his chair and lifted his glass. Yet he found his dinner companion more tempting than his favorite Mendoza wine.

Damn, she was pretty. Carlo prided himself on his strength and character, but God help a weak man who found himself attracted to her.

"Is your tasting room open daily—or just by special request?"

"We're open in the afternoons, and we have a host

who handles the regular tastings for us. He also works at La Viña in the evenings, so I'd prefer to use someone else during our special events."

"So that's where I come in."

"Exactly. And as part of your pay, I'll do whatever I can to help you be that fly on the wall with the Fortunes."

"I'd really appreciate that." Her eyes were an interesting and unusual shade of blue. They also were assessing him just as carefully as he'd studied her moments ago.

"I'm not blowing smoke," he said. "There's going to be a Valentine's Day party at the Mendoza Winery on the fourteenth, and a lot of the Fortunes will be there. You can be the hostess that night and 'work' the room."

Her smile practically lit the entire restaurant, extinguishing the need for the votives on the table. "That would be great, Carlo. You won't be sorry. I'll be professional and discreet."

He hoped she was right, and that his belief in her hadn't been unfounded. After reaching into the pocket of his sports jacket, he pulled out his business card and handed it to her. "In the meantime, why don't you stop by the winery tomorrow morning. I'll give you a personal tour."

"I'd like that."

Interestingly enough, Carlo would, too.

Bright and early the next day, while Schuyler was sound asleep in her suite at the Monarch Hotel, the alarm went off.

Normally, she hated wake-up calls or sticking to a

schedule. But not this morning. Without a grumble or even a yawn, she threw off the covers, rolled out of bed and padded to the bathroom.

She stopped long enough to glance in the mirror, expecting to see her hair a sleep-tousled mess, but it didn't look all that bad. That in itself was a surprise, but even more so was the smile that stretched across her face. She'd always had a natural effervescence, but it didn't usually begin to surface until after her first cup of coffee. But then again, today was different. Her wish was about to come true. In less than two weeks, she was going to be face-to-face with some of the Fortunes.

How cool was that?

Yet there was something else giving her reason to celebrate. She was going to see Carlo again.

Dinner last night had not only been delicious and filling, it had been...well, interesting—to say the least. It had also bordered on romantic.

As a rule, she steered clear of men who might want a serious relationship with her. She didn't need any more people trying to pressure her into conforming to their expectations. But she suspected that Carlo was different.

For that reason, before turning in last night, she'd set the alarm on her smartphone to give her plenty of time to get ready.

An hour later she was driving out to the winery and following the directions Carlo had given her. After turning into the driveway, she couldn't help easing her foot from the accelerator and slowing down to take in the acres of grapevines growing in the Hill Country.

Another storm had passed through during the night, drenching the area in rain. But after watering the plants and flora, as well as cleansing the air and leaves, it had passed through and the sky was now clear and blue.

It was certainly pretty here in the country. Schuyler had always been a city girl, but that didn't mean she didn't enjoy breathing in fresh air and watching the sun set over rolling hills and greenery. Not that she'd be invited to stay at the winery that long, although she'd be up for extending her visit.

She'd no more than parked and shut off the ignition when Carlo came out to meet her. If she'd thought he looked handsome last night, he was even more striking today in khaki slacks and a white cotton shirt—button-down, crisply pressed. Definitely not a Texas cowboy. More like a tall, dark Miami Beach hottie.

"Welcome to the Mendoza Winery," he said.

She left her purse, a big black Chanel she'd filled to the brim with various items she might need at any given moment, and locked the doors. Then she placed the keys in the front pocket of her jeans and greeted him with a handshake. The formality wasn't necessary, but she wanted to touch him again, and a hug didn't seem appropriate. Maybe she'd offer him one when she left.

"What do you think of the place so far?" he asked.

"It's impressive. You'd never know that your cousin bought it recently. It's been so well cared for that you'd think your family has owned it for years."

"It was in the Daily family for generations, and Alejandro purchased it from them."

"Either way, the grounds are beautiful."

"Thanks. It's been a team effort. Actually, it still is. We're going to expand more so we can offer it as a venue for parties and weddings. Come on. I'll give you that tour, starting with the sculpture garden around the back."

Schuyler fell into step beside Carlo. In addition to taking in the lovely grounds, she couldn't help breathing in his alluring, ocean-fresh scent and losing focus. As they turned the corner and she spotted the sculpture garden, she realized why he thought the setting would be perfect for weddings or special events.

"This is amazing." She scanned the rose garden, and the manicured lawn that had been adorned with several large sculptures.

"We're going to plant more flowers," he said. "And we've ordered a Spanish-tiled fountain, which a local artisan is going to create. The stone sculptures were already here—and permanent. But we're going to bring in other outdoor art pieces and rotate them."

"That ought to be a nice touch." She stopped to admire the statue of a cavalry officer mounted on a horse. "This is pretty cool."

"I think so, too."

She circled to the front of the horse and placed her hand on its nose, stroking it as if the animal was real. Then she looked at Carlo and grinned.

"Come on. I'll show you the tasting room next." He placed his hand on the small of her back. Her spine tingled at his touch, an electrifying flash that shot through her like a sparkler on the Fourth of July. Her legs wobbled, and she nearly stumbled before making a quick recovery.

If Carlo noticed, he didn't comment. Instead, they crossed the garden, returned to the back of the main building and entered. Just down the hall, a sign on a large, rough-hewn wooden door announced the tasting room hours. He gripped the brass handle and opened it for her, then he followed her inside.

She scanned the open reception area, which boasted high, vaulted ceilings and dark beams, as he led her to a marble-topped bar. Shelves of corked wine bottles awaited the next batch of wine enthusiasts who would come to taste the best vintages the winery had to offer.

"Has your family always been in the wine business?" she asked.

"No. When Alejandro was in college, he got a part-time job working at a South Beach wine bar to put himself through school. And that's where it all started. He changed his major to agricultural operations and went on to get a master's degree in viticulture and enology. He also spent a summer in France interning at a vineyard and another summer in one located in Napa Valley."

"I can see where his interest took off from there. I told you about my friend Calista, whose family owned that villa in Italy. It wasn't quite the same for me, but her enthusiasm was almost contagious, and I learned a lot during my visits. For a while, I thought about moving there, but my dad had a fit and threatened to cut me off for good." She turned and studied Carlo. "But what about you? What made you leave Miami to work at a winery?"

"I come from a long line of restaurant and nightclub owners, so I've got a solid handle on the food industry, as well as wine. One of my jobs with Mendoza Winery is to run La Viña."

"Are you the manager?" she asked.

"I suppose you could say that. Alejandro let me have free rein in remodeling the restaurant and hiring a chef and waitstaff."

"I'd love to see what you've done."

"We'll end the tour there, then have lunch. In the meantime, I'll show you the vineyard and the cellar, where we make the wine."

Carlo led her outside and to a barn, where a red electric car awaited them.

"Oh my gosh," Schuyler said. "How cute is this? It looks like a cross between a golf cart and a limousine."

"It's new," Carlo said. "And another of my suggestions. I thought it might be a nice touch for small, intimate tours. And Alejandro liked the idea."

So did Schuyler. "You've got a great business sense. I'm impressed."

"Thanks." Carlo glanced at her, his brow slightly scrunched.

"What? You don't believe me?"

"No, it's not that."

"Then what's wrong? And don't tell me *nothing*. Doubt is splashed all over your face."

He slowly shook his head and smiled. "It's not doubt. It's surprise."

"Don't tell me that you don't realize how bright and creative you are."

His mouth tilted in a crooked grin. "Actually, I've never had a problem with self-confidence. I just hadn't..." He paused, clearly trying to choose his words carefully. "Well, I didn't think you'd look at the business side of things."

Her brow shot up, and she folded her arms across her chest. "You didn't think that a trust fund dolly could spot a potentially lucrative operation or notice someone with a clear head for business?"

"I didn't mean to question your intelligence. It's just that some women would be oohing and aahing about the winery and more impressed by the family's successful new venture."

"You mean your family's financial status?" Schuyler rolled her eyes and clicked her tongue. "You've definitely been dating the wrong women."

Carlo laughed. "I'm not sure about that, but I can tell you this—you're not like any of them."

She brightened. "You know what? I'm going to take that as a compliment."

"You should." He swept out his arm toward the classy golf cart in an after-you fashion. So she climbed into the front seat and waited for him to join her.

Moments later, he started the engine and took off to show her the property, stopping several times to point out different vintages of grapes.

Despite the sun, there was a bit of a chill in the air, especially as they zipped along the narrow blacktop road just big enough for the cart, but Schuyler wasn't about to complain. Not when she was getting a private tour of a beautiful Hill Country vineyard by a hand-some Latino.

When she'd mentioned the women he dated, which had been his cue to reveal whether he was committed to anyone in particular, he hadn't even blinked. She could probably come right out and ask, but she didn't want him to think she was interested in him.

Okay, so she was. More than a little—and more than she cared to admit.

Carlo probably had his contact list filled with the names and numbers of beautiful women, each of them eager to have his attention. Schuyler would bet her trust fund that he wasn't the kind of guy who spent many Saturday nights alone.

She didn't, either. Not that her dating life was all that active. She preferred to keep things light, fun and unencumbered. And that meant that she almost always came home alone. It was easier that way.

But maybe she ought to reconsider her philosophy on men and dating. She wouldn't mind going out on the town with Carlo Mendoza on a Saturday night—or any night of the week for that matter.

They turned to the left, onto a small dirt path that was still damp from the recent rain, dodging several puddles along the way.

Schuyler didn't like taking vehicles off the road. When she was fifteen, Glammy took her out to practice driving her classic Volkswagen, a hot pink Bug Glammy called Mary Kay.

Since you don't have a learner's permit yet, Glammy had said, *your father will freak if I take you on the pub-*

*lic highway. Let's go out in the country. I know just
the place.*

It had been raining earlier that day, and when they
got out onto the dirt road, they'd soon sunk axle deep.
So much for Glammy's good intentions. Daddy had
freaked anyway, especially when he got the towing bill.

"Aren't you afraid of getting stuck?" Schuyler asked
Carlo.

"No, I drove out here with Alejandro yesterday, before he left for a seminar in California. And we didn't
have any trouble getting through."

The vineyards continued to stretch along the right
shoulder, but when Schuyler's gaze turned to the open
hillside on the left, she gasped and pointed. "Look at
those bluebonnets. I'd heard they were going to bloom
early this year. Would you mind pulling over so I can
get a picture?"

"Not at all." Carlo stopped along the side of the path-
way and waited while she pulled her smartphone from
her pocket and headed off to get a good shot.

Schuyler might have dropped out of art school, but
that didn't mean she didn't appreciate natural beauty.
And sometimes, she liked to dabble in watercolors. If
the painted version of that hillside turned out as good
as she hoped it would, she'd frame it and hang it in her
bedroom at home.

She caught movement to the right and spotted a long-
horn cow lumbering toward a rusted-out farm tractor.
Now there was an unusual sight. She raised her cell
phone, snapping a picture first, followed by a video.

How cool was that? As she backed up, continuing to

film what she suspected was a stray cow, she stepped in a puddle that practically swallowed up her Jimmy Choo ankle boot and knocked her off balance. Before she could blink, she plopped to the ground, splattering muddy water.

"Dang it," she muttered, as she glanced at her drenched leather boot, hoping it was waterproof and not ruined. Sheesh. She'd had the pair for only a few months.

Before she could get to her feet, Carlo was at her side. "Are you okay?"

"Just a little dirty and wet. But it's no big deal."

He reached out his hand, and she took it, allowing him to pull her to her feet.

"I'll take you back to the winery so you can clean up," he said.

"That's not necessary. A little mud never hurt anyone, but that puddle did a real number on my Jimmy Choos." She brushed her dirty hands together, then wiped her palms against her denim-clad hips and smiled. "Oh, well."

His eye twitched, and one side of his lips quirked into a crooked grin. "You're something else."

She wasn't sure what he meant by that, but a humorous spark in his eyes indicated he hadn't meant it as a criticism.

"In what way?" she asked.

"Most women would be flipping out about the dirty water and mud, not to mention the ruined boot."

"I told you that I'm not like most women."

"You were right." He studied her face for a moment,

his gaze locking on hers. Then he lifted his hand and brushed the pad of his thumb against her cheek.

"Did the mud splatter up that high?"

"Just a little." His cleaning efforts turned soft, gentle, tantalizing. Surely her face hadn't gotten that dirty.

She could have stepped back and taken over wiping her cheek of a lingering smudge, but she liked his soul-stirring touch. His eyes seemed to be caressing her face, too, setting off a quiver in her belly.

"Did you know that the color of those wildflowers is the same shade as your eyes?" he asked.

Her breath caught. "No, I didn't."

"They're pretty."

"The bluebonnets?"

"Your eyes."

About the time she thought he might kiss her, he nodded toward the cart. "Let's head back to the winery so you can dry off and clean up before you catch cold."

She didn't much care about the mud or the wet foot or the chill in the air, but she headed back to the cutesy little cart like a soggy damsel who'd been rescued by a handsome prince.

"I can't believe you're not concerned about ruining that shoe."

"It's not that I don't care. But whining about it isn't going to help."

Besides, their budding friendship or whatever was sparking between them just might prove to be a lot more valuable than a pair of pricey shoes.

Chapter Four

"Do you have a change of clothes?" Carlo asked Schuyler on the way back to the winery.

"I keep a packed gym bag in my car, which always has yoga pants, a shirt and shoes."

"Good." He drove the cart to the parking lot, pulled alongside her BMW and waited until she removed a black canvas tote from the trunk. Then he took her to the entrance of La Viña and parked in front. "There's a restroom inside. After you clean up, we can have an early lunch."

Once they climbed the steps and reached the double glass doors, Carlo pulled out his keys while Schuyler studied the hours posted on the sign.

"The restaurant doesn't open until five o'clock," she said.

"That's right. We offer a brunch on weekends, but we

only serve dinner on weekdays. That's going to change in the future. Word has already spread about our menu and the service, so we've been seeing an increase in the number of diners."

"So you were right," she said. "Word of mouth is the best promotion of all."

"Ah, you were listening."

"Always." Her eyes sparkled with mirth. Or flirtation. It was hard to tell. "But I'm a little confused. If the restaurant is closed, how are we going to have lunch?"

"Don't worry." He tossed her a smile. "I don't need a chef to put out a nice meal. Go change your clothes. I'll wait for you here, then we'll raid the fridge."

"That sounds like fun, not to mention clandestine." She winked, then disappeared into the bathroom.

Women, especially the pretty ones, tended to take a lot of time fussing with their appearance, so Carlo expected a long wait. But when Schuyler returned just moments later wearing a lime-green tank top, black yoga pants and gray running shoes, he was again reminded that she wasn't anything like his usual dates.

She'd run a brush through her hair and applied pink lip gloss. He couldn't help noting that she rocked that stylish, curve-hugging outfit. The good Lord had blessed her with a great shape, and it seemed that she worked hard to keep it that way.

Apparently, she hadn't noticed his admiring gaze, because she scanned the restaurant interior, her blue eyes wide, her lips parted. "This is amazing."

She was amazing. But she was talking about the renovation he'd designed. She pointed to the large windows that provided an unrestricted view of the vineyard, as well as the rounded oak-paneled ceiling that resembled the shape of a wine barrel. "I'm impressed. This would be the perfect venue for a wedding reception."

"You'd consider getting married here?"

At that, she balked. "Who, me? Oh, no." She slowly shook her head, those luscious blond locks tumbling along her shoulders. "I'm too much like my grandmother to consider making a lifelong promise like that."

"Your grandmother never married?"

"No. At one time, she'd actually hoped Julius Fortune would follow through with his divorce, which he'd told her was in the works, although it really wasn't. I can't believe that lothario was able to juggle so many affairs without his wife catching him."

"Who says she didn't know? I'll bet some people would put up with just about anything for money."

Schuyler blew out a *humph*. "Not me."

He believed her. She wore wealth and status well, but he figured she didn't consider money to be a cure-all. Neither did he, which meant they might make a perfect match, one that wasn't encumbered by well-intentioned vows most people found hard to keep.

"Come on," he said. "I promised you lunch, although it's going to be a joint effort."

"I'd be happy to help, but will the chef be upset to find out that we're taking over his kitchen? I'd suspect that he'd be a little territorial."

"I do this all the time, so he won't mind."

Once in the kitchen, Carlo pulled out the fixings for

a garden salad, along with some grilled chicken and a small container of dressing left over from last night.

"What can I do to help?" she asked.

"Why don't you fix a fruit and cheese platter? I'll make a salad."

While they worked, Carlo put a small loaf of French bread in the oven to warm.

"Where'd you learn your way around a kitchen?" Schuyler asked.

"I've worked in restaurants for years and learned a few tricks from several of the chefs. How about you? Do you like to cook?"

"Not especially. But then again, it's not too much fun preparing food for one. So I eat most of my meals out." She reached for a bunch of grapes, rinsed them and placed them on the cheese platter, alternating clumps of green and red. Next, she added apple slices.

"Good job," he said.

"Thanks." She glanced at the bowl he'd filled with a spring mix of greens, tomatoes, mushrooms, avocado, pine nuts and chopped chicken. "That looks good, too. I'm impressed."

He gave a slight shrug. There didn't seem to be any reason to tell her that most of the women he dated liked having him cook for them. He'd have them sit on one of his kitchen bar stools and pour them a glass of wine. Then, while soft jazz played in the background, he'd fix one of his special dishes, like chicken marsala. It was part of the foreplay.

Yet this was different.

Or was it?

He kept his thoughts to himself as he and Schuyler set the food out on a table in the dining room, next to a window that looked out on the sculpture garden. He held out her chair, and after she took a seat, he sat across from her.

"That cheese platter looks great," he said.

"I have an eye for color and design. Or so I've been told."

"Did you ever think about doing something with that?"

"Actually, I went to art school for a while, although I dropped out—something that upset my dad." Schuyler plucked a green seedless grape from the cluster on the cheese board and popped it into her mouth. "He couldn't understand that my time there wasn't a waste."

He found himself leaning forward, intrigued. Maybe even entranced. "I'm sure you benefited from your time there. Why did you find it valuable?"

"I learned a lot and I definitely have an eye for color and design, but I really haven't put any of it to good use—as my dad reminds me sometimes."

"So you're a colorful, fun-loving tumbleweed for the time being."

Her smile dimpled her cheek. "I guess so. But I have another focus right now. And that's to sort through the family mystery, although it's not the least bit mysterious to me."

"The Fortune connection."

"Exactly." She reached for a rice cracker. "In fact, I'm going to take a drive out to Paseo tomorrow and visit Nathan Fortune."

"That's one long-ass drive for a little chat."

"I figure Paseo is about five hours from here. If I leave early in the morning, I should be back by late afternoon or the evening."

Carlo nodded, as if it all made sense to him—this quest to meet her family. "So why Nathan? How does he fit into all of this?"

"He's pretty much an outsider, so he probably has an interesting take on the dynamics. When I read his sister-in-law's articles in *Weird Life* magazine, I remembered some of the things Glammy told me about my dad's biological father, and I connected the dots."

"Glammy?"

"Sorry." She smiled and placed a small slice of white cheddar on her cracker. "I was trying to call her Grammy, like the other kids in the family, but I had a speech impediment when I was a little girl, so that's how it came out. And the nickname stuck. Anyway, Glammy and I were very close."

"She sounds like an interesting character."

"She's gone now, but Glammy was pretty unique, and I idolized her. On the other hand, her unique personality sometimes embarrassed my dad."

"In what way?"

"Well, for example, I went to a private high school in an exclusive part of town. On the night I graduated, she showed up wearing a tie-dyed T-shirt and a pair of fluffy bunny slippers. I thought a vein on my dad's forehead was going to burst."

"Did it embarrass you?"

"No, not at all. Glammy showed me how to tie-dye

one summer, and we had fun making matching tops. So that was her way of letting me know she remembered the fun we'd had that day, which was pretty special. And the slippers? I'd given them to her for Christmas. Besides, she'd had an ingrown toenail, and she chose comfort over style."

"You must have loved her a lot."

"I really did. You have no idea how much I miss her. We were a lot alike. Two orange peas in a purple pod, my dad used to say."

"Does that mean you own a pair of bunny slippers?"

She laughed. "I wish I did, but no. My dad wasn't too happy that my grandmother and I had so many similarities. For example, she had a penchant for art, mostly retro stuff, psychedelic colors and that sort of thing. She was the first one to encourage me to express myself artistically. And she stepped in and convinced my dad that it wasn't a bad thing for me to transfer from college to an art school. He'd just about gotten used to the idea, when I decided to come home after two semesters. He doesn't let me forget that I sometimes disappoint him, like she used to."

"Tell me more about your grandmother."

Schuyler brightened. "She was amazing. Years ago, when she lived in San Francisco, her name was Mary Johnson. She was working at a nightclub and met Julius. That's when he told her he was in the process of getting a divorce. They hit it off, and he put her up in a fancy Houston condominium. She'd assumed that he would eventually be free to marry her, but Julius wasn't interested in making an honest woman out of any of his lovers."

Carlo poured them each a glass of iced tea. "When did they break up?"

"When Glammy got pregnant with my father, it was the beginning of the end. Julius asked her to sign a confidentiality agreement, promising to give her the deed to her home and to leave her financially comfortable. He also insisted that she name their son Kenneth rather than one of her unconventional suggestions. She agreed, and the affair ended."

"Did she admit to you that Julius was your grandfather?"

"Not in so many words. She honored that confidentiality agreement, although keeping that secret just about killed her. When my dad was six, she legally changed their last name to Fortunado. I think she chose a Latin form of the name she believed we all deserved but could never claim. She also changed her first name to Starlight, which my dad never understood."

"Starlight? Sounds like a hippie name."

"Yes, but you have to remember she lived in San Francisco in the 1960s. And just between us, I think the name suited her a lot better than Mary did." Schuyler used her fork to spear a piece of chicken from her salad. Before popping it into her mouth, she added, "My dad loved his mother, even though he considered her to be a little too flamboyant and over the top. I'm sure that's why he chose a quieter life for himself."

"And you didn't?"

"Life wasn't meant to be boring. And just so you know, Glammy wasn't a flake. She was one of a kind."

"It's easy to see that you admired her."

"And adored her. She loved all of her grandchildren, but there was a special place in her heart for me. Over the years, we became especially close, and when she died, I was heartbroken. I was also determined to live my own life the way Glammy had."

"And that means being a little out of step with the other members in your family."

"Yes, but that doesn't bother me. Although I must admit, that's one reason I'd like to ease into the Fortune family. I'd like to get to know them before they have a chance to judge me."

"I can't imagine them finding you lacking in any way. And I'm surprised your father doesn't appreciate you for being unique."

"That's nice of you to say." She paused, as if pondering whether she should share more or not. "I'm happy with things the way they are. But to be completely honest, when my younger sister, Valene, started working for Fortunado Real Estate, it stung a bit."

"Why is that?"

Her response stalled again. "I'd never be happy working in an office, but it's a little disappointing to be bypassed in the hierarchy of the family business, especially by my younger sister."

"I'm sorry."

"Thanks, but I'd never be a good fit anyway."

"So here you are," he said, "doing your own thing and searching for your family roots."

"Pretty much. I'm also doing it for Glammy. She always dreamed that her son and grandchildren would be recognized as Fortunes, and that's my dream now. Hopefully, they'll end up being the kind of people I wouldn't mind knowing or claiming as family."

"I guess there's only one way to find out. You'll just have to meet them." He reached for a cluster of purple seedless grapes and pulled off a couple. "Are you going to keep your room at the Monarch Hotel?"

"Yes, of course. I have a nice room there, so why pack up and look for someplace else to stay?"

"So you're not planning to get a room in Paseo tomorrow night?"

"I'm going to leave early in the morning and will head back in the afternoon. I'm determined to make the trip to Paseo and back in one day. From what I can see from the map, there's not much between here and there."

"I'll be in town again tomorrow," he said. "Maybe I can buy you a drink when you get back to Austin. Then you can tell me how your visit with Nathan went."

"That's sounds fun. We can be partners in crime."

"I don't know about that, but something tells me it might be a lot of fun getting into trouble with you."

"Now there's an intriguing idea."

Wasn't that the truth?

Carlo was eager to see Schuyler again, for drinks and a debriefing.

An evening couldn't be more intriguing than that.

Schuyler peered out the bug-splattered windshield. Her GPS indicated she was getting close to her destination. And from the looks of the small town up ahead, she was. That is, if the meager set of single-story buildings that hadn't seen any new construction since FDR's New Deal was Paseo, Texas.

Talk about being down in the boondocks. She'd driven hours to get here, and within a blink or two, she'd be leaving the town in the dust. Even though she hadn't seen a car in ages, she hit her turn signal and turned off the highway, following the directions she'd been given.

Nathan Fortune knew she was coming. She'd mailed him a letter to begin with, asking him to please call her. When they'd talked on the phone, he'd been pretty quiet. But she hoped to draw more out of him when she met him in person.

"Hi there," she said, practicing her announcement aloud, "I'm your long-lost cousin."

No, that wasn't true. You couldn't lose a relative you didn't know existed. And none of the Fortunes, legitimate or otherwise, realized they were related to the Fortunados—a soon-to-be-revealed secret.

Her family had always teased her about being too impulsive, about following her heart rather than her mind. But how could she do otherwise? She often got a gut feeling about things and couldn't let it go until she saw it through. Besides, she seemed to have a killer instinct for knowing when something felt right. And, like it or not, meeting her Fortune relatives felt better than right. So when her father had told her to back off on her quest, she hadn't been able to.

It wasn't like she planned to waltz right up to the

upper echelon of the family hierarchy and blatantly introduce herself.

She scanned the countryside. Wow. Talk about living outside the inner circle. Nathan must be a hermit. Of course, living way out here, in the middle of nowhere, he'd almost have to be.

When she spotted a line of bent and rusted-out mailboxes along the side of the road, she muttered, "There it is." Then she followed the graveled drive to a two-story house.

She'd no more than parked near the big barn and gotten out of the car when she was met by a shaggy brown-and-black dog with a red-and-white Western bandanna tied around its neck. It barked several times to announce her visit.

Then again, maybe it was in warning. For a moment, she wondered if she should climb back in the safety of her BMW, but the mutt really didn't look all that mean or vicious.

"Hey," she said, "don't worry about me, doggie. I'm friendly. Gosh, I'm actually family."

The dog seemed to understand and trotted up to her, giving her a curious sniff. Moments later, a man walked out of the barn, all big and buff and cowboy.

"Hi there," she called out, as she reached across the dog to greet him. "You must be Nathan. I'm Schuyler Fortunado. But you probably already gathered that."

"Yep. I figured as much."

She scanned her rustic surroundings, which were also clean and neat. "I don't expect you get too many visitors way out here."

"You've got that right." He gripped her hand and gave it a sturdy shake. "But I kind of like it that way."

She supposed he'd have to. "You have no idea how happy I am to meet you. Thanks for agreeing to see me."

After releasing her hand, he lifted his hat and wiped the sheen from his forehead with his sleeve. "I can't imagine why you'd come all the way out here to talk to me. It's a long drive just to say hello. You must have something on your mind."

Schuyler might be a little impulsive, but she was as honest as the day was long. "First of all, like I mentioned in my letter, I've been on a hunt for my family roots, and I finally solved the mystery when I read your sister-in-law's articles in *Weird Life*."

His brow creased, but he didn't respond.

"Don't get me wrong, Ariana is a great writer and investigative reporter, but she came up short in uncovering all the Fortunes out there. There are more of us than she could've imagined."

Nathan continued to stare at her, his unspoken questions deepening the furrow in his brow.

"Your father didn't corner the market on infidelity," she said. "Julius Fortune was as big a tomcat as his son was."

Nathan adjusted his hat on his head, then folded his arms across his broad chest. "What are you getting at?"

"I'll cut to the chase and hit the high points. Years ago, Julius had an affair with Mary Johnson, my grandmother. While she was pregnant with my dad, they split up."

"I've never heard of a Mary Johnson, and I've read Ariana's columns."

"Well, that's probably because she legally changed her and my father's last name to Fortunado. She was always partial to things with a Latin flair. Or any kind of flair, really."

Nathan continued to gaze at her as if he didn't know what to make of her. Or her story.

"So why'd you come to see me?" he asked. "Why not go all the way to the top with your claim?"

"Because I'd like to observe the family for a while."

The front door squeaked open, and an attractive brunette in her late twenties stepped onto the porch. She lifted her left hand to shield her eyes from the midday sun, revealing a diamond ring, and made her way to Nathan.

His expression softened, and his eyes brightened at the sight of her. "Bianca, this is Schuyler Fortunado, another one of my cousins, it seems."

Bianca had to be his wife, the woman he'd recently married. She crossed the yard, her long straight hair sluicing down her back, and greeted Schuyler with a smile. "It's nice to meet you."

Was it? Schuyler had pretty much just dropped a bombshell. At least, that's how she'd feel if the tables had been reversed and Nathan had shown up at her condo in Houston and made a similar announcement.

"I'm sure you didn't expect to hear that there are more of us," Schuyler said.

Nathan and Bianca looked at each other, as if weighing how to respond.

"Well, actually…" Nathan began, "we're not all that surprised."

Schuyler frowned. *Had* they known about her?

"Ariana spent months tracking down elusive Fortunes and was the one who'd found me and my brothers," Nathan said. "She mentioned that there was another branch of the family, but I made a point of not listening. So if you're looking for information about any of them, I'm not the person you want to talk to."

"But that's exactly why I'm here. I want an honest, unbiased opinion from someone who isn't swayed by the family's money or influence or even its drama."

"I'd be happy to give you one, but I've never met any of them, including the man who was my sperm donor."

Now it was Schuyler's turn to be surprised. "Aren't you interested in meeting Gerald Robinson—or should I say Jerome Fortune?"

"It's a little late to be looking for a daddy at my age. I'm more interested in keeping him away from my mom, Deborah. So the less contact I have with the man, the better."

That was an interesting flip. Schuyler was dying to meet them all, while Nathan wanted to avoid them. "Is something wrong with Gerald—or with the rest of the family?" That thought hadn't crossed her mind, but maybe it should have.

"Some of them are okay, I guess. Why?"

"I'd like to meet with them. Any of them."

"I can't tell you much about the Robinson branch of the family. You'll need to go to Austin for that. You can also go to Red Rock and Horseback Hollow to learn about the others, some of whom are married to Mendozas. But for the record, some of them may not be as welcoming as others. Kate Fortune has been subjected to plenty of phony gold diggers over the years."

Schuyler had, of course, heard of the family's matriarch. "I'm not the least bit interested in the family money or in Kate's cosmetics company. So she doesn't scare me."

"Then maybe you should talk to her or one of the others," Nathan said. "I'm not privy to or interested in any of the family dynamics."

Before she could remind him that she didn't want to make a big splash, the screen door creaked open, then slammed shut as a small boy dashed outside. "Mommy, can I have another cookie? I'm super hungry and I've been good all morning."

Bianca smiled. "You also picked up your Legos without me asking, so yes. But let me get it for you, okay?"

"This is our son, EJ," Nathan said, boasting a happy grin.

Schuyler couldn't help but admire the little guy. "He's darling."

"He can also be a real pistol at times," Bianca added. "But he's been exceptionally good this morning, so if you'll excuse me, I'd better get that cookie before he tries to get it himself. I'd be happy to put on a pot of coffee, if you'd like to come inside."

"Thank you," Schuyler said, "but I need to go."

As Bianca and EJ returned to the house, Nathan studied Schuyler. "So will you be heading to Austin to talk to some of the Fortune Robinsons?"

"Eventually, but rather than barge in on them, I have another connection. The Mendozas."

"Sounds like a viable option," Nathan said. "Good luck."

She thanked him for his time, then headed for her car. She had another long drive in front of her. She wanted to be back in Austin before the end of the workday.

Or to be more exact, before the cocktail hour began at the Monarch Hotel.

Chapter Five

Carlo sat in the upscale lounge of the Monarch Hotel, a red glossy gift bag resting discreetly on the floor next to his chair. Nearly an hour ago, just after four o'clock, Schuyler called to let him know she'd hit the Austin city limits and to ask where to meet him.

He figured she'd been on the road long enough, so he'd suggested the hotel where she was staying.

Now, here he sat, watching the happy hour crowd with a glass of wine in front of him. He'd ordered the Lone Star, the Mendoza Winery's prize chardonnay, from the cocktail waitress, a quiet-spoken blonde in her thirties who'd introduced herself as Patty.

He'd taken only a couple of sips when Schuyler entered the lounge with a bounce in her step and a pretty smile on her face. You'd never have known that she'd spent the last ten to twelve hours driving.

She must have gone upstairs to her room to freshen up and change into the stylish little black cocktail dress she'd worn for a couple of hours for the tasting two nights ago. She looked just as sharp this evening, just as sexy. Maybe even more so.

As she approached his table, he stood to greet her, then he pulled out a chair for her. "How'd your visit with Nathan go?"

"It went okay. He's a nice guy, and I'm glad I had the chance to meet him, his wife and their sweet little boy. But he really didn't say anything to quench my curiosity about the family."

"Did you expect him to?"

"No, not really. But at least I've met him face-to-face. And now I have an in with him and his brothers."

"You'll also have a chance to meet more of the Austin Fortunes at the Valentine's Day party," he reminded her.

"That's true."

Carlo took his seat, motioned for Patty the cocktail waitress, then asked Schuyler, "What would you like to drink?"

"What are you having? Is that the Lone Star?" When he told her it was, she said, "I'll have that, too."

Once Patty arrived at their table, Carlo ordered another chardonnay.

"I poured quite a few glasses of Lone Star at that tasting, and several people raved about it. So I'm looking forward to trying it."

"I'm glad to hear that. You can't very well sell our wines if you haven't tasted them all."

"I agree."

He studied her a moment, the way her vibrant personality shined in her eyes, the way her blond tresses tumbled over her shoulders.

"What's the matter?" she asked. "Don't tell me I have spinach in my teeth."

He laughed and slowly shook his head at her humor. "No, I don't see anything out of place."

Only trouble was, he couldn't blame her for wondering why he was gawking at her. And he'd be damned if he wanted her to think he was caught up in his attraction.

"I was just admiring that pretty dress," he said. "It looks nicer on you each time I see it."

"Thanks. But don't worry. I'm going to do a little shopping while I'm in Austin. I have a closet full of appropriate evening wear at home, but I'm not going to drive back to Houston to get them. Especially after the tiring road trip I just made."

"I'm sure you're beat after going all the way to Paseo and back, but as a side note, you don't look all that tired to me."

"Maybe not. But I'm going to turn in early tonight. I have a feeling one glass of wine is going to do me in."

He didn't know what he'd been expecting, other than having a drink or two with her tonight. Dinner afterward, maybe. And possibly a visit to her room. But she'd just set the parameters.

Patty returned with Schuyler's drink, as well as a

small silver serving dish filled with mixed nuts. After she left them alone, Carlo reached under the table for the surprise he had for her. "Since you're going to kick back and relax after that drink, I thought I should give you this."

At the sight of the red gift bag, Schuyler's eyes widened. "I don't understand. What's this?"

"It's no big deal. Just something to show my appreciation for a job well done." He hoped she didn't think it was an early Valentine's Day gift. Of course, maybe it didn't matter what she thought until she peeked inside.

So he handed her the bag, eager to see the look on her face when she opened it and saw what he'd scored while shopping earlier today.

Schuyler loved surprises. She also loved presents, no matter what the cost. Over the years, she'd learned that it was often the least expensive things that meant the most. Yet before looking inside, she studied the bag in her hands for a moment, stunned that Carlo would give her a gift. "This is so unexpected."

"Aren't you going to open it?"

"Yes, of course." She pulled out the tissue paper and gasped at the fluffy white items inside. "I don't believe this." She withdrew one bunny slipper by the ear, then the other.

"I guessed at the size. So if they don't fit, you can exchange them."

"I'm sure they're perfect." As her eyes filled with tears, she did her best to blink them away. "I don't know how to thank you. This is the best gift ever. Where'd you find them? I mean, you must have taken the day off work and scoured every store in Austin."

He tossed her a boyish grin. "I'm not about to reveal all my secrets. But I have to admit, this is the first time I've given a present to someone who really appreciated it."

"Seriously?"

"Yep. And that smile on your face means it was a great investment."

An investment? "Were they expensive?"

"So asks the multimillionaire's daughter." Carlo laughed. "Don't worry. They were running a sale on bunny slippers at Dillard's in The Domain mall."

"I find that hard to believe, but thank you for putting so much thought into this. You're something else, Carlo. I can't believe a woman hasn't snatched you up and put a ring on your finger."

"Yeah, well...I was married once, but it didn't work out. I've come to believe that I'd be better off not making serious commitments."

Musical chords sounded in the background, followed by a microphone sound check. Schuyler glanced across the room, where a long-haired musician with a guitar and another with a keyboard were setting up so they could entertain people in the bar. But she was more interested in the handsome Latino who'd proved to be both generous and thoughtful.

He'd admitted to being married before, and if he'd decided not to make that mistake again, he must have been hurt by it. "I take it your divorce was painful."

"Actually, it was more disappointing than anything.

I'd never failed at anything in my life, so it was a hard pill to swallow. But then again, my parents didn't have a good marriage, either. So you can't blame me for being realistic about people not following through on those kinds of promises."

"Tell me about her."

"Who? Cecily? What do you want to know?"

"Whatever you feel like sharing. I'm curious about the woman who stole your heart."

"I don't know about that. I mean, I thought I loved her at the time, but in retrospect it was probably just lust. In the bedroom, things were good. But outside? There were problems from the start."

"Why's that?"

"I was only twenty-four, and she was two years younger. We were both headstrong and naive, and within a year, we were divorced."

"You don't think you could have worked things out, even with counseling?"

He shrugged a single shoulder. "I doubt it. To make matters worse, Cecily wanted babies right away and I wasn't ready. Besides, I didn't think we knew each other well enough."

"Maybe you didn't ask yourselves the right questions."

"That's possible." He grew solemn for a moment, then glanced at his nearly empty wineglass. When he looked up, he slowly shook his head. "I'm not sure why I'm telling you this. I have friends—good ones back in Miami—and I never shared any of the details with them."

"I'm easy to talk to, I suppose." That was probably why Glammy had told Schuyler more details about her love affair with Julius than she'd told her other grandchildren.

As one of the musicians sang the Otis Redding hit "(Sittin' On) The Dock of the Bay," Carlo reached out his hand. "Dance with me. This song reminds me of the ocean and my old stomping grounds."

He didn't have to ask her twice. She'd always loved this song. So she took his hand and let him lead her to the dance floor. He opened his arms, and she stepped into his embrace, swaying to the sultry tune.

The scent of Carlo's unique cologne reminded her of late-afternoon walks in Galveston, where she and Glammy had sometimes slipped away for what they called "girl time."

But as Schuyler rested her head against Carlo's shoulder as they moved to the sensuous beat, she wasn't having thoughts about afternoons on the bay. She was thinking about nighttime in an Austin hotel.

But that was crazy. It was too early, too soon to have thoughts like that. And as impulsive as she could be at times, making love with a man she'd met only a couple of days ago was sure to be a mistake.

When the song ended, and Carlo released her, she nearly swooned. She blamed it on the long drive and on that glass of wine that had gone right to her head, giving her romantic thoughts she didn't dare trust.

"I hope you don't mind if I call it a night," she said.

"No, I understand."

They stood on the dance floor for a moment, which

only gave her second thoughts about saying good-night. He'd said that since his divorce, he'd been avoiding serious commitments. That ought to make her feel better about having a short-term affair with him.

But for some reason, she wasn't opposed to striking up a relationship that might last a little longer. Because a man who'd gone out of his way to find her a pair of bunny slippers just might turn out to be a keeper.

She placed her hand on his chiseled jaw and placed a kiss on his cheek. "Thank you so much for the slippers."

"You're more than welcome."

That was her cue to leave, but she found herself vacillating. She was tempted to hang out for another glass of wine and one last dance. Either that or she could take him by the hand and lead him to the elevator.

She wasn't that buzzed. If and when she invited Carlo to her room, she didn't want her thoughts distorted by alcohol, lack of sleep or starry eyes.

"I'll make this up to you," she said.

"You already did."

He probably thought she meant her appreciation of his thoughtfulness and generosity, but it went beyond that.

"I'll see you on Thursday," she said. "And don't worry. I'll be there early, fully rested and prepared with my A game."

He gave her a dazzling smile that nearly stole her breath away. Then she walked back to the table and retrieved her purse and the gift bag. After taking one last glance at Carlo, she turned and headed for the elevator—alone. And wondering if she'd just made a big mistake.

* * *

True to her word, Schuyler arrived at the winery on Thursday afternoon an hour early and wearing a stylish red dress. On another woman, Carlo might have considered it a classic. But on Schuyler, it looked downright sexy. Talk about bringing her A game.

"You look great," he said. "Apparently you had a successful shopping trip yesterday."

"I certainly did." She gave a little twirl. "Will this do?"

He admired the red dress that hugged her curves. "It's perfect. Red is my new favorite color."

She laughed. "Oh yeah? What color used to be your favorite?"

"When we were at the Monarch Hotel, it was black."

"Great line, Carlo. But then again, I'm sure you've had a lot of practice charming the ladies."

True. But he hadn't been trying to charm Schuyler. That compliment was genuine and had just rolled off his tongue.

"Come on," he said. "I'll show you how we've got things set up for this event."

She fell into step beside him, and he took her inside the winery and to the tasting room, where they'd placed a sign on the large, rough-hewn wooden door that read: CLOSED FOR PRIVATE PARTY FROM 3 PM to 5 PM. PLEASE COME AGAIN.

Carlo reached for the brass handle and pulled open the door for her. Once she'd entered the reception area, he walked her to the marble-topped tasting bar, where she would be posted for the next two hours. Behind her was a tall linen-draped cocktail table holding an array of wineglasses, and a shelf with the corked bottles she would serve this afternoon.

"When it gets closer to three, the chef will send out a variety of gourmet crackers and cheeses, as well as sliced baguettes and fruit on that wooden trestle table."

"Is there anything else I need to know?" she asked.

"You certainly don't need instructions on how to be a hostess. Just do what you did the other night."

"Will do. But just so you know, I'm going to try and break my last sales record."

"Maybe I should pipe in music to set the mood. Something like 'Lady in Red' would be perfect."

"Hey. Are you trying to sell me or the wine?"

Actually, the thought of any other men ogling her and having romantic ideas didn't sit very well. But then again, he didn't have a claim on her. So he shook off the momentary jealousy and smiled. "You don't need any props, honey."

"Neither do you." If his term of endearment surprised or bothered her, she didn't let on.

He nodded toward the door. "Do you want a snack before the bus gets here?"

Her eyes sparkled with mirth. "Why? Do you want to raid the chef's fridge again?"

"No, we'll have to ask what he can spare. He's already back there, preparing for dinner."

"Cool," she said. "I'd like to meet him."

For a moment, Carlo's gut clenched. Bernardo Santos, the new chef he'd hired, was in his mid-thirties and had an eye for the ladies. Not that it mattered, he supposed. Schuyler was free to date anyone she wanted.

"Then come on. I'll introduce you." Carlo placed his hand on Schuyler's back and ushered her out of the tasting room and toward the kitchen. He could have walked next to her, his arms at his sides, but oddly enough, he didn't let go.

Instead, as their shoes clicked upon the tiled floor, he let his hand linger on her lower back as if staking his claim.

The tasting was in full swing, and the software execs seemed to be enjoying the wine Schuyler served them. She had to admit, they weren't the nerdy and boring group she'd expected them to be. Some of them were actually bright and witty.

Of course, there was usually one in every crowd that proved to be a jerk. And the guy wearing a ninja T-shirt and a black sports jacket was no exception. One of the others mentioned that Ninja Guy had been downing tequila shots at the restaurant where they'd had lunch.

With each sip of wine he took, Ninja Guy grew louder and more political. But it was impossible to decide whether he leaned to the left or right, because he voiced a loud and contrary response to any opinion.

"So how 'bout those Broncos?" he asked, switching from politics to sports. "Are you into football, pretty lady?"

"I'm not a huge fan, but I'll probably watch the Super Bowl on Sunday."

"I've got tickets to the company skybox," Ninja Guy

said. "Let me show you how the rich and famous watch the game."

A couple of the others at the table rolled their eyes. Schuyler was half tempted to do the same thing, but she'd promised Carlo she'd be a professional this afternoon.

In the meantime, she was cutting off Ninja Guy. He'd had way more than his share of wine, not to mention the tequila buzz he'd had when he arrived.

Carlo, who'd stepped out of the tasting room to write up several orders, returned to announce that dinner was being served in the main dining room. Those lingering in the tasting room began to file out the door. But not Ninja Guy.

He sidled up to Schuyler as she was replacing the cork in an open bottle. "Hey, sweetie. Why don't I help you clean up, then you can join me for dinner."

Carlo stiffened, but he clamped his mouth shut. She suspected he was tempted to speak up, to put the guy in his place. But he couldn't very well make a scene, especially when Ninja Guy had ordered several cases of the Lone Star, as well as the Red River. Why set him off?

"Thanks for the offer," she said, "but I've already eaten. So you go on to La Viña without me."

"Then join me in there for a drink. We can talk about watching the Super Bowl in that skybox."

"Sorry," she said. "I already have plans to watch the game with friends."

"You gotta be kidding me." He reached across the marble-topped bar and grabbed her hand.

The moment he touched her, Carlo moved across the

room, no doubt planning to come to her rescue. But he didn't know Schuyler very well. She was capable of taking care of herself.

She jerked her hand away and pointed her index finger at Ninja Guy, jabbing it at his chest. "Listen, jerk. I don't like to show off, but I've had years of karate training and have a black belt. You wouldn't want to limp back into the restaurant, sporting broken ribs, would you? I'd think that would embarrass you in front of your colleagues."

"Sheesh," he said, taking a step back. "I had no idea you were so temperamental."

Okay, so she'd lied and claimed to have a black belt, when she'd gotten only as high as green before telling her parents she was done with sports and had moved on to country line dancing.

"Mr. Layton," Carlo said. "Your friends are looking for you."

"Okay, I'm going." He nodded toward Schuyler and told Carlo, "Watch out for that one. She might be pretty, but she's got a mean streak."

As he shuffled out of the room, listing to one side, Schuyler looked at Carlo, who was shooting daggers at the drunk. His glare offered a warning that was as tough as any bouncer she'd ever watched in action.

When the door clicked shut, Carlo's expression softened. "I'm sorry about that. Usually, the people who come to our tastings are classy and don't arrive already liquored up."

"Don't worry about it. No harm, no foul."

Carlo slowly shook his head. "It took all I had not

to kick his butt all the way to the bus that brought him here."

"Maybe it'll do him good to get some food in his belly."

"Speaking of food, let's go get something to eat."

She tucked a strand of hair behind her ear, hesitant.

It's best to keep a man guessing, Glammy used to say. And in this case, maybe it was.

"Actually," she said, "I was thinking about heading back to the hotel. I'd rather not have to cross paths with Ninja Guy again. Otherwise, I might have to prove my skill at karate."

"Were you serious about being a black belt?"

"I'm afraid I was really stretching the truth. Not that I don't know some defensive moves I could have used on him."

A slow smile stretched across Carlo's face, creating boyish dimples in his cheeks.

"Just so you know," she said, "I can take care of myself. You wouldn't have had to kick his butt."

"I'll make a note of that." He nodded toward the door. "If you're dead set on heading back to the hotel, I'll walk you to your car."

"That's nice, but again, I'm not afraid of that guy."

"I didn't make the offer to protect you, although I'm definitely willing. But my mom insisted that I respect women, whether they have black belts or wear sexy red dresses."

"Aren't you a charmer."

"You say that like it's a bad thing."

"No, actually I'm a bit in awe of it." Then she reached out and slipped her arm through his. "Let's go."

As they stepped outside, the sun was setting, taking what little warmth it had provided earlier, and a crisp winter chill filled the air. Schuyler leaned into Carlo, absorbing some of his body heat and savoring his ocean-fresh scent.

She had half a notion to change her mind, to tell him she'd stick around after all. It wasn't like Glammy had been an expert on men or romance.

Did Carlo have any idea how appealing Schuyler found him? And not just as a person or a boss. But as a man. The guy was smart and personable. Generous and thoughtful, too. Who else would have thought to give her bunny slippers?

When they reached her car, she kept her arm in his, unwilling to let go yet. Apparently, he wasn't in any hurry, either, because they remained like that for a while.

"What do you have planned tomorrow?" he asked.

So he wanted to see her again? That was a good sign. At least, they seemed to be on the same page. "Not much. I got some shopping done yesterday. Did you need me to hostess another tasting?"

"Actually, I plan to scout around the downtown area and check out a few properties that are for sale. We plan to open a nightclub later this year, and there's a board meeting next week, so I'd like to have a few ideas to report, as well as some numbers. I realize you're not interested in real estate, but I thought I'd tap into your artistic and creative side."

It wasn't often that someone asked her opinion, especially when it came to business deals, especially real estate ventures. And the fact that Carlo had—and that he acknowledged her creativity—made her heart swell. "I'd love to go with you."

"Even to check out properties that are for lease or sale?"

"Believe it or not, that sounds like fun."

Carlo laughed. "Does anything *not* sound fun to you?"

"I'm not big on root canals—or dental visits in general."

"I'll make a mental note."

She turned to face him, still reluctant to get in her car and leave. As their gazes met, something passed between them. Something too big and powerful to ignore.

Carlo must have felt it, too, because he slipped his arms around her and drew her close. She suspected he intended to kiss her, which sounded a lot more fun than anything else he'd ever suggested.

When he lowered his mouth to hers, she closed her eyes and held on for what she suspected would be the ride of her life.

Chapter Six

Over the years, Carlo had experienced plenty of kisses, but he'd never had one quite like this. It began slowly and shyly, as he and Schuyler tested the sexual waters. But within a couple of heartbeats, it deepened and exploded with passion.

Schuyler leaned into him, and he pulled her close. Yet try as he might, he couldn't seem to get her close enough. While his hands caressed her back, exploring her curves and the slope of her hips, he relished her sweet taste, the floral scent of her shampoo and the feel of her in his arms.

He was never going to be content just spending the cocktail hour or a romantic dinner with her. Somehow, some way, he had to convince her that they had to take this newfound relationship to a deeper, more intimate level.

Of course, with the way she was kissing him back, convincing her wasn't going to take much effort on his part. Their mating tongues had kicked things up more than a notch already.

A car door opened and shut, bringing Carlo back to reality—if not his senses. He didn't especially care who'd caught them wrapped in a heated embrace, only that they'd been forced to stop.

With reluctance, he withdrew his lips from hers, glanced over his shoulder and spotted his father getting out of his car. Even in the waning light, he clearly saw the grin on his old man's face, one that shouted, *Attaboy, Carlo.*

"Good evening!" Esteban Mendoza's jovial tone damn near echoed through the vineyard. "I came to see how the tasting turned out, but by the look of things, I suspect it went especially well."

Carlo was never going to live this down. His father had been a ladies' man for years, maybe before his parents had actually divorced, although that was just his speculation. Either way, Esteban could appreciate the kind of kiss that was sure to spark a romantic liaison.

Schuyler, who seemed completely undaunted by the unexpected interruption, tossed his father a carefree grin. "I think it's fair to say everyone had a good time."

"Apparently." Esteban made his way closer, his smile deepening.

But then again, did Carlo even care what his old man thought, or what he might mention in front of his brothers? He was proud to have Schuyler in his arms. And if his luck held, in his bed.

"I certainly enjoyed the tasting this evening." Schuyler turned to Carlo, her eyes boasting an impish glimmer. "How about you?"

Whose side was she on? "I'd have to admit that it was probably the best I've had to date."

"That sounds promising." Esteban's smile widened. "I hope I didn't interrupt your…um…debriefing."

"Not at all," Schuyler said. "We're finished with that, and I was just leaving."

That's what she'd said, although Carlo wasn't ready to call it a day. Or rather, a night. And he'd hoped that the kiss they'd just shared might have changed her mind.

"Then I'll leave you to your goodbyes." Esteban pointed toward the new restaurant. "I'm going to see how things are going at La Viña."

As his father walked away, Carlo turned to Schuyler. "Should I apologize?"

"For what?"

Kissing her had been his first thought. Being caught had been his second. And his father's interruption of a heated moment came third. But she didn't seem to be the least bit concerned about any of it.

"I'm not going to dance around the issue," he said. "I like you, Schuyler. A lot. And there's definitely some mutual attraction at play."

"I won't argue that."

"Then why don't we let things play out between us and see what happens?"

She laughed. "I thought that's what this kiss was all about. And just for the record, I thought it played out nicely."

So it had.

"We clearly have chemistry," she admitted. "And I'm not at all opposed to seeing where a little romance might lead. But I'd hate to complicate things."

He supposed that she was talking about their working relationship. It was also possible that she was concerned about her upcoming introduction to some of the Fortunes who were in the inner circle. But he wasn't about to renege on the deal they'd made—even if a short-term affair didn't work out.

"We've both admitted that we're not interested in a serious relationship," he said. "So we can certainly keep things light and easy. And fun."

"Now, that's an interesting thought."

He figured she'd like that idea, since she'd made no secret of having a playful side.

"Why don't you sleep on the idea?" he suggested. "We can talk more about it tomorrow."

She blessed him with a bright-eyed smile that nearly lit the evening sky. "That works for me."

It definitely worked for him, too.

He kissed her one last time for the road. And to give her more romantic fodder to sleep on.

When Carlo drove into the porte cochere at the entrance of the Monarch Hotel, Schuyler was seated on a wrought iron bench near the valet desk, a disposable Starbucks coffee cup in her hand and that big black Chanel purse resting beside her.

That morning she'd pulled her hair up into a messy but stylish topknot and wore a red long-sleeve T-shirt, snug black jeans and running shoes. The moment she spotted his car, she flashed a happy grin and got to her feet.

Before either Carlo or the valet could get the door for her, she opened it herself and slid into the passenger seat, clearly eager to set out on their latest adventure.

But heck, so was Carlo.

As her breezy scent, something soft and floral, infiltrated his car and invaded his senses, he said, "I didn't expect you to be ready, but I'm glad you are."

"I'm always ready for an adventure."

Apparently so. For some reason, he'd assumed a pretty, stylish and wealthy woman like her would relish her beauty rest and take her time getting ready in the morning. But it hadn't taken Carlo long to realize Schuyler was unpredictable and not at all like other women.

He liked that about her.

In fact, when it came to Schuyler Fortunado, there was a lot to like. And he wasn't just counting those luscious blond locks, sparkling blue eyes and soft pink lips that could kiss a man senseless. She had an effervescent personality that kept him interested, intrigued. And completely engaged.

A man who had preconceived ideas about romance could find himself at a disadvantage with her. If he expected to tie her down in any way, he'd risk being disappointed or hurt. And if the poor guy thought he'd fallen in love with her, he might just convince himself that he actually liked having his life turned upside down.

Carlo would have to stay on his toes around her,

although he really wasn't worried. He always kept his romantic relationships lighthearted and simple.

As he pulled onto the city street, she asked, "Where are we going first?"

"I heard about an old bank building downtown that's vacant and for sale. It will need renovating, but it might have a lot of potential as a nightclub."

"Are you meeting the listing agent?" she asked.

"No, not this time. I'm just scouting the area before reporting back to the family."

"When you're done with the preliminary footwork, and if you decide to check out that property, you should consider calling my sister. Maddie works out of the Houston office, but she's really good at negotiating commercial deals. And while you could work directly with the seller's agent, the buyers should have someone who can watch out for their best interests."

Carlo had planned on getting an agent to represent the family. If he still lived in Florida, where he had a lot of contacts and connections, he'd know just who to call. But he hadn't researched any of the local agencies yet.

Still, Schuyler's suggestion was sound. Fortunado Real Estate had a solid, statewide reputation, with offices in Houston, San Antonio and Austin.

"I just might call your sister," he said. "But I have a question for you. Why didn't you suggest that I call your father?"

"No reason, really. My dad is the best commercial Realtor in the state, if not the entire country. But he's pretty busy."

"That's not surprising. He's built an impressive company."

"That's true, although my mom would like him to slow down, if not retire."

"For health reasons?"

"No, that's not it."

Schuyler had made no secret of the man's financial success, so Carlo assumed his wife would like him to enjoy the fruits of his labor.

"My dad worked very hard to build the company, so he's reluctant to pass the baton. But there's no reason he can't slow down some. My sister could run things blindfolded and with her hands tied behind her back."

"Do you think he'll eventually let her take over?"

Schuyler shrugged. "My mom would love that, but who knows?"

She grew silent as Carlo drove to the downtown area. He wasn't sure what Schuyler was thinking about. Her family and the successful empire her father had built, he supposed.

As his own thoughts drifted to finding the right property, making a good deal and jumping into the renovations, his enthusiasm soared.

Going to work with Alejandro and his brothers had been a smart move for him, a good one in which he'd found his true calling. He had a growing fervor to help build the winery and to expand the family's interests.

When he left Miami, he'd hoped that would happen, but he hadn't been sure it would. In the past, his initial passion for a project would peak then wane, and after a while, he'd become disenchanted and bored.

The same could be said for his love life, he supposed. After dating a woman for a couple of months, he'd lose interest in her, too.

He shot a glance across the seat at Schuyler, who was watching the city skyline, her eyes aglow. There was something special about her, something vital that sparked his excitement.

A smile tickled his lips. He had a feeling that he wasn't going to lose interest in this woman anytime soon.

As he pulled in front of the empty three-story brick building that had once housed a bank, he pointed it out to Schuyler.

"Wow," she said. "You were right. This place has a lot of potential."

That's what Carlo had thought when he'd first checked out the pictures on the internet and researched its history. "It was originally built in the mid-1880s and then renovated in the 1920s. But when the depression hit, it closed down."

"Has it been vacant all that time?"

"No, it's had several owners since then. It's also housed various offices and businesses. A couple years ago, a guy bought it with the intention of turning it into a trendy restaurant, but he died before finishing it. There were some legal issues when his heirs divided the estate, but from what I understand, the property is going on the market soon."

"I think you ought to snatch it up," Schuyler said. "What an awesome location for a nightclub. My mind is abuzz with ideas. I can't wait to see the interior."

Carlo felt the same way. His mind was spinning with the possibilities, too. And interestingly enough, he wanted Schuyler to be with him when he got his first look inside.

Maybe it was time to call Maddie Fortunado. But talk about complicating things. All he needed was to be knee-deep in a real estate negotiation with Schuyler's sister when—not *if*—their romantic relationship went south.

But he wouldn't let things become so involved that there'd be a blowup when they parted ways. Besides, they'd already decided to take things slow and easy.

Of course, if he kissed her again, things could escalate faster than either of them anticipated. But would that be bad?

Not unless he didn't handle their breakup well and things went up in smoke at the end.

"What other properties are you considering?" Schuyler asked.

With her sudden interest in the bank property, you'd never have known she'd been reluctant to work with her father's company. But then again, family dynamics could be difficult for outsiders to understand.

"There's an old warehouse about a mile from here," he said. "It has a lot of potential, too, but I'm not thrilled with the location. It's a little too far away from downtown."

"You might be surprised when you see it," she said.

"I agree."

Carlo took her to see that property, as well as another that was located a bit farther outside town. But they both came to the conclusion that the bank property would work best—if it went on the market. And if they could negotiate a good price.

As they left the last warehouse, Carlo was about to suggest they drive back to town and have lunch at a new café that had opened up across the street from her hotel, when Schuyler stiffened, pointed out the passenger window and yelled, "Stop."

"What's the matter?"

"I need to get out."

Stunned, he pulled to the side of the road. Had she gotten sick?

While the engine idled, Schuyler opened the door, jumped from the car and hurried across a vacant lot. He glanced in the rearview mirror, then turned in his seat and looked over his shoulder. He watched as she approached a big scraggly bush, its branches and leaves rustling.

She knelt down on the dried grass, as if paying homage to the wild shrub, and patted her hands on her thighs. Moments later, a scruffy little dog crept out from its hiding place, followed by another mutt that looked just like it.

Strays, he suspected. Was that why she'd wanted to stop?

She cooed to the small critters, then reached out to pick them up. Once they were both balanced in her arms, she carried them back to the car.

Seriously? What did she plan to do with them?

Now, there was a silly question. Obviously, she was

bringing them back to his car for a reason. And not one he was likely to appreciate.

Upon her approach, she called out, "Can you please get the door for me?"

He had half a notion to object, but instead, he leaned over, reached across the seat and opened it for her.

"Look what I found. Puppies. Two of them. And just look at the sweet little things. They're darling."

Actually, they were dirty and scrawny. And flea-bitten, no doubt.

"Can you believe someone would just drop them off on the side of the road like that?" she asked.

Actually, he could believe it. It wasn't right, but some people abandoned animals all too often. "What are you going to do with them?"

"If I can't find a home for them, I'm going to keep them."

His brow lifted. "You're staying in a hotel, remember? And I don't think a place as nice as the Monarch is going to let you keep them there."

"I know. But we can't leave them here."

Carlo had to agree, even though he wasn't what you'd call a dog lover. Sure, he and his brothers had pets as kids, but once they'd gotten into high school, their interests had turned to sports and girls.

He shot a glance across the seat, wondering what the dirty critters would look like once they had a bath. One pup, the smaller of the two, licked Schuyler's cheek. A love offering for being rescued, it seemed.

Apparently, she'd interpreted the doggie kiss the same way he had because she said, "Aw, sweetie, you're welcome. I wasn't going to leave you back there to starve to death or get hit by a car."

"What if the hotel won't let you keep them?" he asked.

"I'll think of something."

Hopefully, she didn't expect him to take them. His life wasn't conducive to caring for pets, for pooper-scoopers and walks in the park. Besides, he lived in a high-rise apartment that probably wasn't any more dog friendly than the Monarch.

"You'd better come up with a plan B," he said.

"I know." She grew somber for a moment, then said, "They've got to be hungry—and thirsty. I'm going to have to find a place that sells dog food."

"They're also in need of a good bath. And a flea dip. I suspect that a place that works with pets will have food and water for them, too."

"Then I'll have to find a groomer."

No wonder her family found her a bit on the impulsive side. But she clearly had a big heart, and he had a hard time finding fault in her for that.

As he headed back to the city, he picked up his iPhone, brought up Siri and said, "Directions to the nearest pet groomer."

When Siri responded with the name of The Pampered Fido, Schuyler got on her own smartphone and called to see if they had any openings today—and sooner, rather than later. As luck would have it, they could fit in both dogs if they came now.

"I hate to have you drive me all over town," Schuyler

said. "Do you have time to drop off the dogs and then take me back to the Monarch?"

"I'll make time." Otherwise, she and those dirty pups would be turned away before they could step foot onto the hotel premises. And where would that leave Carlo?

Besides, as much as he'd like to deny it, he had a heart, too. Not just for animals, but for pretty blondes who were more impetuous and loving than they ought to be.

Still, he had to admit this was a first. No other woman he'd ever dated, including Cecily, his ex-wife, would have been able to talk him into driving dirty, stinky dogs to the pet groomer. But hell, for some reason, he found himself on a constant adventure with Schuyler. One that, in her words, sounded like fun.

For the next ten minutes, Carlo followed the directions Siri gave him. At the same time, Schuyler juggled the pups in her arms while fiddling with her smartphone.

"What are you doing?" he asked.

"I think you were right about the Monarch Hotel, so I've been looking for a small studio apartment that's pet friendly and will allow me to sign a month-to-month lease."

So she planned to extend her stay in Austin, at least for the time being. He supposed that was good. He couldn't very well expect her to continue being a hostess for his special wine tastings while staying in a hotel. Besides, a month-to-month lease made good sense financially—no matter how healthy her trust fund might be.

And since she wasn't making a permanent move,

it suggested that she considered their relationship—either working or otherwise—to be temporary. And that meant she and Carlo were both on the same page.

"Are you having any luck?" he asked her a few minutes later.

"Actually, I am. There's an intern in my dad's Austin office who's been helping me, and he just found the perfect place." She slipped her phone into her bag, then glanced up at him and bit down on her bottom lip. "I'm sorry. I'm not trying to monopolize your day or take advantage of you. Once we drop off the dogs at The Pampered Fido, you can take me back to the hotel."

"What are you going to do there?"

"I'll check out and take my own car to pick up the dogs. Then I'll move into my new digs."

Carlo had plenty he could do this afternoon, but for some crazy reason, he didn't mind spending more time with her. "As long as I can get to the winery before La Viña opens for dinner, I don't mind helping you and the pups get settled."

She blessed him with a grateful smile. "I really appreciate this."

"No problem."

Her expression grew serious, and he watched her for a moment as her brow furrowed. When she looked up, she blew out a little sigh. "I'll also need to pick up some dog food, chew toys and maybe a couple of pet carriers."

Hopefully, they'd have enough hours in the day to accomplish everything she needed to do. But she couldn't very well adopt two puppies without getting the proper supplies.

Carlo had planned to take her to lunch, but since time was of the essence, their eatery options were limited.

"I've got an idea," he said. "Why don't we pick up sandwiches at a deli and find someplace outdoors where we can eat?"

"A picnic? That sounds fun."

Carlo chuckled and slowly shook his head. "I think *fun* is your middle name, Schuyler."

"It probably should be."

No doubt. Then he continued the drive, feeling as though he'd just agreed to be her partner in crime.

And hoping he didn't live to regret it.

Chapter Seven

While Carlo waited in the car, Schuyler dropped off the two pups at The Pampered Fido to be bathed, dipped and groomed.

"My goodness." Trudy, the shop owner, reached for one of the dirty dogs. "They're a mess."

"I found them in an abandoned lot," Schuyler said. "I couldn't just leave them there."

"I'm glad you brought them to me. And that I was able to fit them in. But I can't groom them unless they've had their first round of shots and been seen by a vet."

"I'd planned to have them examined, but I haven't gotten around to it yet."

"You know," Trudy said, "there's a new veterinary clinic across the street. Dr. Mayfield just opened his practice and isn't very busy yet. I'm sure he'll be able to check them out for you today."

"I wonder how long that'll take. My friend is in the car and doesn't have a lot of time." Schuyler bit down on her bottom lip, wondering if she'd have to take a rain check on that picnic after all.

"You're in luck," Trudy said. "The vet has a real heart for strays and people who rescue them. I'm sure I can get him to examine the dogs. He's probably on his lunch hour and might come right over."

"That would be awesome."

Trudy made a phone call, then gave Schuyler a thumbs-up. "Dr. Mayfield will be here in five minutes. He also said their first exam and shots are free."

Schuyler hadn't expected to get a deal, but the gesture was nice. And it was a good way for the vet to get new patients.

"You mentioned that your friend was on a time schedule," Trudy said, "so if you need to go, the vet can examine them here. I'll give you a call if he has any issues or concerns."

"That's really sweet of you. I need to shop for pet supplies, plus I'm moving into a new place this afternoon."

"I'll need two hours for their doggie makeovers," Trudy said. "You won't recognize these little guys when you come back."

"How much do I owe you?" Schuyler asked.

"Not a thing. Their first grooming is on me. I'll even feed them while you're gone."

The smallest pup whined as Schuyler walked out the

door, but she continued to Carlo's car, knowing they'd be in loving hands.

Once she climbed in, he started the engine and glanced across the seat. "Are you ready for lunch?"

"I'm hungry, but I think it would be best if we picked up the puppy supplies first."

"Sounds like a plan." Before backing out of the parking space, Carlo asked Siri for directions to the nearest pet supply store, which turned out to be a ten-minute drive from the groomer.

Once they arrived and began walking down the aisles, it took Schuyler another ten minutes to find everything on her mental shopping list. Only trouble was, one cart wasn't enough, and Carlo had to retrieve a second cart to fit everything she wanted to buy.

As they stood at the register, Schuyler turned to Carlo. "I can't believe you're being such a good sport about this. If the men in my family had to follow me around a store, especially one like this, they would have moaned and groaned about it."

"To be honest, I usually avoid going to malls or stores with women. In my experience, they tend to lollygag and ponder their purchases way longer than necessary, which only makes me grumpy. And then afterward, they can't seem to figure out why I'm in a bad mood."

"When I go to a store, I don't mess around. I make quick decisions." Too quick, if you asked her father.

Schuyler studied Carlo carefully, that dark hair a woman could run her hands through, those sparkling brown eyes, that dazzling smile. No sign of a bad mood there. And he hadn't uttered a single groan or moan.

She nudged him with her elbow and gave a little wink. "Apparently, going shopping with me doesn't make you the least bit grumpy."

"That's not surprising. I was more in awe than anything. You zoomed through this store like you were on a television game show, competing in a winner-take-all shopping spree."

She laughed. "See? Like I told you before, you've been dating the wrong women."

He winked back at her. "You might be right about that."

For a moment, she wondered if they'd stumbled onto a good thing, a special relationship that might last longer than a few weeks. Either way, they seemed to have become friends. Teammates, even. And that realization sent a little thrill right through her.

In the past, she would have been tempted to put on the brakes, but with Carlo... Well, the thought of nurturing whatever it was they'd found struck a chord. She felt almost hopeful.

But just in case her thoughts took a wrong turn, she reminded herself that Carlo had made it very clear that he wasn't into long-term relationships. And that he didn't make romantic commitments.

Schuyler didn't make them, either. Maybe that's why she felt good about this. About them.

Carlo would make the perfect fling. Yet something else niggled at her, causing her to question her long-held beliefs. He might also be the one man who could change her mind about what she wanted out of a romantic relationship, what she needed. And that might lead to disaster.

As the clerk bagged the last of her purchases—two doggie beds—Schuyler studied the carts loaded with the bagged items and scrunched her brow. "Uh-oh."

At that, Carlo laughed. "What's the matter? Now that you're calculating the cost, are you having a little buyer's remorse?"

"No, it's not that. I'm just worried that we can't fit all of this stuff in your car."

"I have a good-size trunk. And a backseat."

"Oh, good. That's a relief. I didn't want to have to put anything back."

He laughed. "Those two strays must think they died and went to doggie heaven. They've gone from rags to riches in one lucky day. Now they'll have everything a mutt could ever want."

Schuyler handed her credit card to the clerk, then turned to Carlo and slapped her hands on her hips. "Are you making fun of me and my new pets?"

"No, not at all. In fact, I'm enjoying this more than I'd expected. But for a while, I thought we'd need a third cart. And I wondered if we'd have to make two trips to lug all this loot back to the Monarch."

"Um... You know what?" She looked up at him and smiled. "We might have to make two trips to my new place, though. I've done some shopping, and my new suitcases alone are going to fill my trunk."

He glanced at his wristwatch. "Unless your studio apartment is clear across town, and you drag your feet until we have to deal with rush-hour traffic, I should be able to make it back to the winery before the dinner hour—and with time to spare."

If they'd been in Houston, Schuyler would have known the best route to take, but she wasn't the least bit familiar with Austin and could only relate what she'd been told. "According to my dad's intern, my new place is about ten minutes from the hotel."

"Then we should be fine."

That was good to know. She didn't want him to be late for work.

When the clerk returned her credit card, Schuyler pushed one cart out of the store, while Carlo pushed the other.

"If we run late," she said, "and it looks like you can't get back to the winery on time, I'll take a rain check on that picnic in the park."

"We'll see how things work out. But if we can't find time to eat, then maybe we can have that picnic at the winery tomorrow or the next day."

"That would be awesome. But can I bring the dogs?"

"Seriously?"

"Absolutely. I'm not going to be an irresponsible pet owner."

Carlo froze in his steps and studied her as if she'd placed a bird's nest on her head.

"Uh-oh," she said. "Don't look at me like that."

"Like what?"

"Like you've just lumped me in with all the women you date—the boring and predictable ones."

A slow smile slid across his face, and he reached out and cupped her jaw. "No way, Schuyler. You might surprise me at times, and maybe even exasperate me, but I'd never lump you in with anyone. You're in a class all by yourself."

She'd never had a compliment like that, one that praised her uniqueness. A gush of warmth filled her chest.

"I'm touched," she said. More than he could possibly know. But the years she'd spent trying to explain and defend herself and her uniqueness brought out the skeptic in her. Rather than question him or herself, she nodded toward his car. "Let's get out of here. I'd like to squeeze in that picnic with you today. And as my hero, John Wayne, would say, 'We're burning daylight.'"

"So you're a John Wayne fan?" he asked, falling into step beside her.

"Glammy was. And since I used to watch a lot of Westerns with her, I liked him, too."

"The Duke was definitely a hero," he said.

That was true, but right now, Carlo seemed to be Schuyler's hero. And she wasn't sure if she should embrace that thought or run for the hills.

While Carlo waited for Schuyler to check out of the Monarch Hotel, he talked to the valet who'd brought up her Beamer from the garage and asked about their pet policy.

"Service dogs are okay," the young man said. "But the management really frowns on pets."

That's what Carlo had thought. But since Schuyler had already found another place to stay that would allow her to keep those puppies, she'd managed to circumvent the problem. And he found that to be interesting. She might be quirky, fun-loving and a bit impulsive at times, but she also seemed to think things through.

Just as the valet brought up her car, Schuyler exited the hotel, along with a bellman pushing a loaded luggage cart. While she tipped both men, Carlo helped them put everything in her trunk. Then he followed behind her car on the drive to her new, temporary residence, which was located on a tree-lined street in what appeared to be a quiet neighborhood.

He parked behind her along the curb in front of an older two-story brick home. They both got out of their cars, and he followed her to the front door.

"My place is in back," she said, as she rang the bell.

Moments later, a gray-haired woman wearing a blue-and-green muumuu and pink slippers answered the door. All the while, a big orange tabby cat threaded in and out of the woman's legs.

Schuyler introduced herself, and the woman reached out her hand in greeting. "I'm Dorothy Coggins, but you can call me Dottie."

"It's nice to meet you," Schuyler said. Then she turned and introduced Carlo as her friend. "He's helping me move in."

"Isn't that nice? And he's a good-lookin' fella to boot."

Schuyler glanced at Carlo and gave him a little wink. "That he is. Lucky me."

"That nice young man I talked to from the real estate office transferred the deposit and the first month's rent into my bank account. He looked over the lease I emailed him and said you'd sign it when you got here."

Once the paperwork was taken care of, Dottie lifted her arm, which sported a key connected to a red stretchy band around her wrist. She removed it and handed it to Schuyler. "Here you go." Then she stooped down and lifted the fat cat into her arms. "This is Rusty, our resident mouser."

"Aren't you a sweetie," Schuyler said, as she stroked the feline's head.

Dottie smiled, clearly pleased by the affectionate gesture, then she scanned their parked cars, her brow furrowed. "Where are the puppies?"

"They're at the groomer," Schuyler said. "As soon as I bring them home, I'll ring your bell so you can meet them."

A smile tugged at one side of Carlo's lips, and he slowly shook his head. He liked animals, but he doubted he'd ever become so attached to one that he'd introduce it to the people he'd just met. But it was nice to think that Schuyler and her new landlady had something in common.

Dottie seemed to be a real character, a bit like he'd imagined Schuyler's grandmother had been. Maybe that was why they seemed to hit it off so well—and so quickly.

"I suggest you follow the graveled drive to the back," Dottie said. "That way, it'll be easier for you to unload your things. And just like I told that nice young man from the real estate office, that apartment isn't much. But it's clean and fully furnished."

"I saw the pictures he sent me, Dottie. I'm sure it'll work out just fine."

Ten minutes later, Carlo had helped Schuyler unload her purchases and her luggage into the small studio apartment. Dottie had been right, it wasn't much to shout about, but it had been scrubbed clean. He just hoped Schuyler's new pets didn't tear the place apart. If they did, that "nice young man" would have to forfeit whatever deposit Fortunado Real Estate had paid.

Finally, as the afternoon sun began a steady descent in the west, they returned to the groomer for the dogs. The happy pups didn't look anything like they had when they'd been dropped off. Their black-and-white fur was no longer dirty and matted down. Instead, it was glossy and puffy.

"Dr. Mayfield said they appear to be in good health," the groomer said. "He thinks they're about four to five months old. He also left you his card."

Schuyler pocketed the vet's contact information. "I'd certainly use him again."

"He also thought they had some cocker spaniel in their genes—and a little terrier. I think they might even have a little poodle in them, although it's hard to say."

Carlo hated to admit it, but the darn little mutts were actually cute. And those matching red collars fit perfectly.

"Look at them," Schuyler said. "Aren't they darling?"

"They do look a lot better now that they're clean," he admitted.

Schuyler turned to the groomer. "Thanks so much, Trudy. You did an awesome job."

"You're more than welcome. I hope you'll bring them back here for their next grooming."

"I'll definitely do that, although I'm not sure how long I'll be in town. I'm more or less a tourist. In fact, I have a couple of questions for you. Where's the nearest deli? And is there a park nearby where we can eat?"

"Well, there's a sandwich shop a few doors to the left. And there's a dog-friendly park about two blocks down from that and across the street."

"Great." Schuyler glanced at the clock hanging on the wall. "That'll work out perfectly. Thanks so much."

"Have you thought about what you're going to name the pups?" Trudy asked.

"I was going to call one of them Scruffy, but that was before their baths. I think Fluffy is more fitting now."

Trudy chuckled. "Since that little one really packed away his puppy food, you might want to call him Stuffy."

Schuyler laughed. "I like that. But maybe I'll shorten it to Fluff and Stuff."

After taking Trudy's business card, Schuyler placed both pooches on the sidewalk and let them try out their new leashes. But unfortunately, the neglected pups didn't like being under submission to humans. They each pulled this way and that, eager to go in different directions—and not to the left, where the sandwich shop was located.

"When it comes to training those dogs," Carlo said, "you're going to have your work cut out for you."

"Maybe so. But I think these little guys are going to turn out to be very bright. Besides, other than being a hostess at those special tastings you set up, I have plenty of time on my hands."

Actually, Carlo might just take up some of that free time himself.

"Why don't you let me carry Stuff." Carlo stooped and picked up the smallest pup. "Like you and the Duke said, 'We're burning daylight.' And I'd like to enjoy a little time in the park before I head to the winery."

"Good idea. I'm really hungry."

Fifteen minutes later, with their sandwiches, chips and sodas packed in two white sacks, they arrived at a small grassy area that wasn't quite what Carlo would call a park, although it had several picnic tables and a very small playground. It also had a green dispenser that provided plastic baggies. "So that's what Trudy meant by saying this park was dog friendly."

"I guess so. And it looks like we're the only ones here."

Carlo nodded to an empty table near a water fountain. "Should we sit there?"

"Yes, that's perfect." When she reached the spot, she placed Fluff down on the grass.

The critter didn't seem to mind its leash now, as it sniffed around, checking out its surroundings. Carlo set Stuff down next to Fluff.

While he removed the food from the sacks, Schuyler reached into her Chanel bag and pulled out several wipes. "Here. Now we can clean our hands."

"Thanks." He wondered what else she carried in that big bag. "Apparently you think of everything."

"I try."

He liked that about her. Hell, he liked too damn much about her. If pressed, he could probably create a list of things as long as the park bench on which they sat.

That ought to bother a man who'd made up his mind to keep his relationships simple and unencumbered, but that philosophy didn't seem quite as ingrained in him as it was before he'd met Schuyler.

He glanced at the tabletop, where someone had carved initials. He traced the letters with his finger. *B.K. Loves R.L.*

Who had defaced the public property in the attempt to proclaim his or her affection? A starry-eyed teenager? Or someone old enough to know better?

When it came to love, Carlo had been there, done that and bought the souvenir shot glass. So he was certainly old enough to know better.

Or was he? Each time Schuyler smiled at him, flashing those cute little dimples, or whenever he caught the soft lilt of her laugh, he found himself wondering if…

Now *that* was troubling. What in the hell was Schuyler doing to him? It was as if he'd morphed into a guy he no longer knew.

He scanned the small grassy area where they ate, then glanced at the table again, at the turkey sandwiches, half-eaten and resting on paper napkins, at the two cans of soda pop—root beer and black cherry.

Carlo enjoyed fine wines and classy restaurants. He didn't do parks or picnics. Yet here he was, listening to Schuyler tell a story about the time she and her beloved but eccentric grandmother made a trip to an animal shelter in Houston.

"Glammy told me she just wanted to look at the puppies and maybe play with the kitties in what she called the cat house. But when we entered the office and she spotted a three-legged cat and a one-eyed dog in the office, she was toast."

"What'd she do? Adopt them and take them home?"

Schuyler nodded. "That's exactly what she did. Their numbers were up, and they were going to be put to sleep at the end of the day. So Glammy adopted them herself. She called them Tripod and Pirate. I thought it was pretty cool, but my dad couldn't understand why she'd want to pour her love and attention on a couple of old, defective animals. But I don't think he ever really understood her need to make some kind of difference in the world. Instead, he only saw her as *being* different."

Schuyler's eyes glistened with unshed tears, and Carlo found himself sympathizing with the damaged pets, the quirky grandmother and the little girl who'd loved and admired her Glammy.

As a flood of compassion swept through his chest, he found himself smiling and admiring Glammy, too. "I wish I could have met her. It sounds like she had a lot of pluck, as well as a big heart."

Schuyler gave a little laugh, one that sounded bittersweet. "She did. I wish you could have met her, too."

"Whatever happened to Tripod and Pirate?"

Schuyler let out a sigh. "I wish I could tell you that there was a moral to the story."

"What do you mean?"

"You know, like on Facebook? When a family rescues a dog, then it eventually alerts them to a fire or a burglar or pulls their drowning toddler out of the pool?"

Carlo nodded, although he wasn't a big Facebook fan. And on those rare occasions when he did check out his home page, he usually passed right over those kinds of posts.

"It would have been pretty cool to tell my dad that one of those pets saved Glammy's life, but Tripod nearly broke her neck. One day she was bringing in her groceries from the car, and Tripod dashed out the door, tripping her and causing her to fall down. Before she could get up and chase after him, he was hit by a car."

"Dang, that's terrible."

"I know. It was very sad, but he died instantly. And the vet insisted that he didn't feel any pain."

"And what about Pirate?"

Schuyler's lips quirked into a crooked grin. "He spent a lot of time in the proverbial doghouse, but she finally found him a new home after he chewed up her vintage white go-go boots."

"She booted the dog out?" Carlo asked. "No pun intended."

"At first, she only scolded him and sent him out into the backyard to sleep. She had a soft heart and would have forgiven him by morning, but he howled like one of the hounds of hell, and she was afraid he'd wake the neighbors. So she brought him inside. The next day, she gave him to a friend who lived in the country and needed a watch dog." Schuyler tossed her hair over her shoulder. "Still, you have to give Glammy credit for at least trying to give Pirate and Tripod a loving home and new leases on life."

Carlo glanced at the frisky little puppies whose luck had changed the moment Schuyler spotted them.

Was Carlo's luck about to change, too? He'd never thought he'd needed it to. Not after his and Cecily's divorce was final and he'd picked himself up, dusted himself off and created a new philosophy on romance and dating, which meant that a helpmate was no longer in his future.

But something told him a change was in the wings. What kind of change, he really couldn't say. And that possibility left him more than a little unbalanced.

Over the next week, Schuyler represented the Mendoza brand at several of Carlo's special tastings and at an industry-wide event that was held last night in one of the downtown luxury hotels. She consistently brought in new orders that increased business, and the entire Mendoza clan not only thanked her, they raved about the amazing job she was doing for them.

Yet it was Carlo's praise that pleased her the most. He always made a point of complimenting her efforts at the wrap-up of each event, but he really didn't need to say a word. While he observed her from the sidelines, she could read his appreciation in his supportive stance, in the tilt of his smile and in the intensity of his gaze as it focused on her every move. And that pretty much said it all.

He'd watched her the same way today, during an

afternoon tasting at the winery. Then he'd slipped out of the room with the last of the guests, leaving her alone.

Outside, Fluff and Stuff frolicked on the grass. She could see them through the big bay window that looked out at the sculpture garden, where they rolled around, nipping at each other. It was a game they liked to play.

She supposed she should take them home now, but she decided to first wipe up a small spill that had splashed on the bar. So she bent to retrieve a dampened cloth she kept on one of the shelves underneath.

Before she could straighten, a familiar male voice called out, "Hey."

She glanced up to see Carlo entering the room wearing a sexy grin, and her heart rumbled in her chest. She tamped down the sudden thrill at his return, offered him a breezy smile and called out a "Hey" right back to him.

"Thanks for another successful day," he said. "That group just placed over two thousand dollars in orders. Good job."

"You're welcome." It wasn't often that people took Schuyler seriously, so she appreciated it when someone did. Especially this particular someone.

Silence filled the room. Sometimes, when they faced each other like this—neither of them saying a word, his praise stoking her pride—they seemed to be tiptoeing around... What exactly? She didn't know for sure, and it was probably best that she not put too much thought into it. So she broke eye contact and wiped down the marble-topped bar, even though it no longer needed it.

Still, she couldn't keep the thoughts from churning

in her mind. They'd talked about making love. At least, they'd done so indirectly. But so far they'd shared only a few heated kisses.

Sure, they flirted with each other when no one was around, but they'd yet to take that extra step. She was ready, though. She just hadn't done anything to instigate it.

And why was that? She'd never had trouble taking a bold step before. She'd never sat on the sidelines when something needed to be done. But she'd never actually made a brazen sexual move.

Schuyler might be quick to react at times, but for some reason, she was more cautious with Carlo. And there was good reason for it. He was a dyed-in-the-wool bachelor who only played at romance, and she knew better than to expect any more from him than fun and games.

Still, wasn't that what she'd wanted? A lighthearted fling while she was in Austin?

"You don't need to clean up," Carlo said, as he approached the bar where she worked. "The janitor will be here this evening."

"I know. I just want to wipe up a few splatters of spilled wine."

As he leaned against the bar, coming dangerously close as far as her hormones were concerned, she caught a whiff of his sea-breeze scent. Her heart rate, which was already escalated, slipped into overdrive. Dang, the guy did something to her. Something that made her hands tremble. But she'd be darned if she'd let the sexy Latino know that.

Attempting an unaffected pose, she reached under the bar, where she kept her purse, pulled out a pack of breath mints and held it out to him. "Would you like one?"

"No, thanks. I'm still enjoying the taste of the chocolate truffle I just stole from the kitchen."

"And you didn't think to bring one to me?"

"That was pretty thoughtless, huh?"

She chuckled. "Chef Bernardo ought to ban you from his territory for snatching so many snacks." She popped one peppermint mint into her mouth and replaced the rest in her bag.

Focus, she told herself. But that was hard to do when rebellious hormones were telling her brain to stand down.

As she retrieved the damp cloth she'd been using and swept it across the marble top one last time, her elbow brushed against a stack of paper cocktail napkins, causing them to flutter to the floor. "Oops."

She and Carlo bent at the same time to pick them up, and their hands met. Their fingers touched. Their gazes met and locked, setting off a flurry of pheromones that darn near knocked her for a loop.

Was she ready for this?

Yes, but what if things turned serious for her? It certainly wouldn't for him.

She really ought to laugh off their obvious attraction— or at least ignore it, like she'd been doing this past week.

Instead, she placed her hand on his jaw, felt the light

bristle on his cheek, and common sense turned to mush. Without any thought to the consequences, she drew his mouth to hers.

Chapter Eight

Carlo didn't know how many more heated kisses he could share with Schuyler before he completely lost his head and said something stupid, promised something he couldn't give her. But right now, all he could think to do was to wrap her in his arms and take each moment as it came.

So they knelt on the tasting room floor, hands caressing, tongues mating, breaths mingling. Yet the only tasting going on right now had uncovered a tantalizing blend of peppermint and chocolate. It was enough to make him want to eat her up, if not feel her up. And try as he might, he couldn't seem to get enough of this amazing woman.

As the kiss intensified, he wondered where they could steal away for a more private sexual exploration.

Before he could rack his brain for options, the door creaked open.

Dammit. Who'd caught them this time?

He slowly pulled his mouth away and turned to the doorway, where his father stood, that atta-boy grin lighting his eyes once again and shaving twenty years off his face.

"Apparently," Esteban said, "I've done it again. You must think I have lousy timing."

He had that right. Carlo might be frustrated by the interruption, but he certainly wasn't embarrassed by it. His old man wasn't, either. And judging by that twinkle in his eyes, he was getting a big kick out of it.

Too big, it seemed. Word of this was soon to hit the Mendoza rumor mill.

Schuyler, who seemed a wee bit more bothered by Esteban's arrival this time than last, leaned back and combed her fingers through her hair. Then she reached for a handful of napkins on the floor. "Carlo was helping me pick up the mess I made."

"I can see that." Esteban winked at Carlo. "I've taught my sons to always offer their assistance to a young lady in need."

The innuendo didn't go unnoticed, but there wasn't much Carlo could say at this point. Besides, he was too stunned by his growing attraction to Schuyler—and his growing desire to take her to bed.

Now, there was an idea. Once a relationship turned sexual, his interest in the woman began to dissipate, and he'd pull back. So if he and Schuyler actually made love, they just might be able to put this blasted attraction behind them and move on.

Not that he was the least bit tired of her yet. Nor was he ready to put any distance between them. But he wasn't at all comfortable with the skewed idea that kept cropping up. One that suggested he might actually be falling for her.

Schuyler hadn't made any secret of the fact that she liked to have fun. And she was just the kind of woman he'd like to play around with.

But it wasn't going to be the least bit fun if he let his feelings get in the way.

Esteban Mendoza couldn't keep his mouth shut if it was covered in duct tape, especially when he had four sons and a nephew to entertain.

Carlo had no more than entered the winery yard after Schuyler drove off with the puppies in her Beamer, when all the good-hearted but unwelcome teasing began.

"Hey, bro," Mark called out, a smirk plastered across his face. "Do I hear the sound of wedding bells in the distance?"

"Very funny," Carlo said.

Rodrigo laughed. "That's not the story we heard."

That wasn't surprising. His father had been connecting a lot of romantic dots that weren't there. At least, there wasn't anything going on until he and Schuyler actually addressed the issue—and pursued it.

"What pumped-up story did you hear?" Carlo asked his brother, although he had a darn good idea.

Rodrigo folded his arms across his chest, his grin rivaling that of the Cheshire cat. "Just that you and Schuyler were steaming up the windows in the tasting room."

It was hard to argue that. Still, Carlo shot a thanks-for-nothing glance at his father, who was an irrepressible flirt and a natural-born ladies' man.

"Better watch out," Chaz said.

Carlo shook his head. "You guys are making something out of nothing."

"That kiss on the tasting room floor wasn't the first one I saw," his father said. "And I damn sure wouldn't call either of them 'nothing.'"

"It's not what you think." At least, Carlo didn't want them to make that assumption. He glanced toward the restaurant, where Chef Bernardo was prepping the waitstaff before the dining room opened for dinner. He ought to attend that meeting, which gave him the perfect excuse for a quick escape.

"I'm glad to hear that kiss didn't mean a thing," Stefan said. "I assume that means I'm free to hit on Schuyler. I've always been attracted to petite blondes, especially one with a great personality, big blue eyes and sexy curves. And if she's free for the taking, I wouldn't mind making a move."

Carlo stiffened. He loved his brothers. He really did. But he didn't want any of them staking a claim on Schuyler. Not yet, anyway. And maybe not ever.

"Okay," he admitted. "There's a little something brewing between us. But I'm not sure what it is. And just so you know, Schuyler feels the same way I do about marriage and commitment."

"So it's just a drive-by romance?" Chaz asked.

It certainly should be. That was the plan.

"Hey," Carlo said, "even if there might be a little more than that going on, Schuyler lives in Houston. So it couldn't be more than a temporary thing."

Chaz placed his hand on Carlo's shoulder and gave it a brotherly squeeze. "For a divorced guy who swore off making any more romantic commitments, I'd say you're playing with fire."

There might be some truth to that statement. A part of him recognized that he could develop deep feelings for Schuyler, but he didn't like the thought of becoming vulnerable. So he shrugged it off and addressed the elephant in the winery. "You can't blame me for being gun-shy when it comes to long-term commitments."

He knew they'd all assume he was talking about his failed marriage, which was a good reason in itself. But on top of that, Carlo and his four brothers had grown up in an unhappy household.

Their father had traveled for business, but even when he was home he spent a lot of evenings with his friends. He might be stone sober now, but he'd had a drinking problem back then. Still, that was no excuse for practically abandoning their mom and forcing her to raise the boys mainly on her own.

Needless to say, they'd fought a lot—over his absence, his drinking and, while it was just speculation on Carlo's part, a little lipstick on Esteban's collar had probably been an issue, too. After each blowup, they'd make up, only to start the cycle all over again.

Carlo, who'd been the oldest, had a front-row seat

to the family drama. Sure, he'd known his parents had loved each other. They'd had moments of passion and affection interspersed with the arguing, but eventually his mom got tired of it and left his dad. Their divorce had taught Carlo a lesson about love.

"Just to keep the record straight," Carlo said. "There won't be any wedding bells for me."

At that, his cousin Alejandro, who'd just returned from a weeklong seminar in California, stepped forward. "I know how you feel."

Did he? Alejandro had recently married Olivia Fortune Robinson and was happier than he'd ever been.

"But you should give love a chance," Alejandro said.

Carlo had done that once. And it had blown up in his face. "Some people might be able to have a committed relationship, Alejandro. And you're one of them. But I'm not."

After his divorce, Carlo had poured himself into his work, managing restaurants and a nightclub in Miami. And his move to Texas hadn't changed that.

"Listen," he said, nodding toward La Viña, "I'd love to stay here and chew the fat with you guys, but I've got work to do."

Yet as he walked away, a beautiful blonde had him thinking about sexual fun and games. And he'd be damned if he'd let it become any more than that.

Formal invitations had gone out more than two weeks ago for the Valentine's party that would take place in just three short days, and the entire Mendoza family—at least those living in Austin and involved with the winery—had been busy, pulling out all the stops for what was sure to be an impressive event.

Carlo and Bernardo had put together a tantalizing menu. Esteban had negotiated a special deal with a talented string quartet to provide the music during dinner, as well as a popular local DJ for the dance to follow. And Alejandro, with the help of Carlo's brothers, was planning to go all out decorating the grounds and the restaurant.

True to his word, Carlo had announced that they would have a special wine tasting during the cocktail hour, and Schuyler would be the hostess. That would allow her to meet the many Fortunes who would be in attendance. Needless to say, she was delighted to have the opportunity to see them up close and observe them in a social setting. So she'd offered to help with the party preparations.

The evening weather had been unseasonably temperate for February, and if it continued, they planned to hold the tasting in the sculpture garden.

Schuyler intended to bring the puppies with her to the winery today, which she often did. She liked giving them a chance to play outdoors. But Dottie, her landlord, had taken a real liking to Fluff and Stuff. She'd also been helpful in housebreaking them and teaching them to walk on a leash.

"When my Punky crossed the rainbow bridge," Dottie had said, "I swore I'd never get another dog. It's too painful to lose them. But these little rascals have made me reconsider that decision."

So it was no surprise when Schuyler was heading for her car, Dottie caught her in the yard.

"Oh." The older woman's smile faded. "You're leaving. I was going to invite you and the puppies to the dog park today. It's Bailey's birthday."

"Bailey?" Schuyler asked.

"You know, Donna Mae's Pomeranian mix? I introduced you to her last week, when we took Fluff and Stuff on a walk."

"Oh, yes." In Schuyler's defense, they'd met several dogs and owners along the way. "If you want to take them to the park, it's fine with me. But I could be gone until later this evening. Do you mind keeping an eye on them that long?"

"Not at all," Dottie said. "I used to take Punky to the park all the time. And I met a lot of really sweet people there. I miss not chatting with them, but after Punky died... Well, it was a little...tough."

"I understand." Schuyler handed her landlord the leashes. "Go ahead and take them. I'm sure you'll all have a great afternoon." Then she climbed into her car, knowing the pups were in good hands.

If she wasn't so determined to check things out for that Valentine's Day tasting, she might have gone with Dottie. She'd never attended a dog's birthday party, and it sounded like it'd be a hoot.

Twenty minutes later, as Schuyler arrived at the winery, she spotted several of the Mendozas' cars in the parking lot, including Carlo's. But she didn't see anyone milling about. She supposed she'd run into them soon enough. So she headed for the sculpture garden to determine the best place to set up the portable wine bar.

She'd no more than decided on a spot near the new fountain, when a car engine sounded out front. Curiosity got the best of her, and she went to see who'd arrived. She circled the perimeter of the tasting room, entered the yard and spotted three women getting out of a white late model Cadillac.

Schuyler didn't recognize the driver or the two others with her—a redhead in her twenties and a middle-aged brunette. Since no one else seemed to be around, she embraced her inner hostess and greeted them with a friendly smile.

"Hi there," she said. "Can I help you?"

The woman who'd been driving, a forty-something blonde who was professionally dressed in black slacks and a tailored white blouse, reached out her hand in greeting. "I'm Betsy Wilkins, a wedding planner with White Lace and Promises, and these are my clients, Joelle Pearson and her mother, Mavis."

Schuyler introduced herself, saying she worked for the winery, which was true, albeit temporarily.

"We've been checking out several possible venues," Betsy said. "But we haven't yet found a place that hits the mark. One of my colleagues mentioned that the Mendoza Winery might be scheduling special events in the near future, so I thought we'd drop by and see if we could get a tour of your property."

Schuyler would love to show them around and schedule the very first Mendoza Winery wedding, which would be a real feather in her cap. But she didn't want to step on anyone's toes.

Wow, now that was a first. She didn't often tamp down her enthusiasm—or the compulsion to act quickly. But she'd come to respect Carlo and his family. All of them—even Esteban, who'd assumed that she and Carlo were romantically involved and liked to tease them about it every chance he got.

"I'm a hostess for special...events," Schuyler said, pumping up her actual title. "I'd be happy to show you the property. And if we're lucky, we'll run into Alejandro or Carlo, who can provide even more details about the winery's calendar. When is the wedding?"

"Saturday, July eighteenth," the bride said. "I know we're getting a late start, but my fiancé and I are going to attend graduate school in August, and we want to get married here before we have to move."

"Congratulations on all counts," Schuyler said. "I'm not sure what you're looking for, but I have to tell you, if I were getting married, I'd love to have an outdoor ceremony here, followed by a dinner reception. Follow me, and I'll show you what I mean."

When she led them to the sculpture garden, the mother let out a little gasp of surprise. "This is lovely!" Then she turned to her daughter. "What do you think, honey?"

"I like it. And I love that fountain. The blue Spanish tile matches the color of the bridesmaids' dresses."

"There are a lot of possibilities," Schuyler said. "If you should decide on an evening ceremony, we can put up twinkly white lights on the trees."

"Oh," the bride said. "That's a great idea."

"We also plan to add a permanent gazebo in the very near future," Schuyler added.

Okay, so that wasn't entirely true. No one had mentioned anything to her about that, but she'd certainly push for one if the Pearsons decided to hold the wedding here.

"Why don't you come with me," Schuyler said. "I'll take you to see La Viña, our restaurant. And if we're lucky, I might be able to introduce you to Bernardo, our chef."

"That would be awesome," the bride said.

The women followed Schuyler. All the while, they chattered to themselves about guest lists, dinner menus and cake flavors.

When they entered La Viña, which had already been set up for the dinner hour, Mavis, the mother of the bride, made her way to the nearest window, which reached from the hardwood floor to the arched oak-paneled ceiling. "Oh my gosh. Would you look at that view of the vineyard?"

"It's absolutely gorgeous." Betsy reached into her purse, pulled out a business card and handed it to Schuyler. "I have several other clients who are also looking for a wedding venue. So I'll be calling you to set up a couple of tours in the next couple of weeks."

Schuyler hoped she wasn't overstepping her bounds, but Carlo had told her that he wanted her to be the winery hostess for special tastings. Maybe he'd also meant special events. At any rate, that would be her response when they broached the subject.

"If you'll give me a minute," Schuyler said, "I'll check and see if the chef is available to meet you."

Sure enough, when she entered the kitchen, Chef Bernardo was hard at work, seated at his desk and sketching out a list of some kind. But it was Carlo who caught Schuyler's eye.

He was dressed casually today in khaki slacks and a white button-down shirt, the sleeves rolled up his muscular forearms. When she approached, he turned away from Bernardo and flashed a dazzling smile her way. "Hey, I'm glad you're here. I wanted to go over a few things with you."

She was delighted to know he was as happy to see her as she was to see him. "Me, too. I was checking out the sculpture garden a few minutes ago and I had an idea to add twinkly white lights on the trees for the party. But before we get into that, I ran into some people you need to meet. They're in the dining room."

He scrunched his brow. "Who is it?"

"A bridal consultant and her clients. They're interested in having a wedding here in July."

"That's great. And the timing should work out perfectly—if they're interested in having it here." Carlo followed Schuyler through the swinging doors and back to the restaurant.

The women, who were still standing at the window gazing at the lush vineyard that grew on the hillside, turned around at their approach.

"Betsy," Schuyler said, "this is Carlo Mendoza, the vice president of the winery."

"It's nice to meet you." Betsy shook his hand. "We

were just marveling at the view. This would make a lovely backdrop for a wedding."

"Thank you," Carlo said. "You should check out the sculpture garden while you're here."

"We've already seen it. Your special event co-ordinator was very helpful. She also gave us some ideas to consider."

Schuyler stole a glance at Carlo, wondering how he would accept the title Betsy had given her. But he didn't even blink.

"Betsy is a wedding planner with White Lace and Promises," Schuyler added. "And these are her clients, Mavis and Joelle Pearson. Joelle is getting married in July."

Carlo moved toward the women, reached out and shook their hands. "It's nice to meet you. I'm glad you stopped by. And yes, we're scheduling special parties and events beginning in June."

"Do you have a brochure we can take with us?" Betsy asked.

"I'm afraid it's still at the printer," Carlo said. "We've just begun to take reservations."

Schuyler hadn't realized that they'd started booking events. But then again, she really wasn't privy to those kinds of things.

"Would your chef be willing to talk to us about possible menus? We'd also like to set up a tasting for the bridal party."

"Absolutely."

"Great. We'll need to talk things over when we get

back to my office," Betsy said. "I'll let you know once we've made a decision."

"I've already made my decision," Joelle said. "I want to get married here. I want an evening wedding in the garden, with white lights adorning the trees, followed by a dinner reception."

"That can be arranged." Carlo reached into his pocket, pulled out a business card and gave it to Betsy. Then he and Schuyler followed them back to their car.

"We'll need a deposit to hold the date," Carlo told them. "Give me a call and I'll get you a contract with all the details."

"I assume that means we'll be working with Schuyler as your on-site coordinator." Betsy turned to Schuyler. "Can I have your card, too?"

Schuyler wasn't sure what to tell her. *I don't have any business cards because I was just blowing smoke when I told you my position with the Mendoza Winery.* Before she could come up with a response, Carlo spoke for her.

"Schuyler is a new hire," he said, "so her cards are still at the printer, along with the brochure."

Bless his heart. He'd played along with her white lie. She was so grateful, she could kiss him.

Of course, kissing him would only make things more complicated, since she had every intention of returning to Houston.

Or had her plans begun to shift?

She'd told him that she'd give lovemaking some thought. And she'd done just that. Day after day, she'd relived their heated kisses. And night after night, she'd slept on his suggestion to let passion run its course.

And each morning, she'd awakened to the same conclusion. They really should see how a short-term affair would pan out. Like it or not, she wanted to make love with Carlo.

Of course, becoming intimate could complicate their working relationship. Then again, her position at the winery was only temporary. So scratch that complication.

But there was also another consideration. She'd begun to feel more for Carlo than she'd felt for any other man. And while she'd never thought of herself as marriage material, she might reconsider a more serious relationship with a guy like him.

Carlo continued to charm the women as they discussed further details. Then, as they watched Betsy drive away with the Pearsons, he turned to Schuyler. Truthfully she was a bit nervous to hear what he had to say now that they were alone. Would he be angry at the way she'd inserted herself in winery business? She braced herself for a dressing-down. Instead, his face lit up with a smile.

"You're amazing."

Her heart soared at the compliment. "I am?"

"You're the perfect hostess for our tastings. And now you've pretty much locked in our first wedding. Betsy was obviously impressed." He slowly shook his head, that dazzling smile still stretched across his lips. "For a woman who's sworn off romance and marriage, you have a real knack for this sort of thing."

"Yeah. Well, a wedding celebration and a reception is just another kind of party, right?"

"Good point. Either way, I'm going to talk this over with Alejandro, but I think he'll agree to offer you a permanent position at the winery."

"Seriously?"

"Absolutely."

Wow. She hadn't seen that coming. Usually words like *permanent* made her want to cut bait and run. But she didn't feel that way now.

"Thank you," she said. "I'd have to think about that, but I don't mind you two talking it over."

"Good. I'm glad to hear that."

Was he? She hoped there was more to the offer than the service that Schuyler could provide the family business. Was he hoping to keep her around so they could strike up a romance?

"Have you seen *Jersey Boys*?" he asked, throwing her for yet another loop.

"No, but I love Frankie Valli and the Four Seasons."

"Good. It's playing at the Paramount Theater, and I have two tickets for the show next Saturday. Would you like to go with me?"

She'd have to ask Dottie to dog sit for her, but there wasn't anything she'd rather do than go out on a real date with Carlo. "That sounds like fun."

"Good. I'll pick you up around five o'clock so we can have dinner first."

"I'll be ready." That date was sounding better and better. Dinner and a show and...

She wondered if he'd be ready for a romantic wrap-up to their date. She certainly was.

Chapter Nine

The Valentine's Day party at the Mendoza Winery was sure to be everything Schuyler hoped it would be and more. It was also the kind of elegant event she would have loved to attend as an invited guest. But she was content to serve the Mendoza wines and discreetly observe the Fortunes.

As Carlo planned, the evening would kick off with a wine tasting in the sculpture garden so the guests could see the impressive improvements he and Alejandro had made to the property. Soon the winery would be bursting with happy chatter, but the only sounds now came from the water gurgling in the new fountain.

The sun had just set, and the white twinkling lights gave the grounds a festive and romantic ambience. There seemed to be a magical aura, too. As if something special was about to happen.

And wasn't it? Schuyler had dreamed about meeting some of her Fortune relatives, and she was about to do that tonight.

Alejandro had invited Mendozas galore to celebrate, and from the many RSVPs that had rolled in, it seemed that quite a few had jumped at the chance to attend. Several would be coming from Horseback Hollow, including Alejandro's brother, Cisco, and his wife, Delaney nee Fortune. Their sister Gabriella and her husband, Delaney's brother Jude Fortune Jones, would be traveling with them. Counting those from Red Rock—and the ones living in Austin—it would make a full house.

Schuyler might have read Ariana Lamonte Fortune's articles in *Weird Life* magazine, but she was afraid she wouldn't be able to keep everyone straight. Still, she'd do her absolute best to match every face to a name and remember every family connection.

Carlo had done his part to help her with that by giving her a primer on which Fortunes would be in attendance, although Schuyler wasn't sure she'd be able to pick them out of the crowd without his assistance.

Eager to see the Fortunes, she'd spent way more time getting ready than she usually did.

She'd worn her red dress tonight, which had both a scooped neckline and a low-slung back. It was stylish and flattering, and while she'd worn it before at other tastings, she thought it would be especially appropriate for Valentine's Day. Her hair was swept up into a stylish twist that revealed her diamond stud earrings, a birthday gift from her parents. And as a final touch, she'd used a bit more makeup than was her usual habit.

When she'd taken one last look in the mirror at home—
or rather her temporary Austin residence, she'd been
pleased with her appearance.

Taking a deep breath, she walked into the winery
garden. She wanted to make a good impression tonight,
even though she wouldn't introduce herself as Julius
Fortune's granddaughter. Still, she was finally here—
ready and eager for the night to unfold.

She was glad someone had already set up the portable bar, but the wines she'd be serving hadn't been
brought out yet. She was just about to go inside the
tasting room to get them when Ricardo, the man who
hosted the daily tastings at the winery, came outside
pushing a cart loaded down with wineglasses. He also
brought out bottles of Sunny Days, a chenin blanc, and
Desert Sunset, a Syrah.

She wasn't sure why he was here. Perhaps to pass
out appetizers or serve dinner in the restaurant. Either
way, she thanked him for setting things up.

"No problem," he said, as he uncorked the bottles.

"Are we serving any other wines tonight?" she asked.

"I'm not sure. Carlo specifically asked me to bring
out this cart. But there's another one still in the tasting
room. I'm going back for it. It's possible that he has a
few others in mind."

Schuyler had yet to spot Carlo or any of his brothers.
She assumed they were making last-minute preparations
in La Viña. She was about to go in search of him, but
when a car engine sounded out front, signaling that the
guests had begun to arrive, her steps stalled.

She whipped out her cell phone, which held her Fortune family cheat sheet, and gave it one last read. It was impossible to ignore the Mendoza connections to them, which convinced her that she'd made the right decision by starting her quest at the winery distribution center in Austin Commons.

Okay, she told herself. *You've got this.*

Alejandro Mendoza, Carlo's cousin, was at the top of the list. He owned the winery and was married to Olivia Fortune Robinson. Interestingly enough, four of Alejandro's siblings were also married to one of the Fortune Robinson clan. Joaquin was married to Zoe, and Matteo was married to Rachel.

Several others of the Robinson Fortune clan would be here as well, including Ben and his wife, Ella, Wes and Vivian, Kieran and Dana, Graham and Sasha, Sophie and Mason… Wow. Would Schuyler be able to remember who belonged to whom?

It wasn't likely. Still, she was glad to have the chance to meet them all.

As the guests began to enter the garden, dressed to the hilt and ready to party, she couldn't help noting that all of the Fortunes and Mendozas were dazzling, good-looking and well dressed. It was an embarrassment of riches, both literally and figuratively.

She wasn't sure whom she should approach first. Not that she'd forget to be a hostess. In fact, she'd walk up to them and invite them over to the wine bar for a tasting. She peeked at her phone once more. She'd scanned only the first few names on her list when Carlo came over and placed an arm around her shoulders.

"Don't be so obvious," he said. "If you're not careful, people will become suspicious."

"I'll try, but this is a big night for me. And I'm a little nervous."

He stroked her back, his fingers resting on her bare skin, sizzling her with his touch. "I know you came to work this evening, but I'd rather you were a guest instead of an employee. So I asked Ricardo to cover for you."

Seriously? That was a sweet thought.

"How are you going to introduce me?" she asked.

He blessed her with a smile. "You're my date tonight."

Her heart spun like an ice skater about to score an Olympic gold medal, and she returned his smile with a confident grin. "I shouldn't have any problem pulling that off."

He drew her a little closer, and as she caught a tantalizing whiff of his sea-breezy cologne, she leaned into him. Pretending to be Carlo's date was going to be an easy role to play.

Ricardo, who'd just returned from the tasting room with the other cart, gave her a thumbs-up. "I'm back, Schuyler. I'll take it from here."

"Thanks." She turned to her handsome escort. It was nearly intoxicating to think of herself as his special lady. Would people think they were lovers? She wouldn't mind if they did.

Carlo looked great tonight in that stylish black suit, crisp white shirt and red tie. In fact, they matched so well, one might think they'd gotten dressed together.

"Come on," Carlo said, taking her by the hand. "I'll introduce you to some of our guests."

This was what she'd been waiting for, the chance to meet some of her cousins, and she had Carlo to thank for it. Yet her enthusiasm paled ever so slightly, making room for the swell of pride she felt at being with him all evening. His date. And, hopefully soon, his lover.

As they crossed the grass, Carlo squeezed her hand and whispered a soul-stirring compliment that bolstered any lack of confidence she might have had. "You look gorgeous tonight. I love that dress."

She brightened, and her heart took flight once more. The only thing he could have said that would have made her happier was that he loved *her*, but that didn't make sense. Why would something like that pop into her head? She shook off the silly thought as quickly as it crossed her mind.

They made their way over to Alejandro, who stood next to a pretty brunette. That had to be his wife. Schuyler had had the pleasure of meeting him only twice, since he'd been out of town all last week. But she'd been especially eager to meet Olivia, a bright young professional at her father's company, Robinson Tech. A woman who had no idea that she and Schuyler shared the same grandfather— good ol' Julius Fortune, who'd left a trail of illegitimate children in his wake.

Olivia had married Alejandro last year, and while her last name was now Mendoza, she was every bit a Fortune by birth. Just as Schuyler was.

Before Carlo could make any introductions, Alejandro reached out and shook Schuyler's hand. "I'm glad you're here. I want to thank you again for all you've done for us in a very short period of time."

"It was my pleasure," Schuyler said, reveling in the praise that made her sound like the Mendoza Winery employee of the week. "But to be completely honest, your wines practically sell themselves."

"I'm glad you like them." Alejandro turned to the brunette standing beside him. "Olivia, this is Schuyler Fortunado. For the past two weeks she's worked for us as a brand rep at Carlo's special tastings. And just a couple days ago, she scheduled our first wedding and reception."

"It's nice to meet you, Schuyler." Olivia extended her hand in greeting.

Schuyler took it, but a customary response balled up in her throat. And she'd be darned if she knew why. She never found herself at a loss for words and rarely suffered any insecurity. But dang. Olivia was one smart cookie. What if she saw through the fake-date thing? What if Olivia figured out who Schuyler was and why she was here?

Finally, in what seemed like forever but had been only a couple of beats, Schuyler rallied her senses, tamped down her worries and blurted out, "You have no idea how glad I am to meet you."

Okay, so that was way more truthful and sincere than she'd planned to be. She hadn't meant to sound like she was having a fangirl moment, but the thrill of meeting her Fortune cousin had just tumbled off her tongue.

Luckily, Olivia didn't seem to notice. Nor did she look the least bit suspicious about Schuyler having any ulterior motives. And even though Schuyler did, she didn't mean anyone any harm.

Moments later, two other brunettes bearing a striking family resemblance approached them, and Olivia introduced her sisters, Zoe and Rachel, to Schuyler.

This was so cool. In one fell swoop, Schuyler had met three of her cousins. Counting Nathan, the reluctant Fortune who lived in Paseo, that made four. But she didn't expect to see him tonight. He seemed to prefer living out in the boonies, which suggested that he wasn't very social. On top of that, she doubted that he and Bianca would want to make that long drive.

"If you ladies will excuse me," Carlo said, "Alejandro and I have a little business to discuss." He gave Schuyler's hand a gentle, reassuring squeeze before releasing his hold. Then the two men left her and her cousins to get better acquainted.

The three Fortune Robinson sisters, all of whom were stylish, beautiful and smart, chatted about normal things. Family things. And Schuyler hung on every word. She wasn't sure what she'd been expecting to learn when meeting them, but clearly some of the media accounts had been exaggerated—as they often were.

Maybe, if she played her cards right, they'd provide her with more information about the others who would be arriving soon.

Schuyler glanced across the garden, where Carlo and Alejandro stood. Did they really have something to talk about? Or had Carlo just given her another unexpected and thoughtful gift?

Girl talk with Olivia, Zoe and Rachel might prove to be sweeter and better than a pair of bunny slippers.

"What did you want to talk to me about?" Alejandro asked Carlo, as they crossed the lawn to a more private spot.

In truth, Carlo didn't have much to say that couldn't wait. He'd just wanted to give Schuyler some time to get to know her cousins. But that wasn't something he would admit.

"There were a couple of things I wanted to mention," Carlo said. "I didn't get a chance to tell you that, while you were at that seminar, I drove by a few properties that might work out for us if we go forward with that nightclub project."

"What'd you think of them? Did any of them have potential?"

Carlo related his thoughts and his opinions of all three. "I'm really interested in that bank building. It might be a little small, but we could expand it during a remodel."

"What's the asking price?"

"I have no idea. It hasn't been listed yet, and I haven't approached a real estate agent who can provide any comps. Schuyler suggested that we talk to her sister Maddie. If we want to go forward with this, I think that's probably a good idea."

Alejandro nodded his approval, then glanced over to where his wife, her sisters and Schuyler stood. Each smiling lady held a glass of wine and seemed to have found plenty to chat about.

"We lucked out when you stumbled upon Schuyler," Alejandro said.

"Yes, I know." But it wasn't just the Mendoza family business that had scored with her arrival. Carlo felt as if he'd lucked out, too. Of course, the jury was still out on that.

"Your father seems to think that you're serious about her," Alejandro said.

Was he? He hadn't planned things to get that deep, although he felt a lot more for her than he'd expected to. Yet to be perfectly honest, at least with himself, he was reluctant to ponder his feelings for her. "I admit that I enjoy being with her."

Alejandro, who'd yet to celebrate his first wedding anniversary, nodded sagely, as if that's exactly how he'd felt when he started dating Olivia.

Had he enjoyed her company so much that he would have let her rescue two stray mutts, then drive her all around town with them until she found a groomer and a vet? Would he have gladly helped her move into a temporary residence that she'd found on a whim and secured with a lease just as quickly?

Carlo doubted it. And if he listened to his better judgment, he'd realize that Schuyler might prove to be too flighty for him, too prone to change direction with a shift in the wind.

Yet he could just as easily argue against that assumption. Schuyler had found the perfect place in record time. Didn't that imply that she had wisdom, determination and the ability to make things happen?

"So what's holding you back?" Alejandro asked.

From what? "I'm sorry, I'm not following you."

"You might have walked away from the ladies, cousin. But your gaze has been locked on Schuyler for the past five minutes." Alejandro laughed. "Your dad was right. She's got a hold on you. And you've got it bad."

He wanted to object, but it had really begun to feel like that. And that worried him. If he was ever going to consider settling down with a woman, it would have to be one who'd make a lifelong commitment. And Schuyler had made no secret of the fact that she was interested in only fun and games.

But no way would he admit the truth, even to a man he respected to keep his secret. "No, you're wrong. She just amazes me. That's all." Then he changed the subject back to business. "I also had another idea I wanted to run by you."

"What's that?"

"We both have our hands full already, and if we decide to go forward with that nightclub, we'll be busier than ever."

"Actually, if we decide to open that club, you'll be the busy one. It's what you do best. And with that being the case, I'll be here most of the time, doing what I do best."

That was a fair division of labor. And now it was Carlo's turn to nod his agreement.

He took one last look at Schuyler, watched as she told her newfound cousins something that made them all laugh. It would have been nice to have been privy to whatever she'd said. He liked hearing the lilt of her voice, the melodic sound of her laughter.

Unwilling to let Alejandro make any more assumptions, Carlo shook off the distraction and again focused on business. "By the way, Schuyler impressed the hell out of that wedding planner who stopped by the winery a few days ago. The woman thought she was our on-site special event coordinator, and I didn't correct her."

"I see where you're going with this," Alejandro said. "If you think she'd be a good fit for us, I'm okay with it. She's done a great job so far, and I have no reason to doubt her abilities to lock in other weddings and parties. She'd be working with you, though. Do you foresee any future problems?"

Actually, quite a few. But none of them had anything to do with Schuyler's ability to take the ball and run with it.

"No," Carlo said. "I think it'll work out okay."

Now all he had to do was to offer her the position and hope she'd say yes.

"You know," Alejandro added, "if Schuyler wasn't a rock star at representing our brand and so darn good for business, I'd think that you might be trying to strike up points with her for your personal gain."

Carlo stole a glance at his cousin, who was eyeing his pretty bride and probably hadn't realized that his comment had struck a chord.

It was true that Schuyler was a great hostess during those special tastings and a natural-born saleswoman, so it made good business sense to offer her a permanent position with the company, but Carlo's motives were selfish, too. He wanted the opportunity to see her each day.

And there lay his problem. Spending that much time with her was a risky move for a man who didn't make long-term commitments. So he'd better watch out.

The last thing he needed was to get too emotionally involved, especially if his efforts to keep her close for the time being led to a big complication in the future.

Schuyler had always thought La Viña was the perfect place to dine or hold a party. But she'd never guessed that, with a little careful decorating, it would look so festive and romantic. Each linen-draped table had been adorned with white tulle, vases filled with gorgeous red roses and flickering candles.

The string quartet Esteban had hired for the dinner hour had serenaded them all while they dined on oysters in the half shell, a lobster salad on butter leaf lettuce with a citrus vinaigrette, fingerling potatoes and filet mignon with lump crab and hollandaise. As if that wasn't filling, the dessert was to die for: individual chocolate soufflés and long-stemmed strawberries dipped in white chocolate.

Schuyler had attended plenty of other classy parties in the past, each with lovely settings, great music, amazing service and a delicious menu. But none of them had ever energized her quite like this one, which was sure to become a memory she'd never forget.

As the waitstaff began clearing the tables and the disc jockey set up to provide the music for the dance, some of the intriguing people she'd met, as well as a few she'd been observing from a distance, began to mill about the dining room.

Moments ago, after spotting a business associate, Carlo had asked her to excuse him so he could greet the man. Schuyler took the opportunity to get up from the table where they'd been sitting with his father and brothers. She could have continued to chat with his family and gotten to know them even better, but she wanted a chance to not only stretch her legs but to scout the room. So she asked them to excuse her, as well. Then she took a stroll across the room, weaving through the tables until she reached the nearest window that provided a view of the vineyards.

Outside, seated on a wrought iron bench, an older woman with silver-streaked auburn hair seemed to be holding court with several other well-dressed women. She had enough diamond bling around her neck and on her fingers to light up the night sky.

When she turned around, Schuyler realized it was none other than Kate Fortune, the matriarch of the entire Fortune clan. Kate was fiercely devoted to her famous cosmetic company, although she'd recently handed over the CEO reins to Graham Fortune Robinson, a rancher. That move, from what Schuyler had read, had taken the entire family by surprise. But Graham apparently had a business background and just enough out-of-the-box thinking that he impressed Kate. And now that he was in charge, he was doing quite well.

Kate, who was in her nineties, was just as attractive in person as she was in pictures Schuyler had seen. She also appeared to be twenty years younger, thanks to very few facial wrinkles. Her skin had a healthy glow, something that came from having good genes,

Schuyler supposed. Yet it was just as likely a result of the Fortune Youth Serum, which she'd developed and turned into a very successful company that had made her a billionaire.

Schuyler had been intrigued by the stories she'd read about Kate, so to see her in person, even behind a wall of glass, was unbelievably cool.

"Fancy meeting you here," a man said from behind her, his voice laced with the hint of a Texas drawl.

Schuyler turned away from the window to see Nathan Fortune, who'd changed his flannel and denim ranch wear for a stylish suit. "What a surprise." She offered her newfound cousin a friendly smile. "I didn't expect to see you here."

"I make my way to the city every now and then. Besides, I thought Bianca would enjoy a special evening on our first Valentine's Day as husband and wife."

"I'm glad you came. It's nice to see a familiar face."

Nathan scanned the dining room, his eyes taking in the hardwood floors, the wall-to-wall windows, the rounded oak-paneled ceiling. "I heard the restaurant was recently remodeled and expanded. The Mendozas did a great job."

"Yes, they did." Schuyler found it a bit odd that Nathan seemed more interested in the party setting than in the people who'd attended, many of them his relatives. She suspected he was trying to keep his distance and not get too chummy. Hopefully, he wouldn't blow her cover. "I…um…haven't mentioned anything about my…grand-father."

"Don't worry. I won't say anything or reveal your secret. But tell me. I'm curious. What have you found out?"

"Not much. Just that I really like Olivia, Zoe and Rachel, the three cousins I met earlier. But I'm still making my rounds, and the night is young."

"So how are the Mendozas treating you?" Nathan asked. "You must have eased your way into their good graces if you snagged an invitation to the party."

"They've been great." Especially Carlo.

Her gaze drifted across the room, scanning the crowd until she spotted her tall, dark and handsome boss. Her attraction to him continued to grow, which had made her decide to stay in Austin longer than she'd expected to. Maybe, while she was here, she'd be wined and dined—and courted.

Should she invite him back to her place after the party tonight? Or was it too soon? She certainly didn't want to come on too strong. This was one relationship she'd like to last longer than a couple of weeks. In fact, the word *indefinitely* came to mind.

She supposed that was an odd thing for her to ponder, when she'd never thought she'd ever settle down. Not that Carlo would ever want to get married or anything. He'd made it clear how he felt about remaining single. But for some crazy reason, whenever they were together, she found her imagination going off her tried-and-true grid. But that might be due to his kindness to her, his respect for her uniqueness.

"How long do you plan to be in Austin?" Nathan asked, as if reading her mind.

"I'm not sure. I'm actually working for the Men-doza Winery."

"Really? Doing what?"

"I'm a sales rep at special wine tastings. It's only part time, which suits me fine. And, of course, it's just temporary."

"How long is temporary?"

"Who knows? I tend to go with the flow, but I really like it here. The Mendozas are easy to work for."

She'd grouped them all together, even though the one Mendoza she actually answered to was Carlo. But it was true. She liked them all, even Esteban. But it was Carlo who'd caught her eye, touched her heart and held her thoughts.

Sure, he was drop-dead gorgeous. But it was more than sexual attraction that drew her to him. He seemed to accept her and her quirky nature, just as she was. And that didn't happen often.

The two of them had also become a team. Equal partners, it seemed. And her pride, which sometimes faltered when people criticized her, had grown exceptionally strong while working for the winery. She was doing a bang-up job, something all the Mendozas recognized, which gave her a thrill. She wished she could say the same about the feelings her own family evoked.

That, in itself, was enough to make her wonder if it would be in her best interest to consider something more long-term. And she wasn't just considering a professional decision. She was pondering a romantic one, too.

But did she really want to screw up the admiration

she'd achieved and her growing self-respect by letting herself become sexually involved with Carlo?

She glanced across the room again, and her brow furrowed as she spotted him talking to a beautiful brunette who was dressed to the hilt in a flashy red dress and spiked heels. And dang. He was grinning from ear to ear, clearly enjoying their little chat.

When the woman laughed at something he said, Schuyler stiffened. That wasn't good. No, not good at all.

She'd never been the jealous type. Heck, she'd never had reason to be. She'd never cared enough about a man to worry about losing him.

Not that she had any claim on Carlo, but she didn't want to lose him before she even figured out how she felt about him.

Her reason for attending the party in the first place fell by the wayside. All she wanted to do was interrupt that woman's flirtations before… Well, before…

"I'm sorry," she told Nathan. "It's been nice catching up with you, but you'll have to excuse me. There's something I have to do." Something she had to stop.

Before waiting for Nathan's response, she hurried to Carlo's side so she could make her presence—if not her claim on him—known.

Chapter Ten

Carlo had no more greeted Wendy Fortune Mendoza, who'd come all the way from Horseback Hollow with her husband, Marcos, to dance the night away, when Schuyler swept up beside him as if all hell had broken out and the devil was on her trail.

Before he could introduce her to Wendy, his cousin's wife, Schuyler grabbed his hand, gave it a good tug and said, "I need to talk to you."

He had no idea what had her wound up so tight, but he figured it had to be important. And urgent. So he asked Wendy to excuse him, adding, "I'll be back in a moment."

"That's okay," Wendy said. "I was just making the rounds. I'm sure we'll run into each other more than once before the night is over."

Schuyler asked to be excused, too. Then she practically dragged him across the room, her strides causing him to pick up his pace. Something was clearly wrong. Had someone discovered her identity and her reason for being here? Then again, maybe she'd landed a big sales contract for the winery. Or she'd lost one.

Either way, making a mad dash through the restaurant wasn't getting him any answers. He'd at least like a hint. So, as they briskly walked along, he asked, "What's going on?"

Without slowing her steps, she said, "I'll tell you in a minute."

Since they'd just approached a recently vacated table, where no one could overhear their conversation, he pulled back on her hand, making her stop. He studied her intently. "Are you okay?"

She bit down on her bottom lip, and her once-determined expression turned pensive. And a bit flustered.

Before he could suggest that they go outside for some fresh air and privacy, the disc jockey's voice rang out. "Good evening, everyone! What would Valentine's Day be without Elvis Presley singing one of his romantic classics?"

At that, "Fools Rush In" began to play, lulling the crowd and drawing several couples to the dance floor. The familiar tune seemed to work its magic on Schuyler, too.

Her blue eyes widened, sparkling bright. "Oh my gosh, Carlo. I love this song."

The abrupt change in her mood nearly floored him,

but he tamped down his surprise, as well as his confusion. "What did you want to tell me?"

"It can wait for now. Dance with me, Carlo."

He should have balked and demanded an explanation, but he let her lead him to the dance floor. If truth be told, he'd wanted to get his hands on her all night.

So he opened his arms, and she stepped into his embrace. As they swayed to the sensual tune, he savored the feel of her in his arms, the soft feminine curves he would stroke and caress if they didn't have an audience.

Yet several beats later, he felt compelled to ask again. "What was so important that you pulled me away from my cousin's wife?"

Schuyler stiffened, drew back and gazed up at him. A crease marred her pretty forehead. "Your cousin's wife? Is *that* who she was?" She slowly shook her head. "She must think I'm a ditz. And a rude one at that. I'd better apologize to her as soon as this dance is over."

It was beginning to all make sense now. She'd been jealous. He wasn't sure if he should take that as a compliment, laugh or be offended. "Did you think I'd try to hit on another woman when I was with you?"

"Well…you've made no secret about the fact that you're dedicated to the bachelor life."

"Maybe so, but I'd never be disrespectful of the lady I'm with. That's not my style."

"I'm sorry, Carlo. I don't know why I reacted like I did. That's not my style, either."

So he'd been right. Jealousy had provoked her impulsive reaction. He actually took a bit of pride in that and pulled her back into his arms. A wise man might reconsider a relationship with Schuyler, but as he held her in his arms, her head resting against his shoulder, her tantalizing scent doing crazy things to his heartbeat, not to mention his head… Well, hell. He felt like a fool tonight.

In fact, as they continued to dance, he forgot all about business, family and parties. Instead, it seemed as if he and Schuyler were the only people on the dance floor.

Except they weren't. As he steered her through the other couples, he spotted Alejandro and Olivia dancing cheek to cheek, their love for each other apparent.

When Alejandro looked up and caught Carlo's eye, his lips quirked into a crooked grin. *Give love a chance*, he'd told him once. And it seemed that Alejandro was repeating that advice again tonight, only he didn't have to say a single word.

The next couple to ease their way next to him and Schuyler was his father and one of the sales reps, a newly divorced brunette in her early forties. Using some fancy footwork, his wily old man spun his attractive partner to the side, long enough to give Carlo the thumbs-up sign and flash him another atta-boy grin.

Carlo had no more than rolled his eyes at his dad when Chaz and a blonde companion joined them on the dance floor. Carlo would have thought that romance was in the air tonight, that his younger brother had found a lady to woo. But when Chaz let out a slow whistle and gave him the okay sign, Carlo realized that wasn't the case. His family clearly approved of Schuyler, but they were also taunting him, reminding him of all the times he'd sworn to remain single.

Normally he'd be annoyed, but right now he was too caught up in his attraction to Schuyler and his growing arousal.

They danced as if they'd known each other forever—or as if they both planned to get to know each other really well tonight.

What the hell. Whom was he kidding? There was no reason to pretend neither of them knew what was happening.

"I've been thinking," he whispered into her ear. "Maybe we should give a temporary relationship a chance."

She turned her head just enough to catch his eye and smiled. "I'm willing if you are."

Her agreement shot a zing right through him, amping up his desire. "I'd hoped you would say that." He pulled her closer and whispered, "I have to stay until the last guest leaves and the restaurant closes. But if you'll hang out with me, I'll take you home."

Her lips quirked into a sweet but sexy smile. "To your place or mine?"

"Does it matter?"

"Not to me." Then she went up on tiptoes and brushed a kiss on his lips, letting him know they were definitely on the same page. "There's nothing I want more than to be with you tonight."

"Ditto," he said. "It's too bad we have so long to wait."

"I know, but the anticipation will make it all the better."

"And more fun."

"Hey," she said. "Isn't that supposed to be my line?"

"That'll be my motto, too. At least for tonight."

"I have another one," she said. "Life wasn't meant to be boring."

She might be right, but he knew one thing for sure. When it came to being with Schuyler, life would never be dull or routine. But for now, all they had to do was decide where they'd spend the night. So he made the decision for them. "Then my house it is."

The only thing left for them to decide was what they'd have for breakfast.

Schuyler had figured it would be well after midnight till she got to go home with Carlo. But right before the disc jockey announced the last dance, Alejandro had taken Carlo aside and told him to feel free to cut out early.

So they'd left her car at the winery and drove to his place, a luxury apartment in a snazzy high-rise building in downtown Austin.

After he parked in the underground garage, Schuyler walked with him to the elevator. Once inside, they rode it to the fifth floor. Usually, when she was on a date, she'd start having second thoughts long before this. She'd see signs that the man would become possessive and that he'd have unrealistic expectations when it came to her or to their relationship. So she'd find one excuse or another to say good-night and go home alone. She'd found that it was easier to end things rather than risk losing herself or her independence.

She didn't have those same doubts and concerns with Carlo, though. He truly seemed to like her—

unconditionally and just the way she was. He didn't criticize her, and so far, he hadn't made any attempts to change her. And he certainly wouldn't try to tie her down or stake a claim on her. He'd made that pretty clear.

She had to admit that she was a little nervous coming home with him tonight, yet at the same time, she felt a thrill of excitement. The thought of spending the night in his arms and in his bed trumped any butterflies swarming in her stomach.

When they reached his apartment, Carlo unlocked the door and let her inside. The living room was decorated nicely in leather, dark wood and glass. Colorful artwork depicting ocean scenes, sailboats or beach life adorned the walls. But it was the large window that looked out at the city lights that drew her immediate attention.

She walked straight to it and peered into the night. "What an awesome view." She could have stood there indefinitely, admiring the sight, but after all the dancing they'd done this evening, her feet ached. So she kicked off her heels.

The moment she did, she looked over her shoulder at Carlo, then down to her bare feet. "I hope you don't mind if I get cozy."

"Not at all." He removed his suit jacket and placed it on the back of a chair. "Please. Make yourself at home. *Mi casa es su casa.*"

She smiled. "If I was at my house, I'd put on my bunny slippers."

A grin stretched across his face. "Too bad I didn't

buy two pairs. One for you to keep at your place and one to have here."

She liked the sound of that. Apparently, he didn't think one night together would be enough, and she had to agree.

"You never told me," she said, as she turned away from the city view. "How in the world did you find those slippers?"

"I did an internet search for places in Austin that sold funky nightwear. Then I called around till I found them." He loosened his red silk tie, removed it and draped it over his jacket. "Like I said, it was no big deal. Besides, if I would have hit a brick wall, I wouldn't have mentioned anything about them, and you never would have been the wiser."

The fact that he'd put so much thought and effort into finding those slippers pleased her. Carlo was truly one of a kind. A keeper. That is, if he ever wanted to be kept.

"Thanks again," she said. "You scored a lot of points with that gift."

"Oh, yeah?" His eyes twinkled, competing with the stars and the city lights—and winning hands down.

"Yep." In fact, he was racking up points each time she saw him, each time they were together, whether at work or play.

He crossed the room to where she stood. "Can I get you something to drink? Coffee? Water? A nightcap of some kind?"

"No, thanks. I'm not thirsty." Neither was she coy. She knew why she was here. And what she wanted. So did Carlo.

Only trouble was, while he might think otherwise, she wasn't all that experienced sexually. So, rather than making the first move, she'd better let things play out naturally. After all, Carlo had to be a skilled lover. He'd know how to proceed from here, and she'd be in good hands.

But dang. He wasn't making any moves, and she was getting antsy. She'd never been patient when her heart and mind were set on something. And right now, that something was Carlo.

So she stepped forward and slipped her arms around his neck. "I might not be thirsty, but there's something else I'd like."

Apparently, he'd been waiting for her to make the first move because he wrapped his arms around her waist, pulled her flush against him and kissed her as if they'd never stop. Within a heartbeat she was lost in a swirl of heat, passion and desire. An ache settled deep in her core, and Carlo was the only one who could fill it.

She seemed to be stirring up something in him, too. She could feel his blood pounding, his heart beating. Or was that her own?

As their tongues mated, her head spun, and her knees nearly buckled. All she could do was hold on tight and kiss him back.

Their hands stroked, caressed, explored. When he reached her breast, the fabric of her dress bunched up. She had half a notion to stop kissing him long enough to remove the darn thing. Before she could offer the suggestion, his thumb skimmed across her nipple, sending her senses reeling.

About the time she thought she was going to melt into a puddle on the floor, he broke the kiss and said, "Let's take this to the bedroom. I'm not sure how many people are awake at this hour, but with the blinds open and the lights on, we're probably giving them one hell of a show."

She hadn't thought about that. She should have, though. Yet for some reason, it really didn't matter. It wasn't like they were naked. Not yet, anyway.

Carlo took her hand and led her to his king-size bed. If their kisses meant anything at all, making love with him was going to be unimaginable. Amazing. Magical.

Everything about this night felt so good. So right. She was about to tell him that when he caught her jaw in his hand and brought her mouth to his in another earth-spinning kiss that stole her thoughts, her words and, quite possibly, her heart.

Carlo couldn't get enough of Schuyler. As his hands slid along the curve of her back and down the slope of her hips, a surge of desire shot clean through him. He pulled her hips forward, against his erection. She must have realized how badly he wanted her because she whimpered into his mouth and arched forward, rubbing against him, making him grow even harder.

She was driving him crazy, and by the time he thought that the urge to make love would turn him inside out, she tore her mouth away from his, ending the kiss.

Her passion-glazed eyes locked onto his, capturing him and holding him hostage. He ought to run like hell.

Instead, he didn't dare move. In fact, if she had any requests, he'd promise her damn near anything.

She slowly turned around, revealing the back of that alluring red dress. "Unzip me. Please?"

"My pleasure." He did as she requested, then watched as she pushed the fabric over her shoulders and let it drop to the floor.

She stood before him in a skimpy black bra and a matching thong. When she turned to face him, a sexual flush revealed her arousal, her readiness to join him in bed.

Her body, petite yet lithe, was everything he'd imagined it to be and more. He couldn't help marveling at her perfection.

She reached up, removed the clip from her hair, then shook out the thick, glossy strands in a move that was almost his undoing.

While she unhooked her bra, tossed it aside and removed her thong, he unbuttoned his dress shirt and shrugged it off. Once he'd taken off his shoes and the rest of his clothing, he eased toward her, his heart pounding, his blood racing.

She skimmed her nails across his chest, sending a shiver up his spine and a rush of heat through his veins. He couldn't wait any longer. He filled his hands with her breasts, firm and round, the dusky pink tips peaked and begging to be touched, to be loved and kissed.

As he bent and took a nipple in his mouth, she gasped in pleasure. He lavished first one breast, and then the other. All the while, she gripped his shoulder, her nails pressing into his skin.

"I don't know how much more I can take," she said, her words coming out in slow, ragged huffs. "I need to feel you inside me."

Happy to oblige, he lifted her in his arms and placed her on top of the bed. Her luscious blond hair splayed upon the azure blue pillow sham while her perfect body stretched out on the comforter. She lifted her arms toward him, silently urging him to lie with her.

He paused for a beat, drinking in the angelic sight, then he reached into his nightstand drawer and removed several condoms from the box. Something told him they'd need to have plenty of them handy tonight.

With that taken care of, he joined her on the bed, where they continued to kiss, to taste and to arouse each other until they were both eager to become one.

He tore open one of the packets and rolled the condom in place. As he hovered over her, she reached for his erection, opened for him and guided him where he needed to be. The moment he entered her, joining their bodies, a burst of pleasure shot through him. She arched up, meeting each of his thrusts.

This was unbelievable. Staggering, yet in the most surprising sense of the word. He tried to tell himself it was only sex. That it was the same lust that had driven him to propose to Cecily. But nothing he'd ever experienced, ever felt, compared to this. And after tonight, he didn't want to experience it with anyone else.

As Schuyler reached a peak, she cried out and let go. That was all it took to send him over the edge. He shuddered, releasing with her in a sexual explosion that had both his heart and his head spinning.

But as his climax ebbed, realization dawned, and he had to face a startling truth, one that shook him to the core and knocked him for a loop.

He was falling for Schuyler, a woman who claimed to be a romantic tumbleweed, just as he'd once been. And that scared the hell out of him. Schuyler Fortunado had the power to break his heart in two.

They'd both entered this thing—whatever it was—because they thought it might be "fun." But feeling this way about her wasn't fun, and falling in love wasn't a game.

Still, as they lay in the afterglow, Carlo pulled her close, spooning with her in his bed. She seemed to be taking it all in stride. Wasn't she the least bit worried about what was happening? Or did she consider it all fun and games?

He damn sure wouldn't ask. He couldn't face the fact that he'd fallen for a woman who didn't love him back.

For now, he would hold her until the last wave of pleasure subsided, wishing it would never end and knowing it would. Like it or not, it was just a matter of time till Schuyler got a wild hair and moved on to something or someone else.

It was nearly dawn. Schuyler was lying in Carlo's bed, wrapped in the comfort of his arms. Yet it only made her antsy, eager to run away, and she hadn't slept a wink.

She'd spent the last hour reliving each heated touch, each tantalizing kiss. Never in her wildest dreams had she imagined how good their lovemaking would be.

Nor had she realized that she'd end up wanting to spend every night with him. Not just while she was in Austin, but for the rest of her life.

How was that for bad luck?

For as long as she'd been old enough to date, she'd sworn that she didn't want a serious relationship with anyone. And then she'd met Carlo, and she'd begun to reconsider that belief.

At first she'd told herself that her fondness for him was due to the fact that he was fun to be around. And since he felt the same way about commitments that she did, he didn't threaten her independent spirit. But now she realized there was a lot more to it than that. He wasn't the threat. She was.

She'd fallen hard for him, head over heels, heart over brain. And now she had no idea what the morning sun would bring.

He kept a box of condoms handy, within easy reach of his bed. Undoubtedly he had reason to use them often. So what happened if she pushed for something more serious with him, something that might require a commitment from him, if not a ring?

He'd run for the hills. She had no doubt of that. And where would that leave her?

She'd be out of a job, one she really liked and the first she'd ever had that allowed her to shine on her own merits. And worse than that, Carlo's rejection would break her heart.

He lay next to her, his breathing soft and steady, clearly at peace and oblivious to her worries. She glanced at the clock on the bureau. It was nearly five o'clock. If he hadn't brought her here, if she hadn't left her car back at the winery, she would have slipped out of bed quietly and driven home. But she was stuck.

Oh, God. What a mess. And she had only herself to blame. She should have known better.

She rolled to the side. Carlo hadn't yet told her that all good things came to an end, and her heart was already battered and aching. She needed to talk to someone. The only one who'd ever truly understood her was her grandmother, but Glammy was gone. There was one other person she could call. Someone wise and kind. Someone who'd offer her compassion and guidance without judgment.

Of all her brothers and sisters, Everett was the one she looked up to, the one whose judgment was always sound. He was also the one she went to when she was confused or her feelings were hurt.

Everett had made the perfect career choice when he went to medical school. He was a born physician, a healer in every sense of the word. And he'd always been able to put things back to right.

But not this time. She didn't think he could help her straighten out the mess she'd made of her life. Nor could anyone mend her broken heart.

Still, she'd call him the first chance she got. In the meantime, she carefully slipped out of Carlo's embrace, trying her best not to wake him. Then she picked up her discarded clothing and tiptoed to the bathroom.

By the time she'd showered and done her best to

freshen up, the sun had finally risen. And Carlo had woken up.

"Good morning," he said. "You're up early."

"I…um…need to check on the puppies. I called Dottie last night and told her I'd be late coming in and that I'd get them in the morning. But I don't want to take advantage of her, especially when I might need to leave them with her again."

Carlo threw off the covers, revealing his long, lean sexy body in all of his masculine glory. "As soon as I shower, I'll fix a quick breakfast."

Her tummy clenched at the thought of food and after-the-lovin' small talk at the dining room table. But she couldn't surrender to the urge. "That's okay. I'm not hungry. And I rarely eat before nine."

"How about a cup of coffee to go? Or a glass of orange juice?"

She tossed him a breezy smile, hoping he wouldn't see right through it. "I'd better take a rain check."

He nodded. "Sure. No problem. Next time."

Only there wouldn't be a next time. She couldn't allow herself a luxury like that. Not when her emotions were spiraling out of control.

Again, she feigned a smile. "Thanks for a great evening."

"Don't thank me. It was my pleasure." He nodded toward the bathroom. "Give me five minutes, and I'll take you to your car."

True to his word, he was dressed and ready to go within minutes. He hadn't taken the time to shave, which gave him a rough-and-rugged edge, one she found appealing.

On the drive to the winery, neither of them said much. Those fake, carefree smiles had been hard enough to manage. She wouldn't have been able to fake a happy-go-lucky conversation.

Heck, she couldn't even glance across the seat to check out his expression. She was too afraid of what she'd see—and how badly it would hurt.

He pulled into the parking lot and stopped next to her car, but he didn't turn off the engine. No doubt, he was eager to be on his way. Gosh, it hurt just to think about it.

"Thanks again," she said, trying her best to be upbeat. "It was a great party. And last night, at your house, was amazing. We'll have to do it again sometime."

How was that for breezy and carefree?

"You got it." His brow furrowed. "Are you having regrets?"

"About what? Last night?" She waved off the thought with a limp hand. "No, not at all. It's what we both wanted. Right?"

"Yeah."

She lifted her fingers to her lips and blew him a kiss. "I'll talk to you later."

"Yeah."

She grabbed her purse and headed for her car.

Love. Ha! No wonder she'd been so determined to remain single. But even sarcasm didn't take the edge off her ragged feelings.

Carlo didn't drive away. He waited until she got behind the wheel and started her engine. Then he continued to watch until she backed out of the parking space and headed down the driveway.

She'd barely reached the highway when she dialed her brother's number. She usually called him at the office, but not today. He'd still be home.

When he answered, it took her a moment to gather her thoughts and to blink back her tears.

"Hey," she finally said. "What's for breakfast, Doc?" She'd meant her comment to sound normal, as if she wasn't about to burst into tears. But she couldn't squelch a sniffle.

"What's wrong, Schuyler?"

Darn it. He always knew when something was off, even though she rarely cried.

"I…well, I think I've screwed up."

"Didn't I tell you not to chase after the Fortunes?"

"It's not them. I've met quite a few, and all of them have been nice. It's just that…" Her eyes filled with tears, and she tried to blink them back.

"Are you crying?"

She sniffled again. "It's just allergies."

"You don't have allergies."

"I do now. I'm allergic to tall, dark and handsome men."

"Where are you?" he asked.

"I'm in Austin."

"Still? When are you coming home?"

"I don't know. I'm…" Her voice waffled, and her

eyes welled once again. Dang it. She never cried. Well, rarely. She blew out a sigh. "Okay, here's the deal. I've fallen in love with a guy who's determined to remain single the rest of his life."

"You met a man with the same philosophy you have?"

"Yes, that's about the size of it. Only I seem to have changed my mind about weddings and a home in the suburbs with a swing set in the backyard. And it's killing me to feel this way."

"And you've only been in Austin for two weeks? I knew your impulsivity would get you in trouble eventually."

"So it happened fast. But it's real. And it hurts. What should I do, Doc?"

"Pack your things and come home."

"Just like that? I can't. I've got…responsibilities."

"Like what?"

"A job for one thing, although I probably need to quit. It's at the Mendoza Winery, and Carlo—that's the guy I'm dating…well, *was* dating. Anyway, he's the vice president."

"If you don't feel comfortable around him you should leave."

"That's the problem. I've never felt so comfortable around a man in my life. But he's a heartbreak waiting to happen. And it's tearing me up to think about it. I don't want to stay, but I can't leave… I'm so confused."

"Have you talked to him about any of this?"

"Heavens no. I don't want him to flip out. It would

ruin our working relationship. But then again, it's practically ruined already."

"Listen, Schuyler. I'll need to shift some appointments around and change a meeting, but I'm coming to see you in Austin within the next day or so. Hang tight. We'll work through this. And hopefully, by then, you'll be ready to come home."

It was nice to know she had someone in her corner. "Thanks, Doc."

"Where are you staying?"

She gave him the address. "But call first. By the time you get there, I could be at the winery. Or at the dog park."

"Why in the world would you be—" He paused. "Don't tell me you adopted a dog."

"Not one. Two. And they're puppies."

"Do you think that was a good idea?"

"Probably not, but my landlord, who's also my neighbor, has taken a real shine to them. And she looks after them for me sometimes. I guess you could say we're sharing custody at the moment."

When he didn't respond, she said, "Oh, come on, Everett. Don't tell me I'm too irresponsible to be a pet owner, let alone…" She left the rest unsaid.

"I'd never say that, Schuyler. One of these days, when the right man comes along, you're going to be an amazing wife and mom. And you'll get that home in the suburbs."

"You have no idea how much I appreciate your saying that."

"I mean it."

She knew he did. Everett never minced words or tromped on hearts. "I love you, Doc."

"Hang in there. It'll all work out—one way or another."

She wanted to believe him. But something told her that her current problem was one that even Everett couldn't fix.

Chapter Eleven

Twenty minutes after ending her telephone conversation with Everett, Schuyler arrived at her temporary home. She'd told Carlo she needed to check on Fluff and Stuff, and that was on her to-do list. But first she had to get inside her studio apartment before Dottie spotted her wearing the same outfit she'd left in last night.

Not that it mattered. It wasn't anyone's business what she did. At least, that's what she'd always told herself when defending one of her choices in the past.

She'd no more than entered her small digs and kicked off her heels when her phone rang. She assumed Everett had forgotten to tell her something, but when she grabbed her cell and saw Carlo's name on the lighted display, her heart dropped to the pit of her stomach.

As her eyes began to well with tears, she nearly silenced the darn thing. If just seeing his name could set off that kind of visceral response, what would the sound of his voice do to her, let alone the words he might say?

Still, her fingers froze, and the blasted phone continued to ring. If she didn't answer pretty soon, the call would roll over to voice mail before she made the decision to take it or not.

What was wrong with her? She hadn't always made the best choices in the past, but she'd never been indecisive.

Get a grip, Schuyler. What would Glammy do if this were happening to her? She certainly wouldn't put her tail between her legs. She'd take the call.

Schuyler swiped her finger across the screen to answer, just as the ringtone stopped. Great. Now what?

She cleared her throat, shook off her apprehension and returned the call.

When Carlo answered, she let out a nervous little chuckle. "Sorry about that. I couldn't get to my phone in time."

Okay, so that was a lie. And even though it was just a little one, guilt still warmed her cheeks.

"I called to see if you got home okay," Carlo said. "You seemed a little…off when I dropped you at your car. Are you all right?"

Heck no. She was dying inside. And her heart had cracked right down the center. But no way could she reveal that to him. The last thing she wanted was for him to think that she was flaky or weak. That she was a woman who was afraid she couldn't get through life without a man.

"I'm fine," she said.

The conversation stalled for a moment. She tried to rally her thoughts and come up with some kind of feasible script, but it wasn't working.

"You told me you were okay earlier," Carlo said. "But for some reason, I can't buy that."

Probably because she'd told him a lie. A big fat one.

"For the record," he added, "last night was amazing, and I have three empty condom packets to prove it."

He was right about that. Their lovemaking had been everything he said it was. "I couldn't agree more."

"I don't usually make follow-up phone calls," he said. "I never need to. But this is different. I wasn't happy about the way things ended this morning."

She'd take the blame for that. But if she hadn't left when she did, things might have ended a lot worse. She wasn't about to admit that, but she did have to say something. And she couldn't leave him hanging.

"I had a great time at the party," she admitted. "And making love with you was…" A golden memory she'd never, ever forget. "Well, it was awesome. And it could become habit forming."

"And that's a habit you'd rather not have."

Was he expecting confirmation? She could give him that, but it would be yet another lie. She could easily get used to waking in his arms each morning. But they'd agreed to keep things simple.

Hadn't he said he kept his sexual relationships simple?

She'd even assured him that she preferred not to become attached. And then she'd ruined everything by doing an about-face.

"I've always been a little uncomfortable with the after-sex talks," she admitted. And this time it was a whole lot worse.

"Me, too. Those chats can get pretty awkward."

Especially when the two people involved had such different expectations and hopes for the future.

"Don't get me wrong," she added. "Making love was better than good last night. And I really enjoyed it." In fact, way too much. "But can we talk more about this later? I just walked into the house to change my clothes before going to Dottie's to pick up the pups. I'd like to take them for their morning walk before she has to do it."

Now there was an excuse that sounded believable. And it was also consistent with what she'd told him when he dropped her off at her car.

"Sure," he said, "we can talk later. Or we can drop the subject completely. Just keep in mind that I'm the last one in the world who'd ever push you. Or ask more from you than you're willing to give."

Yes, he'd been up-front about that early on. And she'd tried to do the same thing. Then she'd flipped and done a complete one-eighty. And now she was no longer opposed to an exclusive relationship. She was even pondering words like *forever*. And that really should run against her grain. It always had.

"I'm not worried," she lied.

"So you don't have any regrets about last night?"

She had a ton of them, but rather than admit that,

she looked heavenward, hoping she wouldn't get struck by a lightning bolt for her dishonesty. "No, not at all."

"Good. Then there's nothing more to talk about. Let's just take things one day at a time, okay?"

"Sure." She closed her eyes, willing them not to tear up. "It sounds like we're still on the same page."

"By the way," he added, "I scheduled a special tasting at the winery on Saturday afternoon. Are you available to pour at two o'clock?"

Apparently he thought everything was status quo, which meant he wasn't trying to put any distance between them. Of course, he hadn't mentioned anything about that full-time position. But then he probably still had to discuss it with Alejandro.

Still, if that job offer came through, she'd have to turn it down. She couldn't risk being in daily contact with Carlo. Not feeling the way she did.

"I'm free on Saturday afternoon," she told him. "I'll even arrive an hour earlier to make sure everything is set up the way I like it."

"Sounds good. Saturday is also the same night we're going to see *Jersey Boys*. So I'll make sure you're finished in time. Just in case, I'll have Ricardo in the wings as a backup."

With all the emotional upheaval, she'd nearly forgotten their date. The real one she'd been looking forward to.

"I'm not worried about the timing." Her biggest concern was figuring out just how and when to back off.

But then again, wasn't that what she was already doing?

Silence hung on the line.

Finally Carlo said, "I'd better let you go."

That's exactly what she'd been afraid of since early this morning—that he'd make that very decision. And that's why her pride insisted that she let him go first.

Carlo had sensed that Schuyler was withdrawing from him the moment he woke up and saw that she'd already gotten out of bed and showered. In the past, he might have felt relieved that things had gone so smoothly, but that wasn't the case with Schuyler.

He hated to see things end before they even had a chance to get off the ground. Just the thought of her leaving town and going back to Houston nearly choked the breath out of him.

Like it or not, he'd gotten attached.

It's not as if he hadn't seen this coming, either. Ever since he met her, she was all he'd been able to think about. At first, he'd considered her unique and a real novelty. She'd been able to lift his spirits in a special way. She was fun to be with, to laugh with. And for that reason, he'd wanted to spend more and more time with her.

But it was more than that. He'd fallen for her— headfirst and hard. And now that he'd slept with her?

He slowly shook his head at what had become a stark reality. He wanted to stake a claim on a woman who'd made it clear that she was interested only in having fun. And that left him in one hell of a fix.

It also made him feel like a love-struck fool.

He walked across the room, turned and strode back

again, hoping to shake off the compulsion to level with Schuyler, to tell her how he really felt. But how could he do that when she'd obviously sensed it and was pulling away already?

And why wouldn't she? She owned a condo in Houston, where she also had family and had created a life for herself, so she had every reason to return. Hell, even though she was in Austin now, she'd rented that place on a month-to-month lease. She'd moved there from the Monarch Hotel only because of the dogs.

He raked his hand through his hair, then continued to pace his apartment like a caged jungle cat. He needed to talk to someone. Maybe then he could put things in the proper perspective.

Alejandro came to mind, but his cousin was too wrapped up in his new bride and thought everyone else ought to find their own happily-ever-after.

Give love a chance, he'd told Carlo.

Yeah, right. Carlo had tried to do that with Cecily, and where had that gotten him? Hot sex had gone cold within a couple of months. It didn't take a brain surgeon to realize that what he'd thought was love turned out to be lust.

So how could he consider throwing his hat into the marital ring again?

Yet that's the direction his damn thoughts had been leading him. He had to be losing his mind.

Sure, sex with Schuyler had been out of this world—hotter and sweeter than anything he'd ever experienced. But sex wasn't the great equalizer. It took more than that to solve life's problems. He'd learned that lesson when he'd been married to Cecily.

Of course, he'd never smiled as much with her as he did with Schuyler, never enjoyed her company as much. And in the bedroom? There was no comparison.

But Schuyler was sure to blow him off in a few short weeks, if not sooner.

He had to clear his head from fruitless thoughts. He really ought to talk to someone, another bachelor who understood the appeal of great sex, the disappointment of a failed marriage and the need to remain single for life.

The best person would be his father, a man who was the happiest single guy Carlo had ever known. Esteban Mendoza would know just what to say to set things back on track. And the sooner he said it, the better.

Carlo grabbed his cell and made the call. It wasn't until his father answered, his voice sleep-laden, that he realized what time it was.

"I'm sorry," Carlo said. "I didn't mean to wake you."

"That's okay. What's up?"

Carlo blew out a ragged sigh. "I've got a problem, Dad. And I need you to talk me through it."

"Sure, but hang on a minute."

Carlo waited, listening as sheets ruffled, as a groggy feminine voice uttered, "Huh?"

Obviously Carlo and Schuyler weren't the only ones to go home together after a romantic party.

"Shh," his father said. "Go back to sleep, babe. I'll take this call in the other room."

A door clicked shut. Moments later, his father said, "Okay, Carlo, I'm back. What's the problem?"

"I didn't realize you had company. This obviously isn't a good time. We can talk later."

"You rarely call, especially claiming to have a problem. What's going on, *mijo*?"

Carlo raked his hand through his hair, then proceeded to tell his old man what happened and how he was struggling with his feelings.

"I'm not surprised you fell for Schuyler," Esteban said. "I saw it coming before you did."

"You mean when you caught us kissing?"

"No, that's not what clued me in to what was happening. You've kissed plenty of pretty ladies in the past, but I doubt you've ever looked at any of them the way you look at Schuyler. I've seen you smile more in the past couple weeks than in the past ten years. You're happy again, and if you want my opinion, I think you should go for it."

But Carlo *wasn't* happy. He was miserable.

"Thanks for the advice, Dad. But Schuyler isn't interested in having a serious relationship."

"With you?"

"With anyone."

His dad let out a *humph*. "Kind of like you felt before, huh? But you've changed your mind. Maybe, given time, she will, too."

"I doubt that." Carlo slowly shook his head. "And even if she did, I don't want to face another failed relationship. So the only thing I can do is to pull back."

"That won't be easy to do with her working at the winery."

"I'm not sure how long that will last anyway. And so I've been thinking that I'd better not offer her a full-time position. In fact, having her hostess for those special events isn't a good idea, either. Not when she isn't feeling the same thing I am."

"What about that tasting Saturday afternoon?"

"I already asked her to do it, but Ricardo can handle it."

"You'd fire her?"

"If I have to." Wouldn't it be best? Then again, maybe he wouldn't have to go that far. What if he didn't make her working environment so comfortable?

"You could be making a big mistake, *mijo*. Schuyler's done a great job so far."

She'd also done a real number on his heart, and if he didn't figure out a way to send her back to Houston, he'd be toast.

"Yes, I'm sure." He couldn't handle the frustration, either sexual or emotional.

He had to let her go.

"Thanks for letting me talk through this," Carlo said. "Go on back to bed. My head's clear, and I know what to do now."

"Don't do anything rash. You might wind up regretting it in the end."

"I won't." He thanked his dad again, then ended the call.

Once he put away his cell phone, he went into the kitchen and brewed a pot of coffee. He needed a heavy dose of caffeine before setting his plan in motion.

He was going to act cool and unaffected, which years ago had helped him break things off with a woman who'd forgotten their agreement and gotten clingy. If he kept his distance from Schuyler, maybe she'd quit and return to Houston on her own. Either way, he had to end things.

Starting right now.

Everett called Schuyler early on Saturday morning and apologized if he woke her up.

"You didn't. I've already showered, gotten dressed and had breakfast." She didn't blame him for thinking she might still be in bed. She tended to be a night owl, but ever since she'd gone home with Carlo, she hadn't been sleeping very well.

"Where are you?" she asked.

"I just hit the Austin city limits."

"Then you're only ten minutes away from my place. Just meet me here." She'd already given him the address, so she provided him with the easiest directions from the interstate. "I'll see you soon."

While Everett was en route, Schuyler took Fluff and Stuff outside for a potty break. Once her brother arrived, she was going to ask Dottie if she'd dog sit again today.

The front door squeaked open. Schuyler glanced over her shoulder and watched her sweet, pet-loving landlord step out on the porch.

"Good morning," Dottie said. "You're up early."

"My brother is coming to visit."

"That's nice. Will he be staying with you? Not that it matters. I'm just curious."

"I'm not sure." If Everett had his way, Schuyler would be following him home tonight.

And maybe that wasn't such a bad idea after all.

"How long will he be visiting?"

"Just a day or so. I thought I'd take him around Austin and show him the sights."

"I'd be happy to watch Fluff and Stuff—unless you're going to take them with you."

"You don't mind?"

"I'd love to. I'm growing very fond of these sweet little rascals."

"That would be great. Thanks, Dottie."

The women and the dogs were still in the front yard when Everett arrived.

"Hey," Schuyler called out as he got out of his car. "You found me."

"It wasn't hard."

Gosh, it was good to see him in person. Not that he'd provide an instant cure for her heartbreak, but having him here would help.

Schuyler introduced him to Dottie. "Everett is a doctor in Houston."

Dottie reached out to shake his hand. "How nice to have a physician in the family."

Yes, that was true. But there was more to Everett than his medical degree. He was one of the smartest men Schuyler had ever met. He did get a little hyperfocused at times, but only because he was determined to be the best doctor in the world. He also had a kind and sympathetic heart.

Schuyler was actually surprised he hadn't gotten married yet. She would have thought some woman would have snatched him up by now.

He was attractive, too. At six feet tall, he was both lean and buff. With his dark hair and expressive blue eyes, he reminded her of a young Christian Bale. Not so much today, though. He was wearing glasses, which he sometimes did.

Schuyler liked seeing them on him. They made him look even extra bright and not the least bit geeky.

"Well," Dottie said, stooping to pick up Stuff, who'd jumped up on her leg, "it was nice to meet you, Doctor. If you'll excuse me, I'll take these little rascals inside and leave you two to visit and take that drive. Maybe you'll see why Austin is so appealing."

"Thanks, Dottie. And don't worry, I'll show him all the sights." Then she turned to her brother. "Have you had breakfast yet?"

"Yes, before I left Houston. I'm not hungry now, but I'll probably want an early lunch."

"That works for me."

Everett scanned the yard, taking in Dottie's two-story brick house, the tree-lined street and the quiet neighborhood.

"What do you think of my temporary digs?" she asked.

"It seems like a nice place to live, but this isn't anything like your loft condo in downtown Houston. And it seems a little too much like suburbia to suit you for very long."

He might be right, but she'd found it peaceful.

"Have you given any thought to coming home with me?" he asked.

"Yes, but I have some commitments. I have a wine tasting to hostess this afternoon." She also had a date tonight, but she was going to cancel that, using her brother's "surprise" visit as her excuse. She couldn't have made up a better one than that.

"So where are the sights you're going to show me?" Everett asked.

The only one that came to mind was the winery. So why not take him there? After all, that's what had kept her in Austin. Well, that and the handsome Latino vice president who didn't love her back.

As much as she'd like to avoid Carlo, maybe it would be best if she did find him there. That way, Everett would understand why she was so taken by him and why she was so confused about what to do.

"You know," Schuyler said, "let's drive out to the Mendoza Winery. I think you'll like seeing it, and it'll also give me a chance to introduce you to my new friends."

"That's fine with me. Do you want to take my car or yours?"

"I'll drive."

Twenty minutes later, they arrived at the winery and parked near several familiar cars, including Carlo's. Her heart made a swan dive, then belly flopped. Had she made a bad decision to face him?

"This is impressive," Everett said, as he unbuckled his seat belt.

Well, there really was no getting around it now. Worst-case scenario, upon seeing Carlo she'd break into tears. And if that happened, she'd drive home, pack up her things and her dogs and follow her brother back to Houston.

It wasn't the greatest game plan, but it was the best she had. "Come on, Doc. I'll show you around."

She pointed out the tasting room, as well as La Viña, then led him to the winery office. She opened the door and found Esteban and Alejandro bent over a desk and going over an order.

Esteban straightened. He glanced first at Schuyler, then focused his gaze on Everett. He wasn't wearing his usual smile, which was odd, but she'd probably interrupted a business conversation.

Schuyler introduced the men to Everett, mentioning the title he'd earned and explaining he was her brother. At that, Esteban seemed to forget business matters and smiled.

"Where's Carlo?" she asked.

Esteban was the first to answer. "He and his brothers took the truck and went to the distribution center at Austin Commons."

The fact that Carlo wasn't around was both reassuring and disappointing. She realized that was why a relationship with him wouldn't be in her best interests. Her feelings for him were too complicated, too confusing.

"Doctor, how long will you be in town?" Alejandro asked.

"Just a day or so. I'm trying to talk Schuyler into going back to Houston with me."

Esteban arched a brow. "Is it working?"

Tears welled in her eyes, and she blinked them back. "I never expected to remain in Austin very long."

"Then I guess that means you won't be interested in taking on a full-time position here," Alejandro said. "I'm sorry to see you go, but if you ever decide to relocate to Austin, you have a job here."

A single tear overflowed, and she swiped it away, hoping no one had seen it. She had to clear her throat before she could trust herself to speak. "Thanks, Alejandro. Anyway, I guess I'll be back around one o'clock this afternoon for that wine tasting."

She glanced at her brother, then nodded at the door, signaling she was ready to leave. She'd held it together the best she could, but if they didn't go now, she'd fall completely apart.

After a quick tour of Austin, which didn't take very long since Schuyler was pretty much a tourist herself, she and Everett stopped at a trendy sandwich shop not far from Austin Commons. They ordered lunch at the counter, then found a quiet table nearby and waited until a teenage server brought them their food.

When the young man had gone back behind the counter, she picked up her fork, then said, "I'd like for you to go with me to that tasting at the winery this afternoon. Regardless of how things turned out for me here, I love their wine. And I know you will, too. I dare you not to order a case or two to take home with you."

"With *us*, right?"

Reluctantly, she agreed. It was for the best.

Everett bit into his sandwich, and Schuyler had no more than taken a forkful of her salad when the door of the eatery opened and two women walked in. Schuyler didn't give them a second glance, but Everett did.

He straightened, then set down his sandwich.

"What's the matter?"

He didn't answer right away. Instead, he watched the women order a couple of brownies to go.

"Do you know them?" she asked.

"The redhead is Lila Clark."

Schuyler put down her fork and studied her brother's rather perplexing expression. "Who's she?"

"A girl I dated in high school." He continued to study her, as if the surprise sighting had thrown him for a loop.

Schuyler could see why. There was a quiet beauty about Lila. And her long straight auburn hair was striking. She wore a floral-printed skirt and a matching pale green blouse. She also had on a pair of ballet flats, which made Schuyler wonder if she was a little self-conscious about her height. Not that she was *that* tall.

"I was just a kid when you were in high school," Schuyler said, "but I never knew you dated anyone. You always had your nose in a book."

Apparently, he'd set those books down once in a while.

"What's she doing in Austin?" Schuyler asked.

"I have no idea. I haven't seen her in more than a decade."

"You should go say hello."

Everett slowly shook his head. "No, that's not a good idea. We've both moved on, created different lives."

Maybe so, but he continued to watch Lila, his eyes pained. Did she dare ask what had gone wrong? Why they'd split up?

"Lila looks good," he said. "But her eyes aren't as bright as I remember."

"Maybe she's having a bad day."

"Maybe." Everett studied her a bit longer. "But there's something sad about her."

Schuyler had no way of knowing. And she wasn't sure what to say.

Oddly enough, after Lila and her friend left with their brownies in a small bag, Everett stopped talking to her about leaving Austin. Instead, he looked up, his gaze locked on hers. "If you love Carlo, you should fight for him—the way I should have fought for Lila."

If Schuyler hadn't been so wrapped up in her own hurts, she might have quizzed her brother more about his broken teenage romance.

Instead, she pondered his advice. *Fight for Carlo.*

Schuyler had never needed to fight for anything. But then again, she'd never wanted anything that badly.

Meeting the Fortunes had come close, which was why she was here.

Carlo was definitely worth fighting for—if she could guarantee a win.

What would Glammy do?

Maybe there was a better question. What was Schuyler going to do?

Chapter Twelve

Everett remained quiet and pensive on the drive to the winery. Schuyler suspected he was reflecting on Lila and his high school days. Then again, he could just as easily be pondering a medical issue facing one of his patients back home.

She might have asked him to share his thoughts with her, but she was too busy trying to figure out what she was going to say to Carlo when she got him alone.

When Everett suggested that she "fight" for him, she'd agreed. But she wasn't sure how to go about that. It wasn't like she could actually do anything to change his mind or convince him to give up his bachelor lifestyle and settle down with one woman, namely her.

Maybe she should start out by laying it on the line. She could tell him how she felt, then apologize for not sticking to the agreement they had to keep things light and simple. At that point, the ball would be in his court.

She stole another glance at her brother, who was gazing out the passenger window, watching the landscape pass by. She was tempted to draw him out of his musing so she could practice what she was going to say to Carlo, but that was one speech she'd have to come up with on her own.

When they arrived at the winery, she didn't see Carlo's car, which was a little surprising. Was he trying to avoid her? Her chest tightened at the thought, squeezing her heart, which was already crushed.

Well, she'd just have to wait until he returned. Then she'd face him and whatever resulted from her confession, whether that was tears or hugs and kisses.

But hey. Life wasn't meant to be boring—or predictable. Right?

Rather than take Everett with her to the tasting room, she stopped by the office first. That way, she could ask someone where Carlo went and when he'd be back.

That someone was Alejandro, who sat at his desk. When Schuyler and Everett entered, he looked up from his work and smiled.

"Is Carlo around?" she asked, even though she knew he wasn't.

"He *was* here." Alejandro set his pen aside. "But he left when Esteban told him you were planning to leave town."

What was that supposed to mean? Was Alejandro suggesting that Carlo had reacted negatively to the news? That he might actually feel more for her than he'd admitted to? That he was saddened to hear she was going back to Houston?

Maybe she'd read him wrong.

"I get the sense that you care for him," Alejandro said.

"You're right. I didn't want it to happen, and neither did he. But I fell in love with him." She bit down on her bottom lip, then looked to Alejandro, hoping he had some answers for her. "Did he say anything about me? About us?"

"No, he was pretty tight-lipped. But don't follow his lead. You two really need to talk it out."

Alejandro was right. She glanced at Everett, who was nodding in agreement.

"All right," she said. "Where did he go?"

"Home. He lined up Ricardo to pour at the tasting this afternoon and then gave him a list of things to do for him while he was gone. He said he needed to get away for a while."

That didn't sound good. Something was definitely wrong. And a phone call wasn't going to fix it.

She turned to Everett. "I need to talk to him alone."

"You're right."

And that meant she had to leave Everett here. "Alejandro, do you mind entertaining my brother while I'm gone?"

"No, not at all."

"Maybe you could let him have a taste of the Red River. Everett has always been partial to merlot." Then she hurried out the door, reaching into her purse for her keys before getting anywhere near her car.

* * *

Carlo had never felt such a strong compulsion to escape, to get his head together. Schuyler was leaving. And not some day in the near future. Apparently she was going *now*.

When his father had told him that she'd made plans to return to Houston, the axis that held his world together had shifted, leaving him stunned.

"Her brother was with her," his father had added. "He's a doctor and seems like a nice guy."

The good doctor must have influenced her decision to go, although Carlo wasn't entirely sure anyone could actually persuade Schuyler to do anything. But that didn't really matter.

She was going. He was hurting. And he'd be damned if he wanted anyone to know that she'd had that big of an effect on him.

That meant he couldn't hang around the winery, where someone was bound to pick up on his mood. And he couldn't very well slip off without letting his cousin know what he had in mind. So he'd gone in search of Alejandro and found him in the office.

"Listen," Carlo had said, "I'm going to need to take some time off."

"Sure. It's not like you haven't earned it. When?"

"Now. I'll fill in Ricardo on the things he'll need to do to cover for me, then I'm going home to pack."

Alejandro studied him for a moment, as if he could see right through him. "Does this have anything to do with Schuyler leaving town?"

Carlo'd slowly shook his head. "No, it's a coincidence. I just need some time away."

"Will a week be enough?"

Maybe. Hopefully. "Yes," he'd said.

"Where are you going?"

"I'm not sure." The place would have to be warm and
tropical, somewhere he could find a beach and let the
ocean lull him and allow him to heal. "The Bahamas
maybe. Possibly Belize or Cancún. I'll figure it out on
my way home."

Damn. When had he ever taken off on a whim to
parts unknown? He was behaving as impulsively as
Schuyler. Still, it seemed to be the only thing he could
do right now.

"Are you going to talk to Schuyler before you go?"
Alejandro had asked.

"No, that's not necessary." It's not like Carlo would
be able to change her mind about leaving. Besides, she
had her life to live, and he had his.

"Do you want to talk about this?" his cousin had
asked.

"No, there really isn't anything to talk about." And
certainly not with a happily married guy who'd probably forgotten what it was like to be single and carefree.

Alejandro wouldn't understand what it felt like to
have his life upended by a beautiful bohemian, to have
his heart broken and then to have to figure out a way
to pick up the pieces before anyone realized his vulner-
ability and his pain.

After thanking his cousin for understanding his need
to get away, as well as his desire to keep his thoughts

to himself, he went home to retrieve a few things he'd need on his upcoming trip—boxer briefs, casual shorts and T-shirts, a couple of swim trunks.

As he stacked them on top of the dresser, he couldn't help noticing the tickets he'd purchased for tonight's performance of *Jersey Boys*. He wouldn't be using them now. Should he give them away?

Maybe Schuyler would like to take her brother. Then again, that would require him to talk to her, to meet with her so he could give her the tickets.

He'd just pulled his suitcase from the closet when his doorbell rang. He rarely got uninvited guests, so he couldn't imagine who it could be.

He left his suitcase on the bed and went to open the door. His breath caught when he spotted Schuyler. She was dressed in that killer black dress she wore when she was a hostess for some of the wine tastings.

She offered him a shy smile, and his knees nearly buckled, weakening him even further. It wasn't a good feeling.

He meant to act cordial, unaffected by her presence. But his tone came out a little harsh when he asked, "What are you doing here?" He didn't apologize for it, though. Her arrival had taken him by surprise, and he was too broken up, too scattered to be polite.

She tucked a strand of hair behind her ear. "I came by to…check on you."

"Why? I'm fine."

"Alejandro said you were taking some time off."

He nodded. "Yeah. I've got some things to do that I've been putting off."

"Does this have anything to do with me? With...us?"

Of course it did. Any fool could see that. Hell, Alejandro had figured it out, even if Carlo had refused to admit it. Surely Schuyler had, too. Wasn't that why she was here? To tell him she was sorry that he'd let himself get in too deep? To explain why it was best for both of them if she left town? If it weren't so freaking sad and painful, he'd laugh.

"No, Schuyler, my vacation doesn't have anything to do with you."

"Are you sure?"

At that, he almost laughed. If he told her the truth, she'd take off at a dead run back to Houston faster than a speeding bullet.

Don't show any emotion. Think about your pride. You can do this.

"I'm sure." The polite thing to do was to invite her inside, but he couldn't do that.

"When are you leaving?" she asked.

"As soon as I finish packing." He thought of the suitcase on the bed, the clothes he'd stacked next to those tickets.

Realizing they'd go to waste—and that she was already here—he said, "I'm not going to be able to see that show tonight, but I'll give you the tickets. Your brother may enjoy seeing it."

Her eye twitched, then she slowly shook her head. "No, we'll be on the road to Houston by then. You'd better give them to someone else."

"Okay. Drive carefully. If I don't see you again, I hope you find everything you're looking for."

"Thanks. You, too." She nodded toward the hall elevator. "I'd better go. My brother is back at the winery, waiting for me."

He was tempted to tell her to keep in touch. But it was hard enough watching her go now. He'd be damned if he wanted to put himself through the pain again.

As the door clicked shut, he pondered his next move while regretting he had to make this one.

By the time Schuyler reached her car, hot tears were streaming down her face. She'd no more than swipe them away, when they'd spill over again.

She'd been wrong. Carlo didn't feel anything special for her.

You two need to talk, Alejandro had said.

Yeah, right. And just look where that stupid advice had gotten her. Her heart ached more than ever, and her pride had all but been crushed.

On the upside, he'd offered to give her the two tickets to *Jersey Boys*. She rolled her eyes at the absurd gesture. There was no way she'd be able to go out this evening and enjoy the show. As it was, she'd have to avoid her favorite oldies radio station so she wouldn't hear a song by the Four Seasons and remember the man she lost.

When she reached the winery and parked, she glanced at her image in the rearview mirror. Her eyes were so red and puffy, she'd never be able to hide the fact that she was heartbroken.

Everyone would know, and then they'd tell Carlo.

But so what? At this point, nothing seemed to matter anymore.

She got out of the car, slammed the door and made her way into the winery office, where her brother was sipping on red wine. A fancy white cardboard box bearing the Mendoza label rested next to him.

So she'd been right. He did like that merlot enough to purchase a case to take home.

When Everett looked at her face and realized she'd been crying, he got to his feet, set his wineglass aside and gave her a hug. "I'm sorry, Schuyler. I take it things didn't go very well."

"Good guess." She pulled free of his brotherly embrace and gestured toward the door. "Come on. Let's go. I need to get out of here. If we get on the road within an hour, we'll be back in Houston before dark."

All she had to do was pack. It wouldn't take long to get her things together, but she'd need to get the dogs' stuff, too. She'd also have to tell Dottie she was leaving.

She had a feeling that Dottie would offer to keep Fluff and Stuff, but Schuyler couldn't leave them behind. Having the dogs to care for might help ease her pain, if that was even possible. But at least she wouldn't be entirely alone.

Since Dottie was on a limited income, Schuyler would offer to pay her several months' rent. It was only fair. And it would tide the kindhearted woman over until she found another tenant.

Everett had no more than picked up the case of wine, when Esteban entered the office.

"Before you leave," Carlo's father said, "I'd like to have a word with you."

She couldn't imagine what he had to say to her, but

he'd always been kind. She couldn't refuse him. "All right."

Esteban made an after-you gesture with his hand, pointing to the door. "Let's go outside where we can talk privately."

She agreed, and they stepped out into the yard.

"I heard that you were leaving today," he said.

"Yes, I'm going back to Houston."

"That seems like a pretty sudden decision."

"Not really. But I've always been a little impulsive."

He nodded, as if giving that some thought. "Did you know that Carlo is leaving, too?"

"Yes, he told me."

"My son has never been impulsive."

Schuyler's eyes filled again. "Maybe not, but I think he's trying to distance himself from me."

"That's probably true. But your red, swollen eyes suggest you're not happy about that."

She blew out a sigh. "I guess it's not a big secret. We started flirting with each other, and we both were determined to keep things simple. But then I went and ruined it all by falling in love with him."

"Have you told him?"

"I was going to, but he wasn't at all happy to see me and practically threw me out of his apartment."

"He told you to leave?"

"No, but he was pretty cold. He told me to have a good life."

Esteban reached out and placed a fatherly hand on her shoulder. "Carlo didn't mean to hurt you, *mija*."

Schuyler rolled her eyes. "So you say. But you

weren't standing in his doorway, wondering if he'd invite you inside and realizing that he couldn't send you away fast enough."

"All of my boys are headstrong and love-shy. After growing up in a house with two unhappy parents who fought more often than not, they've all pretty much vowed to be single. Especially Carlo, who gave marriage a try, only to see it end within a year."

"Yes, I know about that. He told me."

"But what he didn't tell you is that, in spite of himself, he loves you."

"That's not the vibe I got twenty minutes ago."

"That's because Carlo's afraid to tell you how he really feels."

She wanted to believe that, but she couldn't risk finding out that Esteban was wrong. That if Carlo had any feelings for her, they weren't strong enough to last. "I'm sorry, but I'm not going to face him again. Not after the words he said and the tone he used today."

Still, she didn't rush back into the office and tell Everett her chat with Carlo's father was over, that she was ready to go now.

"Carlo has my number," she finally said. "If he changes his mind, he can call me in Houston."

Before Esteban could respond, she heard a car engine. Schuyler suspected the people who were coming to this afternoon's tasting had begun to arrive. But when she glanced into the parking lot, she spotted Carlo.

She watched as he strode forward, clearly approaching her. But this time, when they were face-to-face, she was the one to ask, "What are you doing here?" And not very nicely.

"I came to apologize."

"For what?" she asked, not about to make it easy on him. "For being a jerk?"

He nodded. "After the party, we got off on the wrong foot. And things got progressively worse."

"Actually, it wasn't until I woke up in your bed that things went downhill."

Esteban folded his arms across his chest and looked at Carlo sternly. "Since you refused to admit it, I told Schuyler how you really feel about her."

Schuyler studied Carlo, wondering if what his father had said was true. If so, would Carlo actually admit it?

Carlo wasn't happy that his father interfered with his love life, but his dad was right. And just looking at Schuyler's splotchy, tear-stained face told him that she might care more for him than she'd let on.

"I do love you," he told her. "I know it's not what either of us planned. But I couldn't help it. And I was afraid to tell you because I thought you'd retreat and move back to Houston."

"Seriously?"

There was no point denying it now. Thanks to his dad, the romantic cat was out of the bag. "You're all I think about, Schuyler, and once I realized all I stood to lose…well, I started to withdraw."

"But you're here," she said.

"After you left, I realized that I'd just shot myself in

the foot. So I figured I'd better try to make things right. I'll do whatever I can to convince you to stay."

"Okay," she said.

"Okay, as in you'll give me a chance to prove myself and make things better between us?"

"No," she said, shaking her head while a smile danced on her lips. "Okay as in I'll stay. I'm not leaving. And if you would have given me a minute to explain, I would have told you that I love you, too. It's clear to me that we belong together."

Any apprehension, any fears Carlo once had, dissipated in the air, replaced by hope. "You've got that right, honey."

Esteban, who'd been eavesdropping and clearly enjoying it way too much, laughed. "Then what are you waiting for, *mijo*? Don't let me stop you. Go ahead and kiss her!"

Carlo couldn't think of anything he'd like to do more—other than taking her home with him and making love until dawn. But that could wait.

For now, he wrapped his arms around Schuyler and kissed her with all the love in his heart, all the hope he had for a future together. By the time they came up for air, Alejandro and a guy who had to be Schuyler's brother had joined them outside.

"I believe I hear wedding bells," Esteban said.

"I hope you do," Carlo told his father. "Because I'm going to propose as soon as I buy a ring. And hopefully, she'll say yes."

Schuyler laughed. "I don't need a ring. So if you're proposing—and I have witnesses—I'll tell you right now my answer is yes." Then she threw her arms around his neck and kissed him soundly and with assurance that she'd heard those bells, too.

This time, when the kiss ended, Schuyler was crying.

"What's the matter?" he asked. "You're not having second thoughts, are you? Was a proposal too much, too soon?"

"My mind is set, Carlo. These are happy tears. I can't wait to be your bride."

Carlo turned to his cousin. "I still plan to take some time off, but now Schuyler will be with me. Can you get by without us for the next week or so?"

"Are you going someplace?" Alejandro asked.

"We'll see how we feel after all the fairy dust settles, but I'd be content to hole up at my place."

Schuyler laughed. "That sounds like an amazing plan to me."

Esteban elbowed Alejandro. "Well, what do you know? The two people who never wanted to tie the knot realize they can't live without each other."

That was the truth.

"Schuyler," her brother said. "Aren't you going to introduce me to your future husband?"

"Oh my gosh. I'm so sorry." She turned to Carlo. "This is my brother, Dr. Everett Fortunado."

The good doctor reached out his hand, but Carlo embraced him instead. "It's nice to meet you, Doctor."

"Call me Everett. And the pleasure is all mine. I'm glad to see my little sister so happy." He turned to Esteban and Alejandro. "It was nice meeting you both. I'm sure we'll see each other again soon."

Esteban wore a proud, father-of-the-groom grin. "No doubt at the wedding, if not sooner."

Everett reached out his hand to Schuyler. "Let me have your car keys."

"Where are you going?" she asked.

"It looks like you have another ride, so I thought I'd take your car back to your place, exchange it for mine and hit the road."

Schuyler went inside for her purse, then handed the keys to her brother. "Thanks for coming."

"You're more than welcome. I'll see you soon." Then he turned and walked away.

Carlo glanced at his watch. "You know, since we both have some time off, why don't we go to my apartment. I still have those tickets to *Jersey Boys*."

"That sounds like a great idea. We can go…if we don't get sidetracked."

Carlo liked the sound of that. "Let's see how the afternoon unfolds." Then he took Schuyler's hand and led her to his car.

"I can't wait to see what life has in store for us," she said.

Neither could he. But right now, he was looking forward to spending the afternoon in bed with her.

The sun had just begun to set, darkening the bedroom, as Carlo and Schuyler snuggled in bed, enjoying the afterglow of another heart-stirring, star-spinning climax.

"We can still make the show," he said, as he rolled

to the side, bracing himself with his elbow. "That is, if you want to go."

"I'd like that, if you don't mind." Still, neither of them moved.

"I was thinking," he said. "Maybe we should find another place to live. Since I'm going to marry you, that'll make me a dog owner. So we'll need a house, one that's pet friendly and has a big, fenced yard."

"That's sweet of you. Just so you know, I talked to Dottie earlier, and she agreed to keep the puppies for a while. I have a feeling it'll be hard for her to give them up. We might have to take one and let her keep the other."

Carlo laughed. "Let's take Fluff. She won't be as expensive to feed. Stuff eats a ton."

"Good idea." Schuyler brightened, then rolled to her side, facing him. And loving the sight of him, naked and stretched out beside her.

"I have a question for you," he said, as he trailed his fingers along the slope of her hip. "What do you plan to do about the Fortunes? You've met quite a few, and you've told me you liked them. Are you going to announce that you're related to them?"

"Maybe, but not right away." She brushed a fallen hank of hair from his brow and smiled. "Now that I'm going to be a Mendoza, there's no rush. I have a feeling there'll be plenty of Fortunes in my future."

And if Carlo had anything to say about it, there'd be some little Mendozas in her future, too.

* * * * *

MILLS & BOON

Coming next month

BABY SURPRISE FOR THE
SPANISH BILLIONAIRE
Jessica Gilmore

'Don't you think it's fun to be just a little spontaneous every now and then?' Leo continued, his voice still low, still mesmerising.

No, Anna's mind said firmly, but her mouth didn't get the memo. 'What do you have in mind?'

His mouth curved triumphantly and Anna's breath caught, her mind running with infinite possibilities, her pulse hammering, so loud she could hardly hear him for the rush of blood in her ears.

'Nothing too scary,' he said, his words far more reassuring than his tone. 'What do you say to a well-earned and unscheduled break?'

'We're having a break.'

'A proper break. Let's take out the *La Reina Pirata*—' his voice caressed his boat's name lovingly '—and see where we end up. An afternoon, an evening, out on the waves. What do you say?'

Anna reached for her notebook, as if it were a shield against his siren's song. 'There's too much to do . . .'

'I'm ahead of schedule.'

'We can't just head out with no destination!'

'This coastline is perfectly safe if you know what

you're doing.' He grinned wolfishly. 'I know exactly what I'm doing.'

Anna's stomach lurched even as her whole body tingled. She didn't doubt it. 'I . . .' She couldn't, she shouldn't, she had responsibilities, remember? Lists, more lists, and spreadsheets and budgets, all needing attention.

But Rosa would. Without a backwards glance. She wouldn't even bring a toothbrush.

Remember what happened last time you decided to act like Rosa, her conscience admonished her, but Anna didn't want to remember. Besides, this was different. She wasn't trying to impress anyone; she wasn't ridiculously besotted, she was just an overworked, overtired young woman who wanted to feel, to be, her age for a short while.

'Okay, then,' she said, rising to her feet, enjoying the surprise flaring in Leo di Marquez's far too dark, far too melting eyes. 'Let's go.'

Continue reading
BABY SURPRISE FOR THE
SPANISH BILLIONAIRE
Jessica Gilmore

Available next month
www.millsandboon.co.uk

LET'S TALK
Romance

For exclusive extracts, competitions
and special offers, find us online:

- facebook.com/millsandboon
- @millsandboonuk
- @millsandboon

Or get in touch on 0844 844 1351*

For all the latest titles coming soon, visit
millsandboon.co.uk/nextmonth

Want even more
ROMANCE?

Join our bookclub today!

'Mills & Boon books, the perfect way to escape for an hour or so.'

Miss W. Dyer

'Excellent service, promptly delivered and very good subscription choices.'

Miss A. Pearson

'You get fantastic special offer and the chance to get books before they hit the shops'

Mrs V Hall

**Visit millsandbook.co.uk/Bookclub
and save on brand new books.**

MILLS & BOON